The Story of the Night

COLM TÓIBÍN was born in Ireland in 1955 and lives
in Dublin. He is the author of five novels including
The Blackwater Lightship (shortlisted for the Booker Prize)
and *The Master* (shortlisted for the Booker Prize and winner
of the *LA Times* Book Prize and the IMPAC Book Award).
His non-fiction includes *The Sign of the Cross* and
Love in a Dark Time, and his short-story collection,
Mothers and Sons, was awarded the inaugural
Edge Hill Prize.

Also by Colm Tóibín

Praise for The Story of the Night

'This troubling and haunting book is one of shadows and
secrets, half-lives and losses, endings and tears . . . we are in
the atmosphere of surreal apprehension that colours some
of our best contemporary fiction'
Hermione Lee, *Observer*

'He writes sentences of classical elegance with staccato
insistence . . . Tóibín is not a writer who lets readers go
once he has them in his grasp. There is always, you feel,
the potential for surprise, that silences will be
exploded, that a revelation is coming'
Alan Taylor, *Scotsman*

'A brave and remarkable novel, the impact of which
no reader will shed'
Dermot Bolger, *Sunday Independent*

'Colm Tóibín is a writer's writer: fastidious, unshowy and
capable of thrillingly accurate perceptions'
Victoria Radin, *New Statesman*

'A fascinating mixture of the real and the imagined
. . . Tóibín's is an explosively emotional subject, and
we cannot fail to be shocked and moved by it'
Catherine Storey, *Independent on Sunday*

Colm Tóibín

The Story of the Night

PICADOR

First published 1996 by Picador

First published in paperback 1997 by Picador

This edition published 2010 by Picador
an imprint of Pan Macmillan, a division of Macmillan Publishers Limited
Pan Macmillan, 20 New Wharf Road, London N1 9RR
Basingstoke and Oxford
Associated companies throughout the world
www.panmacmillan.com

ISBN 978-0-330-52088-1

1 3 5 7 9 8 6 4 2

A CIP catalogue record for this book is available from
the British Library.

Typeset by SetSystems Ltd, Saffron Walden, Essex
Printed and bound in the UK by
CPI Mackays, Chatham ME5 8TD

in memoriam

GERRY MCNAMARA

PART ONE

DURING HER LAST YEAR my mother grew obsessive about the emblems of empire: the Union Jack, the Tower of London, the Queen and Mrs Thatcher. As the light in her eyes began to fade, she plastered the apartment with tourist posters of Buckingham Palace and the changing of the guard and magazine photographs of the royal family; her accent became posher and her face took on the guise of an elderly duchess who had suffered a long exile. She was lonely and sad and distant as the end came close.

I am living once more in her apartment. I am sleeping in her bed, and I am using, with particular relish, the heavy cotton sheets that she was saving for some special occasion. In all the years since she died I have never opened the curtains in this room. The window, which must be very dirty now, looks on to Lavalle, and if I open it I imagine there is a strong possibility that some residual part of my mother that flits around in the shadows of this room will fly out over the city, and I do not want that. I am not ready for it.

She died the year before the war and thus I was spared her mad patriotism and foolishness. I know that she would have waved a Union Jack out of the window, that she would have shouted slogans at whoever would listen, that she would have been overjoyed at the prospect of a flotilla coming down from England, all the way across the world in the name of righteousness and civilization, to expel the barbarians from the Falkland Islands. The war would have been her shrill revenge on everybody, on my father and his family, and on the life she had been forced to live down here so far away from home. I can hear her screeching now about the war and the empire, her voice triumphant. I can imagine trying to silence her, trying to escape her.

Her brittle old bones are firmly locked in the family vault, with my father's middle-aged bones, and my grandparents' bones, and the bones of one uncle and the small, soft, delicate bones of a cousin who died when she was a baby. Recently, I have felt unwilling to join all the rest of them in that dank underworld beneath the ornate angel and the stone cross. I can imagine the vague stench of ancestors still lingering, despite everything, despite all the time they have been dead. If I have enough money left, I will find my own place of rest.

I was the little English boy holding my mother's hand on the way out of the Church of England service on Calle Rubicón on a Sunday morning, my mother smiling at the members of the British colony, my mother wearing her good clothes and too much make-up and putting on her best accent and the weird, crooked smile she used on these occasions. She loved my name, Richard, the Englishness of it, and she hated it when anybody used the Spanish version, Ricardo. As I grew older, she loved me sitting quietly in some corner of the apartment away from her reading a book. She liked the bookish part of me, she drooled over the English tweed suit which I had specially made by a tailor on Corrientes. She mistook my reserve and my distance from her. She thought that it was real, and she never understood that it was fear. She liked my teaching at the university, even if it was only two hours a week in what passed for a language laboratory. And when I lost those hours and worked solely in Instituto San Martín, teaching repetitious English, she never mentioned it again, but saved it up to contemplate in her hours alone in her study, another bitter aspect of the way things had declined. She was disappointed.

Maybe that is what lingers in her bedroom, her disappointment and all the time she had alone to savour it and go over it in detail. Some of that dull energy is left there, and I can feel it when I go into the room and I still call it Mother.

She wanted me to have friends, to move around in groups, but in some deeper manner which I have never understood she taught me to distrust people, to want to slip away and spend time alone. She hated me going to the movies on my own. Do you not have a friend, she would ask. In my first year at university I did have a friend, who was studying economics, and who approached me one day and asked me to teach him English. His parents would pay, he said. I met him three times a week for lessons. His name was Jorge Canetto and he became important for me then because I fell in love with him and thought about him all the time. I loved how tall and strong he was, and how strangely blue his eyes were against the darkness of his hair and his skin. I loved the slow ease with which he smiled, the softness in him.

My mother noticed that I was happier, and asked me if I had a girlfriend. I told her that I did not. She laughed, as though the possibility caused her infinite mirth, and said I had, I had, she knew I had, and she would find out soon, someone would tell her the girl's name. Soon, she would know, she said. I told her again that I did not.

At five o'clock three days a week in an empty classroom in the university I taught Jorge English. A few times he came to the apartment and I gave him the lesson in the dining room, my mother hovering in the hallway. I taught him how to ask questions in the present tense, I made him learn vocabulary. And I listened for some clue that he might understand. That is the word they use here. *Entender.* To understand. There are other words too, but this one is still common. *Entendés?* you could ask and this would mean Do you? Are you? Will you?

Sometimes I became tense with worry that I might blurt it out, summon up the courage to ask him on the way out of a lesson. It would just take one moment to say it. 'There's something I want to ask you. I've noticed that you never mention girls the way most men here do, and you never look behind at a woman who passes on the street, and there's something I've wanted to ask you, you may guess what it is . . . Do you understand. *Entendés?*' And if he had said yes, perhaps I would not have wanted him as much as I did in this twilight time when I taught him English and did not know about him. Maybe I wanted whatever part of him was unavailable. Maybe if he had understood I would have despised him. Maybe I am being too hard.

The generals were in power then, and nobody stayed out late, even though the cafés and bars in the streets around us remained open, eerily waiting for the lone customer who had missed his train to finish up and go, or for time to pass, or for something to happen. But nothing happened. Or, as we later learned, a great deal happened, but I never witnessed any of it. It was as though the famous disappearances we hear so much about now took place in a ghost city, a shadowy version of our own, and in the small hours when no sounds were made or traces left. I knew – or thought that I knew – no one in those years who disappeared, no one who was detained, no one who was threatened with detention. I knew no one at that time who told me that they knew anyone who was a victim. And there are others who have written about this and come to the conclusion that the disappearances did not occur, or occurred on a lesser scale than we have been led to believe. But that is not my conclusion.

My conclusion centres on the strange lack of contact we have with each other here. It is not simply my problem, it is a crucial part of this faraway place to which our ancestors – my mother's father, my father's great-grandfather – came in search of vast tracts of land: we have never trusted each other here, or mixed with each other. There is no society here, just a terrible loneliness which bears down on us all, and bears down on me now. Maybe it is possible that I could watch someone being dragged away in front of my eyes and not recognize it. I would somehow miss the point, and maybe that is what I did, and others like me did, during those years. We saw nothing, not because there was nothing, but because we had trained ourselves not to see.

I do not remember when precisely I began to go directly home after my day at the university. In those years you moved carefully; without knowing why, you watched out. It was something in the atmosphere, something unsaid and all-pervasive, rather than anything printed in the papers or broadcast over the radio. You did not want to be the lone figure in the street at night. But I often went for coffee with Jorge after the lesson, nonetheless. And I waited for some sign from him. I expected him to mention a girlfriend. I observed him when girls passed for some sign of desire or interest, but there was nothing. His clothes in those years were old-fashioned and formal. I liked that about him. I imagined him in one of those old-fashioned bathing costumes that covered the torso as well, and I thought of the shape of him, and that was exciting.

A few times I found pleasure in the city. It would always begin in the same way: a sharp glance at a stranger as he walked by, a turn of the head, and then the watching and waiting as he stopped to look into a shop window and I moved nonchalantly towards him. And then the approach, the discovering if he had a place to go to, and then the setting out, conspirators laden down with desire. Often, because I am tall and fair-skinned and blond with blue eyes, they would want to know where I was from, and I would say that I was half-English, and that would be a subject we could discuss as we made our way home.

I remember one such encounter not for the sex we had, but

because of a sound that came into the room as we made love, the sound of car engines revving over and over. I asked my partner – I remember a dark-haired man in his thirties with white skin – what the noise was. He brought me to the window to show me the police station opposite and the cars outside, driverless, but still revving, with wires going from the engines to the basement of the building. They need power, he said, but I still did not understand. They need extra power for the cattle prods, he said. I still do not know if what he said was true, if that was one of the centres in the city to which people were taken, and if we fondled each other and came to orgasm within moments of each other to the sound of the revving of cars which gave power to the instruments of torture. It made no difference then, because I did not pay much attention to what he said, and I remember the pleasure of standing at the window with him, my hands running down his back, more than anything else.

It is only now years later that it seems significant, perhaps the only sign I was ever given of what was happening all around me. I cannot remember the name of my companion that evening, the man I stood with at the window, but I have often wondered how he knew or thought he knew, or if he imagined, what the revving of the cars' engines meant in our city at that time.

★

ONE FRIDAY WHEN we had finished our class, Jorge walked into the centre with me. We went into a bar together and had a beer. He asked me if I had been to England, and I said that I had not, but I had often thought about it. I would like to live there, I said, at least I think I would, even though I have no relatives there. I think that you could be free there, I said. I think people are more relaxed about things, about sex, for example. I noticed him looking up from the table at me as I spoke. I could feel my heart thumping. I was going to do it. I was ready now. Everything is easier, I said. I mean if you wanted to go to bed with another man, to have an affair with him, no one would care very much. You could do that. It would be hard to do that in Argentina. He nodded and looked away and then took a sip of his beer. He said nothing. I waited.

I mean, I said, do you know anyone here who prefers men to women, I mean a man who prefers men to women? I almost ran out of the bar as soon as I had said it. I was trying to sound casual, but I had not succeeded. I wanted him to say yes he did, and then make clear that it was himself he was talking about. Or maybe I wanted him to leave silence, leave everything suspended. You mean queers, he asked. No, he said, he did not know anybody like that. He sounded sure of himself. Most men liked women, he said, in England as much as in Argentina. And did I like women, too, he asked. I felt a terrible weight in my chest. I wanted to find some dark corner and curl up. No, I said, no, I did not.

Does anyone else know that, he asked. Does your mother know? Have you never told her? I needed to tell him how much I had wanted him, how much I had dreamed about him, how my hopes had depended on him and now things would change. But he wanted to talk about my mother. I wanted him to go and leave me there.

I don't think that your mother has had things easy, he said. He looked like a parody of a responsible teenager as he sat and tried to discuss my mother with me. And maybe I looked like a parody of something too: a homosexual foolish enough to believe that a man he fancies is homosexual too. You should tell her, he said, and maybe there is something that could be done. I did not ask him if he meant that if I talked enough about it, or sought medical help, I might start watching girls as they passed on the street instead of making embarrassing propositions to fellow students. I was going to tell him that when I was a baby I was homosexual, and I laughed to myself at this vision of myself in a pram.

He asked me what I was laughing at, and I said that everybody always felt sorry for my mother, but they were usually older people. I had never expected him to join the chorus, and I found it funny that he had done so. I told him that maybe he could tell her himself and perhaps he could listen to her every day and he could live with her and I could go home to his house, to his rich parents in the suburbs.

We continued our English lessons; I was glad of the money. More and more he came to the apartment to learn English. My mother often made him tea. I often wondered if he took a secret interest in me, but could not admit this to himself or to me. But, as I later discovered, I was deluding myself. I told him how easy it was to pick up a man in the street. I asked him to check out the toilets in the railway station for himself some day if he did not believe me and see if he noticed anything. He became worried about me. What if I was caught? If I went home with the wrong type? If it was a policeman just checking me out? It would kill her, he said. It would kill your mother. What would it do to me, I asked him. He shook his head and told me that I must be careful.

My mother's health was beginning to give. She was mellow and quiet for much of the time, sitting in an armchair in the square tiled hallway of the apartment, and, much as I do now, examining the sky and the backs of buildings and the cats manoeuvring their way along the ledges and rooftops. When she looked at me sometimes she seemed old and frightened.

The hallway looked like a porch with its huge window which gave light to the living room during the day through a glass partition. My mother enjoyed being sandwiched between these two pieces of glass; often, we turned on a lamp in the evening until everything seemed all shadow and reflection. One evening as we sat there, she asked me about Jorge, she said that she liked him and wondered if I enjoyed teaching him English. I said that I did. Did I know much about him, she asked. Had I been in his house, for example, or met his family? I said I had not been to his house, but I knew that his family were rich, that they had their own tennis court and swimming pool and that his father had been involved with Perón.

Had it ever occurred to me, she asked, that he was homosexual? I had never heard her say the word before, and she pronounced it as though she had recently learned it. She looked at me sharply. I looked straight into the glass of the window and saw her shape in the armchair. No, I said to the glass, no, it had not occurred to me. Well, I think he is, she said, and I think it is something you should consider before you become too friendly with him.

I stood up and walked through to the bathroom. I closed the door behind me as though someone were following me. I wet my hands and my face and I stared into the mirror. I stood up straight. I was breathing heavily. I looked at my own eyes and then turned and opened the door. I did not stop walking as I began to speak; she watched me, her expression defiant, unafraid, her duchess look, and that made things easier. I was tired of her acting high and mighty.

Jorge is not homosexual, I mimicked her accent as I spoke. I am the one who is homosexual and I always have been. She did not flinch; she held my gaze. I stood still.

Like you, I said, I thought he was too, indeed I hoped he was. But we were both wrong, weren't we? By this time I was standing in front of her, shaking. I felt like kneeling and burying my face in her lap but I could not do that. She smiled and then shook her head in wry amusement. Somewhere in her expression there was utter contempt. She sighed and closed her eyes and smiled again. It has been so difficult for me, she said, and now this, now this, now this. She stared at herself stoically in the polished glass of the window. I stood there in silence.

So tell me about it, she said. Sit down here, she patted the chair beside her, and tell me all about it. Maybe we should stay up late tonight.

There were things I could not say, things which were too intimate, details which were too explicit. She wanted to know if there was anything she could have done, if there was anything we could do now. I said no, it was always there and it would not go away. And when did it start, she asked.

I looked at her in the glass as I spoke, I told her what I could, and sometimes she asked a question. What I said became distant from us, as though I were reading from a book, or reciting a story I had been told. We were actors that night in the old hallway of the apartment, me talking and my mother listening to the lurid tales of a wayward son, my mother infinitely patient, but not reacting, making clear that she wished to know everything before she could pass judgement.

*

I HAVE A MEMORY of a dark evening in Buenos Aires when I must have been five or six. I was with my father in the street, I was catching his hand. He had come with me to the dentist. I remember that I had been lying back with my mouth open crying with pain and fear; everything the dentist did seemed to make things worse, and my father trying to calm me, standing there holding me, telling me that it would be all right, it would be over soon, the dentist just needed to do a little bit more. I think I remember this because it was the first time anyone had used Spanish to soothe me and calm me down. Usually, if I was sick or afraid or crying about something, it was my mother who spoke to me and she always spoke in English. I have a feeling also it was the first time that my father really noticed me, the first time that he believed that I cried or wanted attention for a good reason. I remember that I tried not to cry because I did not want to alarm him, and then I could not stop myself, and he held my hand and tried to distract my attention.

I remember us both in the streets leading up to our street; I must have sensed his relief that the drama of the dentist's surgery was over. He bought me plums. I could not eat them because my mouth was sore, but I liked having them. I must have asked for them, and even still I love the smooth purple texture of plum-skin, and the tight soggy flesh inside.

They had been married for ten years when I was born. My mother had suffered two or three miscarriages in the early years of their marriage, and then nothing. She was forty-three, nearly forty-four, when I was born, and he was fifty. His family, the Garays, owned a small shipping business, which was slowly declining, and he was the third son. My mother was the English secretary in the firm, and I think his family saw the marriage as another example of my father's lack of imagination and enterprising spirit. They were not, as far as I know, hostile or outraged, but they did not pay her much attention.

My parents treated me as a small adult in the household from as early as I can remember. If I was frightened in the dark, or if I was sick, or if I woke in the night, I could move quietly, without crying, into their bed, either in between them or beside my mother, and fall back asleep. My father would complain that I woke too early in the morning and wanted to sing or have a story read while he tried to sleep. I do not know what language I used when I spoke to them both. I suppose it must have been Spanish. I know in later years it was Spanish. But my mother always spoke to me directly in English, and in school I spoke in English, and because of my colouring I always believed I was English.

My mother had come to Argentina with her father and her sister, Matilda, in the early 1920s just after her own mother died. When I was a small boy I always wanted her to tell me the story of the voyage one more time. Days and days at sea, without a single sight of land, the sea flat and monotonous, going on for ever. The story of the man who died and whose body was thrown overboard. And the storm that blew up. And the moment when they passed the equator, and the seasickness, and the terrible food. And the ship rocking and rocking, and the first-class passengers. And then the port of Buenos Aires, the long wait to disembark, and this new language, how they did not understand a single word anybody said. I knew this story as though its details were more real and absolute than anything that happened in our apartment, or in school, or in our lives during those years of childhood.

And even then I knew that things had been disappointing for her. The story created expectations of future wealth and romance and excitement. The story should have been the beginning of something, but it was not. I was not yet born when her father died, but I heard her telling the story of his last days, when he could talk only in English, how he had never really learned to understand Spanish, and how she and her sister had buried him in a new graveyard at the edge of the city, and how she felt that from the moment he arrived in the new country he wanted to go home, and now he was trapped in Argentina for ever.

I do not know at what point I began to feel separate from my parents, when I stopped feeling comfortable about touching them and being close to them, when I was prepared to lie in the dark on my own rather than walk into their room and get into their bed. It would be easy if I could connect this with puberty and sexual awareness, but it has to do with something else. It has to do with how at a certain age I began to see the world as separate from myself, I began to feel that I had nothing to do with anything around me. I stood back and watched as my parents moved about the apartment, or the teacher drew on the blackboard, and I felt apart. Maybe I began to feel then that nobody loved me, maybe that is what I am talking about, and maybe everything that happened afterwards was a way of making people want to include me. I have always been surprised by anyone liking me, or approving of me, and I have always been ready to do what is necessary to stay close to them.

I began to notice how old my parents were compared to other parents, how slowly they walked, how much they disliked noise, how their clothes seemed dowdy and my mother's straight grey hair seemed strange. I have a memory of walking into their bedroom, I don't know what age I was, and seeing my father standing with his back to me naked. I felt then in a way that I can remember sharply how separate he was from everybody else, how he was alone too with his hairy body and his flesh, just as I was alone observing him, and we had nothing to do with anybody else, we were all separate in our bodies, all nobody to each other and everything to ourselves.

And this may explain how I felt when he first began to stay in bed and found that he could not eat and then went to hospital and then came home. I felt that this was not happening to me. I sat in his room sometimes because my mother told me to, and I realized that he was in pain, but I stood back from it. Perhaps that is the only way you can deal with watching your father dying, and perhaps it takes an effort, although it did not feel like an effort, and the results may stay with you, and they may shape how you behave. But I do not know if any of this is true.

We did not see my father's two brothers or his sister very much in all those years. I remember that we met his sister on the street one day and I did not recognize her. But now they appeared in the house in all their gravity, and they spoke in whispers.

I went into my parents' bedroom a few times in those days; the room was darkened because the curtains were drawn, but I could still see that the figure in the bed had grown thin, and his face now was like the face of an old man. I did not want to touch him or go too close to him, and I was glad when I was told by my mother that I was not to go into the room again. A doctor came and went, and then a nurse arrived and sat in the room and came out and whispered something. I watched her but I did not hear what she said. I remember it as a time when there were hardly any sounds: light footfalls, soft voices, doors being noiselessly opened and closed. I did not go to school for days on end, but drifted around the apartment or stayed in my room. I was not allowed to listen to the radio. I did not think that my father was really alive in there. He did not talk, and he could not eat. Sometimes, they said, he slept, but I did not know what he did when he was awake. He was part of a world I could not imagine, his body fading away in a darkened room, his family keeping vigil. I did not think about him then at all.

He must have died in the night. My aunt came and whispered the news to me in the morning, and told me not to cry or make any noise. Just to get up quietly and put on my clothes. I was not surprised. I hoped that they would bury him and then we could come home. I pictured us coming back up the stairs without him, into the empty apartment, and opening up the curtains in the bedroom, and making dinner, and turning on the radio, and continuing as though he had never existed.

But I wanted these days to be over. I wanted the apartment to myself again. I hated the hushed voices. I tried to imagine what they would do now. Would they take all his clothes off? How would he get from here to the church to the grave? How soon would his body rot and his teeth fall out? I was just past my twelfth birthday and I was growing all the time. My uncle took me out of the apartment to buy me a new set of clothes. I passed my mother in the hallway, but she was surrounded by people and had a handkerchief to her nose. My uncle and I sneaked by her, tiptoed our way out of the apartment.

It is strange how quick and easy certain actions are. I saw the coffin being carried into the apartment, and then I went into the kitchen with my aunt and uncle and when I came out my father was in the coffin and they were carrying him out the door. In two or three minutes they had carried the coffin down the stairs, and, except for his clothes and some books and papers, it was as though my father had never been in the apartment. I thought that it would be fine without him; soon, I expected, we would be used to it.

In the days after the funeral my mother grew distant from the household. I watched her type out letters on an old machine that suddenly appeared on the dining room table and then tear them up. I don't think she slept at all and we did not have proper meals. I do not think she understood that my father's family were in debt, and my father's share of the business was worthless. She was sure that there was money but there was none. There was the lease on this apartment which guaranteed a low rent. She could not be evicted, but she had no income. Maybe my uncles and my aunt had money invested. She was sure that they did, and she began to write to them and scream at them to demand her share, if not for her sake, then for mine.

I sat in on the final meeting she had with them. Two unsmiling uncles and a frowning aunt, and the chairs set out in the hallway, as though she would allow them to go no further. She asked them if they were going to leave her destitute, if that's what they were going to do. If the company could pay my father his salary, then they could pay her a pension. Did they want her to wash floors? Did they want her to beg on the street? There will be no need for that, my aunt said. How dare you tell me what there will be no need for, my mother said. I will stand outside your offices with Richard and I will beg. She leaned over and grabbed my arm. I will shame you all, she said.

A small amount of money would be set aside, my uncle said, for my school fees and my university fees, and the lease of the apartment would be put in my mother's name, although the lease technically belonged to the family and was potentially valuable. But there was no other money available; even the cost of my father's last days and his funeral would make a difference to the family. It might not have occurred to my mother, he said, but shipping between Argentina and England had declined and the company was running at a loss, and when the ships were sold, as they would be in the near future, the money would be used to pay off debts. If she thought she was marrying money, my aunt said, then she had married the wrong man. But we do have friends in Buenos Aires, my uncle said, and we could help find you work, and maybe you could talk to some of the English community in the city, they might know of work.

I will talk to lawyers, my mother said, and I will see you all in the courts. I will prove that you owe us money, and your name will be a disgrace all over the city. And that will be the next time you will see me. She stood up then and asked them to leave. She had not offered them tea or coffee or a drink. They sat there and said nothing, and then she walked over and opened the door. Quietly, one by one, they left and went down the stairs. She closed the door and stood with her back to it, as though she expected them to return and wanted to bar the way.

Within half an hour she had her typewriter on the table and she was typing a letter to her sister, Matilda, who lived on an estate in a place called Molino in La Pampa. I had seen photographs of the huge house which the owners lived in. I knew that Aunt Matilda and her husband lived in a smaller house and I knew that they had two boys, who were older than me, but I had never met them. I don't think that my mother had seen her sister for more than ten years. She wrote to her, outlining what had happened, and she asked her for help, or for shelter, or for advice. I am not sure what she asked for, but she waited with great impatience and nervousness for the reply.

I had gone back to school by this time, and I remember

coming in one afternoon and my mother telling me that we were leaving the city, at least for the moment. It might be easier to find work in Molino – she did not say what type of work – and it would be cheaper to live and we could stay with Matilda. I said nothing. I was sure that she meant more than she said, and I listened for any sign that we were going to give up the apartment and pack up everything. I noticed one day when I came back from school that she had cleared out all of my father's clothes, and some of her own clothes, and some of my old clothes. There were boxes of clothes outside the apartment door waiting to be collected. I did not know if she was selling them or giving them away. On one of those evenings, as she spoke about packing and what we would take and what we would leave behind, I reminded her that my uncles and aunt had agreed to pay for my education. What school would I go to in Molino? If I left my English school for too long I would lose my place. I knew that there was no English school in Molino so what school would I go to, I asked her, and how would I get used to school in Spanish?

Maybe if she were alive now and could give her version of this, these remarks of mine would not figure. It is possible that she thought about me all the time, that every decision was made because of me. But I think not. I think my father's death shocked her and left her forlorn to the extent that she noticed nothing around her, and she did not know what to do. She was intensely wrapped up in herself. I spoke carefully that day, I prepared what I was going to say. And I remember that within a few minutes she came down to my bedroom and stood at the door.

'Are you saying that you don't want to go to Molino, that you want to stay here? There's nothing for us here.'

'I don't want to go to a Spanish school.'

'Why don't we go and try it? Why don't we tell the school that we are going away for a short time?'

'How long?'

'I don't know how long.'

'And will we leave our things here? I mean everything we own.'

'Yes, we can do that.'

'Like we're going on a holiday?'

★

WE TOOK THE BUS from the city to Santa Rosa and there we waited in the bus station for a late bus to Molino. I loved the bus journey from the minute it started, the seat was comfortable and the air was warm. I soon fell asleep, and when I woke I lay back and closed my eyes and hoped that the bus would never stop, that I could dream and doze and wake again, and take a drink from the flask my mother had and stare out of the window and then doze once more, and that nothing would have any consequences, and that time would stand still. It was cold on the second bus, and I was tired now and wanted to be in my bedroom with the main light off but the door open so I could see the light from the hall. My mother was silent. Now I realize that she was fifty-six and penniless in a country which she did not understand, sitting beside a son old enough to work out strategies, hiding his erection from her as the bus thundered on towards Molino.

Aunt Matilda met us at the bus station. She was with the younger of her two sons, Pedro, who was a tall skinny boy who did not smile. Aunt Matilda spoke in Spanish to us, although my mother addressed her and Pedro in English. We had to wait at the side of the road until a truck came. My mother and I and our bags were hoisted on to the back of the truck. Then Pedro lifted his mother on and jumped on himself and told us gruffly to hold on tight. I had not realized, and my mother had not realized, that Aunt Matilda was poor.

We drove out into the dark countryside and then up a long tree-lined drive to a big house. As we grew nearer I turned and watched my mother look at the house suspiciously as though she were moving forward in water step by step, testing the bottom each time. The truck drove around to the back of the house and stopped. Pedro and the driver helped us off. We each carried a bag as we set off in the darkness across a field towards a cluster of small lights in the distance. My mother had to watch each step because of her shoes. She spoke English all the time, but Matilda spoke only Spanish; Pedro did not speak at all.

Eventually, we came to the door of a small wooden cottage with a tin roof. We walked straight into a kind of kitchen. There was a tall unshaven man, Aunt Matilda's husband, sitting on a chair. He spoke to his wife without acknowledging our presence. I noticed my mother's clothes, how fancy they seemed now, and her make-up and the comb in her hair. My uncle stood up and nodded at us. He took a lantern from over the door and lit it. I looked around the room, wondering if there was another kitchen. I could see no fridge, and no sink with taps, although there was a small, old-fashioned range in the corner. My uncle told us to follow him out with our bags. We walked around the back of the house until we came to a shed with a door and a window. He pushed open the door; there was no handle or lock. Inside there was an old iron bed made up and ready for someone to sleep in, and a smaller camp bed beside it. The floor was plain concrete. There was a table with a basin on it and some soap beside the basin. My uncle showed my mother where the toilet was, handed her the lantern, and then left us there, closing the door behind him.

'We'll talk about this in the morning,' my mother said. 'It might be better if we went to sleep now.'

She handed me my pyjamas from the top of a bag and then brought me outside by the light of the lantern and showed me the small shed where the toilet was. I said nothing. I knew that there was no need for me to speak.

When I woke in the morning her bed was empty. I closed my eyes and tried to go back to sleep, but I wanted to go to the toilet and knew that I would have to get up and dress myself. I did not know what time it was. In the dusty light of the room, things looked even shabbier than they had looked the night before.

My mother was drinking coffee and eating bread in the kitchen. I sat down and was given a mug of cocoa and some bread. Aunt Matilda was there and my other cousin, Paco, who was tall and skinny like his brother. His mother said that he was fifteen, but he looked older. I wondered what it would be like to be so tall and skinny. Aunt Matilda said that I should wear older clothes, that everything would get dirty here, but my mother said in English that these clothes would do for the moment. I did not understand why we had come here, and I wished that my mother would explain to Aunt Matilda that in Buenos Aires we lived in a big apartment in a nice building and we were not used to this, but I imagined that Aunt Matilda might have guessed this from the way we dressed and sat at the table.

On the second day, Paco took me with him to the yard at the back of the farm buildings and then down through the fields to where a large number of boys were gathered. Most of them were about fourteen or fifteen, but a few were younger. Some of them had very dark skin. They divided up into two teams to play football on a piece of waste ground. Paco picked me to be on his team. I did not explain to him that in my school, sport was optional, and I had always chosen to go home in the afternoon rather than stay behind to play football. Also, I was wearing the wrong shoes.

As soon as the game started they realized that I was useless. I tried a few times to tackle a player from the opposing side, but he sidestepped me without any difficulty and left me standing there. A few times I ran to get the ball and tried to work out which way to kick it, but it was taken from me almost immediately. Once, a fight broke out between two players; I watched how fierce and strong they were, and I stayed back. I could not wait for the game to be over. Even though I had hardly taken part, I was hot and sweaty; I realized that no one was timing the game, that they were going to play on and on until they were too exhausted to go any further.

Afterwards, we lay down on a patch of soft grass. It was late spring, but the weather had still not turned. Some of the boys drifted home, a few continued to kick the ball back and forth, and then a few of us went down to the river, which was four or five fields away. One of the boys, stockier than the others and a few years older than me, explained that all their fathers worked on the estate, which was one of the biggest in the area, thousands and thousands of hectares. The owner often used a helicopter to travel over his land. He owned all the houses, he even owned the school in the village and he controlled everything.

At the river some of the boys took off their shoes and socks and paddled in the water, but it was too cold for me. I sat on the grass and watched them. A few days later, when it was sunny, I went down to the water again with Juan, the stocky boy, and two other boys with whom I had played football. We paddled in the water and splashed each other, and then walked over to a big wooden barn across the fields. It began as a game; and maybe it began because I was blond and had freckles on my face and they wanted to see what I looked like with no clothes on. I was nervous at first and refused. I wanted to go home. I promised I would not tell anybody what they were doing. Juan asked me to stay, it was all right, he said, they did this quite often.

The two other boys were young and soft-skinned and only

half-formed; they had a wiry strength which did not interest me — even at that age I must have had preferences. It was agreed that we would all strip at the same time, but the two boys were much slower, so that Juan and I were down to our underpants while they were still fumbling with their shoes. I still did not want to do it, and I stood there watching them. One of them was not wearing underpants, so he was the first to appear naked. Come on, you, Juan said to me, but I did nothing. The other boy took his underpants down; he had a small erection. Let's do it at exactly the same time, Juan said. Now, let's do it now. He had white cotton underpants and I could see that he had an erection. He pulled them down, but still I did nothing. His penis was much larger than I had expected, longer with a huge crown at the top. I realized as I looked at him that I had no choice: I pulled my shorts down, and all three of them looked at me, approached and touched my pubic hair and pulled back my foreskin.

I put my hand on Juan's buttocks, I could sense how strong he was. I put my hands between his legs and felt his balls. I knew that I could not pay him too much attention. One of the other boys began to masturbate me; I did not know what this was, but I let him do it. I put my hand on Juan's penis and felt the tight, smooth skin on his stomach. Suddenly, I began to come. I did not understand what was happening. I closed my eyes and put my arms around Juan and lay against him. One of the boys was too young for all this, but the other boy and Juan began feverishly to masturbate. By the time they came off I was putting my clothes on.

★

MY MOTHER SAT AT the kitchen table in Aunt Matilda's house and went over everything that had happened while Aunt Matilda moved around the kitchen. Every time I entered the house my mother was in exactly the same chair, telling the story of my father's death, and his funeral, and the doctor and the nurse, and his brothers and sister. Sometimes she would remember that she had left out a detail from an earlier part of the story and she would go back to that, but my aunt would then become mixed up and would fail to understand that this was in the week before my father died and not the day after the funeral. My mother spoke as though telling the whole story, going over every moment of what had happened, might suddenly lift her out of her current plight into some bright new future. She acted out her rows with my uncles and aunt while her sister still moved around the kitchen. Not once, in the time we were there, did I see Matilda sitting down.

At mealtimes, my mother switched into Spanish and told my uncle and my cousins what she had been telling Matilda. I listened to her some of the time. I liked the story, because I knew what was coming next; I had been there while some of it happened. My mother left nothing out and made nothing up. My uncle paid her no attention, interrupted her in mid-sentence to ask for more food, or to ask some mundane question, and stood up at the end of the meal and went out. My cousins kept their heads down and left the table as soon as they had eaten. My mother sat at the table without offering to help in the preparation of meals or in cleaning up afterwards. She made it seem natural, part of the deal she had with her sister, and thus neither she nor I noticed the resentment building up against us.

The day after the episode in the barn I looked around for Juan, but he did not appear, and I did not know where he lived, and did not want to ask my cousins. But the following day I met him as I crossed the field. He had a small handball with him; we played with that for a while and then moved down towards the river. We sat down on the dry grass and talked. He told me that he would be leaving school soon and he would probably start working on the estate. At first, his job would be to round up cattle. He would like to learn to drive a lorry, he said. I told him about Buenos Aires, and about my English school. He asked me how to say various things in English and I told him and he smiled. As we stood up to walk back, I asked him if we were going to the barn. He looked puzzled and asked me what I meant. I did not know what to say, but as we walked on I referred to what we had done the previous day, and he said that we would go back some other day. I had presumed that our meeting and walking towards the river and our playing and talking were all preliminaries to our going to the barn.

The next day as I was walking by the river with my cousin Pedro, I found Juan sitting there with one of the other boys who had been in the barn. We sat and talked and then Pedro wanted to go. I said that I would stay by the river for a while. I knew as soon as Pedro left that the other two would come to the barn. We walked in that direction without saying why we were going there. This time we did not strip, but took our trousers down. I played with the other boy and pretended that I was interested in him, while knowing that I would soon be able to turn and pay attention to Juan. He held up his shirt and let us both play with his dick and balls. I buried my face in his neck as I ran my hands over his body. When I brought my lips close to his he turned away. I paid more attention to the other boy, and then turned towards Juan again, but he did not want me to touch his body, and when I suggested that we lie down, he refused. He said that I was acting as if I were a queer. None of us spoke as we walked home across the fields.

I had learned the rules. He had to have somebody else present, but not one of my cousins, or anyone older, and I could not lean against him, or lie down with him, or seem too interested. He liked me touching him, and he preferred me to any of the others, though we never discussed it, or even mentioned it. In the meantime, I began to sense that my mother was causing tension in Aunt Matilda's kitchen, and often when I went in and out of the house, I noticed silence. But my mother still did not move from the chair. When she came into the room we shared at night I pretended I was asleep. I knew that something was going to happen, but I did not know what it was going to be.

One day I came in and found a new atmosphere in the kitchen. My mother had stopped talking about herself and was talking about something else. She was angry about something; over and over again she said that something could not possibly happen. Aunt Matilda moved around the kitchen with her mouth closed and her jaw rigidly set. I sat on a stool in the corner and listened. It seemed that my uncle had found my mother a job as a servant in the owner's house. She would serve at the table and wear a uniform; she would be in charge of keeping the dining room clean. When my uncle came in, my mother stopped talking. No one spoke. My cousins came in. Still no one spoke. It seemed clear to me that they had been talking about us, or that something had happened earlier which I had missed.

As soon as the food was on the table my uncle asked my mother if she was ready to start work. My mother said that she had no experience serving people at table and she had never worn a uniform. How are you going to make a living if you don't take this job, my uncle asked her. My cousins kept their heads down. I am not a servant, my mother said. I suppose Matilda is a servant, waiting on you day and night, my uncle said. Can Matilda not talk for herself, my mother asked. No, I'll talk for her, my uncle said. And I've told the house manager that you will take the job, and there is a possibility now that you will get a small house of your own, and that might be easier for everybody.

You mean, my mother said, that I would live in one of these houses and work as a servant? Yes, my uncle said, and I can't see what else you can do. What did you mean, my mother went on, when you said that it might be easier for everyone if I had my own house? I meant, my uncle said, that I am tired listening to you and looking at you. Nobody spoke then. I thought that my mother might cry or leave the table. Instead, she ate her food and drank some water. Matilda's jaw was even more rigid than it had been before my uncle came in. My uncle kept his head up and looked around the table. He caught my eye for a second, but I looked down. I knew this meant that we would be going back to Buenos Aires, but I understood that we would have to wait until the morning.

My sister, my mother said, is the only person I have in the world, and I thought she might help me. No one spoke. I looked at Matilda but she was busy eating. I hoped that my mother was not going to cry. I wondered if my mother had expected to sit for the rest of her life in that chair in that dingy kitchen while her sister washed clothes and cooked and stored things away. But I do not think that my mother put any thought into anything she did during that time.

She sat for the rest of the evening without speaking, and then when it came to bedtime she asked Matilda if she would lend her the bus fare back to Buenos Aires. And then I learned something which I had not known before – my mother had no money at all, not a penny. Aunt Matilda said that she would ask her husband and she would let my mother know in the morning. I went to bed and buried my face in the pillow when my mother came into the room with the lantern. I wondered how we would eat if we went back to Buenos Aires. I thought of the jars and tins that were in the kitchen. But I did not think it would be enough.

My uncle came and woke us early in the morning. He said that there was a lorry going into the town, and if we packed up now, we could have some breakfast and then get a lift. We would be there in time to get the bus, he said. When he left, my mother said that she was disgusted at him coming into the room like that while she was in bed. He was a pig, she said, just a pig, and he lived in a pigsty. I made a grunting sound from the bed, and suddenly the two of us began to laugh. He has piggy eyes, my mother said, and we laughed more. I grunted as I lay there with my hands behind my head. A fat pig, my mother said.

It occurred to me as we walked along the dirt track to where the lorry was waiting that my mother had not changed her clothes in the three or four weeks we had been there. Perhaps she had changed her underclothes and her stockings, but not her blouse or her skirt or her cardigan or her shoes. Pedro and my aunt came with us to carry the bags, and as we were helped up into the lorry I noticed that my aunt and my mother had the same pursed lips and long-suffering look. I knew that my mother must have been given enough money to pay the bus fares, she also had a bag of food, but I hoped that she had some extra money for when we arrived in the city. And I hoped that she had a plan. As soon as the bus started on the way to Santa Rosa, I began to grunt like a pig, and my mother put her arm around me and shook with laughter. He was smelly, like a pig, too, wasn't he, I said. My mother nodded. Yes, smelly, she said, he certainly was.

*

WE HESITATED as we opened the door of the apartment. Once I stepped inside, I found that I could not hold back the tears. For the first time I felt all the grief about my father's body lying in the dark earth, and fright at the idea that his eyes were closed and his body was slowly rotting. I ran into my mother's bedroom and put my arms around her. I was sobbing now. She held me and said that she would make cocoa and then I would go to bed and she would sit with me until I was asleep.

In the morning, she came into my room and whispered that

29

she had to go out, but she would be back soon, and I could stay in bed, or I could get up, and there were things for breakfast on the dining room table. I did not ask her where she was going, and I did not find out until later that day when the Anglican clergyman Mr Walters, whom I had seen at Sunday school and at church, came to the apartment and sat with us. He was a thin, grey-haired man with a large bottom lip. We should have consulted him much earlier, he said, and of course he and his congregation would be only too willing to help. It was a small community, he said, and something could be arranged. He left my mother an envelope full of money.

Soon, I went back to school, and when we attended church on Sunday now, people came up and spoke to us and smiled at us. Faded old ladies and men with moustaches shook our hands and asked us if everything was all right. Mr Walters found my mother a job in a small English hotel called The Home Counties Hotel in San Telmo. Her job was to take charge of reservations and to sit at reception and give people their keys and make up their bills. It was, Mr Walters said, a very refined hotel, and my mother liked the job and did not have very much to do. The pay was not good, but if she was prudent, Mr Walters said, she would be able to get by. And if she needed extra money for clothes or schoolbooks or some emergency then the English community in Buenos Aires would be prepared to help out. He was sure of that.

When I came home from school my mother would still be at work. I put my school texts and my copybooks on the dining room table. I was alone there, except for some ghostly remnants of my father that hovered in corners, except for some aspects of myself which I did not understand, desires and longings which did not seem part of the everyday world, which would not have been understood by the Church of England congregation as they greeted us on the way out of Sunday service. Sometimes, when I wandered around those empty rooms, I dreamed that I was a woman, not a girl, but a woman like my mother. I opened her wardrobe, and touched her clothes, found that most of her things would fit me. I imagined I was her. I bolted the door of the apartment so that if she came back early she would not surprise me as I put on her clothes. I stripped and pretended that I was a woman; I put on her underclothes, her brassiere, and then her dark skirt and blouse and jacket. I put one of her hats on my head and I moved about the apartment.

There was an old *Life* magazine which someone had given her with page after page of photographs of Kennedy's funeral, of world leaders following the cortège, but, more importantly, photographs of Jackie Kennedy dressed all in black, wearing a mantilla, tearfully walking behind the coffin. I dreamed that I was her, I found a mantilla in a dusty old trunk in my mother's bedroom and I walked slowly around the apartment as though I were following my husband's coffin. I looked at myself in the mirror, my shape, and tried to imagine what it would be like to be married, to take my clothes off in front of my husband, to go to bed with him, to be penetrated by him. I did not do this every day. Sometimes, I went to the hotel and waited for my mother in the lobby. But other days I went home and made myself into a woman, looked at my face in the bathroom mirror pretending it was a woman's face. When people asked me what I was going to be, I found it hard to answer. I had no vision of a real future in which I would take part, in which I would find a job and start a family. I wanted to be a woman, I wanted to have a tragedy and dress in black.

My mother and I talked in the evening about guests in the hotel, where they were from and how long they were staying. We did not talk about my father or his family, or my aunt Matilda or what had happened to us in Molino. As I grew taller, she told me that I should start going out with friends, that I should join a club maybe. I said that I was okay, and slowly we got used to living with each other, the mother and her growing son. She was content at that time, I think, and full of hopes for my future.

★

WE LIVED TOGETHER and we grew close. My mother said that she could tell when I walked in the street below the apartment. She could tell when I was coming up the stairs. Sometimes, we did not speak to each other much; like an elderly couple we behaved as though a great deal could be taken as understood. Often, she became attached to a guest who stayed at the hotel for more than a few days; she relayed to me all the information she had elicited from whoever it was. And she felt sad when they left and went back to England or to some other part of Argentina. She began to view England as the place she most wanted to be, but it was, I think, an England in her mind somewhere.

In ways that she herself did not understand or appreciate she liked me being gay once I told her. I think she thought it meant that I would not leave her; that no other woman would claim me; that she had me all for herself. I think she would have liked me to be an engineer or an architect or a doctor; she would have enjoyed telling everyone who came to the hotel about me. Instead, I had gone to the university to study English. I had a real advantage there over everybody else in the department, including the academic staff, but, nonetheless, others always came ahead of me. I found it hard to study. I could look at something for a while, but soon I would get bored. I found it easy to read the set texts – I understood every word – but it was difficult afterwards to write about or interpret the events and the characters in a novel or the tone and structure of a poem. Every sentence I wrote in those years at the university seemed to be only partly true.

One day, when I had been teaching Jorge for more than a

32

year, his mother telephoned my mother to say that he was about to go to Barcelona in Spain for a holiday with a friend, but the friend had pulled out. The tickets were bought, she said, and the *pensión* was already paid for; they could possibly get a refund, but they were student tickets. She did not want Jorge to travel on his own, as there had been riots and political ferment in Spain due to the death of Franco the previous year. She wondered if I could go, and they would pay for the tickets and for the *pensión*. My mother was disturbed by this. She did not want me to feel that I was travelling as Jorge's servant, or his paid companion. She also was uneasy about letting me too far out of her sight. She told Jorge's mother that I was not in the apartment right now, but she would speak to me when I came in and phone her back. She walked into the kitchen, where I was making coffee. She looked worried and depressed. She would much prefer if I went to England, she said. But if I wanted to go she would give me money and I could use some of the money I had earned from teaching Jorge. However, I had to promise her to be careful. I could pick up all sorts of diseases in Spain, she said. But it would be a good holiday for me. Did Jorge know about me, she asked. I said that he did. He was the only one who did. She shook her head in a mixture of worry and wonder and went back to the telephone and phoned Jorge's mother to say that I would be delighted to go to Barcelona.

She prepared for my trip as though she were going too. It would be the winter in Barcelona, so she made me buy a leather jacket and a woollen pullover. She ironed and folded shirts. She worried about what shoes I would wear. We were going for only three weeks, yet for the weeks before we went she worried whether I would have the right clothes to wear, whether I would have enough money. She did not want Jorge's family to feel that they had to collect me and take me to the airport. She arranged with the general manager of one of the big hotels that I would be taken to Ezeiza free on the hotel's courtesy bus. I would arrive there about an hour too early, but that would be no harm, she said.

I liked the idea of the aeroplane travelling across the world through the night. I said to myself that there were no mothers on aeroplanes. I thought that maybe I would sleep through the night, and I hoped that Jorge planned to sleep too. I saw him arriving in the departures section of the airport with his parents. His mother seemed even more involved in the details of his journey than mine. His father looked around the airport as though he were considering whether he was going to buy it or not. His father said that we would be the tallest boys in Barcelona. He was there years ago, he said, and in Madrid and Seville, and he was the tallest person he met. They were small, all of them, he said. Franco was a tiny little fellow, he said. And he supposed that the new king was small as well. The food is terrible there, he said, that is why they are all so small. Jorge and his mother laughed. I smiled. I wished his parents would leave us now, so that we could check in and wait for the plane without having to listen to his father. I wondered what my father would be like if he had come to the airport with me. He would be older, much older. I saw him now as a gaunt and faded presence, almost here now, standing close to me. I looked at Jorge's parents: they were so confident of their place in the world, they smiled with such ease. I could not imagine how it would be to have parents like that.

I sat by the window, and we agreed that we would change places as the night wore on, but Jorge liked being in the middle beside a Spanish girl who was going home after a visit to her uncle and aunt. Her parents had phoned to say that there had been huge marches and riots in Barcelona, she said. I fell asleep after the meal and when I woke the lights had been turned on, and there was an announcement that we would be landing in half an hour. When I pulled up the blind on the window, I discovered it was bright; there was a raw blueness on the horizon and we were sailing through freshly washed clouds. The Spanish girl told us that we could get a bus from the airport into Plaza de España, and from there we could get a metro or a taxi to our *pensión*.

I do not know what I expected the city to look like: maybe I thought that the buildings would be old and painted white, but the part we drove through that morning looked like Buenos Aires, except it was untidier and busier. We passed by a busload of police; some police were sitting in the bus and others were standing on the street holding rifles and what we thought were rubber-bullet guns. Jorge nudged me in the back of the taxi and we both looked out at them. In Buenos Aires when you saw police like that, it meant that there would be trouble, a raid on an apartment, or an office. But here the police seemed to be just standing there, looking around them.

The *pensión* was on the first floor of an old building down a side street off the Ramblas. There were two narrow iron beds and a tiled floor and no heating that we could see. The bathroom was down a corridor. We had one window, which overlooked the street, and even now, at nine in the morning, there was an extraordinary amount of noise from shutters being pulled up, from cars and motorbikes and voices. We decided that we would have a shower and shave and change our clothes and then go out and take a walk in our new city. Both of us were, I think, intimidated by being there. If Jorge had not been with me I would have gone to bed for a while, and postponed any exploration of Barcelona.

I could not think what made the city different from Buenos Aires: certainly, the shops were brighter, more alluring, entering one of them was like entering territory you already possessed, rather than trespassing; there was more loud talk in the few cafés we went into in that first morning; people on the street examined each other with a kind of openness which was new to us; and if two people walked along together, they could exude an intimacy in public which we had not seen before. Also, as we learned over the next few days, some people spoke Catalan. At first we thought that it was just older people, women in the market, people in shops, but soon we learned that young people spoke it as well. Jorge began to imitate their accents.

I liked being with him. I enjoyed waking in the morning to find him in the other bed. I knew that he was aware of me all the time: he took pleasure in coming back from the shower with just a towel around him and letting the towel fall away and standing there naked going through his suitcase for fresh clothes. He was more beautiful than I had imagined, his skin was perfectly smooth, his body seemed both strong and delicate as he moved about the room. In the evening, we walked up and down the Ramblas, idly looking at people as they passed, stopping for beers, wandering into side streets. One evening, it was maybe our third or fourth evening in the city, it began to rain. We went into a bar for shelter, and we realized when we came out that the air was much colder. The strain of being in one another's company constantly was beginning to tell. I found it hard to sleep all night with someone else in the room. It was still only nine o'clock. We went into a place called Casa José on a corner in an old square, and we had our dinner there without speaking much, and then we drifted back to the *pensión*. Neither of us, I think, was enjoying himself very much.

There was a television in the communal room of the *pensión* and we went in there out of curiosity; it was too early to go to bed. There were five or six people, all in their twenties, sitting in the room, the television was on, but no one was looking at it. Jorge went out to the *portero* and got us a beer each. We sat down close to the television and watched some French comedy that had been dubbed into Spanish. We both noticed that the voices around us were South American. I thought at first that they were Peruvian, but then I realized that they were Chilean. Jorge asked them where they were from, and I was right, they were Chilean. We said that we were Argentinian and immediately they began to include us in the conversation. They were all staying in the *pensión*. Three of the girls were white-skinned and very pretty; another girl and one of the boys were darker, more Indian-looking; and one boy was very tall, his dress and his manner reminded me of a priest. There was one other boy with very dark eyes.

It struck me that there was something strange about them all, it was a while before I could work it out as they talked about Santiago and Barcelona and Buenos Aires. I realized that they lived here, they were not on holidays, and, when they talked about Sweden and the time they had spent there, I knew immediately that they were refugees of some sort.

There was something about their eyes and their manner which made them different, and there was also an intensity in the way they responded to us – they included us too quickly in their world – that made me feel they were homesick and had nothing to do here, except wait for something to happen. I was uneasy with them that night, and I must have half-understood how excited Jorge was at meeting these good-looking girls; I stood up when I had finished my beer and told Jorge that I would leave the key in the door.

I was glad to have our bedroom to myself for a while. It seemed like months since we had stood with Jorge's parents at the airport. I left the light on and read the newspaper: there were articles about the possibility of the communist party being legalized, and I was surprised by this. I did not recognize the names of the main politicians in the article; I thought that we should try to find out more about what was going on in the country. Then I turned off the light and thought about the people we had just met. I believed it was possible that the dark-eyed boy, or the one who looked like a priest, could be homosexual. Then I fell asleep. I did not hear Jorge come in and I did not wake again until the morning.

Jorge was already awake and he wanted to talk about the Chileans. What did I think of them, he asked. They seemed nice, I said, but it was a bit like walking in on a family. They all seemed to know each other very well. All of them, I said, with the exception maybe of the tall boy who looked like a priest, were good-looking. Jorge had stayed up late, he said, hoping that one of the girls would stay behind, but the boy with the dark eyes had stayed up to the very end, as if he were guarding the girls. The three girls stay in one room, he said, and the three boys in another. I said I thought they were refugees, and he sat up in bed and clicked his fingers: that was it, he said, that's who they were, that explained everything.

At about ten o'clock that morning one of the boys shouted at us through the door that they were going to breakfast. Both of us were half-dressed, and we asked them where they were going and then said that we would join them in a few minutes. We met them in a café around the corner. Some of them were studying at the university, but part-time courses only. We watched that morning as the priest, as I nicknamed him, and the boy with dark eyes, who was called Raúl, and one of the girls devoured the morning newspapers, passing pages to each other to read, concentrating fiercely on the print.

There was nothing about Argentina that morning, but the next morning there was a report about an Amnesty investigation into human rights violations there. They handed it to us before they read it themselves since this was our country, and we would need to read the news from there with the same urgency as they followed the news from Chile and the new politics in Spain. We both read it and nodded; neither of us said anything. From the beginning, from the first night in the *pensión* when we met them, I realized that they thought that we too were political dissidents of some sort. And when they learned that we were merely here on holiday, their attitude did not alter. They presumed, because we were young and friendly, that we followed the violations of human rights and the possibility of change in Argentina and Chile as they did. And we were certainly interested in what we read. I was, and I presumed Jorge was too, against the police and illegal detentions and tortures. But it seemed remote from us. I was surprised that the newspapers were not censored.

Soon, we learned that Raúl would always be there. Usually, he said nothing, but he smiled if someone made a joke, and he liked ordering more coffee if anybody needed it, or collecting the money to pay the bill, or getting cigarettes. The priest was the most distant, he was away for much of the day, and in the evening he often went to bed early. The others were all members of the film club the Filmoteca, which was close to the cathedral; they had each bought a season ticket and made us buy one too. They went to one or two films a day. For them the most exciting part of the week was when the Filmoteca programme became available. They asked us what films were banned in Argentina, but we did not know. They went through a list, but we did not recognize most of the names on the list, so we presumed that they must be banned at home. We realized that the girls had talked about us, and decided to match two of themselves with the two of us, but this did not work because Jorge did not like Elena, who after the first few days began to sit beside him and pay him careful attention, as much as Maria José, and I liked all of them, but I preferred Raúl or the boy with the Indian features. We wondered if we should tell them this; Jorge took the view that this would mean a major rethink on their part, and might result in his being able to talk to Maria José. I said that I was not sure I wanted them to know that I was gay.

I had caught a cold in the city and this was a good excuse to stay in the room and let Jorge sort out his own problems. Raúl brought me tea and lemon drinks and sat on the bed and told me what films they had been to. He asked me what age I was; I told him that I was twenty-one. He was twenty-five, he said, even though he knew that he looked younger. He looked at me and smiled; there was something oddly gentle and childlike in the way he behaved. I couldn't decide about him. He asked me if I had been to Chile, although I was sure he already knew that I had not. I think he just wanted to talk, without the conversation becoming too personal. When I asked him if he would like to go back there, he sighed and stared at me as though I should know the answer to that. He told me about the time when he and the girls had found a phone box which was broken and thus they could make free calls to Chile. They used it for a few days until they had spoken to everyone they knew, and then they all became too sad and didn't phone for a day, and when they went back it had been fixed. I asked him if his parents were still alive and he said that they were. When I had finished the tea and the hot lemon, he took the glasses out and left me to sleep.

That night just before midnight Jorge came to our room and asked me to turn off the light and pretend that I was asleep. There was a chance, he said, that he might be able to bring Elena to the room, as Raúl had gone to bed. If I was awake it might embarrass her, he said. I thought that you preferred the other one, I said. Ssh, he put his finger to his lips. I had slept during the day and I was not tired enough to sleep again. I lay there in the dark listening to the footfalls and other sounds in the street and the ringing of the cathedral bells every fifteen minutes. I was almost asleep when they arrived in the room. They did not turn on the light. I moved around in the bed as though I had been slightly disturbed in my sleep and then I lay still. I was facing the other bed. Jorge locked the door. I could hear them whispering. Then there was silence. I wondered what they were doing. I could not look. Then they moved across the room and lay on the bed where I could make out their shape.

Slowly, they began to take off their clothes between bouts of kissing. They lay on the bed and did not move for a long time; then I heard Jorge whisper something. He reached out to the bedside table, and I realized that he was putting on a condom. Then I heard her gasp and hold her breath as he entered her. I was sure then it would be over soon, as his thrusts became harder until the bed began to hit against the wall. He and Elena had to move towards the centre of the bed. I could hear her moaning and I presumed she must be having an orgasm. I could not believe that Jorge was still fucking her. He behaved as though he were going to do this all night. When he finally came I felt that I should sit up in the bed and applaud him, but I lay there instead and closed my eyes, and soon I fell asleep, and when I woke it was still dark, but Jorge was alone in the bed.

When I found the used condom in the waste-paper basket in the morning, I told him he had better get rid of it before the landlady saw it. He smiled and said that it had been worth flying all the way over from Argentina for. When we went for breakfast I noticed Raúl and the priest watching us darkly as we approached. The girls were still in bed. We sat and read the papers with them, and afterwards we went off walking around the city and did not come back until after six o'clock. I wished that we were moving to another *pensión* or another city. I would have liked to go to Madrid or Seville. But I knew that Jorge was happy, and I thought I knew what was on his mind. He would sleep with Elena again if he had to, but what he really wanted to do now was sleep with Maria José.

When we arrived back at the *pensión*, we met the three girls, who had just returned from the cinema. They were talking about a demonstration the following Sunday. The slogan, they said, was Amnesty, Freedom and Autonomy. It would be led by Catalan activists, but anyone else who wanted could march. Everyone thought that it was going to be the biggest march since the death of Franco, Elena said. They were all going to go, and they thought, they said, that we might come with them. Jorge nodded and said that it sounded like a good idea. At the first big march, Elena said, there had been a baton charge, but the most recent ones had been peaceful.

As soon as we closed the door of our room, Jorge said that we would have to be very careful. I did not understand what he meant. We can't go on any demonstrations, he said. Why not, I asked. I had no idea what he was talking about. It would just take one photographer, he said, or just one shot on television, or just one person watching. And what, I asked. He said he was sure that the embassy was noting who was going on the marches. There's no embassy in Barcelona, and nobody, in any case, would recognize us, I said. He turned and looked at me sharply as he spoke. Sometimes, he said, you are the most innocent person I have ever met.

That night he told me to turn off the light and pretend to be asleep once more. I think that he liked the idea of my being there in the bed beside his bed, listening to every sound which he and Elena made, the eunuch beside the sexual athlete, witnessing his prowess. I began to view the length of time it took him to come, all that gasping and sweating, as a form of stupidity, but I am sure that I simply felt jealous or useless and my opinion was formed as a result of that. I woke the next morning wishing I was at home in my own bed with the day to myself. Instead, I had to get up and be Jorge's companion. I did not feel like his companion. We did not discuss the demonstration again, and the Chileans believed that we were going to come with them. I wondered what plans Jorge had to avoid them on the Sunday.

As we walked around the city, and went into a restaurant to

have our lunch, he told me that Raúl had been tortured after the coup in Chile. None of the others had been tortured, although two or three of them had been arrested. But the others were in danger because they had been members of the communist party. The priest, he said, was an important member. They had all gone to Sweden first, and their lodgings were being paid by a Swedish organization. Soon, they would decide whether to go back to Stockholm and apply for Swedish citizenship, or stay on in Barcelona, or maybe wait and see if the situation changed in Chile – although this now seemed very unlikely – or maybe go to some other country in South America, like Mexico.

Was Raúl tortured badly, I asked Jorge. He said that he did not know, that he had not asked too many questions. Elena had told him all of this the previous evening without any prompting. The Chileans had nothing to lose by going on the march, he said, but for us it would be different. Something that seemed entirely innocent could ruin your life, he said. Elena had said that Raúl was not very political; she thought the army had made a mistake when they took him in. He wanted to go home, she had said, but that was now impossible because he had given evidence against the regime.

The following day was the Sunday of the march and Jorge woke me early and said that if we left now, we could catch the train to Gerona and spend the day there. We were careful not to use the bathroom in case we woke any of the Chileans. We left the *pensión* as quietly as we could, as though we were absconding without paying the rent. I slept on the train and walked around museums and churches for the rest of the day in a sort of daze. We sat in a bar in the square beside the river and drank beer and ordered tapas and read the newspapers until about four o'clock, and then we walked back to the railway station and took the train to Barcelona. We went to a movie in one of the modern cinemas on Paseo de Grácia, and we did not arrive back at the *pensión* until about ten thirty. We were hungry and we went to a cheap restaurant with Elena and Maria José and the dark-skinned boy, Enrique. They were high from the demonstration, full of stories about the police with riot shields and rubber-bullet guns watching as the crowd taunted them for being fascists. Elena thought that they had orders not to charge the crowd, but it must have been hard for them. There were all sorts of people on the march – Catalan nationalists, socialists, trade union people, communists, just ordinary people. She was really sure that the government would have to have free elections now.

I was waiting for them to ask us where we had been, but in the excitement and flow of their talk, and in the way we listened as though we were interested in how the demonstration had gone, they never noticed that we had escaped for the day. Elena asked us if we had been on the march and Jorge said no, because we did not know who to march with; instead, we had watched the march, he said, looking out for our friends, but we had not seen them. She nodded and smiled.

I had breakfast with Raúl and the priest the next morning. The newspapers included reports about the march with photographs of crowds in the streets. I looked at some of the faces and wondered if those people would be worried now about their future, but I thought not. It all seemed calm and easy. I had tried to think about Raúl being tortured, but I could not. I looked at him now, and realized that the sort of innocence in him which I had been puzzled by was maybe pain and hurt. But still I could not imagine him being tortured, how anyone could want to make him scream out loud or suffer in any way. I tried to put the thought of it out of my mind.

Two nights later Jorge arrived back in the room with Maria José. It was taken for granted by him that I would leave the communal room in the *pensión* at a certain point every evening and go to bed. Within half an hour I would turn off the light and pretend to be asleep. If he came to bed alone, then he turned on the light and we talked for a while, or I read a book – I had found a copy of Graham Greene's *The Honorary Consul* in a Penguin paperback in a bookshop near the Ramblas – while he looked at himself in the mirror and brushed his teeth and took off his clothes, carefully folding them, and pranced around naked for a while before he got into bed. I do not know how he enticed Maria José into the room. When I left them earlier, Elena and Raúl had been there too. I do not know what he could have said to her. He seemed to have known what he wanted, however, since they both thrashed around the bed, constantly whimpering and gasping, changing position all the time. The cathedral bell had already rung two o'clock in the morning before he entered her. I stayed awake this time until the very end, and I saw her flitting out of the room without making a sound. I asked Jorge if he had enjoyed that, but he lay face down into the pillow and said nothing.

Neither of us appeared for breakfast in the morning. I could not think what to say to Elena, and Jorge did not move in the bed. I had a shower and then quietly dressed myself and slipped out and caught a metro to a stop three stations away. I did not want to bump into anyone I knew. There was a café just beyond the station. I had bought a newspaper but I barely glanced at it. I ordered coffee and a croissant and let time go by and looked at people who came in and out. I wanted to go home. I realized that we had another week to go. I walked back down through the city to the *pensión*.

Jorge had gone out. He had left me a note saying that he and Maria José had gone away for a few days. He would see me when he came back, he said. None of the Chileans was around the *pensión* or in any of the bars or cafés in the area. I presumed that they had gone to the cinema. Suddenly, I did not like being alone, and I did not know what to do.

I walked across to the Filmoteca and waited in the foyer

until the film was over; I felt lighter and better when they all came out of the theatre and stood there smoking. I think they knew that I was not involved in Jorge's seduction plans. They all smiled and wanted to go for a drink. I thought that Elena looked beautiful. I wanted to hug Raúl. Nobody mentioned Jorge or Maria José. I had never been in that area of the city before, except in the small section around the cinema; there were tiny bars down shadowy lanes, and a maze of streets that the Chileans all seemed to know. They spoke about several bars as though they were models of art nouveau and florid decoration, but they turned out to be smoky fleapits with badly tuned televisions and old men behind the bar serving drinks to various lowlife characters. The Chileans laughed as they arrived in each bar; they knew the names of the owners and they moved around these streets with ease. I did not think it was dangerous, but it was dingy. We had a beer in each bar – the prices were incredibly low – and then we moved on. They were all slowly getting drunk, but I remained sober. The beer had no effect on me.

It is only when I began to drink brandy that I got drunk too. As we sat around bars or walked in the street I thought about Raúl all the time. I imagined him coming to our room and getting into Jorge's bed and then, after we had talked for a long time, him slipping across to my bed. I imagined his warm skin and his lips and I kept reminding myself that I must be careful, I must not suggest anything to him. I sat close to him in one of the bars, and we talked about this area of the city, and the Barrio Chino across the Ramblas, and when he talked he always smiled, and as the night wore on, his skin seemed to grow darker and his features change so that I could see he had Indian blood in him, something I had never noticed before. I could not stop looking at him.

At two or half past two when the bars all closed up, the others had already gone home and there was just Elena, Raúl and me. We talked about walking to the Drug Store on the Ramblas, but we were too drunk. I put one arm around Raúl and the other around Elena and we walked slowly back to the *pensión*. I thought that maybe Raúl had been leading up to this; maybe he knew what I was thinking about. I left the door of the room unlocked. I got into bed and lay with my hands behind my head still drunk, wondering when Jorge would come back, wondering if Raúl would come to my room.

I woke alone in the room in the morning with a hangover. I turned and tried to sleep again, but instead I lay there without moving. If I stayed still, I thought, I might feel better. I turned and looked at the door and noticed that it was locked. I must have locked it during the night. It was eleven o'clock in the morning. I waited for some sound in the corridor.

When Raúl knocked on the door and said that he was going for coffee, I asked him to come in. I opened the door for him and then got back into bed. He said that he was feeling bad. He smiled, and went over to the window and looked out. He was wearing baggy jeans and a navy-blue pullover. He came and sat on Jorge's bed and rested his head against the wall. Too much beer is bad for you, he said. Too much brandy as well, I replied. He closed his eyes and put his head back. Neither of us said anything for a while, and then he noticed the English novel on the bedside table. He picked it up and looked at it, but could not understand a word, he said, though he had heard of Graham Greene. I told him that my mother was English. This means, he said, that you could live in England. I nodded. He said that it was hard to get into England now.

We felt too sick to eat anything. We drank water in the Plaza del Pino and decided to go to the movies again. There was a western on, Elena said, and this meant that we would have no trouble following the plot. White man has technology, reason and need, she said, while the Indian rides bareback and causes trouble and loses in the end. Raúl laughed and said that she was always good at making speeches.

I slept through some of the film and left before it was over. I waited outside for them and we went back to the *pensión*. We agreed to meet again at nine o'clock. In the meantime, we would go and lie down. I waited for a while in my room and then I went to the metro station and took a metro to four or five stops up the line. Once more, I found a café and sat on my own drinking coffee. Later, I went back to the *pensión* and had a shower and tried to sleep. As I passed Raúl's room on the corridor, I thought of him lying there asleep, his eyes closed, his face in repose. I would have loved to touch him or stand over him and watch him.

I met Elena as arranged at nine o'clock. No one else was coming out, she said, they were all too hung-over. I said that I wanted a beer, she agreed to have one too, and we went to a bar off the Ramblas. And then we walked to the cathedral and strolled around the strange, dark streets of the Gothic quarter until we found a ledge we could sit on. She asked me when I thought Jorge was coming back. I shrugged. I did not know. I asked her if she minded him going off with her friend like that. She said that under normal circumstances she would mind, but not here and now. She had learned not to mind things.

She asked me if I understood what was happening and I said that I did not. They had all been in Sweden, she said, and had gone through weeks and weeks of group therapy. They knew a lot about each other, and soon they would all have to make decisions about where they would live. The Swedes were paying for them, but soon that money would come to an end. Some of them were contemplating going back to Chile, but others could not do that. It was a decision, in the end, she said, between Spain and Sweden. They knew that they would have to settle somewhere, make a decision to stay so they would not spend much longer – it had already been more than three years

– stateless, homeless, unsure about the future. In the dynamic which develops between people who are rootless and afraid to hope, she said, your friend will want to sleep with the man you have been sleeping with, and you will watch it happen and let it happen, almost want it to happen, you start to will her to behave as badly as she can so that you can feel good.

I asked her about Raúl: what was he going to do? Raúl is the problem, she said, Raúl is why no one can decide what to do. He is the only one who was tortured, everyone else knew fear and lost everything, had to leave in the night and was lucky to escape, but he is different. He was held for three or four months, first in the stadium in Santiago, the famous stadium, and then in a camp near Valparaíso. He hasn't changed on the outside, she said, he was always like that. He was friendly and easy, he smiled a lot. Some people used to think that he looked like Bob Dylan and he did a bit, and he played the guitar, although not very well. But he was always there if there was company, he liked smoking dope and drinking, and he liked girls. He thought that he was living in a free country. He was becoming more political as time went on, but he was never a communist, although a lot of his friends were. Anyway, she said, they got him on the night of the coup, he would have been easy to find, and he never thought that he was in any danger.

I know everything that happened to him, she said, or everything that he is prepared to recall, I know it day by day because I did therapy with him in Stockholm – I had almost finished my psychology degree and I was asked to sit in on the sessions so that I could help him. He saw everything. He saw all the murders and the mutilations. He waited for days before they came for him, he lived in the shadows believing that they would let him go, or they would forget about him. But they forgot about nobody. They used electricity on him, all around his genitals, they put an electrode into his penis, and he gave them everybody's name. This is not a disgrace among us; she said, there is nothing bad about it. This is in the open. He told them the names of his grandparents first, they were dead, and they left him alone for days while they checked this out, and then they came back for him, and he thinks that he was tortured for a whole day and that was when he gave real names. They put him on a bed with no mattress, and then they moved him to hospital, and then to a camp where he was badly beaten, but no more electricity. And when they released him he took refuge in the Italian consulate in Valparaíso, and they got him out, and he was operated on in Sweden. He still has problems.

He cannot let any of us get too close to him, she said, and yet he needs us to be around, and we all understand that. He knows that he will never be all right, not just physically, not just about dreams and memories, but that he will never be able to trust anyone very much, and he feels guilty, and I think he feels shock. He remembers the days and weeks of fear, but then the actual torture seems to be something he cannot recover from. Soon, we're all going to go our own way, but none of us knows what to do about him. I think that he will go back to Sweden, and he will always need a group of people who know how to deal with him. We all love him, of course. I don't know what we are going to do.

*

ELENA AND I WALKED BACK through the Gothic quarter after she had told me this. We were both hungry; we went into a Chinese restaurant on Calle Fernando. We agreed that I would not tell Raúl that I knew his story.

Jorge and Maria José came back to the *pensión* four days before we were due to leave. I found him lying on the bed when I came in from the cinema with Elena, Raúl and the others. He said that he had some spare money and he had asked the landlady if I could have a separate room. He had done a deal with her. Maria José, he said, was going to move into the room with him. He hoped that was all right. I said that it was fine and began to put things into my bag. No, not tonight, he said, in the morning, that's when the room is free. I lay on the bed and asked him where he had been. They had gone to Madrid, he said, and they had loved it there, it was much livelier than Barcelona. And did anything happen here while we were away, he asked. No, I said, nothing.

Jorge and Maria José avoided us over the next few days. I saw them holding hands in the street. Raúl asked me if I knew about what had happened to him in Chile, I hesitated and then I said that I did. He said that sometimes he wished no one knew, and other times he wanted everyone to know. I can't decide, he said, maybe that's the best way. Maybe as the years go by I will forget about it. I nodded, but I did not think he would.

Jorge came to my room on the last morning, and said he wanted to make something clear. We were leaving, he said, and they would want to know our addresses. He was going to give them a wrong address and he thought that I should do the same. It might sound stupid, he said, but they could go back to Chile or come to Argentina, and they could be arrested again, and our names and addresses could be found on them, and that could mean real trouble with the way things are at the moment. Don't be so stupid, I said. I told him he was an asshole. He walked out of the room.

Elena and Raúl wanted to accompany me to the airport while Maria José wanted to go separately with Jorge. I brought Elena for coffee and said it might be better if we could say goodbye here. I gave her my address and she gave me a contact number in Sweden. I did not think that she would write to me or think about me very much. It was Jorge she would remember; it was Jorge they would all remember. Jorge and

Maria José were going to get a taxi to Plaza de España and a bus to the airport from there. I said that I would see them out there. Elena and Raúl came with me to the metro. Raúl carried my bag. I think that they enjoyed having a last coffee with me and seeing me off. It was something normal and everyday; their lives did not depend on it. I hugged them both and waved goodbye as I went through the turnstile.

*

WHEN I CAME BACK from Spain, my mother had changed. It was as though she had waited until I was gone and she had time on her own and free, clear space so that she could age and look worn without a witness to observe the process. She was only in her mid-sixties, but she looked like an old lady. Going to work was difficult. She realized that everything was over and there would be nothing. I think that she made no decisions, that everything she did all her life was done using instinct and whim. She became more involved in the hotel; the guests seemed to love her. She was always punctual and well dressed; her typing was perfect and she remembered everyone's name. And some of the time, when she had the energy, she paid attention to me. At the weekends, on Friday or Saturday evenings, or at Sunday lunchtime, she cooked a large and elaborate meal, and she took time over choosing the wine, and she treated me like someone who was about to go away or who had just come back. I found this disturbing and I noticed that for all of the day afterwards I thought about nothing except how to find sex in the streets.

She was careful not to play the part of the prying mother, so she asked me no questions, but spoke herself, as though she were being interviewed about her life on one of those long television programmes. I think that, prompted by her dinners with me and her English guests at the hotel, she reinvented herself in those years as an Englishwoman of the genteel sort.

One night I told her some of the things which had happened in Barcelona. I was still giving classes to Jorge and to two engineering students as well, but she knew that I liked him less after our holiday together, and it occurred to me one evening that it might help us get through the next hour together if I tried to tell her why. I was so used to hiding things from her that this account of Jorge and me in Barcelona was a relief. I told her about the Chileans in the *pensión* and then I decided to tell her about Jorge taking two of the girls back to our room and having sex with them in the bed beside me while I lay there pretending to be asleep. She was wide-eyed with indignation. The Argentinians are savages, she said, whatever mixture is in them that makes them like that, they are savages, they will do anything. And this became her theme in the months which followed, that she should never have come here, and how refined English people are, how polite and how civilized, how her father should have stayed in England after her mother died, how he could have married again. Compare the generals, she said, or Isabelita Perón with the Queen of England. Compare the Queen's placid smile, her grace, her easy warmth, her modesty, her family life with the half-bred savages who run Argentina.

Perhaps it was easy in those years to invent a whole new set of political views and express them fiercely in your own apartment. We saw newspapers only when something we bought came wrapped in newspaper. We had an old television, but we never watched it. We listened to music on the radio sometimes, but paid no attention to the news. We did not believe the news. I know that the World Cup took place in Argentina in 1978, but I cannot say that I saw any of the matches, or knew when or where they were on, or who won. I remember crowds in the street, men cheering and waving flags, and I remember cutting through side streets to avoid them. We took no notice of anything public; we lived in a small space.

On her days off she stayed in bed. She found the stairs in the building difficult, and did not go out unless she had to. She worried if I did not return early from the university. Sometimes at night when I came in she would be asleep in a chair, her head to one side, her mouth open. I knew that soon she would not be able to work, and I realized that when I graduated I would have to find a job. I wrote to my old school and told them that I was about to qualify, and they wrote back to say that they had a vacancy for a mathematics teacher, but not for an English teacher. My mother could not understand why I did not come first in my class. She suggested that I should study more. I began to do all of the shopping and most of the cooking and cleaning.

I expected that some day the hotel would telephone to say that my mother had collapsed, or had fallen asleep at her desk, but that was not what happened. On a morning when I was about to go and do one of my final exams, she asked me to help her down the stairs, and I realized that her knees would not bend. I had to help her down each step and then go and get a taxi for her. That evening when she came back she rang the bell and I went down and helped her up the stairs. And that is the way it went each day. I told her that I would get a job soon and she could give up her work in the hotel, but she shook her head and said that she would carry on. I took her to the doctor, the same old man who had seen my father out of the world, and he gave her pills, but she was still stiff and weak. He told me that she needed to rest. I was careful not to look at him.

She was elated by the election of Mrs Thatcher. Here is a woman, she said, who knows what is right and what is wrong. And that is what we need here, she said. She showed me Thatcher's face in a magazine, pointed at her, and said how sorry she was not to be in England now. She wondered how the Queen and Mrs Thatcher were getting along. They both, she said, looked so well in blue.

The people in the English Department were preparing a new course on spoken English, and they asked me to come into the language laboratory two hours a week to work with students on their pronunciation. I would make students ask questions so that I could correct their 'h' sounds, which they were pronouncing harshly like the Spanish 'j'. I saw English then as a language which was clear and cold, in which people said what they meant; and I saw the sounds which Spanish-speakers made as full of emotion and wrong-headedness. I corrected the students with icy precision and patience, and made them repeat and repeat and repeat until all the words had lost their meaning. If they learned to say 'have' properly, then, I tried to imply, they would have learned other things too, such as some poise and decorum. But when the results of the finals appeared, it emerged that I had done badly in everything except basic competence in English, and especially badly in linguistics, so it was conveyed to me that I could work with the students for the moment, but soon I would be replaced, and there was no future for me here. I put off telling my mother this news.

Eventually, she could no longer move, and there was no point in pretending that she could go back to the hotel, although I telephoned the manager and told him that she had a flu. Her mother had died of the flu and maybe it was bad luck to use that excuse. I borrowed books from the *Cultura Inglesa* Library for her on the history of the royal family and its present members. I made the mistake one day of bringing home for her a biography of Gladstone. She told me sourly that she had no interest in Gladstone.

That summer I began to teach at Instituto San Martín for the first time, having been recommended by the English

Department of the university, which wanted to get rid of me, and I made my first acquaintance with Señor and Señora Sanmartín. I worked three hours each on Tuesday and Thursday. I knew that they liked me and that I would get more work when the real school term began. They wanted me to sit in on other teachers' classes and report back to them on their performance and command of English. One of the teachers, a young woman called Ana who had studied in North America, made basic mistakes as she taught English, but the children all listened to her. I told Señora Sanmartín that she was remarkably good. I could not think of what else to say.

For the last two years of my mother's life, I was the breadwinner. She managed to move slowly and painfully from the bedroom to her perch in the hall, close to the telephone. She sat in her chair all day, she slept sometimes, she read her books and some magazines which neighbours gave her. She ate heartily, and this led me to believe that she would live for ever. I was not happy. I found her difficult. I hated being asked where I was going every time I got ready to go out the door. I knew that I could never abandon her now, and she could live for another twenty years. In the evenings I sat away from her. I lay on my bed with a book or I stayed in the dining room or the kitchen. And then I would come out and find her asleep, and I would feel sorry for her.

I do not remember when teaching began to bore me; in those first two years I was interested. I taught beginners and I loved controlling what they knew, making them repeat things, learn new words, form questions. I also did some private classes, and I was often tired when I came home to find my mother alert, like a bird waiting to be fed, in her chair, complaining that she had been alone all day and now she was looking forward to a little company. I managed the money now, aware that if I got sick we would both have nothing. We had no savings, nothing to fall back on.

She must have grown weaker as the days went by, but I noticed nothing. She stopped reading for a while, and just stared out of the window. I had, in a few small ways, grown like her. I shared some of her feelings. If she was awake in the night, I would lie awake too. Maybe something in me weakened too during that time. I shared English with her, and that made us different from everyone around. There are more words in English, she used to say, and more things to describe. I told her that made no sense, but she said that I had never been in England so I could not possibly know. She laughed at her own jokes, and I loved watching her cackling there in the shadows of the hallway.

I knew she was dying, but I thought that it would be slow. It was easy not to think about it: I was busy teaching, and then shopping, and cooking, and keeping the apartment clean. I hated washing sheets and trying to hang them to dry from the small balcony off the kitchen. I asked her how she had done it over all the years and she purred in her seat as though I were praising her and thanking her rather than complaining.

She did not want me to call the doctor for her. Even though her awareness was slipping, she knew that we were short of money. She had good days when she pretended that nothing was wrong. She would put her hotel clothes on and some make-up and sit in her chair. Sometimes I found myself looking around the apartment thinking how still and calm and easy it would be when I was alone here and she was dead. I felt guilty about these thoughts, I did not know that they were a way of protecting myself from what was going to happen.

On the morning that she had her stroke I telephoned my uncles and aunt and told them that she was sick. I had already called the doctor. She was lying in bed making unintelligible sounds. The doctor thought that maybe she would be better in a nursing home. I told him that we had no money. He looked at me and said that she would have to remain here then.

Speaking the plain, blunt truth made him satisfied and pleased with himself. I asked him if he knew the name of the nurse who had looked after my father. He said that his secretary had her name and number, but I should remember that a nurse did not come cheaply, and I should not run up bills which I could not pay. I asked him if my mother was likely to regain her speech. He said that it was impossible to judge.

My aunt arrived later that evening. She looked around the apartment as though she owned it and sniffed the air suspiciously. I told her that my mother was sleeping and there was no point in going into her room. I now regretted having phoned her in the heat of panic. I told her what the doctor had said about the nursing home, but she did not offer to pay for my mother to stay there. She asked me if we had any money. A little, I said. Enough for us to get by for a week or two, but not enough for a nurse or for medicine.

I can't pay for a nurse, she said. I did not reply. I was trying to find the energy to say nothing more to her. We sat at the table in the living room. I did not offer her anything. I cannot be here all day, I said, I have to work. I stood up and walked down the corridor to my mother's bedroom. When I looked in she was lying on her back with her eyes open. She did not see me. I went again and sat at the table with my aunt and said that she was still sleeping. She cannot be left alone during the day while I am working, I said. But how long will this go on for, she asked. I told her that I did not know.

That night my uncle telephoned me to say that they had found a woman called Leonora who would come on weekdays when I had to work. She was not a nurse, but she would be able to do housework and keep an eye on my mother and make sure that everything was kept clean. When he had finished speaking, I found that I was staring at the wall and could not say anything. Are you still there, he bellowed into the phone. I was startled by the loudness of his voice. I said that I was still here and that was fine, Leonora could come in the morning. I would have a key cut for her. I almost asked him how many ships he would have to sell to pay for her, but I did not. I thanked him and hung up.

The doctor came a few more times and said that she was not improving. But it was the clergyman Mr Walters's bearing as he came and went which let me know that things were bad. He had spoken to the doctor, and to my aunt and uncles. He came with a prayer book and sat on a chair beside the bed, but I do not think that he opened the prayer book. It is possible that the mournful look on his face offered her some comfort. But I had the idea as I sat with her that there was no possibility of comfort. Her life was over before it began: she had never imagined that things would end like this, that she would be almost destitute in a strange country.

Leonora did not know her, viewed her as an old pathetic lady who could not talk, and moved her roughly. I do not think that I had ever been in a rage before, but one day when I came back I found that she had left my mother sitting in a chair in her bedroom while she changed the sheets. My mother must have wet the bed. Leonora was talking to her as if she were a bad child, almost threatening her. She did not hear me come in, she was so wrapped up in scolding my mother. She was surprised to see me standing in the doorway. I asked her to finish what she was doing as quickly as she could, and then come to the living room. I told her that she was to speak to my mother with respect, that she was to go down now and apologize and I would stand outside and listen. She said she had done nothing wrong. I told her to apologize or leave, I would let her decide. She walked sheepishly down to the bedroom and said to my mother that she was sorry for speaking to her like that.

My mother died on a Saturday evening at about ten thirty. The room was lamplit and the door closed. I had been sitting beside her for some hours. It was not easy; she was desperately trying to speak and to reach out. I asked her to move her good hand if she was in pain, and to keep it still if she was not. Her eyes focused on me, but I do not think that she heard. She babbled. There was an intensity about the way she moved her lips and her chin. She was not getting ready to die, she was resisting whatever was happening within her. I cannot say that I knew she was dying. I thought she might soon fall asleep, and I wanted to make sure that the sheets were dry. I had never yet had to clean her and wash her, and I hoped that I might be spared that. Had her voice been strong enough, I felt, she would have been shouting. I held her hand and told her that I was here, but she was reliving or inhabiting some other part of her life, something which she seemed almost to grasp and then it eluded her.

I concentrated on her, tried to imagine what it might be like now, what she might be thinking about. I had never known her enough; all of her life she had invented ways to prevent people knowing her. I do not think, for example, that England mattered to her at all. Nor do I think my father mattered. What mattered to her were those years between the ages of twenty-five and forty, how quickly they had slipped away, how hard it was that she could not reclaim them. And I mattered to her, and she must have known, she must have known that I was in the room, that I was holding her hand. At some point in those days before she died, she must have recognized me, she must have seen me, but she gave no sign. Everything came from inside her, from dreams and memories and strange urges which made her breath quicken and her body shake. I wish that she had died a peaceful death, but it was not like that at all. Whatever was locked inside her was never released, it did not die with her, and it remains somewhere in the shadows of this apartment; it remains inside me, and I do not know how to get rid of it.

Her shaking became violent for half an hour and then she relaxed. I gave her something to drink and the two pills she took three times a day, but she could not swallow. She almost began to make sense, but I could not make anything out fully. Something like 'she away' or 'she way', but more like grunts than words. And then she died. It was hard to tell at what moment this happened, when there was life and when there was no life. Her mouth was open and her eyes seemed alive, but there was no breath and no pulse. Maybe she could still hear and I should have said something then, maybe I should have told her that I loved her and I was grateful to her and I would be all right, but I kept my finger and thumb on her pulse to see if it would start up again. It did not. It was easy to close her eyes and close her mouth.

I did not know how long it would take for her body to become rigid. I decided to stay with her for a while. I wanted to lie beside her. I held her hand. I looked at her face, trying to make sure that I would always be able to remember what she looked like. The room was absolutely still. I was afraid to open the door, to return to the real world. I wanted to postpone any move, I wanted to let the minutes go by, minute by minute by minute my mother's soul was seeping out of her until there was nothing. I let time pass.

As soon as I opened the door and went out into the hall, I began to cry. I went into my own room and lay face down on the bed. I was alone now, there was nobody in the world who knew me, or who loved me. I had lost whatever anchor I had had in the world: nothing I did mattered to anyone. I went to the telephone and I rang Mr Walters, who must have had an extension beside the bed, because he picked up the phone immediately and said that he would dress himself and come to the apartment as soon as he could.

I thought of the crowds strolling in the streets of the city, the cinemas emptying out, the bars, the restaurants, people driving home, hailing taxis, waiting for buses. The whole bright busy world. And my mother lying dead in a darkened room. I went and sat beside her body until Mr Walters came.

We buried her on a warm spring day beside my father in the family vault. Mr Walters conducted the service in English. A large number came from the English community. They politely shook my hand and left me alone with my aunt and uncles and some cousins in the front pew. Jorge and his parents came; Señor and Señora Sanmartín; some neighbours. I wrote to Aunt Matilda, but I did not post the letter until the funeral was over. My aunt and uncles came back with me to the apartment; they told me that they would have the lease of the apartment put in my name and it was mine for the rest of my life. I could not wait for them to leave. Mr Walters and his wife had invited me for supper and made up a bed so that I would stay the night with them. The community was slowly disappearing, they said, people were always being left alone. They knew what it was like. But I was young, Mr Walters said, and Argentina was my home. In the morning I went back to work. I did not go to the apartment until I had finished my day. I kept the door of my mother's bedroom closed and I did not go in there. I would wait for a while, I thought, wait until I was ready.

★

I BROKE THE SPELL when I brought the first man into the apartment. For the months after she died, and right through that summer, I felt as though someone had numbed all of my nerves. I felt nothing, no desire, no hunger, no thirst, no tiredness even, just an ability to face each day calmly, expecting nothing.

I gave my mother's clothes away. In the wardrobe in her bedroom I found five hundred dollars in cash in an old flattened handbag. I put the notes, which seemed too small to be worth that much money, into the inside pocket of the jacket of the suit which I had worn at her funeral and had not worn since, and then I changed most of it, and slowly spent it. I taught fewer hours in the summer. I slept late, I had a shower, walked a while in these few streets, I had another shower, I cooked my dinner, I went out again, to the cinema, or wandered around some more. I spoke to nobody. I would have loved to go to a beach but I never managed it; I worked a few hours each afternoon, and everything was too crowded at weekends. I remember feeling content, easy with myself, not happy exactly, but like someone who has recovered from something, whose needs are small. I believed then that I would always be like that.

But by the time the autumn came things changed: I would wake in the morning and lie there thinking about sex. I began to masturbate again and fantasize about men. I was aware of a new student in the last class I taught every evening, how he listened to me and watched me. I found that I was thinking about him when I woke in the morning. Sometimes, I would come out of the building and find a group of students outside the door, talking and laughing. I would notice his eyes on me and I would nod and smile and make my way towards home. I do not imagine that any of them realized that I was walking back to an empty apartment and I would spend the rest of the evening sitting in an old armchair in the hallway staring at the window. I tried to appear competent and in control.

On one of those evenings as I walked home I turned into Lavalle and noticed a figure watching me from the kiosk on the corner. It was just a moment, a flash of eyes, and the contact was made. It had been almost a year since I had done anything like this. I was wary, and because I was wary I was excited. I walked slowly away from him and then I turned and looked and he was standing still. He had brown hair and light skin; he was in his twenties. I examined woollen sweaters in a shop window. When he approached, we spoke. He said he was living with his family; I told him that I was living with my family as well. We stood there wondering what we were going to do. It was only when I realized that he might walk away that I said my apartment was empty, there was no one there. Was I sure, he asked, that my family would not return? I told him I was sure. I told him I lived just around the corner. He gave me a look as if to say that this was touch-and-go, he was making up his mind, but he would come home with me despite his suspicions. Then he walked along with me to the apartment building, and we went up the stairs and I opened the door of the apartment as though I owned the place.

That, I think, was the first change, the night when I started to have appetites again. And over the next year a rhythm began. A man I met told me about a sauna in the city not far from where I worked. At first I thought that I could not possibly go there, but he said it was no problem: not everyone was gay and you could just sit around and watch. It was several months before I tried it out, and at first I did nothing, I learned to read the signs, and then slowly it became a place I went to once or twice a week. At that time you had to be careful, but the signs were generally clear.

I found a restaurant two streets away where I often went on my own. A few times I met friends from university, or went for a drink with teachers from the school, or had coffee with students, but mostly I was alone and I was reasonably happy. I never bought a newspaper except to read what was on in the cinema; I seldom turned on the television. Everybody learned to ignore what was going on in public as though it had nothing to do with them. There was, I suppose, a climate of fear which everyone understood, but the fear was like an undertow: it never appeared on the surface and it was never discussed. And no one believed that anything would change.

I remember going down to have coffee one morning and reading in a newspaper headline at the kiosk on the corner that we had taken the Malvinas. But I did not buy the newspaper, and I did not think about it. Either the report was untrue – there were always rumours about taking the Malvinas – or it was not important. It was only when I went to work that I began to realize that something serious had happened. A few of the teachers were unsure about me because I was half-English and they thought that I might be against Argentina taking the islands by force. I had no views on the matter. I went into my class and taught English to the students as usual. None of them mentioned the Malvinas.

I remember that when I was a child my mother laughed when I brought home my first atlas. The Malvinas were too big, she said. They were tiny little places, no one cared about them, and yet on the pages which showed Argentina in this Argentinian atlas, the islands were significant pieces of land in the South Atlantic. My mother thought that this was another example of the lack of proportion, the extreme silliness, which lay at the heart of Argentina.

The night of the invasion I went home and turned on the television. One of the generals was making a speech. It was so full of clichés and the bloated rhetoric about Argentina and its greatness that I turned it off. I do not know when I realized that there was going to be a war. It was certainly not the next day. I had my dinner in the restaurant, where they knew me by now; I usually brought a book to read, but this time I bought that morning's newspaper and read it as I waited for my steak. I did not believe that the English would do anything other than make diplomatic noises. La Nación seemed sure that we would hold the islands. The photograph of the Argentinian flag on the Malvinas across the front page left me cold. I walked home thinking that the invasion was part of the fantasy world that made the army and the navy and the air force feel important, but it would mean nothing to anybody else. I did not turn on the television that night.

Soon, however, I became involved. I found that I was listening to news bulletins on the radio, that I bought all of the newspapers, including the *Buenos Aires Herald*, and read them carefully over breakfast. I now realized that the British were going to declare war on us, but I still believed that any threats they made would not be serious: the islands were too small and too far away from them. I thought that the generals would eventually negotiate a settlement with the British, and the islands would be held by both countries for a time and then would revert to Argentina. In work that day there was still not much talk about the Malvinas.

But something was changing in the atmosphere of the city, something real and clear and unmistakable. Suddenly, the newspapers and the radio and television became interesting, as though a new dimension had been added to our world and people had plugged back into public life. No one needed any more to talk in code, or keep quiet, or confine conversations to foreign holidays and future inflation. Now we could use their names, we could say the words Galtieri or Lami Dozo in the staffroom or in the classroom. We could talk about the government in bars. No one was against the invasion: the islands obviously belonged to Argentina, anyone looking at the map would know that, everyone in the world knew it now.

My students asked me if I supported Argentina and I said of course I did. I said that the entire history of the decline of the British Empire was about forcing the British to leave. The Irish had done it, so had the Indians, indeed so had the North Americans. The British would never listen to negotiations unless there was force, I said. I tried to get them back to the lesson, but the tension was too great for that. No one could speak of anything else. I found it hard to be alone.

One night in the first week of the conflict the school closed early because only a handful of students turned up. It was warm and I walked home and had a shower and went back down to the street. I thought that I might go to a bar and then to a restaurant, but slowly I began to walk through the city. Everything had changed, there was no tension now in the way people walked and looked at each other. I did not deliberately follow a group and I do not think that there was a stream of people going in one direction. But after a while I could hear shouts and I realized that there was a demonstration in front of the Casa Rosada. As I came nearer, the shouts sounded like huge echoing explosions, and then I saw the crowds and the faces, something I had never seen before and never could have imagined, the look of shocked involvement on each face, and the shouting 'Las Malvinas Son Argentinas', all the voices together, all the voices rising towards the balcony. I stood and watched them and felt the pure wonder of us being here together, people who had been unable to speak to their neighbours, who were afraid on the street, and the venal generals who had been our enemies, all of us now were together for these days, proud of our country, glad to be close to each other and shouting with one voice. Afterwards everyone forgot those feelings and there was shame, but during those days in the city we lived in a sort of freedom that we had not known before. We forgot everything in that great first wave of national emotion.

I pushed through the crowd until I could see Galtieri on the balcony. I knew that there had been an American delegation to see him. I knew that Alexander Haig was behind him in the room somewhere and I shouted with the rest of them that the Malvinas were ours. I let my voice rise in the darkness with those of my countrymen and women. We had come after all these years to possess this square once more, these streets. No matter what happened afterwards, I do not believe that anyone

67

who went to those demonstrations has ever regretted it. That night if you found yourself walking along beside a group, you could talk to them. It was something new and strange and I have never forgotten it.

I walked back through the city when it was all over. I felt elated, I felt as though I could walk all night. I was on the way to my restaurant to have dinner and was passing my apartment building when I saw Jorge and his father ringing the door-bell. They had been at the demonstration too, and were worried that I would be harassed because of my English-ness. I told them that there had been no problems, and I began to feel as we stood there that they had called because they needed to talk to someone, that their own company, in this crisis, was not enough for them. When they invited me to come back with them for dinner, I said that it was too late, but they insisted that dinner would not be for a while, and that other people would be coming around. I went with them to their car and we drove to San Isidro, where they lived. They were both excited; they still believed, as everybody else believed, that the British were merely threatening to send a flotilla, but they would not, and that world opinion, and especially North American opinion, would support us. They knew, we all knew that night, that something had opened up in the public life of Argentina which would not easily close down again: even if we had won the war, I think, the generals could not have lasted, but we did not know that then. All we knew was that we needed to talk, and there was a novelty about our need and our freedom to talk that made us want to stay up until the early hours.

There was an armed guard at the gate of their house who let us in when he saw the car. The house was new and painted white – I don't know why I should have expected it to be old – with a flat roof and a long lawn in front with trees and shrubs.

When I asked Jorge's father if he had built the house, he nodded gruffly, saying that there had been a much smaller house on the site in bad repair when he bought it.

A log fire was lighting in the grate in the dining room and the table was set for ten or twelve people. Señora Canetto came bustling into the room with a jug of iced water; she, too, had been changed by the invasion, her movements were jerky and busy and her face was flushed. She said she had been so worried about me when she read an anti-English article in *La Nación* or *Clarín* or one of the magazines. She thought that it was a time for people to stick together and she was glad I was in the house. Soon, a number of men in their fifties arrived, old colleagues of Señor Canetto's from his days in military academy, and then an older man, a retired general whose name I vaguely recognized. The ex-general exuded a dignity and gravity which affected us all as we sat down at the table, like actors in a great and noble tragedy.

Señor Canetto addressed the ex-general formally after we sat down. Señora Canetto was not at the table, and she did not appear again that evening. There were only men at the table. Señor Canetto thanked the ex-general for joining us, explained that everyone here could be trusted, and asked him what was going to happen now in the aftermath of our capturing the Malvinas. The ex-general spoke slowly as though he had learned his lines only with difficulty. He was enjoying the attention. He said that there were things which the British and the Americans did not know: the Argentine air force and navy were equipped with the most up-to-date weapons. No flotilla would have a chance of getting near the islands. He believed that secret and informal negotiations between the British and the generals were already taking place, with the United States government acting as intermediary, and this would result, within a week or two, in the flotilla's turning back and the British agreeing that Argentina could take full control of the islands at a future date to be determined, with the British and Argentinians sharing power in the meantime. He understood, he said, that the British did have a strategic interest in the islands, because of possible resources in the Antarctic which they would lose any claim to if they ceased to control the Malvinas, and he believed that the Argentinians would offer them one of the smaller islands in perpetuity as an outpost. But the main point he wished to emphasize was that the British could not win a military victory.

What he said seemed logical and carefully worked out. He seemed to know what he was talking about. We ate our dinner in silence after he spoke. Later, over dessert, he said that his own son would be part of the air force attack if the British should get too close, and he was deeply proud of this, as was his son. It was not often that you got a chance to fight for your country, he said, and there was agreement about this. I thought about his son, dressed in his uniform, as solemn as his father, but the idea made no sense to me. Later, as Jorge drove me to the railway station, I asked him if he was interested in fighting for the Malvinas. He laughed and said that he liked sleeping in his own bed and hated polishing his shoes. He believed that the islands were ours and would have to be defended now, he said, but someone else, like the ex-general's son, who was a nice guy, could do it. He asked me which side was I really on. I told him I was for Argentina. I wanted Argentina to win.

Over the next few weeks as diplomacy failed and the British forces made their slow journey south, I often went to the Canettos. At first they telephoned to invite me and then they made it clear that I could drop in for dinner any time I liked. Most of the men who came to the house were Peronists of one sort or another; all of them had been in the army. Most of them were rich. Some of them brought their sons, including the ex-general, whose son was much younger than I had expected and sat looking slightly stunned at the table as his father talked about logistics. During the meal itself only the older men spoke; neither Jorge nor I ever spoke. Then afterwards we would break up into smaller groups. Señor Canetto and his friends were indignant about the editorial line taken by the *Buenos Aires Herald*, and each evening I came there I translated articles for them. They were outraged by the references to the human rights record of the government. What choice did the government have, one of them asked, when faced by a Marxist threat? He began to shout at me as I translated an article attacking the invasion of the Malvinas as an illegal act. Señor Canetto had to tell him that I hadn't written the article, I was merely translating it for them.

They had a new toy called the war, and it gave them a reason to gather in the evening. I needed to go out there and be with them, even if I did not agree with some of the things that they said. Sometimes, we listened to news bulletins or watched interviews on the television. At some point in those weeks all of us began to fear Thatcher: there was something ferocious and implacable about her, and her country had conquered the world and won two wars, and she was right when she said that our invasion was illegal. Also, she had been elected and that was something which none of us could understand. It gave her an extra sort of power which helped her to range most countries in the world, including the United States, against us.

The men in that room were quite sure, despite their fear of Thatcher, as the winter approached and her flotilla came closer to us that she could not regain the islands. The British were too vulnerable, we all agreed. But there were moments in that long room in the Canettos' house when we listened to a radio report or watched an item on the television when everyone present showed fear, when everyone sensed that what was floating towards us from the north was defeat. The war was a dream we had that we could snatch the islands and afterwards feel proud and strong and bonded as a community; it was a delusion, a mad play we acted in willingly all day and night in the months between the invasion and the surrender.

The ex-general told us about tensions between the army and the navy and the air force. He was well briefed. This news made us feel like insiders, privy to the machinations of our leaders; it made our gathering feel important. I was there one night when Jorge's younger brother, who lived in the United States, telephoned and his father spoke to him as though he himself were running the war and knew every move that was being made. We would win, he assured his son, we would see the British off.

And as he said it I realized what a wonderful and unbelievable idea it was that we could beat Britain and send the flotilla back north in disgrace. It would have changed our country in a way that I still cannot imagine. I noticed that Jorge's father and his friends began to drink more as time went on, as the heat was turned up. I noticed, too, that I was more optimistic and excited at night, but in the morning when I woke I realized that we were fooling ourselves, that we would not win.

When the British took San Carlos we should have known, but the ex-general was emphatic that our soldiers were still on the island and were ready to ambush and harass the British on rough terrain which we were used to and they were not. His son, he told us one night, was preparing to fight, he had received a special blessing from a bishop.

There was some anti-English feeling in the city. The Plaza Británica had its name changed and its tower defaced, but the students of English at the Instituto San Martín still turned up for class, and things went back to normal in the classroom. At night, there were more people on the street, and the atmosphere was friendlier. A few times, when I brought a man home, everything between us lacked the usual nervous, furtive atmosphere. Things were more casual.

Soon, it was clear to us that we were going to lose the war, even though no one spelled it out. After the sinking of the *Belgrano*, the ex-general stopped coming to the house, and that was a sign. Later, Jorge told me that his son had flown safely and came back home shortly after the war. I was glad about that, because he was the only person I knew who fought and I did not want to think of him being captured or injured or killed. It was bad enough when we thought of all those young conscripts, some of whom must have been cheering in the square the first night I went there, all of them innocent, going down on a big ship. I thought of the English sailors and soldiers as thin-faced and ugly; I wanted us to defeat them, it would not have bothered me if we had sunk one of their ships. In the last days of the war there were conflicting reports and the men who came to Señor Canetto's house were confident right up to the end and even after the end that our forces were superior.

None of us could face the idea that we were going to surrender, that our sojourn in the Malvinas would be a disaster, a humiliation for each one of us. We did not talk about it; we remained silent when the news was black, and we dispersed early. Jorge drove me to the station in silence and I walked home without looking at anybody in the streets. Our country was now synonymous with weakness and stupidity, and there was no future here for any of us. I was in tears when the final surrender came. Maybe I should have felt rage that I had been misled by the government and by the men who came to Señor Canetto's house, but I did not feel rage, I felt shame and I felt powerless and I felt that I had deluded myself and I wondered how any of us would ever be able to face the world in the future.

I had become close to Jorge again without noticing it, and his parents liked me coming to the house. I turned up on time and never stayed too long; my table manners were, I suppose, adequate. I listened respectfully to Jorge's father; I thanked his mother politely for the food. But I still do not know why they wanted me there. It is possible that no one else would have tolerated the self-importance and pomposity of those gatherings.

After the war, I became interested in what was happening. I listened to Señor Canetto when he talked about Perón and the meaning of Perón's movement. I was in that house when all the important things happened: when the elections were declared, when Alfonsín and the Radicals won the first elections, when the trial of the generals was going on. More and more, I joined in discussions. It was an interesting time. By now, I had started to hate my work and I had no other real friends in the city. Thus the daily news on radio and television and in the newspapers began to intrigue me. It was, perhaps, like the way collecting stamps intrigues a child. One of the Canettos' neighbours was in the house on many of those nights, he seemed to have powerful connections in the city. He told me that I should not be teaching English, I should have a better job. I should be working as a translator, he said to Señor Canetto, who nodded. If he came across anyone who needed a translator, he would get in touch, he said. He mentioned this several times.

We watched inflation continue to rise and labour unrest intensify. It was clear to us that Alfonsín would leave no heir or political legacy. And whoever would replace him, Señor Canetto and his friends were sure, would have to have a base in Peronism, without being anti-American, would be more right-wing than Alfonsín, would have no connection to the generals who ran the war, but still have allies in the army. Often, this was discussed late into the night. I had realized early on that Señor Canetto himself had political ambitions, I now realized that his friends had ambitions for him too. Such meetings were, I suppose, held all over Argentina in those years.

I never believed that Señor Canetto had any of the skills

required, but he believed that he did, and so did some of his friends, enough for them to find out what was happening, how they could win support. He learned, through his neighbour, that there were people close to the American Embassy who wanted to fund serious democratic parties in Argentina so that the next elections would see an orderly transfer of power from Alfonsín to a civilian successor. Reagan's administration, it was believed, wanted no more dictators in South America; it wanted to fund and support Christian Democratic parties. I do not know what enquiries were made, but Señor Canetto phoned me to say that there was a series of receptions being held by two people whom he believed were American diplomats. They needed people to attend who spoke English who could talk to them about the democratic possibilities. He had an invitation for me, he said. And that is how I came to meet Susan and Donald Ford.

PART TWO

PART TWO

SOMEWHERE, in the vast underground archive in one of their buildings – in Washington maybe, or wherever it is they store things – there must be a file about my first meetings with the Fords. I imagine strip lighting and shadows and grey-blue metal shelving. As I wander the narrow corridors between the stacks, I imagine the neutral dry smell of paper. And there somewhere – classified as secret, or not to be opened until some year in the future, or coded in some way that few can understand – their account of me and others will be folded, preserved. Will it be in her round, clear, beautiful longhand? Will he have typed it on the small, electric machine he kept on a table at a right angle to his desk? Did they know that they gave me confidence in myself, and, in certain ways, they changed my life?

I knew that I had been recommended to them by Señor Canetto's neighbour. He phoned me to say that this would be a good chance for me. He told them that I knew the scene and spoke two languages and might be useful to them. Thus I had two reasons to be there: to find work as a translator, or local helper, and to interest them in Señor Canetto's candidacy. I remember that I dressed carefully that day, I wore a suit and a tie, I had my hair cut and was shaved, I put polish on my good shoes. But I am sure that I still looked uneasy and awkward as I stood alone with a drink in my hand, having arrived in a taxi and waited at the door while another guest arrived by car and handed the keys over to a uniformed guard who parked it for him. A servant woman in a white uniform guided me to the large square room with long windows on three sides. I recognized nobody. Everyone there must have wanted something as well, must have had a secret reason to be present. No doubt their names are in the archive too, and maybe there's a code to describe their motives. I never saw any of them again, and I noted each face in those first few minutes. I do not know if they had reason to return to this house, if there were more parties where people talked quietly and smiled and gestured subtly as though they were imitating a set of protocols they had learned from a manual or a movie.

A servant came with a tray of drinks and I grabbed a second whisky and added some ice and water, even though I had only half-finished my first. It gave me time to myself, a sudden opportunity to concentrate. But when I lifted my head and sipped my drink and took in the room once more, I had one or two seconds of pure ease. I felt ready for this, whatever it was. And in one of those moments it happened: I was approached by Donald Ford and Susan, his wife. They worked, I already knew, for an organization called the Institute for Economic Development, but they were close to the embassy, and I think their position was understood by everybody who was there, though in all the time I knew them the letters CIA were never mentioned. I remember their white teeth, her blonde smile and her frail frame against his tough, all-male friendliness. It was easy to smile in return, offer a firm handshake, speak in a way which seemed oddly authoritative. It was as though I had hired a double for this first encounter, someone who had known only certainty and optimism, who could choose words with care, hold his glass with equanimity as he introduced himself and told them what campaign he was working on.

I knew how important they were. I still believe that they were involved in every cent which the United States put into the campaign for the election of Carlos Menem and maybe other candidates. I do not know – perhaps they did not know themselves, so shadowy was the chain of command – how much real power they had. But they could make decisions, I was sure, without consulting anybody. I never once underestimated them.

I did not understand that they would change things for me, and then they would fade. I was excited by them, by the idea that they had a hidden agenda here, by the idea that they were outsiders. But in the end there was nothing hidden: they both were simpler and more straightforward than I had ever imagined, perfect diplomats. I glamorized them, I could not imagine life without them, they filled my days. In time, I knew that there would be no drama, there would instead be efficiency, quiet work done, and then they would slip away and go home.

After a while, when we had spoken about my mother's Englishness and my accent, Donald drifted away and joined another group. It was when we were left alone that Susan asked me if it had been difficult for me during the war, if I had had divided loyalties. She listened as though she were memorizing each sentence. I told her how the war had made it clearer to me than ever before that I was Argentinian. I had no divided loyalties during the Malvinas War. I told her that even though we had political problems here at that time, we had right on our side. She narrowed her eyes for a moment in recognition. This was serious. I stood there and watched her believing me. She knew that I represented Jorge's father, who was a Peronist and still had connections with the party, and she knew how important it was for her country to come to terms with all the wounded heat of Argentinian nationalism. I knew as I stood there that I could offer her something, that I could be of use to her, bring her closer to the heart of things. It was a matter of language and gesture, of knowing the key to various codes. It was, in the end, a matter of knowing English.

Donald took me across the room and introduced me to

various Americans working in the oil business. Among them was a small Argentinian in his forties trying to speak English, using a pronounced British accent for some of his words, but without enough grammar and vocabulary to make sense. The Americans seemed irritated by him, and had little interest in what he was saying. They nursed their drinks and looked about the room as though patiently waiting for the party to be over.

I decided that it was time to go. I could not see how anything more could occur that evening which would help Señor Canetto in any way. I caught Susan's eye and made a sign to her. She came towards me.

'Do we have your address, your home address?' she asked. I reached into my pocket and handed her a card. She looked at it and read out my name: Richard Garay. She handed it to one of the men carrying trays of drinks and told him to leave it on the table outside her office. We both stood at the door and surveyed the room. I felt brave and sure of myself.

'Where did you get all of these people?' I asked.

'Actually, we rented some of them.' It was like a line from a movie, something learned and rehearsed. She arched her eyebrows and looked around the room once more.

'Did you rent *me*?' I asked.

'My husband looked after the details. Do you want me to find out?' The look she gave me was one of studied arrogance, and then amusement.

'Not now, perhaps after I've gone, if you remember.'

*

AS I STEPPED OUT into the night, floodlights suddenly lit up the whole front of the house. A figure came towards me out of the shadows; he was the uniformed guard who had parked the cars. I asked him to telephone for a taxi. He motioned me to wait. I wondered as I stood there how many other pairs of eyes were watching me now, what would happen if I made a dart towards the front gate, or if I tried to go around to the back of the house. He returned to say that the taxi would take twenty minutes and told me that I could wait in the hall. Just then, the floodlights went out and the excitement of standing there so exposed, bathed in brightness, faded too.

*

THE STREET BELL RANG at ten o'clock in the morning. I assumed it was the postman, and pressed the entry bell without thinking. A few minutes later my own doorbell rang. I was only half-dressed, and, once more, I went to answer without thinking. The man who had parked the cars and phoned the taxi the previous night was standing there.

'I was asked to hand this to you personally, sir,' he said. He gave me the envelope and then turned to go back down the stairs.

'I'm sorry you had to come up all this way,' I said.

'It's no problem, sir.'

The letter was signed 'Susan Ford' and was written on a blank sheet of paper with just a phone number at the top. The handwriting was perfectly rounded as though done by a machine. 'Donald and I enjoyed meeting you last evening and were sorry you left so early,' it read. 'Would you like to have supper with us? Call me and we'll sort out the details.'

I did not know how long I should wait. Should I call her immediately? Should I tell her that I was free to have supper with her and Donald any time? Also, I did not know what to say to Jorge or his father. I knew that they would telephone and I was unsure how the previous evening had gone. I decided it would be better if I rang them first. I went to the phone and dialled Jorge's number. His father answered. He seemed curt and tired, as though barely interested in what had happened. I was glad that I had telephoned him rather than waiting for him to contact me. I told him I had arranged a further meeting with the Americans later in the week. He asked me if I had put our case to them. I answered that I had done so, and they were interested, but it was hard to be sure, and I would let him know. He said nothing for a while and then grunted a valediction and put down the phone.

I had a private class at four o'clock that day with a fourteen-year-old girl and her mother which lasted until half past five. As I sat there I could not wait for the time to pass and a few times the mother caught me looking at my watch. The girl was clever; she had a good memory. I enjoyed watching her grasp various rules and try to apply them. But the mother could learn nothing and remember nothing. I hated being in the room with them, and when the class was over and I took the train back to the city centre, I managed to put it out of my mind, as though it were a dark, distant memory from childhood, or something that had not really happened. I had another class in the academy from six o'clock to seven and then the course which I taught three evenings a week from eight thirty until ten. After the first class I normally went home for a while; I loved the city in that last hour when the shops were open and the offices still busy. I walked slowly down Lavalle as though I had nothing to do. I relished my freedom from the classroom. But that day there was another reason to go home; I felt as though the season had changed, or I had just been paid, or I was about to meet a lover. I could not tell what would happen when I rang the number which Susan Ford had given me. I was excited by the idea of speaking to her again, by her American accent. I telephoned her as soon as I had closed the door of the apartment. She picked up the receiver on the first ring. I wondered what she was doing and where her husband was. I imagined her at a desk going through names, trying to learn by heart who we all were, what party or splinter party we belonged to, and trying to work out the possibilities. Who should she see? Who should she encourage? Who would she need?

I did not understand then that the two Americans who had seemed in such control the previous night believed that they did not have long to work out how they could best influence the outcome of the next general election. They had, I knew, just arrived. They spoke some Spanish – I was always unclear as to how much Spanish they spoke or understood – which meant that they could read the newspapers and make sense of what was being said on radio and television; they could discuss the future with people in power and people who sought power. They knew just enough to speculate. They knew the questions to ask. They had been briefed by sociologists and political scientists. They knew they should be concerned about the relationship between the provinces and the city, between labour and the nationalists. But what they feared most was that somewhere in the city, or deep in the interior, a number of men in a room held the key to the future. They were desperate to control, or understand, or feel part of such a new movement.

I do not know how many other people they saw regularly during this time, as they saw me. Also, I do not know if everything they did, every gesture and word, was calculated to help them in their work. I like to think that there were days and moments when they were led astray, when they succumbed to things which were not part of their original agenda. They were the first real foreigners I had ever met. I watched them closely, maybe too closely, and I may have misunderstood much about them.

'So what have you been doing?' Susan Ford asked me.

'Thank you for the party,' I said.

'I'd like to see you soon.'

'I'm free, mostly,' I said.

'What about tomorrow, are you free in the afternoon?'

'Yes, I am.'

There was silence for a few moments. I could hear her flicking through the pages of a diary.

'Two thirty? Maybe three? What about the Carlton Hotel? The lobby is usually quiet at that time.'

'Let's meet there,' I said.

★

SHE WORE A YELLOW DRESS and a black jacket and a black band on her hair. She arrived late and when I stood up she greeted me with a fondness and a familiarity which suggested that she had known me for years.

'I like sneaking out of the house during the day. Nobody knows where I am. The city is lovely, really lovely. Do you like it?'

'Yes, I do,' I said. I could not think of anything else to say.

She smiled at the waiter as though she knew him too, and ordered tea with lemon for us both.

'We were very impressed with you, you sounded English to us, even though we know you're Argentinian,' she said as soon as the waiter had walked away. I said nothing. 'We feel lucky to have met you, and would like to see you some more.' I smiled, but still could think of no reply.

'Are you married?' she asked.

'No,' I said. She held my gaze.

'And you live alone? With your family?'

'Alone.'

'That's unusual, isn't it? I believe that most people live at home here until they get married.' Again, I said nothing. I wanted her to ask me about politics, about our campaign.

'Are your parents still alive?' she asked. I told her that they were dead.

'When did they die?' she asked.

'My mother died two years ago next month,' I said.

'And your father?'

'He died when I was twelve.'

'And you're an only child?'

'Yes.'

'It must be hard for you being alone here.' She looked at me across the low table waiting for some response. I wondered if I could ask her now what she thought of Argentinian politics and if I could take her to meet Señor Canetto.

'It must have been hard for your mother when your father died,' she said.

'Yes,' I said.

'How old was he?'

'He was in his early sixties.'

'Did he die suddenly?'

'No. He was sick for a long time.'

'With what?'

'His heart was bad.'

'Did your parents love one another?' she asked. Once more she looked at me expecting me to confide in her. No one had ever asked me such a question before. She waited.

'I don't know,' I said.

'What was your father like?'

'He was dark, he didn't look like me at all.'

'Did you spend a lot of time with him?'

I talked to her about them for more than an hour that afternoon, and she listened as though it were vital for her to know. I told her how he used to pick me up and put me on his back and hold my feet in his hands as though his hands were pedals. I don't know why I told her that. It was the best thing, the happiest memory I had of him. I told her that I loved it when he gave me his full attention, but sometimes, most of the time maybe, he was distant, and it was hard to distract him. My eyes filled up with tears as I spoke about him, how much I missed him after he died and how I could never speak about him to my mother, as though he were a guilty secret between us, as if his death were a crime, something best forgotten, a terrible darkness which neither of us could face. When I stopped talking Susan said nothing, and for some time neither of us broke the silence across the table.

'It was good to meet you,' she said finally. 'It was good to talk to you.' She stood up. I felt that she had trapped me into talking like that, and that I would never be able to speak to her about Señor Canetto and the help we needed. She shook my hand at the door of the hotel. There was a car waiting for her.

★

SHE TELEPHONED two days later to find out if I was free for dinner. It was the first of many such phone calls, her tone brisk, ironic, humorous.

'Formal? Informal?' I asked.

'You mean: what should you wear?'

'Yes, that's what I mean.' I smiled as I spoke, and I could hear her smiling too.

'Something green that will go with your eyes.'

'My eyes are blue.'

'Something blue then.'

★

I WORE A BLUE JACKET and a light blue tie, and once more I took a taxi to their house. The uniformed guard was at the gate this time. He held an Alsatian by a lead, and nodded to me as he opened the gate. The taxi drove through and stopped in front of the house; there were no other cars. The taxi driver looked at me carefully as I paid the fare as though I must be someone important coming to such a big, imposing and secure house. It was almost dark and I waited for the floodlights to come on as I stepped onto the gravel, but nothing happened. I could hear the bell sounding through the house as I rang. I stood and waited until a uniformed servant, a woman, opened the door, and led me up steps to a large room at the back of the house, with windows the same shape as those in the reception room where I had been four nights earlier. I went to one of the windows and looked out over the vast gardens. I could see the red clay of a tennis court behind a hedge across the grass, and over to the right a swimming pool behind a fence. It struck me then that I did not know whether my hosts had any children or not, but it seemed unlikely. I don't know why; there was something about them, some way in which they directed their complete attention at the world around them that seemed to preclude private responsibilities. I listened, as though half-expecting the cries of children telling me how wrong I was.

I was standing with my back to the room when Donald came in. He was dressed in a striped suit of light material which crumpled easily and a bow tie. He shook my hand warmly and then walked over to a table in the corner.

'I think I should mix the Martinis before my wife comes down. She thinks I make them too strong. I hope you like them strong.'

'How strong?'

'Let me show you.'

We had drunk two Martinis. Donald did most of the talking. He told me about the property, and the garden; we arranged to have a game of tennis sometime, but he warned me that he was out of practice. He spoke for a while about food. The talk was lazy; I could not understand where it was leading.

When Susan came into the room she stood in front of me inclining her cheek to be kissed. It was a custom, she said, that she had learned in Kansas City. She laughed. She was wearing a black dress. The material was thick with patterns; I could not tell what it was. She smiled again as she told us that dinner was ready and we walked down a wide corridor towards a dining room where there was a roast chicken and various plates of vegetables on a hotplate on a side table. Susan seemed to behave as if this were an important occasion. The long table had been set for three. She announced that Donald would sit at the head of the table while she and I would sit on his left and right respectively. No servants or waiters appeared and the two doors into the room were kept closed. As soon as we began to eat, Donald changed his tone. He became direct and businesslike and sharp.

'Who are the main players now in with a chance in the next elections?' he asked and looked up from his food. Susan listened and said nothing.

'You must remember that the fears which people have now are not about abstract notions like democracy and dictatorship,' I said. 'Most people are concerned about the disappearances and the stupidity of the war, but they are more concerned about employment prospects, inflation, social welfare and foreign investment. These come first and whoever runs a credible campaign on these issues will win.' I had prepared none of this, but for some reason I was confident when I spoke, as though I knew things about the future of Argentina which were in the possession of very few. Almost every phrase in what I told them, I had heard first, or used myself, at the Canettos' house in the years after the war. But now there was no one to interrupt me, or disagree with me.

'The business of human rights', I went on, 'and how the country is viewed from abroad will matter in the campaign. Anyone who is ambiguous about the democratic institutions will not figure in these elections. But the winner will win on his economic policies, essentially on what he can offer the middle class. Our campaign, for example, will centre on inflation, investment and unemployment, although we will also make clear that we believe the Malvinas should be restored to Argentina through peaceful means, that there must be serious investigations into allegations of torture and official murder over the past ten years, and that the perception of Argentina abroad must be changed. We feel that most other contenders are placing too much emphasis on the disappearances and the end of dictatorship—'

'Have you any surveys to prove this?' Donald interrupted me.

'We have very limited resources. It would also be hard to draft the right questions. These things are delicate. No one has done much research into public opinion because no one has any money.'

'That's not the case,' Susan spoke for the first time. She looked at her husband rather than at me. 'We know of two parties that have done considerable research. It seems vital to us.'

'Yes, but those are the parties which will not figure in the election, irrespective of how much research they do. The main contenders have not yet emerged.'

Since she had contradicted me I felt that it was the only way I could come back. I tried to be convincing and sure of myself, but I did not know whether this was still working. I had no idea whether I was talking to the right people, whether they would offer me work, or offer Señor Canetto professional advice, or simply keep in touch with us, as with all the other splinter groups who sought power in the vacuum that was political life in Argentina during those months. I also believed that this was the best chance I would get to make a deal with them. Before we left the table, I decided, I would ask them what they could do for us, and I would leave silence after the question. If they asked me what we wanted I would say money, money now, and professional advice about how best to market our candidate, advice from the best North American agency about television and advertising and the use of slogans and images.

'How do you think the results of the elections will affect

American interests in Argentina?' Donald asked me. Susan put her knife and fork down and looked at me.

'I think that relations with the United States will improve. Any candidate who hopes to win will have to make clear in one way or another his party's support for economic stability. Some candidates may make anti-American speeches, and use anti-American rhetoric, but this should not be mistaken, especially now, for anything other than electioneering. You must discount it.'

'Nonetheless, a lot of our companies here are worried,' Susan said. She stood up and gathered the plates and left them on a table in the corner. She carried over an apple pie and cream. Donald opened a bottle of white wine which had been in an ice bucket. After a while a servant came with a pot of coffee. There was silence while we ate.

'What about Señor Canetto's campaign?' I asked.

'We are interested, and would certainly be prepared to make some resources available,' Donald said. 'We'll have to talk about it some more, it's hard for us to work out what tone people are using, and there are a few other players we'd like to look at, we'd like your opinions about. Maybe you could translate for us, explain things? You seem very competent,' Donald said.

'Competent?'

'We would value your opinion,' Susan said.

★

A FEW NIGHTS after this I dreamed about being found out. In my dream they came here, Donald and Susan and their advisers, and there were police cars blocking off the street and flashing lights illuminating the whole apartment as men with American accents dragged me from my bed and accused me of fooling them. In the morning I felt all the guilt that was in the dream.

★

I NEVER TOLD them what hours I worked in the Instituto San Martín, or how badly I was paid, or how dingy the place was. I told them where I worked, but they would not have known the other self that climbed the wide, old-fashioned, wrought-iron staircase of the school. They made me perform for them: in their house I was alert and bright. I knew things. In the school I merely knew English grammar and the times of my classes and the names of some of the students. And I knew that the place could close at any time, or that my hours would slowly trickle away, or that they would stop paying me for holidays, as they had already done with one of my colleagues. I hated climbing the stairs and opening that main door, and every day as I went there I dreamed of escaping.

I especially hated classes that lasted an hour and a half. I would walk in and look at the students. At first I would feel I must try, I must make an effort to vary things. I would begin by going over the last lesson, asking the beginners 'Where do you live?' and letting each one name a street or a suburb, and then asking them 'Where are you from?', and, slowly and patiently, like explaining a piece of algebra, like pointing out the difference between a square and a triangle, I would try to make them aware of the difference between 'I am' and 'I do'. 'Where *do* you live?' I asked. And then I would select one of them and ask her or him to put the question, and sometimes I would discover that the person I had chosen, my student, who had been listening to me explaining all of this for an hour and a half at a time, could do nothing, neither ask the question, nor understand my original command. In my eagerness, I must have often confused them.

But this did not stop me going back over everything. I tried to speak slowly to help the ones who could not make out a word of what I was saying. I told them to write their own questions starting with 'do'; I carefully introduced new items of vocabulary. This was how each class began. For the first ten minutes I felt energetic and anxious that these people in front of me would learn and remember. I wrote on the blackboard for them. I moved about as I spoke. But soon the first temptation came to look at my watch, to wonder how much longer I would be stuck in this airless room. And it would always be disappointing, no matter how long I put off looking. Only ten minutes would have passed, or only fifteen, or only seventeen and a half. There was more than an hour to go, and no break.

Then they would open their textbooks. The beginners' book was called *First Things First*. They were always happier looking at the pictures. I sat at the desk and we went through all the drills the book suggested. They asked me questions, they asked each other questions, they answered questions. They practised the negative.

Most days I felt such relief when the class was nearly over that I was able to summon new energy and liven them up before they walked back out into the world. They could catch buses and trains to the suburbs, have coffee or a beer in one of the bars below the school. I had another hour-and-a-half class to teach. When I gave the class pieces of writing to do, or divided them into groups and told them to make up a story, I dreamed that I could walk out of the building and never come back.

And there is something else too that was maybe more important: most of the students were girls in their late teens or early twenties, and it was impossible, or at least I found it so, to be in the room with them all of that time without becoming aware of their sexuality and their sexual expectations. I wanted them to like me, and I must have flirted with them and made myself seem attracted to them. I was uneasy with the men in the class; I always supposed that they wondered what I was doing in this dead-end job. I was careful not to pay too much attention to the one or two that I liked.

Before going to meet Donald and Susan Ford, I went to the bar on the corner of Lavalle and Esmeralda after my day's teaching and sat alone beside the window reading a newspaper and drinking a beer. It was half an hour of pleasure and relief away from the strain of pretending that I liked girls, away from time passing slowly and monotonously. It was the part of the day I loved most: the first sips of beer, the casual noises in the bar, the smell of coffee, the night outside, the shadows around me, the end of work. A few times I stayed for more than an hour, but they found this strange in the bar, and they looked at me oddly as I paid and left. So normally I just had two beers and went home alone after half an hour.

★

THE SECOND TIME they invited me to dinner, I told them I couldn't, that I was busy until nine o'clock.

'Come whenever you can,' Susan said. 'We don't eat until late. We'll wait for you.'

'Who else will be there?' I asked.

'Just you and us, or just us until you come. Please come.'

I found myself smiling as I taught my classes that evening. I realized that I was looking forward to seeing them again. Yet when the time came to get a taxi out to their house, I wanted to postpone it. I stood outside the school wondering what to do. Why did I not want to go? What sudden urge was this to sit alone? That evening I went to my bar as usual, had a beer, watched the minutes passing, wanting them to pass more slowly, so that I could put off this social encounter with these two people who fascinated me and whose company, in those early days, also made me uncomfortable.

As I waited in the hallway Susan came down the stairs. She had just come out of the shower, her hair was still wet, she was wearing a white smock which made her skin seem bronzed and beautiful in the pale light of the small dining area which lay off

95

the kitchen. Her manner was looser, more informal and direct, and abrupt, as though we had been talking to one another all evening and been interrupted.

'We've decided to cut down on alcohol,' she said. 'We're not drinking liquor, except on Fridays and Saturdays. You're free to have what you like, of course. In fact, we'd love to watch you drinking gin or whisky, but we're sticking to wine.'

When we sat at the table, Donald wanted to talk immediately about politics. He wondered how he could best explain Peronism to an American who knew nothing about Argentina. Was Perón a despot, a dictator, a mob leader? What was his vision? He spoke like this for a while. I wondered if I was meant to reply. I thought of something I wanted to say.

'His rhetoric, if you look at it,' I interrupted, 'is full of nuance and ambiguity. If you don't look at it that way, you could misunderstand him and his movement. What he said meant everything and nothing at the same time. I don't think that Peronism threatens America. It merely makes a certain class of Argentinian feel good.'

'You use Argentinian rather than Argentine?' Susan asked.

'My mother always did. It was her way of saying she was still English.'

Susan raised her eyebrows as though she did not see the point.

On nights like this, her sharpness seemed like aggression, or like a cry of pain at her husband's obtuseness. If she gave him the opportunity, or if I did not interrupt, he would talk like someone drafting a bland report. But he seemed not to resent interruptions or moments when his point of view was ignored. I could not help wondering what this implied about their life as a couple.

*

MOST EVENINGS when I went there we ate in the formal dining room at the front of the house; we began with dry

Martinis, went on to red wine and then followed this with bourbon or brandy and coffee. There was, of course, food as well, but increasingly I realized that all three of us were more interested in the alcohol. These were their nights off work, and most of the time the conversation was not serious. I think I can remember the first time I made them laugh. I did not plan to do this. I was trying to explain how hard it was sometimes to leave the apartment building without being seen and waylaid by one of the widows who inhabited the other apartments. They all seemed to be widows, large-sized ones who looked as though they could have quietly beaten their husbands to death or eaten them alive, or little wizened widows who got rid of their husbands through attrition or slow poisoning. You knew them by the sharpness of their eyes; they would do anything for a small item of news which they could sniff out on the staircase. If I had had my hair cut, this would be enough for them. If I carried a shopping bag or a briefcase, their eyes would furtively glance down to see if this would tell them something on which they could ponder during the long, husbandless evening.

I don't remember how or why I began to talk about this. Aimlessly, we discussed everything except ourselves at that table on those nights: there was never silence. But once I began my diatribe about widows, I found that they laughed, that they savoured each phrase, each grimace. They shook their heads as I continued, and the next time I saw them they wanted me to tell them more about the saga of the widows in my building. I enjoyed their attention and their amusement and the sound of my own voice and the new sense of myself. As time went on it was hard to know how to end the evening. Once dessert and coffee came, the servants did not reappear. Usually, we did not move from the table, and often it was late, two or three in the morning, when they telephoned a private taxi service to take me home to the centre of the city. I have a memory of smiling all the way home, of relishing that journey, going over all the things said, all the laughter and easy talk, how much these people seemed to sparkle. I felt as though I had fallen in love without any of love's tensions or risks or responsibilities.

★

SOMETIMES during the day I experienced a pressing need to go to the sauna. As soon as I woke I felt a fierce sexual compulsion. And once I began to think about it I knew that I would soon sneak into the other world and I would find moments of pure satisfaction there. I lay in bed saving myself up for what was to come. The sauna opened at one o'clock. But I waited. I was never the first there. I would not have liked that: empty, the place would have seemed forlorn, full of dead energy. Others always beat me to it, people, maybe, whose needs were greater than mine, or who had a short break from work. By one thirty or two, there were enough men wearing towels around their waists and a look of studied nonchalance on their faces to fill those corridors with possibility.

I remember going to the sauna one day after I had drunk too much of some special brew of American whisky that Donald had imported from the United States. I lay in the sauna the next day sweating the poison out of my body, lying naked on my towel on the hard wood with my eyes closed, paying no attention to who came in and out, as though I did not care. I knew that soon I would begin to prowl, checking out the dressing room for newcomers, waiting around, pretending to comb my hair if I wanted to watch someone undress. Checking out the showers and the corridors and the cabins and the area around the pool and the steam room. Trying to seem casual, as though looking merely for the most comfortable place to rest. Catching eyes.

I knew the rules. And I knew that I had time for maybe two encounters. That day the place was quiet. There was someone sitting on the lowest bench who I had not seen before. He looked unfriendly. He was stocky, with fair hair and skin and blue eyes, some light hair on his chest and legs. When I sat up I moved close to him and put my towel around my waist. He stared straight ahead. As I looked at him I could feel a sort of hostility towards me. There were just the two of us and I expected that at any moment he would stand up and go. Instead, he removed his towel, and I could see his erect penis quivering there, as he continued to pretend that nothing was happening. I unloosed my towel even though I had no erection. He was watching the door now. His hand reached towards my lower back and quickly moved under me. I gripped his penis, watching his face all the time.

And then without warning he stood up and wrapped his towel around him and walked quickly out of the sauna. I covered myself, moved up to one of the higher benches and lay down. I closed my eyes and began to think about following him out into the corridors. Maybe he was in the shower, or in the dressing room getting ready to go; maybe he had done what he came here to do and would be too nervous, too ashamed to do anything else. I waited for a while, enjoying the heat and the sweat and the expectation. When I went out I saw him in the small swimming pool, up to his waist in water. I watched him dive under and swim the length of the pool and then turn and swim back and stand again. I sat at the edge of the pool and let my feet dangle in the water. A few men sat on easy chairs reading the newspaper or staring ahead. I knew that some of them were not here looking for sex, but I always found it impossible to know which of them belonged to that group, so great was the air of staged indifference. I stood up and hung my towel on a hook, aware that my friend in the pool could see me naked now. I plunged into the pool and swam towards him. We both waited there with our elbows on the side looking straight ahead. I let him swim a length; I did not move. But the second time, I followed him and as we passed one another I touched him and he swam back to the end of the pool.

I felt that at any moment he would go to the dressing room, put on his clothes and leave. I knew that I should move slowly, that I should not frighten him or put too much pressure on him, but at the same time I wanted him.

He left the pool and went back to the sauna. The place was becoming busier so that although I followed him and sat close to him there were too many others around for us to do anything. I realized that I did not have much time: it was now after three and I had a class in the academy at four. I could get there in twenty minutes; it would take five minutes to shower and dress.

He seemed, on the other hand, to have all the time in the world to sit there and brood. He did not move from the sauna, but at no time now were we left alone there. I waited. There was nothing else I could do. I looked at him a few times, but he did not respond. I looked at him once more, as if to make sure that he had been worth all of this trouble: his hair was cut short and he was carefully shaved, his skin was soft, his thighs were muscular. He would have found easy employment at a pornographic magazine, and maybe that is why I waited there for so long, and it is possible too that I was attracted by his nervousness, his tense energy, but I am not sure. Something, in any case, made me wait. When he went back to the pool, I followed him and we both hung our towels on a hook and lowered ourselves into the water. We both rested our elbows on the edge, as before, and wallowed there. This time I let my foot touch his leg; he did not flinch or move. Once again, he stared straight ahead as though nothing were happening. And I looked around me at men in towels who sat in chairs at the edge of the pool. No one was watching us. I touched his leg again and he reached his hand behind me as he had done before. I could see his hard penis refracted in the water.

'Querés tomar un café?' I whispered. He took his hand away.

'Sí,' he nodded. The tone was casual and relaxed. I realized now that I was not going to make my classes, and I felt a burden lift from me. We walked towards the small coffee bar close to the steam room.

I told him my name as soon as we had ordered the coffee and the barman had moved out of earshot. He seemed younger in this light, and friendly, eager to talk. I did not know how soon I should tell him that I had an empty apartment nearby and the whole evening free. I still expected him to stand up suddenly and walk away. Or make an excuse: say that he was already late for an appointment. I told him that I was a teacher and I had a day off. I went on to say that I did not come to this place very much, but, I shrugged, I had wandered in here this afternoon. And what about him? I looked at him and he smiled. He asked me if I would wait while he went to his locker and got his cigarettes. I nodded and said that I would be here when he got back. He tightened the towel around him as he stood up.

*

I WAS SHOWERED and dressed and ready to leave when he was still putting on his white vest. I waited for him in the lobby. When he came out he was like a businessman in a blue blazer, grey slacks and a collar and tie. He seemed taller and more ready for the world than the nervous boy I had met in the sauna. He told me that he would be more comfortable if I walked ahead and he followed me. I wondered if he was still contemplating changing his mind and might at any moment hail a taxi and fade like a shadow into the traffic before I had time to turn and notice. I realized that now I should be standing in front of my students desperately waiting for time to pass. Instead, I was free in the city with a beautiful man walking behind me. I pretended I did not know him when we came to cross the street; he let me stride ahead, and, once more, he followed. I felt no guilt about not turning up for work; I felt only delight and expectation.

I held the front door of the apartment building open for him, he slipped in and stood still as I closed the door. He smiled as if to say that we had come safely this far.

'Querés subir?' I asked him as though I were the porter and he an honoured guest. He grinned and put out his arm and indicated that I should go first.

When I opened the apartment door, the space inside seemed darker and mustier than usual. I watched it through his eyes and I saw peeling paintwork and faded colours and dirty glass. I motioned him to follow me down the corridor; I opened the door of my mother's bedroom. It had been several months since I had brought anyone home, and I had never before noticed how shabby the curtains and carpet seemed, how bulky and ugly the wardrobe, and there was an indistinct smell of something – musty and sweet at the same time. I smiled at the thought of her old ghost lingering here, watching over me. I turned to my companion. He was looking around him.

'Querés tomar algo?' I asked him.

'Sí, un vaso de agua,' he said. 'Es viejo, el departmento, no?'

I was about to answer him, and make an excuse about the state of the place, when the phone rang. I guessed instantly that it was the school. I had never let a telephone ring before. I put my fingers to my lips. He was puzzled. He would have been happier, I am sure, if the apartment had been modern and airy and if I had answered the telephone when it rang. I was to learn very little about him, but I knew from the beginning that he was bourgeois and conservative. Had he not preferred men's bodies, I thought to myself, he would have been a pillar of society. He stood still as the ringing came to an end. It would have been easier to answer the telephone and say that I was ill, but then I would have had to explain why I had not called earlier to let them know. I had no idea how I was going to explain not turning up. I went to the kitchen and got my companion a glass of water and took it back to him. I knew by his stance that he was still uncomfortable and undecided, but after he took a few gulps of water he began to unloosen his tie.

★

WHEN HE HAD GONE I took a shower and put on fresh clothes and thought about what I was going to do. Things would be difficult at the school. Señora Sanmartín would view my not showing up for work as a studied insult. I could say that I tried to phone, or that I left a message with someone whose voice I did not recognize. Nobody would believe me. She would say that there were plenty of other people looking for work and they had to turn them away. I would have to try to speak to her husband. Maybe I should contact him now. It was just after six o'clock. I still had two classes to do. I could redeem myself by sheer penitence and by the incoherence of my excuse. I could telephone now and say that they could keep their job, or they could inflict it upon some other unfortunate, but they weren't going to see me any more, and could they send me the money they owed me, they knew my address.

But I made no effort to contact them. I went out and walked the streets for a while and looked at people. When I came to the Arcadia on Lavalle I found that there was a movie just starting. I knew nothing about it but I bought a ticket anyway and sat back in my seat in the half-empty cinema as the lights went down and the advertisements and the trailers came on. I felt as if the world had just begun. The film showed Meryl Streep and Robert de Niro falling in love in New York in beautiful, bright, cared-for rooms and wonderful shops. Their smiles were hopeful. When it was over, I wanted it to start again.

I went to a bar on Lavalle and experienced the first tinges of regret. I felt like a child suddenly. I sipped a beer and ordered a sandwich. I was going to have to change my life. I hated my job. The apartment was dingy and run-down and reminded me too much of my mother. And that guy whom I had spent hours stalking had walked out of the apartment without asking for a phone number, without suggesting that we see each other again. I had liked his white skin and his soft lips. But even so, I was not sure that I wanted to see him again either.

I had agreed to go back to the Fords' that night, to take part in another life that had no connection with anything I had known before. I thought about the food on their table and the red wine they drank, and the talk and the laughter, and I felt better. I smiled to myself as I paid and left the bar. I walked briskly around the corner and hailed a taxi.

Susan, I learned, could sense things about people around her. I still imagine her as a cat with quiet, magical powers to sniff something out. That evening, she knew there was something funny about me. She did not know what it was, but she asked me what was wrong as we sat in the main reception room drinking gin and tonics.

'I hate my job,' I said, 'and I didn't turn up today. I gave them no notice. They'll be pretty upset.'

'Tell them you want to quit,' she said.

'I can't afford to quit. Could you quit your job?' I asked.

'I don't hate my job,' she said. 'You have several advantages: you look good, you speak two languages fluently. We could find work for you. Donald has told you that before.'

'He mentioned nothing specific.'

'There's something you could do in a couple of weeks from now if you would commit yourself,' she said. She lit a cigarette and looked at me.

'Tell me about it. I'm serious.'

'Just let me go and talk to Donald. You stay there, pour yourself more gin.'

Susan was different when she came back: she was looking sternly at a piece of paper in her hand. She could have been a newsreader. Normally, I would have been able to say this to her and we would have laughed and invented some news for her to read. But not now.

'You know the problem of the external debt,' she said, without looking up.

'Los años de la plata dulce,' I said.

'Well, you probably know, too, that the repayments are being rescheduled, and there's some worry about the state of the economy. Government spending is overrunning its targets all the time in almost every department.'

'That sounds likely,' I said.

'Basically, what's happening is this: the International Monetary Fund is sending a team of economists to take a look at this overheated economy of yours. All of them are English-speaking, most are Americans. They don't know the country, but that's not a problem. Their job is to look at figures and make suggestions. They will be taken very seriously. We need someone to look after them for the ten days they're here. It's something that we would often do, or somebody from the government side, but it would be better for everyone if it were someone neutral. We'll want you to stay in the same hotel, eat with them, translate for them, make sure they get all the information and assistance they need.'

'And when that's over?' I looked up and smiled, but Susan remained stern.

'If that goes well, there'll be other work.'

'And what about Mr Canetto's campaign? That's what I came to see you about first.'

'We'll make a decision soon on that. There's a lot of sorting out to be done.'

'And what about money?'

She mentioned a figure in dollars which was more than two

months' salary at the academy. Again, I tried to make a joke and smile, but she did not respond.

'I'll take it,' I said, 'on condition that you stop behaving like a schoolmistress.'

'Wait until you start and then you'll really see a new version of me.'

'Does Donald change too?'

'Let's talk about how we're going to plan this visit and we can play games afterwards.' She studied the piece of paper and then looked up at me as though I were a stranger who had just arrived in the room.

★

IN THE MORNING the phone rang. I knew it was the academy as I lifted it up, but I had prepared no excuse or explanation, I simply knew that I was not going to work that day. It was the secretary, Cuca, who said that Señora Sanmartín wished to speak to me. I waited, unsure what I was going to say to her. Soon, her voice came on the line. She wanted to know where I had been the day before. I had caused such inconvenience. The students were angry, she said, and she was angry. Her husband was angry too. I said nothing. She would have to talk to me, she said. Why didn't I come in now, I suggested, interrupting her, and we could talk face to face?

She stopped for a moment as though I had said something to affront her. This is very serious, she said. This is very serious. I asked her if she would be there in half an hour. I tried to sound reasonable and measured. I'll decide when I'm here and when I'm not here, she responded. Once more, I said nothing. So you've no excuse, she said. You've no excuse.

Eventually, we arranged to meet in her office at one o'clock. I knew as I made the arrangement that I would not turn up. I knew that I would never set foot in her academy again. I went to the movies in the afternoon and I do not know whether she telephoned or not. I was free of her as I walked up and down Lavalle. I sat on a park bench near the railway station and read a newspaper. A few weeks later a large envelope arrived with some books and papers I had left behind and a letter formally dismissing me which read as though it had been copied from a very old manual. I laughed when I read it. I often wondered if I would meet the Señora or her husband or any of the teachers or students on the street, or in a bar or a restaurant, but I never saw any of them again. They faded, the Señora became part of a routine I performed late at night for Donald and Susan Ford: the Argentinian ogre who says everything twice in a shrieking voice. We laughed a lot at her expense, and this may have helped to assuage the memory of all those hours, all those days, locked in a classroom like a cage desperately wanting time to pass.

*

SUSAN TOOK ME SHOPPING. She wanted me to look like an American economist: she said it was necessary. I had to fit in, she said. Her budget, she told me, would allow for the purchase of two suits. The rest, including an expensive haircut, I had to fund. I asked her how she could justify the two suits. She said that they would be listed under sundry items. In the shops she behaved like my wife, instructing the assistants in a Spanish which seemed to me increasingly accurate and fluent as the afternoon went on. She checked the width of the collar and the quality of the cloth. I might have to wear these clothes, her tone to the assistants suggested, but she would have to live with them. When I came out of the changing booth with a new suit on she would stand back, purse her lips, narrow her eyes and examine me, shaking her head in worry, as if to say that things were not quite right, she was not fully happy. It was a new game and we both enjoyed it. It was called making me look the part.

I stood two days later in the arrivals hall of the airport sheepishly holding up a piece of cardboard with the letters IMF on it. I was wearing one of the new suits, a new shirt and tie, new shoes, and a haircut which had not completely worn off. I had an urge to drop the sign in a waste-paper basket, or hand it to some member of the public, and disappear, walk the long trail back to the city slowly discarding my tie, my jacket, my fancy haircut, my shoes, and my new place in the world. I had thought about discarding my smile as well, but as the men from the IMF trickled out through the dividing doors and came towards me, I realized that smiling would not be necessary. They did not smile. They exuded manners which were friendly, but tough, businesslike and to the point. They were aged, I knew from the dossier, between twenty-eight and fifty-two. I wondered if one or two of them might be interesting, but when they all emerged I noticed something dry and clean-cut and neutral about the way they held themselves and behaved, as though the soft part of the self was something they held in check, allowing only members of their immediate family to glimpse it, or come to know it. I could not imagine what it would be like to touch any of them, or spend a night with them.

Four limousines waited outside to take us to our hotel in the city centre. The three men who travelled with me viewed the journey with a mild disinterest, made jokes and bantering remarks. They asked no questions. It seemed that this sort of travel was routine for them, like commuting to work in the morning. All three of them thought the journey was too long and wondered if there were another airport. I said yes, but it was for internal flights. Maybe we should advise the government to allow us to land there in future, one of them said. The others laughed. I wondered if the same conversation could be going on in the other three cars at precisely the same moment.

We met for breakfast in a private room on the first floor of the hotel at eight o'clock the next morning. Donald was there and some people from the embassy and two men from the government. I noticed that Donald had the title of Economic Adviser to the Ambassador. I stood up, as Susan had told me to do, introduced myself and explained, in case I had not made it clear the previous day, that I was available twenty-four hours a day to sort out any problems anyone had, that translators would be available, but if anyone needed me to translate, then I would make time and help in any way I could. I told them, once more on Susan's instructions, that three meals a day were provided at the hotel, but any other expenses, including laundry, room service and phone calls, would have to be paid for. I added that the city was, comparatively speaking, reasonably safe, but perhaps it would be easier if people were to consult me about restaurants and parts of the city they wished to visit. The hotel reception desk would always know where I was. One of them muttered something I did not hear, and all of them, including Donald, laughed. I enjoyed standing in front of them, wearing the same clothes as they wore, mimicking their masculinity, and seeming to be in control. I did not laugh or smile. I finished what I had to say and sat down.

Later that day, at around six o'clock, I was having a drink with Donald in the hotel bar when two of them approached us. One of them was a tall, beefy man with glasses and grey hair, and the other was Irish, he was the youngest of the group. They were the experts on the economics of transport, they told us, and they were getting no cooperation from the local officials. It was not just that the translator was bad, they said, although she was appalling, but the officials did not seem willing to provide figures, costings, projections or any other precise set of details. Their attitude was hostile, to say the least, the tall, beefy one said. The Irishman nodded.

I told them that I would accompany them to the Transport

Ministry first thing in the morning. In the meantime, I would speak to someone there to make sure that things would be dealt with as soon as we arrived. I asked them to join us for a drink. They agreed. Donald spoke to them about the problems of bureaucracy in Argentina. He gave them a figure which he understood was the subsidy for the suburban train system in the greater city of Buenos Aires. When we're finished there, the Irishman said, it'll be a lot lower.

★

MY ALARM CALL came at seven thirty and instantly I was filled with fear. All the bravery of the day before, all the manly confidence, had been replaced by a terrible hollowness in my stomach and my chest. I curled up and hugged myself and closed my eyes. I knew that I would have to shower and shave and put on a clean shirt. When I was dressed I would have to join the others for breakfast. I wondered if any of them might feel the same fear as I did, or if they faced each morning with equanimity and calm courage. I hated the idea of putting on a tie, half-choking myself. I wanted to lie down and go back to sleep.

The economists were all having breakfast. They moved from the buffet back to the tables like bees in a hive. The two experts on transport were at the same table. As soon as I came in, they asked me to join them.

'Are you British?' the American asked me.

'No, but my mother was born in England.'

'I don't know if you know the phrase "to kick ass", but that is what we want to do here today, starting soon,' he said.

'Sure do,' the Irish one said.

We drove in a limousine to the Ministry for Transport. We arrived just before nine o'clock. The American said this would give a shock to the officials they had been dealing with the previous day. I had the feeling that these officials might not have left home yet, but I said nothing. The building was an imposing structure from the turn of the century; the doorway looked as though it had been designed for carriages rather than transport officials; the hallway was vast and dark with a carved wooden ceiling. I spoke to the uniformed porter, a small man in his fifties with oily hair, and informed him who we were. I gave him the name of the officials we were waiting to see. He told us to wait on a polished wooden bench across the hall from his desk, but he did not, as far as I could make out, try to contact the officials. He sat and read the newspaper until another porter came down the steps from the corridor above. They went into a small room together, leaving the door ajar. The two economists sat without speaking. I felt tired and promised myself that I would go to bed as early as I could.

The phone rang on the porter's desk and all three of us sat there watching it ring, with an eye on the door, wondering when the porter would answer it. After a while, it stopped ringing and then it began again until he came out of the room, lifted the receiver and then immediately put his finger on the button, cutting the caller off. He did this casually, as though it were a normal reaction to a telephone call, and went back in to join his friend. When the telephone rang again, he ignored it, and soon it stopped and did not resume.

At about nine thirty, some officials began to arrive. They waved at the porter, who was now sitting at his desk drinking a cup of coffee, and passed by. I could feel the American's rage rising as he announced that he was going to take a walk around the block and would be back in five minutes. His colleague went with him. As soon as they left, the phone rang again, and the porter lifted it and quickly hung up without even putting the receiver to his ear. I walked over and stood in front of him. He managed to pretend that I was not there until I told him that we were waiting for the officials whose names I had given him and we wanted to see them now. If they were not yet in their offices I wanted him to phone them at home, or I wanted the most senior official in the building to be consulted. But I wanted something done now. He looked at me and shrugged and then pointed to the bench where we had been sitting. Your Yankee friends, he said, have left. The phone rang once more; this time he lifted the receiver and put it face down on his desk. I could hear a voice babbling but the porter paid no attention to it. You'll have to wait like everybody else, he said. I looked down at the receiver and I could still hear a voice coming through the wires. Why don't you answer the phone, I asked him, is that not what you're paid for? He picked up the receiver and defiantly hung up. He shrugged as it rang again and he let it ring while staring off into the distance.

I went back and sat on the bench. Soon, the American and his colleague returned. I noticed how uncomfortable they seemed, as if their shoes did not fit them or someone were squeezing their balls. We'll wait ten more minutes, the American said, and then we'll go sightseeing. I went over to the porter again. We need to see someone now, I said. Now, do you understand? This minute? There's no one here, he said sullenly. I want you to find someone now, I said. He picked up the phone and dialled a number while I went back to the bench and joined the two economists. He shrugged and sighed and muttered to himself and then put the receiver down. He had got no answer.

I could feel the breakfast in my stomach still; I felt queasy and tired. The phone on the porter's desk began to ring once more. He ignored it. Suddenly, the American rushed over to the desk, picked up the receiver and brandished it in front of the porter's face. Tell him to answer it, he bellowed at me, his voice echoing against the high ceiling. The porter held the receiver out from him as though it were something live and poisonous. I stood and watched. I said nothing. The American's face had become red. I realized that we should leave. I spoke quietly to the Irishman, suggesting that we go back to the hotel. The American was pointing his finger at the porter, who was standing up now, looking shocked, the receiver still in his hand.

All that day I waited in the hotel as telexes were sent to Washington and then to New York informing the IMF that the officials in the Transport Ministry would not cooperate and asking for instructions. When no reply came by the early afternoon, the American made a collect call to a colleague in Washington and explained in great detail what had happened. The Irishman and I sat in his room as he aired his indignation, listening as he told the story of the porter who refused to answer the telephone and the officials who did not turn up for work. By this time we had a telex number for the Minister for Transport's office and the President's office and the office of the Minister for the Economy. It was agreed that a strongly worded telex would be sent to each office asking that the two economists in question be contacted through me at the hotel. The American wanted an ultimatum given that the team would be pulled out and IMF cooperation reassessed if the problem was not solved by the following morning, but his colleague in Washington, it was obvious from the call, would not agree to this. He argued for a while and then gave up. When he put the receiver down, he turned to us and said: 'They're not going to threaten them, they're going to ask them. It's so typical. Let's offend no one. That's what America's all about.' He threw his hands up in despair and walked out of the room, leaving us to find the key and lock the door and then follow him down to the lobby.

Later that evening the receptionist put a call through to me in my room; it was one of the officials who had not come to work that morning. He said that his office would be open at eight thirty the following morning, and anything that we needed would be made available. I explained that we had experienced certain problems with the porter, and he said he would sort them out before we arrived. He sounded dutiful and polite but he spoke in a strange, slow way as though he had only recently learned how to use that tone.

As soon as we appeared the next morning the porter became a bustling mass of energy and detailed instructions about how to get to the lift. He paid special attention to the American, smiling at him and nodding his head. The American ignored him, moved ahead of us like a man leading his followers into arduous battle.

The officials were waiting. Their leader was even more unctuous than the porter had been, but the American was even more brusque. None of the officials spoke English, and thus I had to stay there for the entire day – the American and the Irishman refused to have a lunch break and sent one of the officials out for sandwiches – translating the American's barked commands for facts and figures about public transport in the greater Buenos Aires area, explaining his efforts to have these facts and figures broken down into administration costs and running costs.

In the afternoon a man sauntered down from the floor above. His hair was cut short and he was wearing a smart grey suit. Susan, I thought, would have approved of his clothes and his bearing. When he shook my hand, I recognized him. He had studied economics and politics at the university while I was there. I had spoken to him once or twice at that time, and seen him in the library, but we were never friends and I had not seen him since. His face had become thinner; he seemed confident as he spoke to the economists. There was something about his reputation in university which I half-remembered: he had come first in his year, or he had won a scholarship. He spoke English with a heavy Spanish accent; on the other hand, with some words he used an emphatic American accent. He discussed the ministry with the economists for a while. He appeared to understand why they wanted a detailed breakdown of the wage bill. He said with some exasperation that there were three separate offices involved in paying wages and another one for pensions and there might even be one more office which pays wages too, but it was merely a rumour; it had never actually been located. The American sat back in his chair and laughed. You're the guy we need, he said. Tell them that we must have these figures and all the figures we asked for by tomorrow morning. Tell them we will wait here all night, he said, and we expect them to do the same.

The new arrival looked at us and smiled. I think this will be very interesting, he said. Two days later there was still a ban on lunch breaks, but the facts and figures were becoming available with the help of Francisco, the economist who had been to college with me, and the three officials who had been uncooperative. Sometimes, the two men from the IMF would huddle together with some new piece of information they had acquired. Did I know, they asked me, that the train system in Buenos Aires lost five times its annual revenue? Did I know that for each driver, ticket checker and ticket seller, there was an administrator? Did I know that the ticket checkers and sellers earned more than the income from ticket sales so that it would be cheaper to run the service without tickets? They and Francisco were like small boys assembling a train set.

★

ON THE LAST NIGHT there was to be a dinner in the hotel in honour of the Finance Minister. Each group was allowed to invite officials from the various government departments; thus the two experts on transport invited Francisco and we arranged to sit at the same table. Donald and I had a drink in the bar beforehand.

'The visit has gone well,' he said. He sipped his drink. 'It has been a success. And there is a great deal at stake.'

'Do you mean the debt repayments?' I asked.

'Well, yes,' he said, 'that's part of it, but for the moment it's a small part. The real issue is oil: we want them to privatize the oil business, there are a number of private companies here already, we want them to have a bigger stake, but we want the state company opened up. That's the priority, that's what this visit, in essence, has been about. It's a delicate issue, and we want to place it in the overall context of debt repayment and the restructuring of the economy.'

We had another drink as some of the guests began to arrive.

'You probably did not notice,' Donald said quietly, 'the group who specialize in the economics of oil, but they noticed you, and they were impressed with the work you did helping the transport guys. They gave you a good report: they said that you were exceptional. The oil guys are going to stay on for a day or two. We'll have a meeting tomorrow mid-morning to talk about strategy, and they want you to attend. They know nothing about politics here, they don't know where they are. I think you would be good for them. There's a lot of work to do. On Sunday we'll take them out somewhere. I'd like you to get to know them, but they're here for the long haul, and if things work out over the next couple of days we'll think of a title for you and put you on someone's payroll. That is unless you've got other plans.'

I nodded and said we could talk about it the next day. 'Some of this country stinks,' Donald said. 'The oil industry is full of corruption, it's unreformable. It will have to be sold off. I think these guys are pretty shocked by what's been going on. Real banana republic stuff.'

*

THE DAYS LIVING IN the hotel had become the real world for me. I had not gone home. Returning there, walking up the stairs to the apartment, or waking in my own bed, was hard to imagine. I had come to like these men; I enjoyed the sound of their voices and I sensed something beneath all the hardness, the brusque gestures and the clipped talk. And yet I somehow also wanted it to be over, it was too much to absorb and I needed time alone. I contemplated more days of this and I was unsure and suddenly low. Donald said nothing. He finished his drink and went over to speak to one of the economists. I stayed at the bar on my own. It struck me that I felt the same as I had before classes began; I wondered would all of my life be like this, full of moments of dread at the propect of facing the outside world, like a machine fitfully shuddering before it starts. Eventually, Donald came back with a man called Federico Arenas who worked for YPF, the government oil company. Donald told him that I had been working with the transport people and would be spending some time now with the oil people. He shook my hand.

The dinner was in the ballroom of the hotel; there was a big display for the foreigners. A roast calf was carried in on a spit by two men dressed as gauchos; the waiters set to work carving it up. There were eight of us at the table, but the four of us who had worked on transport stayed talking together. Several times during the dinner I caught Donald's eye across the room, and he half-smiled at me as though we were involved in some small but lucrative conspiracy. Afterwards, people wandered from table to table; there was plenty of wine and brandy as well as cigars and Scotch whisky. I went to the toilet and then down to the lobby to check a flight reservation for one of the Americans. When I came back I expected that our group would have broken up or someone would have joined us, but the American, the Irishman and Francisco were still talking. As I sat down I heard the Irishman say that he had been that afternoon to the Plaza de Mayo and he had seen the mothers of the disappeared in their white scarves. Was that still an issue here, he asked. What did we think about it? I hesitated and said that I did not really know. I said it seemed strange to me that after all these years I had never seen a list of the names of those who had disappeared, that I myself knew no one who had disappeared. I am not suggesting, I said, that it did not happen. But, for some reason, I realized, I was suggesting that.

I did not tell the story of the night I saw the driverless cars revving outside the police station. I said again that I didn't really know about it, and I thought that most people were more worried about inflation and unemployment. I noticed the American nodding.

Francisco had said nothing. The Irishman looked at him, but still he did not speak. He asked him what he thought. Francisco shook his head and looked pained for a moment before he smiled. He wondered whether the Plaza de Mayo would become a tourist trap, and if you would be able to buy postcards of the mothers with their white scarves. He seemed reticent as he drank some water. But the Irishman would not give up. He looked at him directly and asked again what he thought about the disappearances.

It's hard for me, the economist said, to talk about what happened. I was away for the worst time. He stopped and turned to me as though he needed help. He cleared his throat a few times. I was at Harvard, he said, when my girlfriend was taken. I suppose if I'd been there that night they would have taken me as well. Or instead. I don't know.

And what happened to her, the Irishman asked.

She disappeared. They murdered her. Ask him. He pointed at me. He knows about it.

I looked at him. I had no idea what he was talking about. I didn't understand, I said to him. By this time the two visitors were watching us intently. Who was your girlfriend, I asked.

She was Marta Goméz, he said, you knew her. She studied English Literature with you; that's how I met you.

I knew who he was talking about: she was a tall girl who dressed in black and wore tinted glasses. I did not know that she had disappeared. Like most of the people I studied with, I had not seen her for years. I could imagine her now walking along a corridor with a folder under her arm. I tried to think what else I knew about her. I remembered that she told me once how she would like to study in Oxford and then return here and become a lecturer in English.

She's dead? I tried to sound puzzled and shocked because I really was puzzled and shocked, but I did not know if anyone in the company believed me. What I had said was true, but now it sounded like a lie or a serious evasion.

During the trial of the generals, Francisco went on, Marta's name and photograph were in the press every day for about a week. General Lanusse was a friend of her family's — he was President here in the 1970s — and he gave evidence about her disappearance to the trial. They had gone to him when they could not find out anything about Marta. She had been taken away in the night with two friends who had been involved in the student movement, they were sharing an apartment and getting ready for their finals. They had nothing to do with politics. No one ever knew how their names got on a list or why they were arrested. At the time I believed like everybody else that they could not possibly arrest someone for nothing. But they were never seen again. When the general went to the army, they told him to try the navy or the air force. He was a highly respected figure and when he asked about her and gave details about her arrest, an officer in the navy told him that they could not help him with an individual case, that so many bodies were taken out at night and thrown from helicopters and planes into the sea that they didn't keep records. At first he did not tell Marta's family what he heard because he thought it was a figure of speech, a brutal remark to convey that she was dead, but later when he enquired more, he discovered that it was literally true: they drugged their victims and hauled them into aircraft and threw them into the sea. Maybe that's what happened to her, he said. I used to think I saw her on the street sometimes but I never do now. I know she's dead. I don't know about other cases, except her two friends, one of them was also from a family who had good connections, but they disappeared too.

He turned to me again. You must have known about Marta, he said, because she never did her final exams. Everybody must have known. And I think that you knew one of her friends too. I don't know how you can say that you know no one who disappeared.

He spoke softly. I know her body must be somewhere, he said, as though he were talking to himself. We'd like to bury her properly. And know what happened. That's the worst for everybody: not knowing what day she died, what she looked like when she died, not knowing, but imagining all the time what it must have been like for her. I suppose that they tortured her, and it's hard to think about that, about someone you loved, and still love, it's very hard. Maybe that didn't happen. I'd love to meet someone who could tell me what happened.

Both the Irishman and the American were quiet now. I said nothing. All around us the group laughed and talked. I knew that it would not be long before someone noticed how subdued we were.

I never knew about her, I said. I'm sorry. He looked up at me and shook his head. Eventually, Donald came over and slapped the American on the back. He looked at each of us and laughed. Come and help us liven up the party, he said. I stayed sitting there. I could not think what to do. The others slowly stood up. I wanted to ask my former fellow student if he believed me when I said that I knew nothing about Marta Goméz's disappearance, but he had left the room by the time I pushed my chair back and faced the company.

★

THE DAY THE ECONOMISTS arrived I had packed my bag and closed the door of the apartment as though I were ready to abandon it for ever and start from scratch. It must have been the second or third night in the new world of hotel rooms and men in suits who exuded control and satisfaction with the order of things: we walked from a restaurant in Corrientes up to the hotel and we passed the building where I lived or, rather, where I had lived before these men arrived. I touched the keys in my pocket, as if I were touching a secret part of myself. I could easily have left these men to make their own way home. The streets were safe and the way was clear. And I could have slipped back into my own house. I could have quietly ascended the stairs and opened the door and it would have all been there. As I thought about it, however, I had a vision of opening the door and suddenly finding instead a bright space that was completely blank and insubstantial, nothing except cloudy light, no rooms or belongings, no floors or walls, no beds or cupboard.

I could have mentioned as we passed that this was where I lived and one or two of them might have expressed an interest, might have asked me something about it: how long had I lived there? was it expensive? did I own it or rent it? did I live with my family? But that would have damaged the integrity of the new self I put forward, the person who was solid and business-like, efficient and serious. One of them, on learning that I lived alone in an apartment on the third floor of this downtown building, would have guessed that I was, in some fundamental way, unreliable. This was simply because he would have focused his attention on me for a second, looked at me carefully, pondered on the detail that I had revealed. And that would have been enough. I did not feel that I would survive close inspection. Thus I let the moment pass out of need. I told them nothing. I let them talk among themselves and as we walked through my streets I found that this gave me pleasure.

Now, however, my time was up. Three of them would remain to study the intricacies of the oil industry and the rest would leave to write reports and follow up on other projects and return to the intimacy of their families. There was no need for me to stay in the hotel. I made sure that their taxis for the airport arrived on time and that all the extras were paid and no one was overcharged. I stood in the lobby and made sure that all the bags were carried out. I rang the airport to check that there were no delays. I shook hands with the departing economists, wished them a safe trip, checked once more their time of departure and assured them that they had plenty of time. And then I went to the desk in the lobby and got my key and hurried upstairs to my room. I sat on the edge of the bed and let time pass. I packed and made sure that I had left nothing behind. I sat on the edge of the bed again. I could easily have gone back to bed and slept until lunchtime and maybe then I would have known what to do. I remember that I forced myself that morning to leave the room and go downstairs and hand over the key and pay what extras I had consumed and go home.

There was an electricity bill and two letters which had been delivered by hand. The writing was familiar. I thought it must be Susan's or Donald's and wondered why they had not contacted me at the hotel. When I opened one of them, however, I realized that it was from Jorge. I read it as I stood in the hallway. His father, he said, wanted to step up the campaign and was surprised, to say the least, that I had not been in touch. Had I made any progress with the Americans? With whom had I been in contact and with what results? He had telephoned a few times a day for the past week, he said, and had called around, but there was no sign of me. His tone was formal, as though I were an employee of his, and it struck me that his father must have stood over him as he wrote the letter. I put the other letter in my pocket and went up the stairs. When I opened the door the space inside seemed comforting. I put down my bag and went into the kitchen and glanced around at each object as though it had been specially placed there to reassure me.

The other letter had been written first; it was just a brief note asking me to contact Jorge or his father. I left it on the kitchen table and went down into the street and had a coffee in a bar. Unless Susan, Donald or the oil economists wanted me for anything, I was free for the rest of the day. I thought that maybe I should buy something for the apartment, new sheets or towels or a new chair. I would also have to telephone Susan and ask her what I should say to Jorge's father. Maybe, I decided, I could talk to her later in the week. I felt guilty about Jorge and his father. I had used their contacts to find work for myself and I had done nothing in return. I imagined that Jorge had tried to reach me at the school and knew that I no longer worked there. I finished my coffee and paid and went back to the apartment with a newspaper so I could check the times of the movies in the afternoon.

★

WHEN THE PHONE RANG at eight o'clock the following morning I knew that I was taking a risk when I got out of bed to answer it. It was Jorge and I realized instantly that his father was close to him. He began by saying how hard it had been to contact me, how many times he had tried. I said nothing. The problem was that they could not send anyone else to talk to the Americans until they knew what I had been doing. Did I have any news for them, he asked me. I said that I had spoken to the Americans several times, but things were still vague. Later in the day, however, I was due to see them once more and it was very likely, I said, that things would become more concrete. And this was why I had not been in touch. Maybe, I said, if we arranged to see each other later today, or early tomorrow. I tried to sound businesslike. What time could we meet, he asked. I told him that there was no point in arranging a time until I had seen the Americans, but I would contact him later in the day. I asked where the best place to contact him was. He would be home from seven onwards, he said.

I went back to bed and tried to sleep. But I began to think about how I needed a telephone beside the bed and an answering machine and maybe a computer, or at least an electric typewriter. I tried to work out how much money I had and how much I was owed for the work I had done with the economists. My mind was racing and I knew I could not get back to sleep. I put on my dressing gown and went to the bathroom to turn on the hot water and then I went to the telephone and dialled Susan Ford's number. She picked up the receiver immediately. I arranged to go out to her house as soon as I had washed and dressed and had my breakfast.

She was wearing a bright blue bow across her hair which matched her eyes. It made her look smaller and more ordinary.

'I was going to call you,' she said. 'We have to have lunch tomorrow with the oil experts and some people from the oil business here. And there are also several people coming next week from various oil companies. Most of them are Americans. They will be here just to check things out. We'll need you to look after them and keep them happy. For example,' she looked up and grinned, 'I would rather they did not catch any venereal diseases during their time here.'

'I will make sure of that,' I said. 'Would you like me to make a note of it?'

'Why did you call me so early? It's not like you.'

I showed her the two letters from Jorge and reminded her of my reason for wanting to meet her and Donald.

'Do you think this man could make a good candidate?' she asked.

'Maybe I know him too well to say,' I said. 'He was a friend of Perón's and he is a successful businessman. He could be sold as solid and forward-looking, a safe pair of hands.'

'He sounds awful,' she said.

'I think that he's a credible candidate. Under certain circumstances he could win this election and I think that you should take a look at him.'

'Why does he need us if he is a successful businessman?'

'He has backers of his own, but the general view seems to be that the Americans are prepared to spend a great deal of money on the candidate they choose. I think that he wants some of that money, but he also wants to make sure that it does not go to a rival candidate.'

'Let's have a look at him then, if he's serious. He has a big house, a big garden, a swimming pool, all of that?'

I nodded. She stopped and thought for a moment. She tapped her fingernail against the table.

'He should have a fund-raising party, invite people who are prepared to put money and energy into his campaign. He could invite us as well, and it would be easier then, perhaps, to assess his level of support. Otherwise, all we know about him is what we've heard from you.'

'I'll tell him what you said.'

'Tell him to do it soon. Also, we need your bank account number so we can deposit some money for you. We'll be able to pay you about half in cash, in dollars, but the rest, I'm afraid, will have to be above board. I hope that's okay.'

'That's fine,' I said.

*

THAT EVENING I TOOK the train to Jorge's house, wondering if this was one of the lines that my friends from Washington wanted to close down. I walked from the station until I came to the long road of big houses, all carefully protected. Some had armed guards at the gate; others had dogs. When I arrived at Jorge's house, I had to stand at the gate while a sharp-toothed Alsatian barked at me. Eventually a man in a uniform arrived and put the dog on a lead. He did not smile or make any gesture in my direction. He was good-looking. I would have enjoyed it had he smiled. But he looked like a man in a bad mood, or maybe Jorge's father paid him to look like that. He opened the gate, holding the dog on a tight rein. I walked past him towards the house. I had forgotten how much I hated the heavy furniture in Señor Canetto's house, the hunting trophies, the terrible calfskin rugs. Jorge and his father were in the office when I arrived and I was shown in there. I realized by Jorge's distant, nervous reaction to my entry and his father's vague hostility that they might easily have come to the conclusion that I was to blame for the fact that Señor Canetto was not at this moment being lifted shoulder-high by the masses as the front-runner in any forthcoming election. I let them know what Susan had said. Señor Canetto screwed up his face and then blew his nose on the folded handkerchief which he took out of his trousers pocket. How much money would they pay for the campaign if they were impressed by the fund-raising party, he asked. I said that I did not know. Was I sure that I had spoken to the people at the top who actually make the decisions, Jorge asked. I was pretty sure, I said, but if they had other contacts then they should also use them.

As we spoke the door opened and the figure who came in looked at all three of us without much interest and moved across to one of the bookshelves. Jorge and his father paid no attention to him. He was dressed casually and his attitude was easy and casual as well. He was dark and stocky. When he turned to leave, having found the book he was looking for, I saw that his eyes, like Jorge's eyes, were a crystal blue. Instantly I knew who he was. He was the brother who had gone to the

United States years earlier. I remembered that he had phoned during the Malvinas War one night while I was in the house. He was, I knew, younger than Jorge by a year or two. Jorge and his father continued talking as he left the room, behaving as though he were an ordinary, fixed part of the household. I tried to remember his name as his father droned on about his election campaign, I must have known it at some point, but I could not remember what it was. As I was thinking about this Jorge asked if I no longer worked in the school. I told him that I had left and had found work as a translator with Donald and Susan. He and his father looked at me suspiciously. They did not ask me to stay for dinner. Jorge, instead, offered to drive me to the station. I accepted and shook hands with his father before I left. He was quiet now and surly. I think he had expected the Americans to hand him money which he could spend on advertising his candidacy in the newspapers, letting everyone know that the Americans had paid for the publicity and were thus supporting him. The fact that they wanted him to do something, take some initiative, seemed to make him uncomfortable and depressed.

On the way to the station I asked Jorge if the figure who came into the room was his brother. Yes, he said, about a month earlier his brother had telephoned from the airport to say that he was home and Jorge and his father had gone to collect him.

'What is his name?' I asked Jorge.

'Pablo,' he said.

'Is he going to stay?'

'Yes, he's working with my father as well. They haven't had a single argument yet. They used to argue a lot.'

'What age is he?'

'I'm thirty, which means that he is twenty-eight.'

'And where has he been living?'

'California. He speaks English with an American accent. Maybe we'll send him to talk to the Americans.'

'Yes, he might get better results than I did.'

★

A FEW DAYS LATER Jorge rang to ask me if I thought that Donald would like to come and play tennis. They had bought a new net and the court was in good order, he said. He and his brother could play against me and the American. I telephoned Donald and he agreed. Thus the following Friday, carrying our tennis gear, we caught the train out to the Canettos' house so that we would avoid the traffic; Jorge met us at the station. He was already dressed in white shorts, white shoes and socks and a white tennis shirt.

I saw him as if through Donald's eyes: he seemed glamorous and handsome, a rich Argentinian wearing expensive sunglasses and speaking English carefully and precisely as I had taught him to do. It had been some years since I had looked at him, studied the shape of his long legs. Beside him, Donald looked plain and uninteresting. I stood back, said nothing, and let them watch each other.

The Canettos had clearly decided to make this an important occasion. The father and his two sons had taken the afternoon off. The father was affable, but oddly authoritative and distant as though he had been searching in the mirror for the pose which would most strike the American as presidential. He told us to use the bathroom in the house, if we didn't want to use the dressing room beside the court, and be sure to come for drinks afterwards. No matter whether we won or lost, he said, the drinks were on him. His laugh, I thought, was too loud and hearty. I was embarrassed for him. When Donald spoke to him I noticed how good and fluent his Spanish was. I had always remembered his accent as flat and his speech as faltering.

'Where is Pablo?' the father asked. Jorge said he was in the

128

swimming pool and we made our way down there, the father going back into the house. I dreaded the drinks after the game, I knew that every moment would seem set up to impress our guest and it would all seem forced and false. The terraced gardens led down to a swimming pool; on the level below there was a tennis court. We could see Pablo's body slicing the water, his arms and legs opening and closing like scissors. He was wearing light blue trunks. Jorge called to him that we were ready.

He swam to our end of the pool and put his elbows on the ledge. He smiled at us. I watched him through my own eyes, and then I turned and noticed that Donald was watching him too. I caught Pablo's eye for one second, but found I had to look away in case it became too clear that I was attracted to him. He swam away from us as though he had no intention of joining us. Jorge shouted at him to get out of the pool and come down to the tennis court. We went down and changed into our tennis gear in the dressing room, and then we played around on the court until Pablo came. His thick, black hair was still wet, but he had changed into white shorts and a light blue T-shirt. He joined his brother on the other side of the net.

Donald and I were out of practice. We missed balls or hit them too hard. Jorge's strokes were accurate. He stood on the baseline and lobbed balls to us. He was patient. Even when we were knocking up, however, Pablo was aggressive and made no allowances. When Jorge told him to take it easy, this wasn't Wimbledon, Pablo suggested that we start the match. We spun a racket and we won the spin. Donald would serve first. I stood at the net and watched Pablo's fierce concentration, his nervous movements, even though it was not his turn to receive the service.

Donald's serve was not difficult to hit back. Jorge drove the ball across to Donald's backhand. He barely managed to reach it. The ball rose softly and Pablo stood at the net waiting for it, his eye carefully inspecting the court in front of him to see where he would place it. He raised his racket as though he were going to smash it towards Donald's backhand. Instead, he chopped the ball hard to his right and it hit me on the shoulder. He turned around and walked back to receive the next service as though nothing had happened. I rubbed my shoulder; it was sore. Jorge shrugged as if to say it had nothing to do with him. Pablo turned and rolled his racket in his hand, and stood stooped and alert as he awaited Donald's serve. I stood at the net in front of Pablo, aware how easy it would be for him to hit me again since Donald's serve, once more, was weak. This time he did not try to hit me, he merely sent the ball past me, flying down the line like a bullet.

'This guy takes no prisoners,' Donald shouted.

They won easily; in the last set, Donald and I gained points only when they became too confident and made mistakes. We were exhausted. Pablo remained obsessed with the game and with the score, which he called out in English. When it was over, he shook our hands as though we had been involved in some important championship. It was still hot although the light was beginning to fade. When Pablo said that he was going for a swim, Donald replied that he hadn't brought any trunks with him; Pablo turned and smiled and said he wouldn't need trunks. By the time we reached the pool Pablo was already naked in the water. Donald slowly took off his gear and then ran towards the water and dived in. The cheeks of his ass were white and smooth. His body seemed firm and tough as he swam a length of the pool with his head under water and then raised his head and shouted at me to hurry. Jorge, by this time, had gone down to the dressing room to get towels. I didn't know how to dive. I stripped and walked across to the shallow end of the pool. I was conscious that both of them were watching me now. I lowered myself in and swam towards the deep end. When I turned I saw Jorge slipping off his shorts. I tried not to stare at his bare legs and his balls and his long dick as he stood at the edge and dived in.

I turned on my back and swam slowly up the pool with my eyes closed. After the exertions of the tennis match, the water was pure relief, and the presence of these naked bodies close to me in the water gave me real pleasure and a sense of expectancy. I had not seen Pablo naked. I waited in the water, ready to turn and look at him when he got out. I swam past him with my eyes closed thinking about his body emerging from the water, his hands on the rails.

★

I THINK MAYBE the heat explains some of the things which happened next. In December the days became hot and the nights too. It was hard to sleep. Everywhere I went people were sweating and fanning themselves and complaining about the heat. There were several strikes in factories and marches through the city against rising inflation and falling wages. One day I had to meet two Amoco executives at the airport and accompany them into the city. At the bottom of Corrientes a line of strikers stood in front of our limousine and blocked the way. It looked as though they had chosen us as the first to stop because of the size of the car. The two Americans watched silently as long lines of chanting marchers passed. It became hot in the car, which had no air-conditioning. I could feel the anger of the Americans as though they owned the factories on strike, as though their money were at stake here.

'This is not what we came here to see,' one of them said. The driver, luckily, spoke no English. Some of his language about the strikers would have been hard to translate. I almost suggested that we get out and walk and allow the driver to curse these people on his own and deliver the luggage later, but

131

I said nothing. I sat there watching too. No one had ever asked me before to have views on strikes and strikers. I did not know how I felt.

The exectives asked me about inflation but I did not tell them that the ticket seller in one of the cinemas near my apartment had asked me if I needed dollars changed; as far as I could make out he offered the best rate. I do not know how or why. He changed my money into local currency and thus I was not affected by inflation. I knew that Jorge's father was pleased with the levels of disaffection which inflation caused in the city. The government could not last, he said. The longer things went on, the more there would be a need for change.

Donald was a member of a tennis club near his house where the courts were floodlit in the evening. We often met there and played the best of three sets before going back to join Susan for dinner. Our game was improving, although his shots could be wildly inaccurate; he served a good number of double faults. I, on the other hand, never made a mistake. I never served an ace, I never hit a winner, I simply returned every ball and never served a double fault. Sometimes rallies could continue for several minutes until Donald managed to pass me at the net, or forced me to run from side to side and then fooled me into thinking he was about to hit the ball in one direction and, instead, hit it the other way and won the point.

One night we were the last to finish, and thus the last in the bar to have a beer after the game. The groundsman was sweeping the courts for the next day and turning out all the lights when we went into the dressing room. We stripped and stood under the cold showers. I was used to Donald's body now, and watched him losing weight as the high summer approached, his belly and his breasts less fleshy every time we played. His body was strong; his chest and legs and arms were hairy; there was some hair on his back. But there was nothing graceful or beautiful about him. All the same, I found his maleness attractive and I could imagine sleeping with him and becoming excited by his strength.

I was drying myself while he was still in the shower. I put my foot on the bench to dry my leg. He was talking about renovating his own tennis court. I was standing with my back to him drying my stomach while he spoke. I did not notice him coming towards me. Without warning, he put his arms around my chest and pulled my body against his. I could feel the softness of his dick and balls against me. I could feel his breath on my neck as he tried to lift me in the air. I could have elbowed him in the stomach, but I did nothing. He was careful in the way he behaved to suggest that this was just a friendly moment in a shower room. When he took his hands away, he moved them down to my balls and then felt my ass. When I turned he could see that I had a hard-on. I looked at his dick, but it was hanging down loose.

'It doesn't take much to get you excited,' he said. He was smiling as though he had discovered something that he had always wanted to know. I was embarrassed. I went to my locker to get my clothes. My dick was still hard. He dried himself facing me.

'Do you do that to many guys?' I asked him.

'You enjoyed it, didn't you?'

'Is that why you did it?'

He walked over towards me and put his hand on my ass.

'Yeah, that's why I did it,' he said and smiled at me. He dried himself and put on his clothes without speaking again. I drank a good deal of wine with Donald and Susan that night after dinner, and I became convinced that this was a first move, that Donald would stay up late, or offer to drive me home, or find an excuse to visit my apartment in the days that followed.

But he did none of these things. He had learned all he needed to know in the shower room.

*

THE CANETTOS decided to give a party on a Saturday night in early January. It was arranged that Susan and Donald could bring some American oil executives, but most of the guests were old friends and business associates of Señor Canetto. He felt too important to telephone me with enquiries about what sort of evening the Americans would most like, but Jorge rang me a few times a day in the week before the party to ask me, among other things, what music should there be, should the food be traditional Argentinian, should there be a lot of young people, should there be speeches, did the Americans have a guest list, did they know how best to contact the ambassador if they thought that he should be invited. Sometimes, I made up the replies; a few times I phoned Susan and asked her view.

'Do these people not know how to give a party?' she asked. 'Do they really expect us to tell them what sort of food to have?' The heat, I think, was making her irritable.

She put on red lipstick for the party and dressed all in white. Donald wore a seersucker suit. The other Americans wore casual clothes and they looked strange, as no one else was dressed casually. I wore a dark suit and a tie. I arranged a limousine to collect the oil executives from their hotel and take them back at a reasonable hour.

Señor Canetto and his wife stood in front of their house welcoming all the guests. She pursed her lips as each person approached her, as though smiling would take too much energy. The Canettos had put lights all over the garden and built a big fire to cook the meat. Cooks in white overalls wandered around, and girls in short skirts offered drinks to all the guests. I noticed a huge Argentinian flag sticking out of one of the upstairs windows, as though the house were an embassy or a presidential palace. There were a great number of middle-aged men and their wives wandering around; I recognized some of the men from the time of the Malvinas. One of them came over and greeted me; others shook my hand. I looked around for the ex-general, but I do not think he was there. I found Susan and Donald sitting by the swimming pool.

'We met your Mr Canetto and his wife,' Susan said.

'So?'

'It's a nice house. We took a look around.'

'Have you eaten yet?' I asked.

'No. Let's go and eat.'

We walked up through the garden and past a small group playing Brazilian dance music. By now, the cooks had set up an elaborate *asado*, with carcasses spread out on poles being cooked in their entirety. On the grass in front of the house, tables were set; the oil executives were sitting there, drinks in their hands, looking around them with the same alert, hungry concentration that they would accord a balance sheet or a bottom line. Jorge came towards us; he too was dressed all in white. He had chains of paper flowers in his hands and he made us all put one on. Susan looked beautiful with the colours around her neck. The lights made her look delicate and desirable, almost soft. Donald stood apart, bored, as Jorge talked to her. Jorge laughed at everything she said with a strange, forced, hysterical edge that unsettled me and made me wish he would go away. But it was clear that he was going to stay with us now that he had found us. He called one of the waitresses and arranged for us all to have fresh drinks. I saw Donald turn his gaze on Jorge and keep it there for a while as couples passed and the music grew louder.

Only once that night did I see Pablo. He was wearing blue jeans and an embroidered blue shirt. He had put wax or gel in his hair, which made it seem thicker and blacker than the last time I had seen him. He looked at us with the same disinterest as he had shown me in his father's study the first time I saw him. I was stunned by the colour of his eyes. He came up to Jorge and whispered something to him and Jorge walked into the house with him, arriving back alone a while later. A few times I was tempted to go and look for him, but I did nothing.

As we were eating our steaks, Jorge's father stopped by, once more accompanied by his wife, and greeted us, gesturing with his hands and smiling warmly at Susan. His wife stood back, adopting a pose of serious dignity. She looked coldly at me, but said nothing. I wondered how long it would take for Jorge and Pablo to resemble their parents now, to develop their father's rough skin and hanging jowls, their mother's cold stare. Tonight there seemed to be an infinite gap between the parents and the children. I knew that it had to do simply with time, that in twenty years Jorge and Pablo would be middle-aged men with rasping voices like their father and bodies that no one would lie in bed in the early morning thinking about.

When they had gone and Jorge was busy talking to the oil executives, Donald and Susan sized up Señor Canetto.

'He reminds me of someone,' Donald said.

'He reminds me of Spiro Agnew,' Susan said. 'In fact, I think that's who he is. Imagine Spiro coming all the way down here and setting up in business. It's just like him. Never give up. Dear old Spiro.'

I was not certain who Spiro Agnew was, but I knew that he had something to do with Nixon. I watched Susan draw on her cigarette and look harshly about her. Plates of ice cream and glasses of champagne arrived at our table. A woman in a red dress began to sing a jazz song in Portuguese and all the faces at all the tables close to us looked over at the bandstand, which was bright with lights. She was cool, the woman in the red dress, she closed her eyes and whispered the song into the microphone. Susan looked around, and I could see her wondering what to make of this; she had no idea who these people were. No one from the government was here, and that seemed reasonable: Señor Canetto was opposed to the government. No one from the opposition was here either, and that was reasonable too: the opposition was fragmented and in disarray. No one from the military was here, and that was reasonable too: the military was in everyone's bad books. These men here tonight, I thought, could easily be waiting in the wings to take over power. I whispered something like this to Susan, but she shook her head.

'There's something missing. I don't know what it is, but it is missing,' she said and drew on her cigarette.

Just then, the singer stopped and everyone applauded. I went into the house to go to the toilet. The toilet on the ground floor was occupied, so I went upstairs and walked along the corridor. I wondered where Pablo was now. Could he be in one of these rooms? I wondered which room he was sleeping in. A picture came into my mind of a tossed bed and a suitcase on a chair lying half-unpacked. When I came back to the garden a middle-aged man in a suit was speaking into the microphone. He was talking about the crisis now in Argentina, the levels of inflation, the lack of confidence, the low morale. He talked about the need for a strong and independent government, for new men to take over who were untainted by the past. There were cheers and shouts from some of the men in the crowd. I asked Susan if she understood; she whispered that she understood perfectly.

The man now called on Señor Claudio Canetto to come to the platform. I felt that the atmosphere was too informal for the speech; and when Señor Canetto began to talk about his love for Argentina, for its flag and its customs and its people, I wanted to hide under the table. This was meant to be a party, not a boring political broadcast, and Señor Canetto seemed not at all anxious to stop speaking once he had started. He spoke about the purity of Perón's vision and his own friendship with Perón and then about his own willingness to serve his fatherland, to put his personal interests aside in favour of the interests of Argentina. I could not wait for this to end. I noticed Jorge standing in the shadows watching his father with great attention as though he believed in him. I caught Donald's eye and he winked at me as if to say that neither of us was being fooled by this speech.

After the speech, some men stood up and applauded Señor Canetto, but it was all subdued. Soon, the singer in the red dress returned to the bandstand. We went over to the bar and got some drinks and then walked around the garden. It was a beautiful hot night; the sky was clear. Suddenly, there was shouting behind us and we could hear some chairs being disturbed and some glasses being knocked over. I thought that a fight had broken out. We stood and watched, but it was hard to make out what was going on. Then we saw that four middle-aged men in suits, two of whom I recognized from the Malvinas dinners, the sort of men who had come with their wives as old friends of Señor Canetto's, were carrying a fifth man towards us. He was wriggling and struggling and a woman who was obviously his wife was screaming. She was a small woman with a large bust.

They dragged the man, two of them holding him by the shoulders, two by the legs. His wife was jumping up and down. Her husband tried to kick and punch and pull himself free, his face was red with anger and fear, but the others were determined, they laughed and shouted as they ferried him in our direction. Several other men followed them, roaring encouragement. Susan asked me if I had any idea what was going on. The woman continued singing in Portuguese and some people sat at the tables as though nothing were happening. I could see the man's face clearly, his look of panic as his wife continued to shout and gesticulate, imploring the men to stop. We walked after them in amazement; the oil executives were suddenly animated and interested. The crowd had now reached the terrace below the house. Behind us, Jorge came running down. I asked him what was going on.

'They always throw this man into the swimming pool. They have been doing it since they were in military academy together. My father asked them not to do it tonight. They are crazy.'

'Are they really going to throw him into the pool?' Susan asked. A broad grin had appeared on her face. 'We must go down and look. I told you there was something missing.'

Jorge heard her and stood back as she and Donald walked past him. The man being carried along was quiet now, as though resigned to what was happening, he had given up struggling. His wife was calling his captors names.

'Cerdos!' she screamed.

'What has she just said?' Susan asked.

'She has just called them pigs.'

'That's what I thought. How polite!' Susan laughed. 'Look at her little gold shoes. Wouldn't they break your heart?'

I looked at the woman's shoes; they seemed incongruous beside her great fury, as did her handbag, held firmly around her shoulder. She looked as though she might burst. Jorge appeared beside us again, as we followed the crowd.

'Does his wife always shout like that?' Susan asked him.

'Yes, she does,' he said and shook his head. 'When we were small boys, our parents used to let us remain awake until it was done. But now it is different.'

When we arrived at the swimming pool, the men were playing with their victim at the deep end, going one, two, three, pretending to throw him in and not doing so, and then starting again. The man had given up struggling. We watched the final heave, one, two and then they gently let him go and this small man with a suit and tie landed in the water with a big splash and sank slowly, then flailed his way to the surface like a spider in water. Now Señor Canetto arrived on the terrace and shouted at his four friends and called them animals. The swimmer was at the shallow end, where his wife was waiting for him. He pulled himself out of the water and began to shrug his shoulders and rub himself down. Soon, he was standing in a pool of water. He slowly took off his shoes and socks and handed them to his wife, and then he walked around to our side of the pool. The men who had thrown him in were now laughing and shouting at him.

'Tito, Ti-to, Ti-to,' one of them roared as he approached. The woman was calm now, but there was a sour look on her face, as though she had eaten something which had disagreed with her. She walked past us, carrying the shoes and socks, without speaking. Her handbag was still around her shoulder. Her husband looked like a smudged photograph of himself as he followed her, his clothes dripping.

'Tito, Ti-to, Ti-to,' one of the men repeated. Susan asked me what it meant, but I told her it was just a nickname.

'So who's next?' one of the oil executives asked. His eyes were bright as if he had won a prize.

Señor Canetto caught my eye for one moment and looked at me as though I had caused his friend to be thrown into the swimming pool. Then he turned away and followed the dripping man and his wife to the house. The four men who had done the throwing walked up the terrace too and went back to their tables.

'Maybe we should go now before they pick on us,' Susan said.

'Maybe we should wait,' one of the oil executives said. 'Maybe the fun is only starting.' Just then a waiter came to say that the limousine had arrived for the Americans. I decided to take a lift with them into town.

'Just remember,' Susan whispered as I kissed her goodnight, 'if you have any more friends like that do let us know.'

★

THE NEXT MORNING I WOKE tired and depressed. The party, I supposed, had been a disaster. I felt that I was somehow responsible: I should have told Susan that a party would not be a good idea; I should have convinced Señor Canetto that he would be wiser to establish his candidacy and his power base before seeking support from the Americans. I lay there in the heat with just a sheet around me and went back to sleep.

I was awakened by the phone. I was glad, for once, that I had no extension beside the bed. It gave me time to think about whether I would answer it or not. I lay there and let it ring. It rang out, then started again. This sounded like Susan, who knew I was in bed; she would not give up. I did not want to talk to her. I turned around and tried to doze again. It rang a few times more as I lay in bed. I was to see Susan and Donald and the two oil executives later in a restaurant, so I could talk to Susan then about the previous evening, or whatever else she wanted to discuss.

I had a shower and then dressed and went down to the bar below the apartment for a coffee. I bought a newspaper at a kiosk and went into another bar and had a beer and a sandwich. It was after one o'clock. I was toying with the idea of telephoning Susan and spending the afternoon lying around her pool, or maybe taking a chair and a book up to the rooftop and spending the afternoon in the sun. I knew that the sauna nearby was closed on Sundays, but had an idea that another sauna, smaller and less busy, was open on a Sunday afternoon. I had never been there. I asked the barman for a phone book and found the number; I phoned and discovered that, yes, they opened at two o'clock and would be open until ten that night. I ordered another beer and sandwich and flicked through the pages of the magazine that came free with the newspaper on Sundays.

I went back to the apartment and had another shower and shaved. Although I pretended that I still had a choice, and could still travel out to Susan and Donald's, I had already made up my mind: I checked the address of the sauna and calculated that I could walk there in about forty minutes. I thought about it, and figured that I could get a taxi now and walk back instead.

I made the driver leave me two blocks away; I didn't want him to know where I was going. He tried to talk about something as he drove along, but he must have realized that I was not listening because he stopped. The city was deserted; there was no one on the streets. As I went towards the sauna, I saw a figure going in the door of the building, and I smiled to myself: the city was empty, but here there would be people gathered, men telling lies to their families. I wondered what excuses the man I had seen had made to his wife or parents or friends not to go with them for a drive in the countryside. No one needed a sauna on a hot day in January.

The man at the cash register asked me if I was a member. When I said no, he asked me if I had been here before. I shook my head. When I paid he handed me a key and a towel and told me if I got lost I should come back and he would give me a tour. When he smiled I could see that he was wearing make-up. A thin man in his forties was in the locker room. I stood for a moment and looked at him. I supposed that he was the man I had seen coming in from the street. He was half-stripped and I was aware that I had examined him too carefully: he was now conscious of my presence as he slipped off his trousers and folded them and hung them in his locker. I loved the next moment, the sudden appearance of bare flesh, but he put his towel around him as he removed his underpants so I could not see him naked. I turned away and took off my clothes, before going to have a shower.

The place was dingy and there was a strange foetid smell. There was a tiny sauna and a steam room beside it which was completely dark. Then there was a room with a small video screen which was showing a film of two men in bed together; as I stood and watched, the camera zoomed in on one man as he began to fuck his friend. His friend's face squirming in pain appeared and then there was a close-up of their genitals. They both looked American, all young and blond and blue-eyed, with crew-cuts.

I went upstairs, where there were restrooms which could lock. Most of them were empty. I could hear two men's voices coming from one of them, although I could not make out what was being said. The sound was subdued and oddly soothing. I hung around for a while in case anyone else came up, and when nobody did I went back downstairs and into the steam room, leaving my towel on a hook outside. There were two other towels on hooks, but inside there was no sound. I could see nothing. When I tried to find a place to sit, I hit against a body standing up. The body did not move. I reached out blindly for a seat and found that I had touched the wall. I lay against it and discovered that there was a long bench to my right. I sat down. Soon, I sensed that someone had moved close to me. I shifted my position nearer the wall, but a hand moved towards me and began to grope. I stood up and moved away; I wondered whose hand it was. Had it been the man I saw undressing downstairs, I would have responded, but I could not tell.

I went back to look at the video. There was an older man lying on a bench masturbating under his towel while watching the screen. I looked at the sex for a few minutes before walking back towards the dressing room. I thought that I would have a coffee in the small bar and see who else was around. I felt almost comfortable in this hidden universe of unwritten rules. As I passed by one row of lockers I realized that someone new had arrived. He was on the other side and I walked around casually to take a look. At first I did not realize who it was as he was bending to take off his socks, but when he straightened up I found that I was looking directly at Pablo and he was looking directly at me. He was wearing a T-shirt and nothing else and he had a towel in his hands. I smiled. I was about to say something. I thought at first that maybe we could go for a coffee, or that we could leave together and go into the street, or that we could just talk here about the strangeness of this.

Before I could say anything, however, he had turned the key in his locker and walked away. He was still wearing his T-shirt, but he had put the towel around his waist. I thought of following him, of touching him, of telling him that we must talk. I went into the bar and had a coffee. I wondered if he was afraid, or surprised, if he was upstairs waiting for me to approach him. I wondered where his father and his mother and Jorge thought he was. I wondered how he knew about this place. I thought of us working out where it was at the same time in different parts of the city, both of us full of furtive desire. I hated the idea of him watching the video in the company of that old man, or of him going into the dark steam room, of anybody touching him. As I finished my coffee, I wanted to go and ask him please to leave with me, walk through the streets with me, come home with me.

I went to look for him. He was not in the video room, nor in the sauna. There were still two towels on hooks outside the steam room, so I presumed that he had not gone in there. I went upstairs: two cabins were locked now. Low voices were still coming from one of them as the two men exchanged sweet intimacies in the dark. I thought that he must be in the other one. I listened outside for a sound, and when I heard nothing I believed that he was alone there. I considered knocking and asking him to let me in, but if he was afraid, this would make him more afraid. Therefore I waited.

Over the next hour stray figures arrived and looked around, checked out the cabins which were empty, noted that two of them were locked, looked at me – some with interest, others with none – and, after a while, they ended their ritual upstairs and went back downstairs. The two men in the locked cabin had, by now, stopped speaking; I could hear other sounds from them, heavy breathing and moans of pleasure. From the other cabin, there was no sound and no hint of movement.

Still I waited. I wondered was he lying in there on his own, hoping that I had gone so that he would not have to face me. Maybe he was with somebody, lying with his arms around a stranger, saying nothing. Somehow, I did not think so. Maybe I did not want to think so. I thought instead about his eyes, I wondered if they were open or shut as he lay there. I thought about their blueness, their crystal brightness. Maybe he had fallen asleep: I thought about his body curled up, inert, unaware. I wished I were asleep beside him, my body against his.

I sat there dreaming until I heard the door of the other cabin being unlocked. A tall man with a hairy chest came out and closed the door behind him. He did not look at me as he passed and went downstairs. Soon, his companion came out as well, and stood in the corridor as if he had arrived unexpectedly in a new country. I was on my own here now, except for Pablo in the cabin. I thought of shouting in to him: that it was all right, I would not tell anyone, that I wanted to hold him, to look into his eyes, to kiss him, that I wanted to whisper to him here in the dark in this place where no one thought it strange that two men might desperately want each other. I dreamed of knocking on the door and asking him to let me in. I closed my eyes and concentrated. I prayed that he would find me here waiting for him. As I stayed there, a man came and looked at me and sat down beside me, then moved closer. I shook my head. He stood up and went into one of the cabins and lay there with the door wide open.

After a while, I heard someone moving in the locked cabin. I hoped that he would not walk away as he had done downstairs. The door opened and a figure appeared but it was not Pablo, it was the thin man I had seen undressing when I came in first. He had been asleep; he seemed lost, as though he had forgotten where he was and what the purpose of his visit here had been. He blinked and stretched. I wondered if Pablo had been with him all of the time. I stood and looked in through the open door: the cabin was empty, the man had been alone in there. I went downstairs. There was no one in the video room. There were two men in the sauna. I checked to make sure that Pablo was not there as well, lingering in the shadows.

I went downstairs and sat in the bar. When the man who had been at the cash register came, I asked him if a man – I tried to describe Pablo – who had arrived about an hour ago, maybe more, was still here or had he left. The cashier pretended not to know who I was talking about. He seemed irritated that I had asked. He shrugged, making clear that he was going to tell me nothing. I had another coffee and then went to the shower. Pablo could have left as soon as he saw me, or he could have left later while I was upstairs, or he could still be here. I went upstairs again, hung my towel once more outside the steam room and explored the darkness inside. How would I have known him? I don't know. I suppose that I would have thought that everybody was him, every piece of flesh I touched. I stood there and waited for him, but he must have gone. A figure moved in the darkness. I went over and touched whoever it was and he reached out and touched me too, but he was too tall, he could not have been Pablo. I moved outside and retrieved my towel, knowing that it was time to give up. I got a fresh towel and had another shower, turned the water on hot and then cold, hot and cold, hot and cold, and then I dried myself and put on my clothes. I was shaking as though someone had frightened me. I paid for the coffees at the cash desk and made my way into the street. I wondered if I could tell Susan what had happened, but it would all have seemed too strange to her. I would have to have started a long way back at the beginning. It would have been too hard. The sun was still hot, the sky blue. I walked through the city, wondering where he was — had he gone home to sit by the pool? was he still in the labyrinth I had just left? — and what he was thinking about. After a while, I saw a taxi and flagged it down. I went home and changed into more formal clothes and went into a bar and had a drink before joining the others for dinner. For the rest of the evening I could not concentrate on what was being said even though I smiled and nodded and pretended to be involved in various plans and projects. After the dinner, I was glad to get away on my own. I went home and sat by the window looking out at the night sky and the roofs of the buildings all around.

*

SUSAN AND DONALD thought that I should rent a small office in the city and begin to operate as an independent consultant and translator. Susan put herself in control, forced the landlord to reduce the rent of the two rooms on the first floor, organized the decoration and the furniture. She conducted brisk interviews with several bilingual secretaries, made them take dictation in two languages and made them type while she stood over them. She chose one of them and then chose her desk and chair and electric typewriter, her filing cabinet and filing system, told her what to say when she answered the telephone.

There was hardly anything to do in the new office; one or two phone calls came a day and sometimes a visit from an American oil executive with time free in the city. The serious meetings were held in the ministry building, or a hotel suite, or at Donald and Susan's house. The longest meeting was with an accountant, another of Susan's discoveries, a pale-faced, puzzled-looking man, who advised me on tax.

My office was somewhere to go every day. I read the newspapers in the morning, searching for stories about oil in the *New York Times*, the *Washington Post*, the *Miami Herald*, following the share prices in the *Herald Tribune*, and then I wondered what I should do. I looked out of the window. I had coffee in the bar downstairs. I wondered if Luisa, my so-called secretary, had been alerted by Susan to my abiding interest in my own sex, but then I did not know if Susan knew. Maybe, therefore, this did not explain why Luisa hardly ever looked me in the eye. Maybe this was what she had been told to do in secretarial school. Maybe she did not like me.

I had been in the office about a month when I got a phone call from Federico Arenas, whom I had met for the first time on the night of the dinner for the economists in the hotel. I knew that he worked for YPF, the national oil company, and I remember that he had been introduced to me by Donald. He was about forty years old, with dark eyes, black hair and full lips. He smiled too much and he wore too many rings and he smelled of cigarette smoke. As the party was breaking up that night, he had invited me to come to a club with him, he was full of mateyness and false intimacy. I was too tired and I thought I knew what sort of club he meant and I was not interested.

I asked Donald about him; Donald said that he was important, and that he had become rich while speculating in shares or currency. He did not need to work in YPF any more, Donald said, and, once any reform of the oil industry took place, it was unclear what would happen to him. I spoke to him on two more occasions when various oil executives from the United States or Europe were visiting. He was always friendly and even deferential towards me. Each time, he suggested that we go out together some night, just the two of us, we could go around the clubs, he said.

On the phone he sounded less friendly and more businesslike. He had heard, he said, that I had an office and was running a consultancy and he wondered if he could call around, there was something he wanted to discuss. He sounded like an investigator. I wondered if I should not explain that I did translation for businessmen sent to me by Donald and Susan. This could hardly be called consultancy. Instead, I told him that he could visit the office whenever he liked. He arranged to come the following morning. I asked him if he wanted to tell me what it was about before he came; he said that he did not.

He was dressed in an expensive suit the next morning. I noticed the rich, thin, tight leather of his shoes. He sat down opposite me and lit a cigarette. When he saw me first, he said, he thought that I was attached to the American Embassy, but he had discovered recently that I was just starting, that not too long ago I used to work as a teacher. He looked at me as if to say that there was more he knew as well, but I could not judge how much more. I wanted him to leave the office. He smiled and pulled on his cigarette. He asked me if I knew how the system worked. I told him that I did. I could not think of any other answer. I had no idea what system he was talking about.

This office was perfect, he said. I had a secretary, notepaper, plausible connections. Certainly, he said, YPF would look very favourably on any applications I chose to make, especially if I moved into the technical side of things. I did not understand. I asked him what he meant. He worked in the department which dealt with contracts for services, he said. A huge amount of work was done by outside agencies, and these agencies had to be carefully chosen and checked out and monitored.

He stopped and asked me if I had an ashtray. I handed him a saucer. He stubbed out his cigarette and lit another. If it had been the afternoon or the evening I maybe could have thought of something to say, but now I could think of nothing. His look of self-satisfaction suggested that there was nothing more to be added. Eventually, I asked him if there were any services with which my office could provide him. He nodded and smiled. He presumed I knew, he said, that even if this room were bugged, it would be easy to deny everything. I told him that the room was not bugged.

He said that his office was seeking tenders for a transport contract, not an important one, but worth money nonetheless. He had somebody he thought would be suitable, but the deal had fallen through. If the details were right, he said, he could probably make sure that if I put in for such a contract, I would get it.

I was about to tell him that I knew nothing about transport, but then I realized that he was suggesting something else. What struck me most was how brazen and unafraid he was. He gave me the impression that he was perfectly indifferent about whether I accepted the deal or not. But I wondered if the opposite might be the case: if he was, in fact, desperate to get this through. I said nothing for a while. He blew more smoke out of his nostrils. I asked him to go into detail. The detail was simple, he said. He and two colleagues knew the specifications for the contract; they could write my application for me. They could ensure that I would get the contract. No one would worry too much if there were huge delays in providing the services – half the money would be paid in advance – and no one would check the services when they arrived.

Why do you think I would be interested in this, I asked him. You're young, he said, you're starting, you're on the outside. And I presume, I said, that you and your two friends would get a cut of the proceeds? Yes, he said, you presume correctly. And all this, let us call it corruption, I said, would come to an end with any privatization? You can call it what you like, but yes, he nodded, it probably would. And how much money would I make on this deal, I asked him. He named a figure. It was enough to buy a small apartment in the city. I tried not to look surprised. What are the chances, I asked him, of being caught? Caught doing what, he asked. We cannot be caught. We regulate what happens, and we are close to power. We know what we are doing.

I still don't understand, I told him, why you want me to be involved. You're in with the Americans, he said. You have very few other connections as far as I can make out. You come from nowhere. I don't think that you have much money. It seems likely that you would think about providing services for the oil business. And, he pulled hard on his cigarette, you're alone, you don't have any partners.

When would this start, I asked him. There will be a small advertisement in the newspapers next week, he said. When do you need to know, I asked. I need to know now, he said. I can't tell you now, I need to think about it, I said. You can phone me in the morning and I'll tell you. I stood up and made it clear that I wanted him to leave. He shook my hand and left. I wondered if I was being set up.

★

DURING THAT WEEK Donald was in Washington on business and Susan and I had arranged to have dinner in her house that night. I decided not to tell her about Federico Arenas and I hoped I could refrain from mentioning his visit to my office.

I was nervous and edgy when I arrived and I was afraid that she would notice. The doors of the dining room were wide open and there was a sweet smell coming from the garden and the sound of crickets and the hiss of a garden hose. The wine was rich and strong, and the food was good, and she looked beautiful across the table from me. I enjoyed things about her: her teeth and the smoothness of her hair. In the glow of that dinner I almost loved her and I understood what it would be like for us to want each other, knowing that there was nothing in the way. As I thought about this I felt she knew what was on my mind. I could imagine myself lying with her, caressing her face and her breasts. She smiled. One of the servants came and took the dishes away. She asked me if I was following the shifts in oil share prices and suggested that I might invest some of my salary, perhaps even borrow money, to buy shares over the next six months while prices were still low. The accountant, she said, could probably arrange a loan.

'The accountant?' I said. 'Do you think there is any blood inside him? If you pricked him, do you think he would bleed?'

'I wouldn't relish pricking him,' Susan said.

The servant came in with coffee, a bottle of brandy and brandy glasses on a tray. A small wind blew up and the white curtains billowed in the breeze. It was like a moment from an advertisement for something. I wanted to tell her about Pablo: I knew how sordid it would sound, how alien, and I wondered if it would also sound pointless, if it had haunted me for days but would probably seem to her merely an odd coincidence, hardly worth telling.

We talked until it grew dark and one of the servants came to light a lamp and take the cups away. It must have been the heat of the evening, or the power of the wine and the brandy, but I found myself thinking again about going to bed with her, her arms around me, her lips against my chest.

'What are you thinking?' she asked.

'I'm thinking about shares,' I said.

'There's something funny about you always,' she said. 'Some parts of you are strong and really serious, and then you change suddenly and you seem all weak, you hesitate. I like all that about you, how hard it is to know you.'

'What do you want me to say?'

'No, nothing. I like you, that's all.'

She poured more brandy and then yawned and stretched. I felt that things would never be like this again for us: the quietness in the house, the heat of the night, the way we seemed to spend our days idling, like players on a chessboard waiting to be deployed when the need came. I wanted to ask her about herself, what she was doing here, what her marriage was like; I wanted to bring her closer to me; and I suppose I wanted her to ask me about myself as she had done once before and this time I would answer her and tell her all I knew.

'Why don't you stay here?' she asked. 'There's no one else in the house. The servants have gone.'

I was embarrassed now. She saw this as she stood up.

'You are so strange sometimes,' she said.

I was going to ask how Donald would feel about me staying when he was away, but I did not want to sound too prissy. She went to her office and came back with a set of keys.

'Will you help me lock up for the night?' she asked. She stood on a chair in the middle of the dining room and pulled down a heavy metal grille which was folded into a narrow cut in the ceiling. I had never noticed it before. When it was halfway down she got off the chair and closed the doors to the garden, locked them and turned on a switch beside the door. When we moved to the other side of the grille she pulled it right down and secured it to the floor. I discovered that most of the rooms had a thin metal grille installed in the ceiling. She moved around securing them to the floor and turning on switches. All the windows and doors had alarms attached to them, but even if an intruder made his way into the house, he would not be able to get from one room to another.

'This was here before we came, but we had it upgraded,' she said.

'Do you have this in America too?' I asked.

'They don't kidnap Americans in America,' she said briskly and turned on another switch. We moved upstairs. At the top of a stairs she opened a box in the wall and turned on more switches.

'How does it feel to live in a fortress?' I asked.

'It feels safe,' she said.

I had never been in their bedroom before. The decoration was modern and bright: the walls and the duvet cover and the carpet were all white, but the fitted wardrobes were painted a bright yellow and the woodwork around the windows was painted yellow and the lampshades were yellow. There was an enormous vase full of fresh flowers on a table beside the bed. Two chairs made of cane were painted dark blue. There was a door leading to a bathroom almost as big as the bedroom; one wall was all mirrors. I tried to imagine Donald inspecting his hairy chest in that glass, but it was not easy. But I could visualize Susan looking at herself; the bathroom, like the bedroom, seemed naturally hers. She turned on one of the bedside lamps and turned off the main light.

The room looked comfortable, attractive. I sat on one of the chairs and watched her flitting about like a shadow. I presumed that I was sleeping here beside her in the bed. I did not ask. I said nothing. When she went into the bathroom, I sat back and listened to the sound of the shower. I imagined her soaping herself. I took off my shoes. When she came out she was naked. In the lamplight her breasts were much larger and stranger than I had imagined. They hung down like ripe pears; all the bottom part was nipple. I wondered if many women's breasts were like this: the breasts I had seen in films and magazines seemed floppier and lighter; the nipples were different. Susan's breasts looked as though someone had shaped them, sculpted them.

'Aren't you coming to bed?' she asked.

I stripped and crossed the room and went to the bathroom, which was full of some fragrance she had been using. The mirror was steamed up so I could not look at myself. I had a shower and then dried myself with the fresh white towel which had been left on the rail. My mind was full of questions: what would Donald say if he found that I was sharing a bed with his wife? did Susan have many lovers? did she know that I had only been with men? did she suspect it? I walked out of the bathroom, turned off the light and closed the door. I went across to the other side of the bed and got in beside her.

'Did you ever think of putting one of your metal grilles across the middle of the bed?' I asked her.

'You think we're insane to have so much security?' she asked.

'Yes, I do.'

We moved towards each other and embraced. We remained still and said nothing. Her face was buried in my neck. Her skin was perfectly smooth and soft. I ran my hand up and down her back and then I cupped my hand over her breast. She held her breath and then put her hand on my hand. I took my hand away and moved my face to her breasts and began to kiss her nipples. I put my hand between her legs and felt the soft wetness there. I could smell the moist sweetness which came from her. She was excited. I could feel it in the way she responded and gripped me and kissed me. I waited for the moment when she would reach down and put her hand on my dick. I waited with fear because I knew that my dick was soft. I wondered if I carried on, would it become hard? If I imagined that I was in bed with a man, would I get an erection? I was masquerading, imitating what a man does in bed with a woman, but it was not working. The more I thought about it, the more tense I became. I felt powerless. I fondled her body, caressed her warm skin, but it was like playing with a child, it meant nothing to me: there was no excitement, none of the effortless satisfaction and pure pleasure and sense of ease that I got from being in bed with a man. There was something inside me, something unknowable, mysterious, lurking in the spaces within me which no one could touch, something desperately real and exact, which made all the difference, and meant now that this beautiful body beside me did not excite me and my penis lay limp.

When she discovered that I did not have an erection, she lay back and stared at the ceiling and said nothing. I felt humiliated.

'Is it me?' she asked.

'No.'

'You prefer boys to girls?'

'I probably should have told you that before,' I said. She reached for her cigarettes on the bedside table and lit one.

'I wish I was a boy just now,' she said.

'I wish you were too,' I said and nudged towards her and held her in my arms.

'Have you always been gay?'

'Ever since I was a little boy.' She kissed me on the ear.

'I thought that Donald was gay when I met him first. Maybe it was because he had a moustache and someone had told me that gay men always wore moustaches. But he turned out not to be.' She drew on the cigarette.

'Where did you meet him?'

'We worked together. At the beginning I was his boss, but we were thrown together a lot. We got to know one another very well.'

'Was that in Washington? You never talk about where else you have been.' It was a relief now to discuss something else. We spoke in a hush, making our quiet voices a sort of intimacy.

'No. It was in Santiago. We were there when Allende's

government fell.' She drew hard on her cigarette again. I was waiting for her to continue. She left silence.

'You were in Chile? I didn't know that.'

She spoke in a tone I had never heard before, as though choosing the words and saying them were difficult, as though the implication of what she was saying had occurred to her only now. She held my hand.

'We were very junior then, raw, we had not been prepared for what happened. Later, much later, I realized that I should have known. All the signs were there, and I attended meetings, but I didn't understand the language that they used then. I didn't know that when a military man used words like destabilize, or undermine, or other words that seemed innocent or nearly innocent, they meant something different than when used by a diplomat or a civilian. I suppose I knew that Allende was going to be overthrown, but I thought it would be done slowly, even diplomatically, although I know that, in retrospect, that sounds unlikely. We mixed only with Americans, and some Americans who came had real problems with the Allende regime. There was a lot at stake. We didn't work in the embassy building, we had a floor in a building nearby. It was only afterwards we really knew what happened.'

'What do you mean?' I asked her.

'We were locked in our own world. We saw no newspapers or television. It was years later I read about it and I went with Donald in Stockholm to see the film *Missing*. Have you ever seen it?'

'Yes,' I said. She lit another cigarette.

'We were there for a conference and we had a night free and the film was in English so it seemed like a good idea.' She stopped as though she were short of breath and then continued: 'Some parts of the film were exaggerated, but others were not. Others were exactly like it was. Neither Donald nor I ever saw any bodies, we had to stay in the building day and night, but after a few days we knew where the bodies were, and the film made me sick because it brought it all back again; things I hadn't dared think about. Richard, I saw things in the film that I had only imagined before, but I knew them when I saw them, they were real and they happened. Donald and I have never talked about it. We walked from the cinema to our hotel next door that night; he had a drink at the bar and then I went to bed. We said nothing to each other about it. We could not help each other.'

'What did you do when you were in the building in Santiago?' I asked. She lit another cigarette and lay back. Again, she said nothing for a while.

'We had orders not to leave the building. We were told to stock up on food and be prepared to stay the night. There were about six telephone lines and our job was to man the lines, to keep them free at all times if we could. Everyone involved had our number: we passed on messages, that was what we did most of the time. But then the numbers were passed on to other people – I mean that somehow local people got the number – and people rang us if they needed to know where their son or their daughter or their friend was. Donald spoke better Spanish than I did, so he took most of the calls, but some of them spoke English too and they were all desperate, they were desperate, they were sure that if they gave us the name and the last time the person was seen we could give them information about the person's whereabouts. We wrote down the names and all the details, but there was nothing we could do, and then they would ring back, every time more desperate. We would try and get them off the phone because our instructions were to keep the lines clear and they would implore us to help them. Most of the time there were just the two of us, two American kids, and the telephone ringing all day and all night. I told my parents about it several years ago, but I have never told anybody else.'

'Maybe we should sleep for a while,' I said. I wanted to be away from her. I wanted to get out of the bed and dress myself and leave, but I knew that I could not do that.

'Does what I told you disturb you?' she asked.

'Yes, it does.'

'You sleep. I'll smoke another cigarette and then maybe I'll sleep too.'

'When is Donald coming back?'

'Not for a few days. Are you afraid that he'll find you in bed with his wife?'

'No,' I said and turned away from her. I did not want her to tell me anything more.

In the morning she left the bathroom door open when she went into the shower. I woke to the sound of running water. It was seven thirty. She came out of the steam covered in towels. Already, I was looking forward to getting away on my own. I had a shower too and then dressed and helped Susan to unlock all the security grilles and turn off all the alarms. We had breakfast in the kitchen.

'You were really shocked by what I told you last night,' she said.

'I knew someone who was tortured in Chile,' I said.

'I lay awake', she said, 'and wondered if you thought that Donald and I were going to do the same thing here, but things are different. We are determined that there will be free elections here and an easy transfer of power and that there will be no army coup. That is part of our brief. I can guarantee that.' She drew on her cigarette again and looked at me with her clear blue eyes. I tried as hard as I could to disguise how much I disliked her at that moment.

I left her after breakfast and travelled in a taxi to the office. I greeted the secretary with the usual formality, and I read the papers, running my finger down the index of share prices. I felt heavy and uncomfortable in my old clothes, as though I had not slept for days. When Federico Arenas telephoned to ask if I had made up my mind about the contract, I told him that I was not interested in what he was suggesting. He hung up.

★

A MONTH LATER the days were still sweltering. One morning as soon as I arrived at the office Luisa said there was an important message for me: I must phone Susan immediately. I smiled and said that since I had spoken to Susan the previous evening it could hardly be that important. She says it is important, Luisa said, glancing at me sharply. I wondered if Luisa had been placed here to annoy me and put me on edge. It occurred to me that maybe I should start shouting at her, barking out orders, maybe then she would stop looking so icy and composed and above it all.

I collected the newspapers from her desk and whatever mail there was and went into my sanctuary and closed the door behind me. I realized that I felt just as bored and disconcerted as I had when I was teaching; I felt tired and unhappy until I reminded myself that I had no reason to be tired and less reason to be unhappy. I sat up straight as though a change in posture would help me to face the rest of the day.

When the phone rang I picked it up. Luisa had put Susan straight through. Susan was in one of her serious moods.

'Do you think a real outsider could win this election?'

'Yes, I do. I told you that.'

'I have someone,' she said.

'I hope you didn't make him give a garden party.'

'I'm serious. We've been watching him for some time. I'd like you to look at him.'

'What's his name?'

'He's the governor of La Rioja province. He's called Menem. He's originally Lebanese or Syrian or something. He looks like a cowboy, but he's dead serious.'

'It sounds unlikely,' I said. 'La Rioja is very remote and very strange. But if he's governor, at least he has a machine. And he's an outsider, and even here in Buenos Aires, people hate the capital, and they'd love to vote for a man from hicksville, they hate themselves, I can see it in their faces. My secretary hates herself. Even I hate myself.'

'Have you finished?' She was trying to sound exasperated.

'Let's find out more about this guy,' I said.

'There's a rally on Saturday in La Rioja,' she said. 'Have you been there?'

'No.'

'I don't quite understand the reason for it, something about a new Argentina, and he's speaking and there's a sort of dinner afterwards, I think they cook a cow in a field and we all sit around eating it being good Argentinians. Anyway, I want us to go to the rally and I have tickets for the *asado* afterwards. I'm going up on Friday and maybe you could fly up on Saturday. There are two flights that day and you could come up on either of them and then we'll travel back together on Sunday. Maybe this will come to nothing, but it's time we started to look at anyone who's got a chance.'

After I put down the phone, I rang the offices of *El Mundo* and asked for the library. I had done this a few months earlier when I was looking for a back issue. I had explained who I was – a political and economic adviser to various American oil companies – and asked if I could have a look at their files. Once more the voice at the other end was intensely polite and helpful; suddenly I felt happy and warm as I arranged to call at the offices of *El Mundo* within half an hour.

The librarian was standing with his back to me at a table when I came in. When he turned, he smiled and shook my hand. I told him that I was looking for any files or cuttings he might have on Carlos Menem. He laughed in a half-puzzled, half-knowing sort of way. I have it here in front of me, he said.

You're the third person to ask for it in a few days. It's just been put back. Is he in the oil business too, he asked. No, I said, he's a politician.

He handed me a thin file and said he had something else to do, so I could read it and photocopy any of it if I wanted. He shook my hand again and left the room. I felt cheered by his friendliness, the ease with which he seemed to operate. I sat down and began to pick my way through the life and times of Carlos Menem. The first thing I took note of was his hairstyle and his long and elaborate sideburns. All the photographs were of him smiling, or laughing, or play-acting, or standing beside a beautiful woman, or even between several beautiful women. Six months earlier he had made a speech about the need for resources to be ploughed into the provinces rather than the capital, and then more recently he had called on the government to begin negotiations with the International Monetary Fund about restructuring the national debt. There was a short news item with no date on it reporting his declaration that he would be a candidate in the next Presidential election. The report referred to him as an ex-Peronist.

I put these cuttings aside and perused the photographs again: he looked like a popular singer, one of those crooners you saw on television on a Saturday night, wearing trousers that were too tight and closing his eyes and stretching out his hand at the end of every phrase. Or maybe he looked like someone from La Rioja, maybe they all looked like that up there. And he had views on the economy. And some sort of relationship with Peronism. I did not know whether this added up or not, but I wrote each point down. I knew that I would never vote for him. I hated the look of him, the cheap glamour. But I would never watch television on a Saturday night; my own preferences were not to be relied upon. Also, he was already governor of a province; he had made a large number of people believe in him. As I photocopied the cuttings I realized that Susan would probably have seen the file, she left nothing to chance. The best thing to do, I thought, would be to write a report for her, using what information I had here and adding whatever I had learned from my conversations in the Canettos' house. I should write out for her some account of the strong man in local politics, especially in the north, the idea of the political family, with the leader at the centre and all those for whom he has done favours surrounding him. I knew that there were versions of it in the United States, and in every other country, but in La Rioja, and perhaps in all of Argentina, especially when people wanted something done urgently about inflation and unemployment and national morale, the idea of a strong man from a remote place would have to be taken very seriously. I left the file back on the table with a note of thanks for the librarian and as I walked back to my office I felt efficient and useful, renewed almost, and I looked forward to our trip.

On Friday morning Susan telephoned with arrangements. She was flying to La Rioja that evening, she said, and wanted me to come the following morning. I could collect the ticket at the airport. She was at her most breezy and brisk. She spoke to me as though I were a customer at a bank. We were booked into the Hotel Plaza, she said. It had a swimming pool and we would need a swim in this heat. Also, and here her tone changed somewhat, as if there were something caught in her throat, she would have a friend with her, and they would be at the hotel when I came. I presumed, from the way she spoke, that her friend would be American, and I also presumed, although I did not ask, that her friend would be a woman.

On Saturday morning I carefully folded a number of clean shirts into a holdall. I packed my swimming trunks as well. I enjoyed walking out of the apartments with my sunglasses on, wearing a blue linen jacket and striped trousers which I had chosen myself and summer shoes with no socks. Señora Fernández on the first floor opened her door as I passed and nodded at me sourly. I pulled my sunglasses down over my nose and peered at her. She studied me as though she were about to take a photograph of me. I went on to the street and ordered a taxi.

The plane was half-empty and had seen better days: my window overlooked a wing which had a big line of rust. I could hear the engine grinding as we took off. I slept for a while and when I woke we were flying over creamy clouds. I liked being here away from things, and I would not have minded had the flight gone on for hours more. The airport when we landed was like some final outpost of civilization; a small concrete shack had La Rioja written on the roof. There were a few jeeps and nothing else. The two men who stood watching us as we descended from the plane looked as though they had never seen an aeroplane before and were deeply puzzled by the new phenomenon of air travel. They studied us with mild disapproval. I asked one of them if I could get a taxi to the city centre and he nonchalantly inclined his head to the other side of the building. There were several cars waiting there, and a few people standing around outside, but none of them was a taxi driver.

Eventually, one of the men who had been standing on the tarmac came out carrying two suitcases and accompanied by a middle-aged woman in a polka-dot dress. He nodded at me to follow him. I sat in the front and the woman in the back and we began the long journey to the city. The road was covered with dust; at times visibility was difficult, and the land around us was flat and arid and dusty. The hills in the distance seemed to belong to a different world. They were covered with dark green trees. The heat was dry and fierce and there appeared to be no wind at all. I realized that I knew nothing about this place, other than how far away it was from Buenos Aires, and I had never met anyone who came from here. Neither the driver nor the woman spoke. Somehow the occasion did not lend itself to conversation. I was wondering how anyone could live here, when the driver asked me where I was going. I told him to drop me at the Hotel Plaza in the city centre.

There was an air of laziness and poverty in the outskirts of the city, as though no one had the energy or the money to build anything more than one storey high, and the city itself as we careered along its grid-shaped streets had that odd air of provisionality that I could sense everywhere in Argentina, as though the whole country could fade away, all of us go back to the places from which we came and leave this landscape bare as it was a hundred or two hundred years ago. I remembered the story by Borges about the map of Argentina the same size as Argentina, and pieces of it being found in remote parts of the pampas years after it was made. I used to think it was a marvellous fantasy. Now I thought that it could almost be real. It would be easy for everyone to abandon these towns in the middle of this vast plain and years later bits of what we had brought here would be found: a hubcap, a metal curtain-rail, some rusty nails, and an atmosphere in which someone very sensitive could detect the vague echoes we had left behind us.

I paid the driver and went into the hotel. When I gave my name the man behind the desk became very attentive, and told me that I must go immediately to a restaurant on the corner of Avenida Perón and Rivadavia where my friends were. They would be just starting lunch now, and they had said – I could hear Susan's voice giving instructions – that I was no leave my bag at reception and go there at once. I needed a shower, but I realized that this man had taken his orders very seriously, and he expected me to obey. I handed my bag over the counter to him and I followed the instructions he gave me on a small map of the city to the restaurant where I would find my friends. I walked along the dusty streets, suddenly enjoying my anonymity here, the fact that I was not a part of this place. I walked four blocks and turned left, as he had told me to do, walked one more block and found Restaurante Los Andes.

When I walked in the door I saw them immediately. Susan had a look of triumph on her face, and beside her, looking at me sheepishly, was Jorge. Clearly he was the friend who had accompanied her to La Rioja. As the waiter ushered me to their table I realized that I was a necessary element in whatever relationship they had formed: they needed me here to be with them, to know about them, to become implicated in their secret. They would need me in a nearby room while they made love, like a thief needs an accomplice for a certain sort of crime.

I did not look surprised, from the first moment I saw them together I pretended that this was normal, to be expected, no big deal. I did not say: what are you two doing here? I did not exclaim: what a surprise! I sat down and told them in English how insistent the hotel people had been that I should drop my bag and come here now. Susan looked at me and smiled as if she were deeply amused by what I was saying. Jorge looked at me blankly. Susan asked what I wanted to drink, and when I said a dry Martini she raised her right hand to attract the waiter's attention and then she touched Jorge's elbow with her left hand. She held it there, almost gripping him, offering me a token of their intimacy, letting me know that touching him was natural, something she did without thinking. I opened the menu, and asked if they had made friends with Carlos Menem yet. I realized when I said 'made friends' that I had begun to circle them and their new-found friendship, that I had suggested that they 'made friends' easily with the most unlikely and strange people.

'The meeting is on at ten,' Susan said. 'There's going to be a torchlight parade.'

I was going to ask Susan if Jorge still took ages to come. I could not sit with them without imagining them in bed. I said nothing. I realized that I was not just jealous of them, but irritated that they had connived behind my back, had not allowed me to make the connections for them. How had they started? I was sure that they had met for the first time at Jorge's father's party. How had they met for the second time? Who had taken the initiative? Had they met by accident? I did not think that was possible as I ordered a steak and a salad and commented on the feeling I had that the city of La Rioja would not last long.

Susan remarked about the hotel, how old-fashioned it was, how there was an enormous ledger with names and dates and future bookings like something from a Victorian hotel in the nineteenth century. Jorge spoke in Spanish, saying this was one of the places in Argentina he knew nothing about, but it had a bad reputation for bully boys and corrupt political leaders. I said nothing. I realized that I blamed Susan for this, that she had decided to have him, since she could not have me. He was flattered by her attention; he had probably, just like myself, never turned down a sexual opportunity in his life. He looked at the world through the eye of his dick, and she had noticed this when she met him and now she was parading him in front of me, like an owner walking a sleek dog.

The bar of the hotel was darkened against the heat. We ordered coffee and cognac, and then went to the desk and collected our keys. I picked up my bag. They were staying in separate rooms. We walked up the stairs together and arranged to meet at the pool at six thirty. They walked and spoke in an odd, distracted way, making clear to me that while I might be going for a siesta, they were going to make love. I smiled at them and turned down the corridor to my room. I felt elated once I was on my own, and amused at what I had just witnessed, and excited as though the chemistry between them had been somehow passed on to me as well, the way a baby must feel when its parents make love.

I had a shower and dried myself, and then pulled back the crisp white sheets of the bed and lay there thinking about what they were doing now, imagining that I was one of them and then the other. I was too involved to masturbate. I fell asleep for a while and then woke in the sweaty heat of the afternoon, feeling as though several days had passed since I had met them in the restaurant, and that I had spent all the time since trying to absorb what I had seen, trying to work it out, imagining and reimagining everything that had gone on between them.

That night we went out into the crowded square. There was a big platform and a band and people stood around staring towards the platform and then stealing glances at each other, eyeing each other up and down and then looking away again as though nothing mattered. Susan wore a black dress and a black band on her hair; her skin was tanned. Jorge was dressed casually. I could not stop thinking about them being together. We walked up towards the front, where the crowd was thicker, and we waited there looking around us wondering what was going to happen. It was getting dark and small coloured lights were turned on in the trees and more people came into the square so we could hear the humming of voices all around us. Susan put her hand on my back and rubbed me as though I had a pain there. She and Jorge did not touch.

Suddenly, over to the left there was a shout. There were too many people in front of me; I could not see what was happening. I jumped in the air, but there was a tree blocking my view. The crowd was pushed back from the platform and we had trouble keeping together and stopping the people in front of us from stepping on our feet. When Susan said something to me in English, several people in front turned and looked at us. Their gaze was not exactly hostile, but it was curious and unfriendly and tinged with darkness. We did not speak again. Now we could see a cavalcade of white horses, their riders carrying flaming torches and wearing gaucho hats, moving towards the platform. There was cheering and shouting and whistling as the crowd focused on the man who was clearly Carlos Menem. When the men in gaucho dress dismounted they accompanied him to the platform and stood behind him, their torches in their hands. His speech was patriotic and full of clichés about the future and the past of Argentina, but he held the crowd with the power in his voice. I watched Susan examine him; it was the first time I had seen a sort of awe in her face. Menem had now begun to shout and the crowd was transfixed; it reminded me of that night in Buenos Aires when the war had broken out and Galtieri came on to the balcony. This crowd had the same rawness, listening as though no one had ever spoken words like this before. I thought that it was possible that all over Argentina now there were men who could talk like this, and town squares full of people listening to them, and that this meant nothing, our country had never been short of demagogues and easy language; but afterwards Susan and Jorge were absolutely sure that this was an important moment we had witnessed.

We had dinner that night at a corner table in the hotel restaurant with a small man in his early forties. His name was Polish or Hungarian and he lived in Buenos Aires. He was the man who had alerted Susan to the existence of Menem, and he was the campaign manager, as far as we could make out, although he was not a Peronist and had no background in the movement. It was hard to work out what his background was. I could not even tell whether he was rich or poor. He spoke no English; he said very little, and when he spoke he addressed himself entirely to Susan, and treated Jorge and me as though we were her bodyguards. As the meal progressed, it became clear that he had known Susan for some time, and that he had a determined campaign strategy, and from now on could depend on her full cooperation. When he stood up to go, I noticed that he had a limp. I watched him leave the hotel, and then I turned towards Susan and Jorge. They were watching him too. None of us said anything. We went to the desk in the lobby and collected our keys. I kissed Susan goodnight and nodded at Jorge and went ahead of them up the wide stairs of the old hotel to bed.

★

AS AUTUMN GAVE WAY to winter I grew friendly with Federico Arenas. He was always there at the end of any dinner, ready to have more drinks or to go to a club. I went one night across the city with him to a country club where he was warmly welcomed at the door. Inside there was a quiet, darkened bar full of plush velvet upholstery; drinks were served by girls. You could have one of the girls if you wanted, Federico said. We could ask her to join us; there were even rooms upstairs, but you would have to pretend that you were staying the night, this was no two-hour joint. Maybe we could do a foursome, he said. Some night we could do that. He loved calling the barman over and impressing him with talk about money; he loved smiling at the girls and giving them large tips. I was there to witness all his charm and munificence. He treated me as though he were a man of the world and I a mere novice. He showed me photographs of his wife and children, all fast asleep, he said, at home. His wife was a good woman, he said. She knew him and trusted him.

I sat up late with him out of boredom and laziness. He spoke to me as though I were interested in girls, although he must have known that I was gay. He knew various friends of Menem's, but he was still worried about his future under the new regime, especially if it sold off the oil industry. On one of those nights, when we had had dinner together and had drunk too much wine and brandy, I agreed to apply for a contract. When I arrived in my office the following morning the details were on my desk. I got the impression that Federico Arenas did not sleep much. He was happier prowling than resting. By that afternoon we had filled out the application, worked out the details of how and when the money would be paid, and how and when he and his cohorts would get their share. This time I had no problem agreeing to the deal; I knew the industry better and I understood that I was not being set up. He smiled as he walked out of the office with all the documents under his arm. I wondered how many other such deals he made. If there were a problem, I realized, I would be able to claim that I had acted in good faith. But in the climate of that time I did not think that there would be a problem.

★

SEÑOR CANETTO became resigned to the idea that he might never be President of Argentina. He grew lighter and more good-humoured and he invited me to dinner regularly. He was impressed by my new status, by my secretary and the address of my office, by the fact that I knew so much about the oil industry and its future. He began to take an interest in oil shares, and, from what I could make out, he had vast resources, money in Miami, which he moved around every day. He rang me in the morning when he had gone through the newspapers and we discussed what was worth watching.

I told him everything I knew, except about Federico Arenas. I told no one about him, I made sure my secretary did not know what was happening. I prepared a file on transport and shipping and got to understand the details of the deal we had made, even though they were pure fantasy. I made sure that they existed on paper.

And when Americans came to the city I would learn everything I could about possible investments, about small banks and subsidiaries of oil companies which were likely to become very profitable once certain changes were made in the industry. It was a slow process; for months on end nothing happened, and then one day the prices would start to move. It would just be a line of small print on one of the back pages of a newspaper, but Señor Canetto would notice it and I would notice it and we would know immediately whether to buy or sell. He introduced me to a friend who worked in an investment bank who agreed to lend me the value of the shares I already had at a good rate of interest. When I sat opposite this man in his office I did not feel that I was playing a role. I knew what I was talking about. I knew that he would give me the money, and I knew how easy it would be to make the repayments. By the time Carlos Menem was elected, between the money I had made from the first Federico Arenas deal and loans organized by Señor Canetto, I had borrowed a hundred thousand dollars, but my assets were more than double that, and increasing all the time.

I bought Italian suits and expensive shoes and shirts and designer ties, and I promised myself that some day soon I would have the apartment redecorated or I would move somewhere new and bright and I would stop leaving clothes all over the floor and greasy plates on the dining room table. One day Susan asked me if she and Jorge could use my apartment during the day when I was not there. I told her how untidy it was. I told her that the paint was peeling off the walls. I gave her a key. That night I cleared a load of junk out of the spare room. I changed the sheets on the bed and I swept the floor and then washed it. The curtains were musty and loose, and the paintwork was old, the wardrobe was like an oversized coffin. Nonetheless, I thought that they might like the room. I enjoyed the idea of them making love here, or, at least, I thought I did. I never let myself think about it enough to be sure.

Pablo was working with his father, but neither he nor Jorge knew anything about the stock market. Jorge had become an expert in currency fluctuation, and sometimes this was useful. When we had sold shares and possessed some spare cash we could move the money from one currency to another, let it earn some more for us – Jorge never seemed to make mistakes – and then reinvest it when the time was right.

I went to the Canettos' for dinner one evening. In the long dining room there was only a lamp in the corner; most of the light came from candles on the table. Pablo was wearing a navy-blue sweater of thick wool. He sat across the table from me. I could not stop looking at him: the tight black curly hair, the light blue of his eyes, the long eyelashes, the full lips. I had to be careful. I did not know whether he noticed me or what he thought about me. We talked about politics. Señora Canetto had no time for Carlos Menem. She thought that he was the worst sort of Argentinian, and she asked us to contemplate what foreign visitors would make of him and his wife. Señor Canetto said that he thought that Menem was going to be a good President.

Jorge and Pablo drove me to the station that night. Pablo seemed preoccupied as he went upstairs and got his coat. We stood in the doorway as Jorge turned the car. Pablo put his hands to his mouth to heat them with his breath. I said that it was cold. He said it would freeze your balls. I said nothing. When the car came I sat in the back seat and Pablo sat in the front. We did not speak as Jorge drove down the long road full of big houses. There was no other traffic.

When I felt something against my foot, I almost cried out. I thought for a moment that there was a mouse on the floor. But it was not a mouse. It was Pablo's right hand confidently opening my shoelace. I reached down and touched his hand, but he paid no attention to this. He was searching for the shoelace of the other shoe and when he found this he opened it as well. Jorge had begun to talk about Menem and his wife's family. I said that the new regime would have to make a deal with the army. By this time Pablo had taken his hand away and my two shoelaces were open.

When we arrived at the station, Jorge and Pablo insisted on getting out of the car and coming into the station with me in case I had to wait too long. I bought my ticket in the old-fashioned waiting room of the station, discovering that a train was due in the next ten minutes, and then I put my foot up on a bench to tie my shoelace. Jorge was reading the timetable. I glanced at Pablo and grinned as I put my other foot on the bench. He looked at me as though nothing had happened, and then he smiled too. I told them I was fine now, I did not need them to wait. I said that I would see them the following week and told them to thank their mother again for the dinner. As they turned I stood watching them, waiting to see if Pablo would look back, but he did not. I walked out and stood at the door as they got into the car. Pablo kept his eyes on me as they drove away. Jorge waved at me, and then I turned and sat on the bench in the waiting room.

PART THREE

FOR DAYS AFTERWARDS I thought about him. I imagined him in bed beside me, fast asleep with his back to me. When I woke in the morning I felt warm and hopeful. I imagined him turning and slowly waking, his face curling into a smile, his tongue wet and supple in my mouth, as though he had woken only to desire. I put my arms around him, feeling the soft smooth skin on the side of his body and then the hair on his chest. I imagined him getting out of the bed to go to the toilet; I pictured myself watching him.

I phoned his house as usual and I spoke to his father or to Jorge, but never to him. I waited. I thought he would answer the phone one day and I would say that maybe we should meet, or ask him if he would be in the city soon. I hoped that he would phone me, or find some excuse to call at the office or the apartment. Maybe, I thought, what happened in the car was merely a teasing gesture, maybe even a gesture of contempt saying look what I could do to you. I felt the way a teenager must feel when he falls in love with a girl for the first time: I felt excitement and fear and insecurity.

Susan came to the office one day to talk about a report on the privatization of the oil industry, one of many such confidential reports commissioned by the new regime. I had been suggested as someone who could work with the commission to represent the views of the North American oil companies, and she wanted to make sure that I would accept membership if it were offered. She and Donald were busy trying to use their influence to confine the membership to economists and academics rather than politicians, who might have a hidden anti-American agenda. The administration was aware, she said, of how easy it would be to stir people up about outside interests gaining control of the oil industry. There were already two academics in the university who had written a paper on the oil industry worldwide and the need for each state to maintain control over its industry. They believed that Argentina handing over its oil to the outside world would result in a loss of sovereignty and less investment in new technology and smaller oilfields. They agreed that there was corruption, but insisted that this was the last chance Argentina had to reform itself.

Susan drew on her cigarette and asked me what I thought. I said that I would like to study the reports of various privatizations in Britain, while I realized that we had to be careful not to use any British experts. It would be good, I said, if we could find an American, or even an Australian, who knew how the British had handled privatization. She nodded. I said that I would make phone calls and find the right person. It would be easier to do so from my office than from any official quarter.

Afterwards, we had lunch in the dining room of the Sheraton. She had a way of coming into these public places with a look of self-importance, almost of belligerence, choosing the table she wanted to sit at rather than allowing the waiter to lead her to a table of his choice, telling the waiter to give her more time to decide, and then calling for the bill, explaining that she wanted it now as she did not have much time. When I knew her first I was always uncomfortable with her when there were servants or waiters or paid assistants close by, but I had taught myself to be amused by her, to let her bully and boss everybody without my sitting opposite her wincing. This time she looked at the menu as if it were a letter of resignation from someone troublesome. The waiter stood there. Then she folded it and left it down and spoke to him in English.

'We'll just have drinks to start with. We'll order later. I'll have a dry Martini.'

'I'll have a gin and tonic,' I said in English. I wondered if the waiter thought I was her henpecked husband.

'What if I wanted to eat now?'

'You don't want to eat now. I want to talk to you about something.'

'Can I not stuff my face as you talk?'

'I want your full attention.'

I looked around the restaurant. A couple of businessmen over by the wall were watching us. When I looked over at them again a few moments later they were still observing us closely; clearly they were talking about us. It struck me that Susan, by now, must be known in the city, must have become a presence for people who were seeking advancement and power or connections with the United States.

'You're not listening to me,' she said. 'There's a new guy at the embassy who's very nice. I think he's a little shell-shocked about being sent down here. He's only been in Europe before. He's quiet, he's nice.'

'That's twice you've said he's nice. Is that a code word for something?'

'Yeah, he's gay.'

'Is he gay, or do you suspect he's gay?'

'No, I talked to him. He's gay.'

'Is he really nice?'

When our drinks came she took up the menu again. She called the waiter back and said that she was ready to order. We ordered. I looked over at the two men who had been observing us, but they were deep in conversation now.

'So you told him all about me,' I said.

'Yes, I did.'

'And he's about to arrive at any moment and look me up and down.'

'Not exactly, but he'd like to meet you.'

'I think I'm in love,' I said.

'With him? Already?'

'A nice American? No.'

'He really is very nice.'

'I think I'm in love,' I said again.

★

WHEN THE SECOND HALF of the money arrived, I became worried. I felt that I had lost my nerve. I had visions of us being caught, our photographs in the newspapers as we were led away. Signing the contract and getting paid seemed easy to live with, but taking money for services never provided was something else. Federico had given me precise instructions once more on how the cheque should be lodged. But I was frightened when I saw it. I had an urge to phone Federico and tell him that I wanted to return it, but that would have been ridiculous. Within a few weeks, I would have to give him three-quarters of the cheque in dollars in cash. I trusted him because I had no choice. I understood that he had made a great deal of money in this way, but people knew about him. He would be the first person to be investigated if the government decided to clamp down on corruption. Also, I did not know who else was in on the deal.

I picked up the telephone and rang him and told him I was having problems. He said that he would come around and see me. As I waited I became more depressed. I knew that I should not have done it. His face looked flushed when he arrived. I told him that taking the second cheque was difficult. I wanted to give him the cheque back, or tear it up. Don't touch it, he said, one-quarter of that money is going to the very top. Did he mean Menem, I asked. No, not Menem, he said, not Menem, but not far away from him. Your application, he said, is completely above board. It was seen by the most senior people, and it was agreed. I have a form which says that the trucks we ordered arrived and the crude oil was transported as agreed from point A to point B. This is why the cheque has been issued. Everything is above board. You are entitled, he said, to withdraw any money in cash you please from the bank without any questions being asked. Go ahead and lodge it, he said, pointing at the cheque, lodge it today. I don't have time to waste like this, he said. Just lodge it and let me know when you're going to hand over the cash. He stood up and walked out. He had left his cigarettes on the desk. As soon as he had gone, I walked down to the bank and lodged the cheque.

★

SUSAN'S AMERICAN FRIEND rang me in the office a few days later. He was called Charles and he sounded nervous. I was sorry that I had not asked Susan to describe him in more detail. I must have sounded less than encouraging because he wondered if it would be better to ring me some other time. I said that we should meet, and that I was usually free. He was busy all this week, he said, but he would have time on Saturday. For the next few days I put Pablo out of my mind, and I thought about Charles – six feet tall, he said, with dark hair and brown eyes. I was going to meet him in the bar of the Sheraton at eight o'clock on Saturday night. Suddenly, I found that it was not difficult to transfer all the longing I felt about Pablo to this American whom I had never seen and to whom I had only briefly spoken. I realized that I was desperate for someone. I felt uneasy about this, and vulnerable. I had always believed that I was self-contained, happier alone.

He must have been in his late thirties or early forties. His face was long. He stood up and smiled when I came into the bar. He put too much energy into his handshake and I could sense that he was making an effort. He was dressed neatly, his hair was carefully combed. When we went into the bar, he ordered the drinks.

'It's great to meet you,' he said as he handed me the drink.

He raised his glass and I raised mine. I liked the way he smiled. There were things about him, even in the first half-hour, that I felt I understood. The humour, the small attempts at irony, the shrugging of the shoulders were all self-deprecating, ways of protecting himself from the world.

I talked about Argentina and told him about seeing Menem for the first time, although I did not tell him that Susan was there. He listened as though everything I said were new to him and some of it astonishing. He smiled in a dry, amused sort of way. He said that soon he was going to start travelling in Argentina; some of it, he said, reminded him of parts of the United States where he had grown up, his family had moved around a good deal, his father had worked for Heinz.

I asked him where he lived; he was careful to emphasize that his apartment was no big deal, that he would have liked something different but he had to placate the security people. I enjoyed watching him, he was smart, and sometimes when he said something interesting or intelligent, or used a funny turn of phrase, he bunched his face up as though he had been caught doing something wrong. When he asked me about being English, I tried to be precise – to tell the truth. I said that one side of me, the English side maybe, was a way of hiding from the other side, which was Argentinian, so that I never had to be a single fully formed person, I could always switch and improvise. I had never said this before, or even thought about it like this, and I suppose I could say it easily to him because I believed that he would understand it; I imagined that he too must have learned strategies. There were other things I could say that I knew he would understand, like how working with Americans had made me feel American, that I knew how to fit into other people's agenda. I could feel that he was like that too, but I said nothing about it because I did not want to say too much.

I presumed as the dinner came to an end that we were going

to spend the night together. When he went to the toilet I thought about it: maybe it was something he did not want to do. But just say he did? Afterwards, then, what would happen? Would I leave him once I had an orgasm and walk back home? Or would I stay the night? Would I see him again? What were the rules? Meeting someone like this was new to me.

He paid the bill on his way back from the toilet. He seemed pleased about this as though he had had his way against considerable odds. I invited him to a bar to have a drink and we strolled up through the city. As we walked along I steered him in the direction of his own apartment. I did not want to take him back to mine, it would have allowed him too much intimacy. I still wanted strangeness. I would have loved to know about his life, when he knew he was gay, or when he had his first experience, but we had not mentioned the word gay; it was taken for granted.

'Come back and have a drink,' he said. He grinned as if he were in a movie and had learned his dialogue off by heart. I nodded and smiled.

The apartment was modern with a long living room and hardly any furniture, there were some giant plants, and rugs which he must have bought in Europe or the East. He mixed two gin and tonics, turned off the main light and put on a lamp instead, then he sat down on the sofa close to me. I wanted this, but still I was uncomfortable. He put his hand on my hair and I leaned against him.

'Would you like music?' he asked.

'No, this is okay,' I turned towards him and smiled. We kissed. We lay together and sipped our gin for some time; we said nothing. I put my ear against his chest. I could hear his heart beating. I could see too that his cock was hard.

'Let's go to bed,' he whispered.

He was careful with his clothes. He took his jacket off and hung it in the wardrobe. He put his shoes neatly beside each other against the wall, and then he took his trousers off and folded them on the back of a chair. Everything in the apartment was tidy and in place. He was a regular guy who liked things to be spare and clean. I was glad that I had not taken him home. I hung my jacket on the back of the door and tried to put the rest of my clothes neatly on the chair. We both left our shorts on as we got in between the clean sheet and the fresh duvet cover. We lay together quietly. After a while, he whispered to me:

'Do you want to put a condom on?' He reached into a drawer in the bedside table and pulled out a packet of condoms.

'Why?' I asked. I was puzzled.

'For protection, we have to be careful.'

'I haven't got anything,' I said.

'Neither have I. We want to stay like that, don't we?'

'Are you talking about AIDS?'

'Yeah.'

'Do you know anyone who's infected?'

'No. But you can't judge, or at least there are no definite signs until the late stages. I went for a test and it took two weeks for the results to come back. I kept thinking I had it, I kept going back over stuff I had done. But I was okay. I made up my mind that I was going to be careful from then on.'

I put my arms around him and held him. I could feel a new warmth from him, now that he had talked about something which was important. I felt that he was vulnerable, someone who could easily be afraid, and who was alone. I made him turn around so that I held him from behind. I pulled him in against me and closed my eyes and experienced a different sort of excitement. I kissed the back of his neck. I felt his nipples between my forefinger and thumb and the soft, warm flesh on his belly. He turned and looked into my eyes. I smiled and began to play with his dick. He reached out and found the condoms. He opened one of the packages and took out the piece of rubber as though it were something precious and he rolled it down on my dick, and then did the same for himself. He asked me if I wanted him to turn off the light, and I said that I did not. I wanted to see him. Quietly, then, by the light of the lamp, we began to make love.

In the morning he put music on a CD player he had imported from the United States and he carried in a tray with freshly squeezed orange juice and coffee and toast. He wore a white dressing gown. We sat up in bed like a married couple and had our breakfast. I knew that he knew that somehow it had not worked; there was a gap between us that would never be filled. We had enjoyed ourselves and we had fallen asleep together without any problem, but there was something wrong, I don't know what it was. The knowledge we shared made the morning easier. Neither of us was insecure, neither of us was full of hope that things would work out, watching for signs of serious attraction. We relaxed and laughed, we put the tray on the ground and made love again in an awkward, almost half-hearted way, and then we slept for a while. When we woke, we talked until it was time for me to go. I had a shower in the pristine bathroom and borrowed a clean pair of socks, leaving my old ones in the laundry basket, which was neatly placed in the alcove outside the bathroom.

I walked through the city. It was almost noon. There was no one in the streets. I felt a strange happiness, the sort I often felt after a day when I had worked hard and written a report, or organized something. I did not feel any urgent need to see Charles again, as we had both quietly acknowledged before I left the apartment, but I knew that I would see him again, and it was possible that he would become an ally in the future. I had enjoyed waking in the morning beside him, with nothing furtive in the air, no strain. I began to imagine what it would be like to wake beside someone you loved, or someone whose body you could not keep your hands off, to spend all morning in bed, and then wash and dress and have the day together, basking in the afterglow of what had happened in the night.

★

As soon as I went in the door of my own apartment that Sunday morning I rang Pablo. I told myself on the way up the stairs that if I rang now he would answer. I did not pray now, or it wasn't really prayer, but I used the words: I asked God to let Pablo answer the phone if I rang the number. I got a drink of water and pulled a chair up and sat down beside the phone. I picked up the receiver and I dialled. The man who answered simply said 'Sí' in a brusque tone. I could not tell who it was.

'Hola puedo hablar con Pablo, por favor?' I tried to sound as businesslike as I could.

'Quién es, por favor?' Still, I could not tell who it was.

'Amigo suyo,' I said.

'Yo soy Pablo,' he said.

I said nothing for a moment.

'I wanted to talk to you,' I spoke in English, 'but I wasn't quite sure how to arrange it.'

'I've dropped by your house a few times,' he said. I had never heard him speak English before.

'I'd like to see you,' I said. And then I stopped. I had not been listening properly: 'You called around to my house?'

'I wasn't sure which bell it was, and so I tried them all. Then a woman told me which was yours, and I tried that again, but there was no reply.'

'I'm sorry I wasn't there.'

'Where are you now?' he asked.

'At home.'

'Can I come around?'

'When?'

'Now. I hate Sunday here.'

186

I wanted time to prepare for him. After all the waiting, I felt a strange resistance, as though I were happier thinking about him than I was facing the possibility of meeting him.

'What about later on?'

'Okay. Like what time?'

'Six, say, or seven.'

'Between six and seven, where?'

'What about the bar of the Sheraton Hotel?'

'I'll come in on the train. That's good. I'll see you there.'

In English he sounded like a different person, friendly, with no hang-ups. I wished that the shops were open so that I could buy a new shirt. I tried to picture myself sitting at the bar when he came in. I did not know what I should wear. I thought about a tie and then dismissed the idea immediately. Maybe he was going to say that he would be glad if I did not tell his family he was gay. Maybe that is why he had called, and why he was now so eager to meet me. I did not know what was going to happen, but when I turned from the phone I jumped in the air as though I had just won money.

I went down to the bar in the street and had a sandwich and then a cup of coffee. Every thought was rushing. I was sure that my heart was beating faster. I am like a girl, I said to myself and smiled. The barman saw me smiling and he smiled too. I had another coffee and wondered what I would do for the afternoon. I thought suddenly that he might telephone now to cancel everything and I would not be there, and I would end up waiting in the hotel bar for hours. I am really like a girl, I thought again, and once more could not restrain a smile.

He came into the bar at a quarter to seven. I had already had one gin and tonic and was just gesturing to the barman for another when I saw him. His hair had grown longer and his skin was less tanned. He looked straight at me as though there were no one else in the bar. I looked at him and then glanced down. It was too much for me.

'I'm so glad you phoned,' he said. 'I've been feeling bad about you.'

'I thought you were amazing from the first time I saw you,' I said.

'You're good at playing the straightest boy in the class,' he said. 'I didn't trust you.'

'Is that why you hit me with the tennis ball?'

'I'm sorry about that too. I was having a very bad time. I had never done anything like that before in my life.'

I ordered him a beer and myself another gin and tonic. We raised the glasses and nodded at each other. I reached over and held his hand and then released it.

'You'd better watch it around here. We're not in California,' he said.

'Why did you come back?' I asked him.

He shrugged and smiled.

'I don't know why I came back. Maybe I just missed it. And there were problems.'

Talking with him was like keeping a balloon floating in the air, punching it higher each time it started to come down. I did not want to ask about problems.

'What's it like at home?'

'Would you like to live there, eat every meal there?'

'Jorge doesn't mind it.'

'About half of Jorge has disappeared.'

I was going to mention that I knew where some of the missing half was, but it was better to say nothing. If I started to tell him about Jorge, then he would have a right to feel that I would tell Jorge about him.

'Maybe you'll get your own place.'

'What's your place like?' he asked me.

'It belonged to my mother. Someday soon I'm going to have it all redecorated. It's in a terrible state.'

'Do you own it?' As he said this, I noticed that he sounded like his father.

'No, but there's a lease on it. The rent is almost nothing.'

'Maybe I'll get to see the inside of it sometime.' Now he did not look like his father at all. The blue of his eyes was delicate and pure, his eyelashes long and dark. We looked at one another.

'Why don't you come up now?'

'Is the bed made?' he asked.

'Yeah, I made sure of that before I came out.'

It was almost dark outside as we wandered through the city. We walked slowly.

'I'm nervous,' I said.

'That's a good sign,' he said. 'I feel calm.'

'I bet you don't.'

As we walked up past Corrientes we passed the shopping mall.

'Let's go down here for a minute,' he said.

'There's nothing open.'

'I know. That's why I want to go down there.'

We walked down the mall, idling as though we were here just to look in shop windows. In the entry to one of the shops we stood facing each other. He smiled and put his warm, soft lips against mine. His tongue was strong and supple in my mouth. I shuddered as he pushed himself against me.

'Be careful,' I said. 'Someone will come.'

'I will come,' he said.

'Don't come yet,' I said. He laughed.

I put my hands on his waist. I could feel his shape, and I wondered if it was like this here, what would it be like when we were at home?

'I want to go,' I said.

We walked along the last few streets saying nothing.

'Is kissing safe?' I asked as we got near the apartment.

'Are you worried about it?'

'I don't know much about AIDS. There's been very little in the papers down here. I read a few pieces in the *New York Times*.'

'Yeah, kissing's safe, and as long as you use condoms everything else is okay.'

He said nothing about the apartment. He went to use the bathroom and I sat at the window in the long hallway waiting for him. When I heard the toilet flushing I thought he would come out and say that this place was in urgent need of someone to dust it and clean it. But he simply asked where the bedroom was and grinned as he gestured to me to follow him there.

At first, he took control. He held me in his arms. Then after we had kissed for a while he quickly took his shoes off and pulled mine off as well. I could not believe how beautiful he was like this, how earnest and concentrated. I took my jacket off and he opened the buttons on my shirt. He knelt up and looked at my bare chest without speaking, as if he were in a trance. He opened the clasp on my trousers and pulled down the zip and then slowly undressed me. He kept his own clothes on.

'And I thought you were such a jerk when I met you first,' he said.

'I thought you were wonderful.'

We lay together for a long time saying nothing, not moving. After a while he turned off the lamp.

'Are you not going to take your clothes off?'

'I'm going to take my socks off,' he said.

'More.' I put my hands under his shirt and felt his skin. He lay still.

When we spoke again it was after eleven o'clock.

'I'm going to have to go,' he said.

'Was it not okay?'

'It was great,' he leaned over and tossed my hair, 'but I have to go.'

'Come here,' I said and pulled him towards me until I could whisper to him. 'Am I going to see you again?'

'Of course, it's okay. I just have to go. Walk down to the train with me. Do you want to see me again?'

'Yes.'

'What about tomorrow?'

'Fine.'

'Let's get ready and go.'

The streets were half-full of Sunday couples on their way home. We walked fast so that Pablo could catch the midnight train to San Isidro. From the time we left the apartment and set foot on the street, I had a feeling I'd never had before. I hesitate to call it love, but it was in my body as much as in my mind, a strange ease and feeling of happiness, a sense that I did not need anything more than this, that this would do me for all of my life. I wondered was this how other people felt, was it something which people took for granted and did not usually mention, was it something all the couples who were walking in the city on this Sunday night felt? Was I the only one who had never felt it before?

The following night we made love in my apartment. Afterwards, he said he liked me. I asked him if he could say it again.

'I like you,' he whispered.

His body was something that I dreamed about at night and felt close to all day. In the evening when I came home, having walked him to the railway station, I loved getting back into the bed where we had been, lying on his side, savouring the faint smell of him from the pillow and the sheets.

On Friday of that first week he telephoned to say that he could not see me that evening, there were problems at home. They had been asking too many questions, he said, and he needed to spend one evening there, and have his dinner with the family. He hoped that I understood. I found it hard to say anything. I told Pablo that I understood, but I needed to know if this was a code for saying that he did not want to see me again. Would I be around on Saturday afternoon, he asked. Yes, I said, I would. What about two o'clock? Okay, I said, I'll see you then.

As soon as I put the phone down Susan rang.

'First, can you have dinner with us tonight? There are a few other people coming, including your friend Jorge. Two, can we use your apartment tomorrow afternoon?'

'Will Donald be there tonight?'

'Yes, he will, and he doesn't know a thing and I want it kept like that.'

'Fine,' I said.

'So that's arranged?'

'Yes.'

It was only when I put the phone down that I remembered Pablo. I tried to phone him at his father's office, but I was sure that the voice which spoke was Jorge's and I put the receiver down without saying anything. I telephoned the house later in the evening and spoke to his mother. I tried to disguise my voice, and I think I succeeded, but she told me that Pablo was not there. I wondered where he was and then I stopped wondering and dressed to go to dinner in Susan's house. The other guests at the dinner seemed to be people in Menem's entourage whom Donald and Susan thought it proper to entertain. Charles was also there. Susan, he said, had spent all week asking him how it had gone between us on the date she had arranged. He had told her, he said, that it went well. Donald came up to fill our glasses and slapped us both on the back, as though he were offering us his seal of approval. Susan neither ignored Jorge nor spoke to him too much. She behaved perfectly towards him, every look, every gesture, every phrase carefully worked out. Nobody could have guessed that they were having an affair, unless they watched me observing them both uneasily. As we were leaving I asked her quietly what time she would visit the apartment in the afternoon, and she said that it would be three or later. That was fine, I realized. Pablo was due to come at two. If he arrived late, I thought, I would wait for him in the street. I knew that I would have to tell him about Susan and Jorge.

I enjoyed waking early that Saturday morning, sitting in the bar downstairs having my breakfast, reading the paper. I bought some new shirts and a new pair of jeans. I even thought about buying a new suit. There were other things Pablo had suggested that I needed to buy: an espresso machine for the kitchen, a machine to squeeze orange juice, a tray to make ice cubes, new lampshades, new sheets, a duvet, new pillows. I moved around the city centre making purchases, preparing for this new life I was going to have.

When he arrived that day, we went for lunch to a restaurant on Corrientes. We got a table in the corner and there I told him the story of Susan and Jorge. He was amazed.

'My mother thinks that he's about to get married. He's been going out with this girl, Teresa. In fact, he is still going out with her, he sees her all the time. I'm sure that they are planning to get married. He must be screwing the American on the side.'

'Jorge has always had a lot of energy,' I said.

'No, Jorge always loves fooling everybody.'

'And what about you?' I asked.

'I fool nobody,' he said, 'although I try real hard.'

He told me the story then of how he came to leave Buenos Aires and go to the States. He was eighteen, he said, he had just finished high school and was about to go to college, although he still did not know what he wanted to do. I tried to work back in time to what I was doing when Pablo was seventeen. I was in college, I realized, and although I knew Jorge I had never been to his house. This was before we went to Barcelona. I must have known that he had a brother, but I could not remember anything about him.

His parents and Jorge were in Bariloche, he said, skiing, and the house was empty, the servants were also getting a break. A friend from school came to stay. They planned nothing, he said, things between them began casually. They played poker, and then they played strip poker, and then they found that they were both naked lying on the living room floor so they went upstairs and got into bed together. The other guy was his best friend, he said, they played tennis and swam together, they had played football on the same team. He had seen him naked before, and for a few years he had dreamed about this, watching him strip and then going to bed with him. The guy was beautiful, he said, and he was enjoying himself. The next night they did the same, and again they went to bed and they fell asleep together. His parents still were not due back for a day or two. In the morning they woke up, he said, and started to mess around in the bed. He could not tell me what they were doing – it was too embarrassing. But at one stage he looked up and Pepita, the maid who had been with the family for forty years, was standing at the bottom of the bed watching everything. He had no idea how long she had been there. When he saw her he covered his face with his hands, and when he took his hands away she had disappeared.

He went in search of her. He thought that he could convince her not to tell and considered trying to buy her off. He sent his friend home and waited in the house for her to appear; when she did not, he waited for his parents to come back. He saw Pepita at breakfast the first morning after their return. She behaved as though nothing had taken place.

About a week later, Señor Canetto began to talk about a scholarship Pablo could win to a business school in Miami and said that if he did not win the scholarship he could go there in any case. Pablo was puzzled by this. It had been mentioned before but only as a vague possibility. Jorge was at the University of Buenos Aires; Señor Canetto had gone there too. He had always thought that he was sent away because of what Pepita had told his father. But maybe there was no connection. His father was making money at that time and the peso was worth a lot in dollars and maybe this was the reason.

He did not want to ask why his father was talking about sending him to the United States. The idea of having to speak to his father about what had happened in the bedroom filled him with terror. Forms and information leaflets about business schools in the United States began to arrive. He applied to several. His English was good enough. He did not want to go, or he was not sure that he wanted to go. He had always believed that he would work in the family business and get married and live in a house like his parents' house. He went to Texas first and hated it, everything about it, and then later he went to Los Angeles and San Francisco. He found work. He got a work permit. He made friends. But he never really wanted to stay there, and after ten years he returned to Argentina for good only to have his mother ask when he was going back to the States. His father had looked at him, and told him that he would have to work hard and prove himself if he wanted to join the business. He had not been home on holiday for two or three years before that. It all seemed so strange and confining.

I did not ask him any questions. Sometimes, as he spoke, he shook his head and sighed as though all this were all too much. When he had finished, I covered my face with my hands. He laughed, and he told me that it would not work, Pepita would tell on me, Pepita had seen the filthy things I had been doing. We had finished lunch at this stage; we ordered coffee.

'Do you think your father knows?' I asked.

'I don't know. I was so afraid of him finding out. I would have gone to the Arctic Circle.'

'And what about the boy you were with?'

'Just married.'

'I don't remember Pepita.'

'She went to live with her daughter soon after that, and then she died. Maybe she died of fright.'

'You should have asked her.'

'I was so afraid.'

'Are you still afraid?'

'Yes, I am. I used to dream when I was sleeping with a man that my father and mother both came in and stood over the bed. This was thousands of miles away.'

I told him about my mother believing that Jorge was gay and about the night when I had told her everything. We were now the last people in the restaurant. I felt depressed by Pablo's story, I wished that I had known him then. We walked out into the busy afternoon and went to the movies. By the time the film was over, I said, Susan and Jorge would have finished whatever it was they were doing in my apartment and we could have it to ourselves.

The story made him seem different. I had believed that he was confident and strong, someone who had made decisions about his life. I had never detected any sign of weakness in him before. The movie was funny: I cannot remember whether it was one of the Almodóvar films or a new Woody Allen – we saw so many movies in that year – but we laughed a lot and held hands in the dark. When we went back to the apartment, Susan and Jorge had gone. Pablo went into the spare bedroom and smelt the air.

'They were here all right,' he said. He pulled back the blankets on the bed and pointed to a small stain on the sheet.

'I thought they would do better than that.'

★

WHEN WE WENT TO BED now things had changed between us. He let me take charge, he seemed to soften as though he wanted me to hold him and comfort him. We slept for a while, and when we woke it was different, we were ready to make love now, we moved fast. I let him do anything he wanted and he did not resist me when I took over. He kept telling me not to make him come, but he came without me touching him, and then he turned towards me and kissed me and made sure that I came too and we lay together until it was time for him to go.

★

I LOVED WAITING FOR HIM. I loved it when he rang the bell of my apartment and I pressed the buzzer and then heard him on the stairs and stood at the door watching him as he came into view. Often, I said nothing for a while. I looked at him and smiled. I could not believe that he was with me, that he was mine, I loved his face, his hair, his skin, his dick. He was always alert to me, to what I wanted. I loved being in bed with him, and not just because of his responses, but because of his shape, I could have spent days looking at his body, touching him.

I told him that I wanted to tell Susan about us, that I wanted to move from having a hidden, secret life with him, to something that would be recognized. He did not want this. The time we spent together was enough for him, our life absorbed whatever needs he had for love and friendship. He did not want anyone else to recognize us, and once I discovered this, I did not ask him for more. Nevertheless, I felt that things between us would be more concrete and that I would worry less about losing him if somebody else could see us together. I would have loved to leave a dinner with Susan and Donald in his company, I imagined us standing at the door putting on our coats and leaving together. But this was not something that he cared about.

I do not know what he told his parents, but soon they got used to the idea that he disappeared after work most evenings and did not come back until late. I asked him if they thought that he had a girlfriend, but he shrugged and shook his head. There was nothing I did not want to know about him, and I had to be careful not to ask too much. I wanted him to leave some of his clothes in the apartment, but I had to be sly about engineering this, because he would not have understood. He was easygoing and took things for granted, but he made it clear, in various ways, that he loved me.

I asked him to come with me to my parents' grave. It was a Sunday afternoon in winter and the sky was low and grey. We got a taxi to the Recoleta; there were people walking around looking at the small, ornate temples built over the graves of the rich of the city. I found as we wandered around that I was glad that my parents were lying here, and I spoke to them in my mind as we stood over their grave. I told them about Pablo and how much in love with him I was and how happy I felt. I wanted them to know that I was all right now, after years of not being all right, years when I missed them, and wished that I could wake in the night and march into their bedroom and snuggle in between them. I've done something with myself, I said to them, and he's here now beside me. I feel loved again and secure, I said. Do you remember how I always wanted a brother, I asked them. Well, I have one now and I love him.

I did not intend to cry, but I found the tears coming and there was nothing I could do about it.

'I'm sorry,' I said to Pablo. 'I'm sorry.'

'You can stay here as long as you like,' he said. 'I'll stay with you.'

We went back to the apartment and lay together under the duvet and I talked about my parents. I don't think it had occurred to him before what it would be like to have both your parents dead. I thought that this was something he understood about me from the very beginning, but it was not. He lived in the present, and understood only what was made clear to him. He imagined nothing and presumed nothing. I wished that I was free like that; I saw his way of thinking as a form of innocence and sweetness. I thought he was shocked by what I had told him, about being close by when someone died, about what the dead body of a loved one was like.

Sometimes I was busy. An executive would come to town, or a group of oil experts, and I would have to spend every evening at dinners or conferences or meetings. Susan and I found Menem's people easy to deal with; they had won an election on the promise of sorting out the economy, and they seemed determined to do so, no matter how unpopular their measures were. People accepted this with a kind of despair: it was bad, but it was needed. I often looked around me at the faces on the street or in a traffic jam and everyone appeared worn and unhappy, moving about the city in a black depression. But no one blamed Menem or his government.

I was trying to persuade Pablo to move in with me. After one of those weeks when I had barely seen him, we decided to go to Montevideo on the last boat on a Friday night. We would arrive around three in the morning, but I had booked a small hotel whose night porter would let us in. I sat on the bench beside the bus which would take us to the boat, waiting for him. I was nervous, thinking that he would not come, and then reassuring myself and then worrying again. When he came he was dressed in a dark suit with a dark shirt and tie and a dark overcoat. If I had not known him, I would have stared at him and tried to sit close to him on the bus.

The hotel room was small and dreary with two narrow single beds. I had imagined plush quarters, I had even thought about a big bath that we could share. The lights were dim and it was cold. We were both tired; we stripped down to our vests and underpants and got into one of the single beds and turned out the light. We made ourselves comfortable together. I felt warm and easy with him, even though neither of us wanted to make love. When I woke in the night, I discovered that he had moved to the other bed.

'Pablo,' I whispered, 'are you all right?'

'I'm sleepy. I'll see you in the morning.'

'Can you hold my hand for a minute?'

He reached his arm out so that I could touch his hand. He gripped me and we stayed like that for a while until I withdrew my hand.

'Goodnight,' I said, 'sleep well.'

In the morning as I came back from the bathroom I saw that all the clothes in his bag had been carefully folded. When I asked him who had folded them, he said that his mother always looked after his clothes.

'Where did you say you were going?'

'To Montevideo with a few friends from school.'

'Did she believe you?'

'I don't know.'

He knew that I wanted him to move away from them. I did not raise the matter again. I sat on the bed with my head against the wall and studied his body as he dressed. I thought of changing the hotel, but in the end it was better to leave everything alone. We had a whole day now to enjoy the city – it was almost ten years since I had been here, and he had not been in Montevideo before. I remembered that the market was turned into one big restaurant on a Saturday, I had already told Pablo about this. We wandered down there, but it was still too early. We went to a bar instead and had coffee and croissants and then went to look at the sea. It was windy and cold, but the sky was blue and we were both wearing coats. We walked along looking at the waves and the glimmering sunlight on the water. There were very few people around, and hardly any traffic. It was strange that Pablo did not have to rush home, or that I did not have an appointment. I could not tell whether he was happy or not. We were both still tired and we did not talk much.

The market was open when we got back there: all the stalls were now busy grilling meat and serving drinks. We sat down on two stools and ordered bits and pieces of meat and some white wine. The place was filling up with well-dressed, fashionable-looking people wandering around the stalls, carefully looking at each other. Most of them seemed to be having a drink and something small to eat at each stall and then moving on to another. We both agreed that there was nothing like this in Buenos Aires.

Soon, the four people standing at our stall heard us talking in English. Two of them, a middle-aged American man and a tall, exotic-looking woman, spoke to us. The woman introduced her companions; they were celebrating this man's birthday, she said, pointing to the mild-looking man standing beside her. He was the American's chauffeur, she told us. The other man was a friend. The chauffeur would have to drink water, or coffee, or maté, she said, because he was driving, so they would have to drink his share too. Her English was perfect, but her accent was foreign. She could have been Italian, or German, because her Spanish, when she ordered drinks for us – a mixture of champagne and muscatel – sounded foreign as well. She was surprised and disappointed when she discovered we were Argentinian, but she soon cheered up and repeatedly raised her glass to toast the chauffeur's birthday.

We ordered another round of drinks. This time the woman wanted to drink to absent friends, and we all raised our glasses. She asked us if our wives or our girlfriends had gone shopping.

No, I said, we were not with our girlfriends or our wives. We were not married. Were we here on business, she asked. No, I said. She stood back and looked at us. She raised her glass again: To the two of you, she said. We drank. Someone else ordered another round. The chauffeur put his hand over his glass to signify that he had had enough water. I could not work out whether she had deduced we were together. I did not know whether I wanted anyone to be able to see us like that. I had always presumed that we could walk around Buenos Aires without anybody suspecting we were lovers. I turned to look at Pablo. He was enjoying this, he was smiling, and he was moving back and forth between English and Spanish. I had never been in anyone's company with him before. I noticed how white his teeth were when he smiled, how his eyes shone when he listened to someone talking. I was proud and happy to be with him. We ordered some more food from the grill and another round of drinks. The foreign woman told us about a shop we should go to where, if we mentioned her name, we would get a ten per cent discount. We told her that we were going home the next day, and she said it was a pity, and made us take down the name of the shop in case we ever returned. Other people came to the stall, a few of them had a drink with us and then moved on. Our four friends looked as though they might stay here all day. I realized that I was getting drunk. I felt that maybe it was time to go, but our companions would not hear of it.

Pablo was now having an animated discussion in Spanish with the chauffeur and the other man. They were talking about Brazil, how different it was from the countries around it; they were imitating Brazilians speaking Portuguese. They all seemed to agree that it was a great place, even though you would never get any work done. I said that Uruguay seemed to be like that too, but the others insisted that every group in the market, except ourselves, was just having one drink and some food before going home to their families. In Brazil, the chauffeur said, everyone has at least two families, and no one minds if they have some more, one for each colour, he said, but Uruguay was like Argentina, everything was strict and normal. We ordered more drinks. The American was saying very little, he smiled a lot, and looked around him. He appeared to be having a good time. Eventually, he said that we must come to lunch the next day, he was having some people to his house. His chauffeur would collect us. He made the chauffeur note the name of the hotel we were staying in. And when he had done this, they drained their glasses and said that it was time to go. The American paid the bill.

The stall did not serve coffee, so we paid what we owed and walked out into the city. We were both drunk. We stopped at a bar on the way back to the hotel and had several coffees and brandies each. I could hardly keep my hands off Pablo in the street. In the hotel room, I realized that the alcohol had had the same effect on him. We stripped without saying anything. He pulled back the blankets on the bed beside the wall. We got into bed together and began to make love. I touched him and held him as though I would never get the chance again. I was so excited that I moved out of myself into a place where there was only his body, the hardness of his frame, the silky beauty of his skin, the softness of his tongue, his frantic breathing against mine, everything about him perfect beyond belief.

We lay together after we came and then we fell asleep and did not wake until night. It was cold in the room; I was thirsty and my head throbbed. Pablo was still in a deep sleep. I went to the bathroom and then got into the other bed and pulled the blankets around me. I was depressed and felt as distant from him now as I had been close before. I tried to sleep, but instead I lay there brooding in the dark, half-hoping that he would not wake now, because I did not know how we would spend the rest of the evening, and I did not look forward to the long night ahead if I could not sleep. But as soon as I realized that he was awake I changed. I whispered to him; I offered to get him a glass of water from the bottle I had carried in my bag. I got into bed beside him, presuming that he too must have felt the blackness that was in me after the euphoria of the day. I said nothing. I kissed the side of his face and put my arms around him. When he asked me the time I was able to tell him that it was after nine o'clock. Neither of us felt hungry, and we were too tired and worn out to think of getting up. I turned in the bed and he cupped his body against mine and we lay together quietly.

Slowly, desire began to stir again in both of us. We did not move. His hands were warm on my chest. I could feel his dick hard against me. After a while I turned and faced him, and we began to make love again. He whispered that he had condoms and some cream in his bag. He asked me if I wanted him to get it. I hesitated and then I said that I did. We had not done this before. I lay on my stomach in the dark while he rolled on the condom and opened the tube of cream. The cream was cold. At first he lay on top of me. I turned my face around so that we could kiss. He gently moved my legs apart and then slowly began to enter. I was tense, and at first I thought that I would not be able to take it. He pulled out and slowly came in again and pushed his dick inside much further than before. He held it there and he did not move. He put his hands under my arms and then gripped my shoulders until I began to relax, until his being inside me gave me pleasure and almost no pain.

After he came he remained still. He asked me if I was all right and I said that I was. All my depression had gone. I was happy with him. As he withdrew he held the condom in place and then he took it off and left it on the bedside table. I still had an erection, was still excited. He knelt over me and started to suck me off, and when I began to come and he took his mouth away the feeling of pure pleasure was stronger than anything I had ever experienced. I cried out and held on to him and then he lay down beside me and pulled the blankets over us and we were calm again.

After a while, we noticed that the heating in the hotel had been switched on. We could hear the pipes crackling and we began to feel hot under the blankets. We decided that it was time to get up. I went into the bathroom and turned on the shower, battling with the control knob to get the water hot enough. When I had got it right I called Pablo, who was still lying in bed. He came into the bathroom and closed the door. We stood under the hot shower soaping ourselves, touching each other's bodies easily, without any tension, desire now replaced by familiarity. We dried ourselves and then dressed in the warm bedroom.

It was cold outside. I had the name and address of a gay bar and a gay discotheque which I had found in an American guidebook. We checked the address of the bar on a map and set out walking. We were hungry now and agreed that we would stop at the first restaurant we came across which was still open. We found a dingy-looking steakhouse down a side street. Because it was half-full of people we concluded that it could not be as bad as it looked from the outside. We ordered a steak and a salad and a bottle of red wine. When the waiter came with the wine, he filled our glasses. Pablo raised his glass and smiled.

'I love you,' he said.

I still found it hard to believe. I wanted to make a joke out of it, to say something casual about it, to shrug it off. I was going to ask him if he was sure that he did not want to hit me with tennis balls when I was standing at the net. But I was careful now not to break the spell of what was going on. I raised my glass and drank the wine.

'Te quiero,' I said.

The gay bar was well lit, glamorous, full of good-looking men who glanced at us when we came in as though they might know us. We ordered gin and tonics and stood at the bar looking around us. I was surprised by how cool everybody looked. In Buenos Aires everything would have been furtive and underhand, and the lighting would have been low. When a man standing close to us began to ask us questions, I did not think that he was trying to pick one of us up; it seemed to me that he was just being friendly. We told him we were having a drink here and then we were going to a disco called Locomotive. He laughed and said that everybody here would be going there, this was the normal route on a Saturday night. We talked for a while about Argentina and the hotel we were staying in. He asked us to look towards the corner of the bar until we saw a slightly built young man wearing an English tweed jacket. We both looked around. He owned, our new friend told us, one of the largest estates in Uruguay, thousands and thousands of hectares. A few years earlier, he would have needed protection, but now things were much easier, and he would be in Locomotive too. The man with him was from New Zealand, they were both sheep farmers, but he did not think they were lovers.

We ordered another drink, and our friend was joined by a tall man with a thin face and black curly hair. Soon, they said, people would be leaving for Locomotive. They both looked over as a woman came in with a black man and another man with dark skin. Did we realize, the thin-faced man asked, that the woman was really a man? Pablo nodded and said he would not be surprised, it was often hard to tell. I looked at the woman carefully; she was not like the transsexuals I had seen in Barcelona. She was not tall enough and her face was shaped like a woman's. We talked about this for a while until one of our companions told us that she was a magician. She could do the most extraordinary conjuring tricks, he said. She moved across the bar with her two friends and sat at an empty table close to us. She was wearing a leather jacket and jeans. One of our companions seemed to know her; he went over and shook her hand and spoke to her and her friends. When he returned he said that when she had had a drink she would perform a few tricks for us. She had just come from a successful show, she had told him, and was in the mood. Pablo smiled at me, he looked puzzled by all of this, but shrugged as if to say that we should wait and see.

Eventually, one of the men with her conveyed the news to us that she was ready. She glanced up at us, pursed her lips like a film star from the 1950s, then stared down at her two hands, which she had placed on the table. She took a coin out of her bag, made each of us hold it in the palm of our hands, then she showed us that it was larger than the top of the beer bottle she had on the table. Her eyes were hard with concentration. She began to move the bottle and the coin around on the surface of the table. By now, several others had come to watch as well. Suddenly, when she lifted the bottle the coin was inside. We applauded, and more people gathered around. She lifted the bottle up to show them and rattled the coin inside. She waved us all back, making clear that she was ready to do another trick. This time she laid her scarf on the table and put the bottle on top of it, and then she began to push the bottle through the surface of the table, her eyes flashing, everybody watching, murmuring, as the bottle went right through the top of the table and she pulled it out on the other side.

Immediately, she took out a pack of cards and asked Pablo to select one. He chose the six of diamonds. She told him to write his name on it, and when he had done this, she made everybody look at it. She then produced a packet of thumbtacks from her handbag, and asked Pablo to take one. She held this up so that everybody could see it. Then she began to conjure with the cards and the thumbtack until the cards landed in a pack on the table but the six of diamonds was fixed to the ceiling above us by the thumbtack. Suddenly, it was there. I watched it happen, just as I had watched the bottle push through the mass of the table surface. I had never seen anything like it before. There was a sort of hush as people looked up at the card with Pablo's name on it stuck to the ceiling. The magician remained tense, as though performing these tricks had drained all the energy out of her. She sipped her drink. Pablo came over and held my hand for a moment and kissed me. He seemed amazed as well. He went back to the magician and raised his glass to her and said thank you. She gave him a crooked, nervous smile.

Later, we went to Locomotive, where we drank more gin and danced and spoke to various men at the bar. We were still touched by the magic, we talked to someone who had been in the bar and witnessed the tricks. He had seen her perform before, he said, but never as well as that. Late in the night, they turned the lights down and played slow music. We left our drinks on the counter and danced again, we were wrapped around each other, swaying to the slow beat of the music. I had never done this before. In my last year in school I had danced with girls, but I had felt awkward and I had not understood that all around me then everybody, or almost everybody, had felt the great ooze of desire that we felt in these moments. It was something that I had missed up to now, and I had, I thought, come across it only by accident. It might never have happened to me. I moved closer and we began to kiss on the dance floor, like the other couples around us.

It was five in the morning when we went to bed but we were still madly excited.

'It's been a wonderful day,' I said. 'It's been the best day I've ever had.'

'Which bed will we sleep in?' Pablo asked.

Both beds were tossed, and the room, once more, was cold.

'Let's pull them together,' I said. I took the lamp from the bedside table and left it on one bed and then I moved the table out of the way. We tried to move the beds quietly, but it was difficult as the legs scraped along the floor. Eventually, we got the two beds as close as we could; the lamp was still on the bed so I had to unplug it and put it back on the table. We undressed and turned out the light and fell asleep together.

I woke to the banging of the door. I turned to Pablo but he was still fast asleep. I looked at the clock on the table: it was almost noon. The banging continued. I got up and pulled on my jeans and went to the door. I half-recognized the figure in the corridor, but I could not think who it was. He was too old to be one of the men from Locomotive or the bar where the magician had played her tricks. He was smiling: but still I could not think. He asked me if we were ready to come with him, and then I realized that he was the chauffeur from the previous afternoon, which now seemed like months ago, and I remembered that we had given his boss our names and the name of the hotel. He smiled at me calmly, as if to say that this sort of thing happened all the time. I explained that we had been out most of the night, but now we would get up and shower and pack and pay our hotel bill and we would be with him soon. Would he like to go and have coffee, I asked him. He shook his head. He would wait outside in the car, he said. As soon as I went back into the room I regretted not telling him that we had to leave for Buenos Aires and thus would be unable to go to the party. I wanted to curl up beside Pablo and sleep. I put my hand on the back of his neck and then I leaned down and kissed him. He opened his eyes and smiled.

'You were awake all along,' I said.

'What happened?'

I explained about the chauffeur.

'We have to get up.'

When we had dressed and packed our bags, we tried to pull the two beds apart and put the table back in its place, but the room still did not look right as we abandoned it. We closed the door behind us and walked down to reception, where Pablo paid the bill. The car looked stately and old-fashioned. The chauffeur got out and opened the boot for our bags and then opened the back door for us. I asked him if he had enjoyed his birthday. He turned and tapped his temple to indicate that his friends of yesterday had not been in their right minds.

The American's house overlooked the sea, about half an hour out of the city. I noticed the security cameras at the gate. Trees and shrubs hid the house from view, the drive was unkempt and overgrown. I expected to find an old house, a ramshackle building, but instead the house seemed new; it was painted white and the windows were shiny. In a long room at the front of the house about fifty people were gathered. Most of them were middle-aged; there was an opulence in the social atmosphere, in the way the guests dressed and looked around them with eyes which had been sharpened by the habit of owning things, by years of making considered choices. I loved the sense of worldliness in the room, the richness of the women's clothes, the purr of amused talk in Spanish and in English, and in broken versions of both. I loved not being in Buenos Aires, where no gathering could be as oddly intimate as this, where everyone would feel themselves on display and voices would be louder, where there would be much false laughter and sexual show. I was glad we were both wearing ties. No one in the room was dressed casually.

Our host shook our hands, made sure we had drinks, asked us when we were leaving, offered his chauffeur once more to take us to the bus station, then stood with us and looked around the room. He seemed older now than the previous day, like a man who would soon retire.

'They're all good people,' he said. 'I think you'll like some of them. Now come with me and I'll introduce you to someone who will amuse you.' There was something about him and his house, some dryness in the decor and some hunger within him for companionship, which made me believe that he lived alone here. I imagined grown-up children, even grandchildren, and a wife somewhere, in one of the great American cities. I imagined his need for them, the pain he so suavely exuded, versus his need now to be alone, to face the world without a consort. He found a group and interrupted a fat man wearing a white jacket and a cravat. He held both our hands as if we were children, announced in English that we were his good friends from Buenos Aires, and told us to introduce ourselves to each other and food would be here soon. He made the food sound like a reward for us all getting along.

The fat man spoke bad English, but his listeners knew him and clearly liked him; one of them was Belgian — she was, I told her, the first Belgian person I had ever met — another was American and there was an old thin lady dressed in black with rich rings on her bony fingers who could have been from anywhere. The fat man asked us if we had ever travelled on Varig. We both shook our heads. We should try it, he said, it was really improving, even ordinary class now gave you a hot towel and the food was good. Pablo began to speak in Spanish to the woman in black. Soon, they were engrossed in conversation. I tried to make a joke about airlines, saying that I usually flew with the Bolivian national airline and then got the train from La Paz, but nobody knew whether it was a joke or not. I said nothing then, and none of the others spoke. We stood there admiring the view, the strange dark patches in the calm green sea, the haze on the horizon, the terrace beyond the window, the shrubs. And all the time Pablo and the woman in black spoke as though they knew each other. She listened carefully as he told her something. It was not a joke, but he smiled and looked at her warmly as he recounted some story, some opinion, some version of things. I did not know what he was talking to her about. I was sorry that I had used up my remark about the Belgian woman being the only Belgian I had ever met.

'Do you live in Montevideo?' the fat man asked me.

Soon, food was served. Everyone became busy handing around knives and forks and paper napkins, and wondering whether those in their group wanted chicken or steak. Pablo and the old lady moved closer to the window and ignored the fuss. I turned and watched him. He was listening to her with rapt attention, there was a smiling light in his eye as he nodded his head. I had not noticed what he was wearing before, but now the blue shirt and the dark blue tie seemed rich against the light from the sea and the blueness of his eyes. He saw me looking at him and smiled and then said something to the old lady. They both laughed. As I looked across the room towards him that day I thought that he was the most charming and beautiful man I had ever seen.

Our host watched the time for us, and came towards us after the coffee saying that his driver was outside and we should be going now. We said goodbye to some of the people we had been talking to, we wrote down our names and addresses and telephone numbers on pieces of paper which our host put into his jacket pocket, and we sat into the car and were driven back to the city. I remarked that no one in Argentina would ever invite complete strangers to a party like that and make them feel so welcome.

'Who was the old lady?' I asked.

'She lived in California too, she went there years ago and now she's back here. We were talking about that.'

I fell into a half-sleep as soon as the bus got going and I leaned my head against his shoulder. I woke a few times and looked at him sitting there wide awake, that half-smile I had watched across the room still on his face.

★

Pablo's family believed that he had a girlfriend in the city. One night over dinner his mother told me, as a way of teasing her two sons, that she no longer knew where they went, that she just cooked for them and made sure they had clean clothes, and in return she received nothing, not even the most basic information about their love lives. Jorge tried to change the subject, but his mother had an audience now and nothing was going to stop her. She went on to tell me how welcome her sons' girlfriends had always been in the house, how much she had liked Jorge's girlfriend Teresa, whom nowadays he hardly ever saw. Jorge asked her to stop. These were, he said, personal matters which he did not want discussed like this in a casual way at table. Then Señor Canetto intervened to tell Jorge that he must not criticise his mother in her own house, and that his mother could judge perfectly well what she could and could not discuss.

I continued eating and wished I could stand up and go home and take Pablo with me. We had now been seeing each other for six months. I wanted him to come to dinner at Donald and Susan's with me, I wanted him to tell Jorge about us, or let me tell Jorge. But he wanted nothing, except secret meetings. He was afraid of his parents and he did not trust Jorge. I expected that he would telephone some day – he would not have the courage to come in person – to tell me that he could no longer see me, that the pressure was too much. I asked him if he was happy, if this was what he wanted, and he nodded and smiled and held me and said he was happy. That night as I sat at his parents' table I felt that they deserved their children. Jorge now seemed to be Donald's best friend; the more he fucked Susan the better he seemed to get on with her husband. And Pablo had fucked me in the dressing room beside the swimming pool just ten minutes before we sat down for dinner. I wondered how they had trained their two sons to be like that, what example had they given them, what lessons had they taught them. I said nothing: I had been furtive too, I was in no position to judge them.

I looked across the table at Jorge and he looked back blankly, as if to suggest that this conversation was not taking place. I glanced at Pablo but he gave no sign that his mother's speech interested him at all. Señora Canetto continued to talk. Her work would not be done, she said, until the two of them were happily married, then she could have a good rest; and she would love grandchildren, she said, she would love them coming around to use the swimming pool, she would love babysitting, but she would not interfere, she was not that sort of mother, she would help and give advice only when she was asked. She was now in full flight. But she would, she said, like to have a say in the weddings, she would love a big wedding, somewhere well outside the city, there were some lovely places, and she would love organizing the seating, even though she knew that this was normally done by the bride's family. And the flowers. It was something she had looked forward to all her life, she said, her sons' weddings, and their first children.

I knew how old she was. I knew that she was fifty-seven, and I could see from looking at her that there was a good thirty years left in her. Pablo was twenty-eight, which meant that he would be nearly sixty when she died. I tried to imagine all the lies and evasions there would be between now and then, his timidity and her refusal to stop dreaming aloud about some golden future she would never have until Jorge decided to clean up his act and become what his destiny and his mother had laid out for him: a husband and a father.

When Pablo went to the bathroom at the end of the meal, I followed him and waited outside for him.

'I want you to come back home with me. You can tell them we're going to a nightclub.'

'What will we tell Jorge?'

'The truth.'

'Not now.'

'Let him guess. He must know something. Just say we're going.'

'He'll want to come.'

I shook my head and walked into the bathroom. I locked the door. When I came out he was still standing there.

'I'll say that I have only two passes,' I said. 'Or else, we'll put your teddy bear in your bed and they'll think it's you.'

'Will you do the talking?'

'I'll do anything to get you out of here.'

I went back to the dining room and began to speak even before I sat down. I said that I had just convinced Pablo to come with me to this new nightclub. I had two special passes. I was going to go on my own, I said, but now it was really wonderful that he was going to come with me. I hoped as I sat down at the table again that they were not going to ask me what the name of it was, or where it was, but I knew I would be able to invent quick names and addresses. His mother immediately became involved: how would he get back? what would he wear? should Jorge not come as well? I said I had only two passes, I said that Pablo could get a late bus back or he could stay with me, I said it was best to wear a jacket and a tie. By the time Pablo came into the room it was all arranged.

I was careful not to look at Jorge. Surely, now, I thought, he must know that I am having it off with his brother. His mother insisted on going upstairs to make sure that Pablo had a clean shirt and pressed trousers. This left me in the room with Pablo, Jorge and their father. I knew if I did not concentrate hard on keeping this forced nonchalance afloat I would be found out. I asked Jorge if he would drive us to the train, and he nodded sullenly. Pablo left the room, saying he had to get ready. The father nervously gathered the coffee cups and carried them on a tray out of the room. It was the first time I had ever seen him perform a domestic chore in the house. This left the two of us. I presumed that Jorge would ask me where the nightclub was. I had no idea what I would say. Instead, he asked me if I was going to lunch at Susan and Donald's the next day. When I said I was, he replied that he would see me there. He could collect me, he said, except that he was going to go there quite early. I understood him to mean that he wanted to fuck Susan before lunch and he needed me to know this. He liked witnesses; I knew him from way back. I wondered if Donald was a witness. For that moment I was happy that Pablo had told no one about us.

Pablo came into the room in a white shirt and a flowery tie and a navy-blue jacket, followed by his mother, who flirted with him proudly as she settled his collar. He smiled at her in the same amused way he had smiled at the old lady at the party outside Montevideo. I knew that his mother, somewhere deep within her, must have known everything about him, and must have known, too, that he was leaving to spend the night with me.

Jorge dropped us at the station and muttered something and drove away. We stood on the platform without speaking. I had to be careful: I did not want to say anything to Pablo about his family. I realized too that moving from his parents' house, where things were folded and neat and polished, to my apartment, which was dingy and dusty, would have its drawbacks. But I smiled to myself as I thought that he could not have sex with his parents whereas he could have sex with me for as long as he liked. I was available all night.

I could still feel the tension of the dinner table as the train trundled towards the city, but I sensed that none of it had affected Pablo very much. He did not dwell on things. He looked out of the window now as though it were an ordinary Saturday evening. My head was full of his mother and his father and Jorge. I decided to calm down. I thought about the shape and feel of his body, the smell of his breath, what it would be like to wake beside him in the morning.

We hardly spoke as we walked from the station to the apartment until I began to tell him my thoughts about his mother living for another thirty years. I told him that some day he would have to make her realize who he was, or some day he would have to free himself from her, live under another roof, iron his own shirts, but he could not go on like this. He said that he wanted to go for a drink so we stopped at one of the bars on Lavalle. Still, he said nothing about his family. He seemed relaxed but tired. As we sipped our beers he told me about a bar he used to like in San Francisco, an old-fashioned hamburger bar which looked over the sea; they were always threatening to knock it down, but people liked it too much and he thought that they never would. In California, he said, people knew how to lobby, they would sign petitions and contact politicians and they would stop something happening if they did not want it to happen. It would be several hundred years before this began in Argentina, he said. I listened and smiled and decided to say no more about his family.

He was different when we went to bed. He curled up, his face against my chest. We did not talk. He took my dick in his mouth carefully, slowly, running his tongue along the crown, then sucking it right in. When he had finished, he reached for the packet of condoms and the jelly on the table beside the bed. He opened the condom, put it on my dick and handed me the jelly. Then he turned around, putting a pillow under his crotch. I had not expected this, and I was touched in a way that was new to me by the idea that he wanted it. I kissed his ears once I had put the jelly on him. He cried out as soon as I pushed into him and I had to withdraw. This time I entered him more slowly. I could feel his nervous breathing under me. I remained still. I felt him relax. I pushed in further. I could hear him whimper as he held his face against the pillow and then he relaxed again. I thought that I was going to come and I tried to hold it back as I began to push in and out.

I held him there under me in the dark. After I came, he curled up against me once more and when I turned during the night he turned with me and held me. There was a vulnerable side to him which he showed sometimes in the deepest privacy of a room with the curtains drawn and the light off. It was something which maybe his mother knew about him, something he had displayed as a child but now kept bottled up inside: he was insecure, in need of comfort and care. I wanted to talk to him about it, it would have meant a great deal to me if we could have acknowledged that this was happening between us, but as he slept in my arms in the middle of the night I knew that he had given me enough, I should not want more, and I was happy as I lay there without sleeping.

I went for lunch at Susan's the next day and he went home to his parents' house. Jorge was there, of course, sitting on the veranda in the weak sunshine with Susan, pleased to tell me that he was wearing new clothes that Susan had bought for him in New York. Donald came out with a drink in his hand, wearing the same thick brown cords as Jorge was wearing. The three of them glowed with happiness, and I wondered if this was what they had wanted from me or from Jorge or from someone else all along, sexual satisfaction for Susan and the right to dress their best friend, as though he were their child. Soon, some other guests came: an American singer who had been performing at the Colón, and her husband, who looked as though he was wearing make-up, a senior adviser to Menem whom we liked and found easy to deal with, and his wife, and Charles. The table was set in the dining room and the food was Argentinian cooked in an American style. The wine was Californian. I knew by now how little to expect from these occasions. The rule was to have no strong opinions and tell no jokes, to talk, if you could, about places, airlines, hotels, cruises, to sound pleasant and clean. I wondered if Donald had ever come into the room when they were fucking, if he had felt Jorge up like he did me in the shower room, if he and Susan still slept together, if this had happened before. When Susan addressed Jorge, she made it clear that he was an intimate, an outsider would have guessed there was something between then, and this, I knew, would have pleased Jorge enormously.

After lunch I had to go with her into her office to look at a fax.

'Oh yes,' she said, 'there's something I should have said to you during the week. There's a man called Evanson – he's one of the deputies at the embassy – he and his wife rented this beautiful modern house down by the marina, he keeps a boat there, but the embassy did a security check on it and it's not safe. They've moved him into one of those secure apartment buildings, and he hates it but there's nothing he can do about it. The problem is that he's stuck with the rent, he's signed a two-year lease. He's looking for someone to take it over. It's expensive. I told him I would ask around.'

'Can I see it?'

'I'll give you his number.'

'Do you think I could see it now?' I realized that I had been thinking about this for days without letting it come to the surface. I would have to move, or make my own apartment more comfortable. I became anxious that I might lose this opportunity which had arrived so casually.

'Today? I'll call him.'

She looked his number up in an address book and dialled. The telephone was answered immediately.

'Can he pick up the keys now? Is he serious about it? I don't know. Hang on, I'll ask him.'

'Are you serious about it?' She cupped her hand over the receiver.

'Yes.'

I heard her saying that I could be there, at the apartment building, in forty-five minutes. It was arranged. She hung up. John Evanson would drive me out to the marina himself.

'You want the bad news?' she asked. 'The rent is two thousand bucks a month.'

'That's high.'

'He says the house is amazing.'

Susan arranged for her driver to take me into the city, which was empty in the late afternoon. The wide streets were beautiful now, full of soft light. I was glad to be away from Susan and Donald and Jorge. The driver dropped me at the address he had been given. I rang the bell of the apartment and an American voice said that he would be down in a moment. He was a skinny, red-haired man in his early forties. He shook my hand briskly; he did not smile. We walked down to the underground car park. As he got into the car he checked that he had the keys to the house he could not live in. I imagined a bungalow with a flat roof, but he told me that it was a two-storey house, all glass and steel. I told him that I had often dreamed of walking out of my apartment some day taking nothing with me, except my passport and some financial records.

'You don't have a family?' he asked.

'No. I have no responsibilities.'

He seemed to disapprove. I was sorry I had told him about walking out of my apartment. I was sure that it sounded immature and silly. We drove the rest of the way in silence. I realized that he probably desperately needed somebody to whom he could sub-let this house. Maybe this was why he appeared so nervous; it also might have explained why he was going to the trouble to drive me to see it on a Sunday afternoon.

It was the kind of house that you see in architecture books. It had a flat roof, the front was entirely glass and faced the water. There were huge windows on each side. When he opened the door everything seemed white. The main room was L-shaped, running the whole length of the house, with a stone floor, sofas, easy chairs and glass tables, and then turning into a dining room, and beyond it a kitchen. On the other side of the hall, there was a small room with a desk, a chair and a sofa. The staircase was made of thick glass. Upstairs there was an enormous bedroom, over the living room, with a huge low bed and built-in cabinets; leading directly off there was a bathroom straight out of a designer book. There were two smaller bedrooms and another bathroom. I watched as John Evanson lowered thin white curtains over all the glass so that no one could see in but light could still come through.

'Susan mentioned a price,' I said.

'Two thousand dollars, with a verbal agreement – we're not allowed to sub-let – that you will stay for twenty-two months until the lease runs out.'

'From when?'

'From now.'

'I'll take it. I'll drop you in a cheque this evening. When can I have the keys?'

'You can have them now. The telephone is connected. We can work out an arrangement about the bill. Everything is working. The deal includes bedlinen and kitchen stuff, but you'll need towels. If you like I'll turn the refrigerator and the freezer on. That's if you're sure.'

'I'm sure.' I did not need to think about it. I wanted it. The money was not a problem. I had never done anything like this before, but that somehow made it even easier.

'Well, if you're sure then you've got me out of a fix.'

On the way back to the city he seemed lighter, but we soon ran out of conversation. He dropped me close to home and I promised I would call around in a hour or two with the cheque. I thought he might say I could leave it until the next day, but he did not. When I got in the door I telephoned Pablo immediately. He answered the phone. I told him what I had done. I told him I wanted him to see it. He sounded less than enthusiastic, as though he had been sleeping and did not want to be disturbed. We arranged to meet the next evening so that he could come and look at it. I rang Susan and left a message on her answering machine to say that I had taken it. I wondered where she was and why she was not answering the phone.

I found one towel that I wanted to take with me. I would buy new towels the next day. I carefully selected some clothes which I thought would be suitable. I took the supply of condoms and cream. My passport and some papers I would need. My bank book. A toothbrush, toothpaste, shampoo, soap, a razor, shaving-cream. Some cassettes and a cassette player. A few books: a volume of Neruda with a poem I had almost learned by heart when I was a student and some paperback novels. I filled a briefcase and a bag. I carried a few suits over my arm. I turned off the light and walked back down the stairs and out into the street. It was almost dark now. I felt as though I had come back from the dead, or from years away, and was roaming these streets with new eyes. I bought all the Sunday newspapers and some English-language papers at the kiosk on the corner. I took a taxi to Evanson's apartment building and wrote the cheque before I rang the bell. When the buzzer sounded I went upstairs on the lift. I handed him the cheque for two months' rent, explained that I had the taxi waiting below and then quickly left.

I directed the taxi driver to the marina. With the keys in my pocket I enjoyed pretending that this was my normal house, where I lived. When he dropped me off, I paid him and took my luggage, and left it in the hall. I went to the telephone in the living room and rang Susan's number again. This time she was there. I told her what I had done.

'It takes you years to make the smallest decision. You are the most cautious person we know. How did you do it? What happened?'

It had never occurred to me before that I was cautious.

'You must come and see it,' I said. 'Maybe I will learn how to cook.'

'That can be your next project. Are you really going to live there?'

'I paid him two months' rent.'

The heating, John Evanson had explained, was under the floors. He showed me the switch where I could turn it on, and a separate switch for the hot water. He had left the curtains down. Some of the lights were in the floor, you could turn the light up or down in the living room. I had a bath and shaved and changed into new clothes. I turned on the television and watched the news, and then I lay on the sofa and read the newspapers. I would have trouble getting to work from here, and getting to the supermarket. I realized that I would have to buy a car and learn to drive. I took out the yellow pages and looked through the entries for driving schools. I wondered if I would need a licence to take driving lessons. I thought that I would get my secretary to investigate all of this in the morning. I lay on the sofa and smiled to myself about the future. I went upstairs and made the bed; it struck me that I had forgotten to take a clock from the apartment. I would have to go back there the next day. I thought about it now, vacant and dark, all my things, all my mother's furniture, some objects which must have belonged to my father, lying there. I imagined them both in the apartment, opening the door together, floating freely in the empty air. I was away from them. I was looking forward to waking up in the morning in my new house. I could not believe what I had done.

I felt elated. I felt that I had achieved something, but it had been touch-and-go all along, a matter of nerves and taking chances, knowing when to make each fragile move. I lay in bed and realized that I would be able to offer Pablo a decent excuse to leave home: this house was too big for one person, he could tell his parents that the rent was low, it was too great an opportunity to miss. I imagined his mother coming here, fussing around the house, opening cabinets and turning on switches while her husband sat uneasily in the white light of downstairs longing to get back to the overdecorated, overfurnished familiarity of his own house in the suburbs.

*

IN THE MORNING I called a cab and I discovered the traffic jams of Buenos Aires for the first time. The driver was gruff. I do not think that he had slept enough. I watched the meter rise in regular clicks. I felt low, and I knew that I had done too much too quickly, and now I was facing the real world on a bleak Monday morning with the traffic stuck. I had expected everything to improve, but now I was tired and uneasy. I watched for the lights changing from red to green, and when they changed nothing moved, just a few cars nudged forward, and they changed back to red again, and the meter clicked once more. I realized that in future I would have to leave for work much earlier, or later. I thought of the short walk between my old apartment and the office, and I thought that maybe I would sleep there some nights when I needed to be in the city in the morning.

I made plans to begin driving lessons and I thought about things I would need to buy. I postponed any further thoughts about the traffic and the old apartment. I sat back and relaxed. I had returned to the real world.

That evening Pablo collected me at the office and drove me out to the new house. He was amused. He said he thought that the curtains were the best thing about the house, but he liked the bedroom as well and then he said that he liked the bathroom too, and the living room, and the small study and the stairs. I guess I like all of it, he said.

I did not tell him that I had high hopes that he would move in. I told him that I had put champagne in the fridge while he was wandering around upstairs, that I had bought these incredibly expensive white towels in the city and two white dressing gowns, one for him and one for me, and I thought, I said, that maybe we should try out the bath. That's all you ever think about, he said, sex. He smiled. You are right, I said. That is all I ever think about, sex and towels and hot water. I added that I hoped it was okay with him. And he said that it was, it was fine with him, it was all he ever thought about too. He loosened the curtains down over the glass, we stripped in the big front bedroom, I moved into the bathroom ahead of him and turned on the taps in the bath. Then I went down-stairs and found the new towels and the bathrobes I had bought that day. By the time I came back the room was filled with steam and he was already sitting in the water. I closed the door and got into the bath. He moved his legs apart to make room for me. I leaned my back against his stomach and my head against his shoulder. His dick was hard. I reached forward and found the soap. I held it in the water until it was slippery and I handed it to him and he began to soap my chest.

*

I TOLD HIS FATHER about the house, how I needed a lodger and a car. He sold me Señora Canetto's Fiat, which was five years old, he bought her a new one, and he said that either Jorge or Pablo would be able to give me driving lessons. He had taught both of them, he said, and they were very patient. He suggested that Pablo would be interested in finding lodgings away from home; he felt that he was restless, he said, but his mother would be very upset if he moved, so perhaps he should stay at home, or maybe he should go. He spoke with such confidence and security that I was sure he knew everything about us, that he was trying to help us. I wished we were not speaking on the telephone, I almost asked him if I could see him face to face to talk about this. He said he would mention it to Pablo, and in the meantime I was to get my papers in order and come out to the house for my first driving lesson.

Pablo was almost frightened when I told him what his father had said. All that evening he remained preoccupied and distant. He wished I did not know his father, he said. I must be careful. Maybe his father knew about us, he said, but only in some deep and unconscious part of himself. He softened when he went to bed. He held me that night as he did sometimes, clinging to me, his arms tight around me, gasping for breath when I touched his dick, as though this excitement were too much for him.

He moved in with me, gradually taking most of his belongings from his parents' house. His mother told him several times that his room would always be there for him, that everything would be ready for him if he wanted to come back. He was still her son. Jorge did not speak to me much, and avoided being alone with me when we met at Susan and Donald's.

Pablo and I got up early in the morning and tried to be on the road into the city before eight o'clock. I loved that sense of normality which began then in our lives, going to bed early together, worrying about shopping or washing clothes or paying bills. I thought a few times of the pleasure it would give me if I were pregnant or if a child that was half mine were growing inside him. I understood something of the world around us, what made people happy, which I had not known before. I loved everything about him, his underwear, his socks, his silences. I felt that he suffered in some strange, withdrawn way which I could not fathom and could not share. Sometimes I felt that I was able to comfort him; mostly in the dark in bed, but sometimes in the evening when we were tired, I sensed some terrible hurt or wound or fear in him. I tried to let him know that I was vulnerable too in ways I did not know and could not express and I would need his help to get through.

I loved driving from the moment I began. It was like being an adult for the first time. Within a few weeks I had mastered the gears and the steering. Pablo was funny and good-humoured and helpful. He was as patient as his father said he would be. He seemed to enjoy working with his father, even though he was paid less than I thought he deserved, and less than Jorge was paid.

At weekends cars were parked all around our house as sailors came to use the marinas and day trippers came out from the city. We watched people taking supplies from cars down to boats; they looked so happy that I said to Pablo we should buy a boat, or at least learn to sail. He laughed and said that I was always making plans and wanting new things to happen. First, a house, then a live-in boyfriend, then a car, and now a boat. I must slow down, he said, stop wanting more, enjoy what I had. He let the curtains fall so that none of the sailors or day tourists could see us, and we made love on the living room floor.

*

WHEN THE SUMMER CAME we decorated the patio at the back of the house with plants and garden chairs and a beautiful wooden table; we hung two hammocks between the wall of the house and two wooden stakes which we had specially made; and I gave up my dream of learning how to sail. We built a barbecue. I often came home early from work and sat in the sun, and then drove to a bus stop about a kilometre towards the city and sat in the car waiting for Pablo. I was never late; I would watch for the bus to arrive and examine each passenger until Pablo appeared. He would wave and smile as he walked towards the car. Often we drove to a swimming pool and went for a swim; he was a strong and fearless swimmer.

We saw his parents a few times. When his mother first came to the house, she behaved like a jealous lover who had lost her loved one to a beautiful building. She ignored the house. She sat in the living room as though she came here every day. She looked at her handbag and smiled in a false, forced sort of way. Señor Canetto, on the other hand, seemed much looser and more good-humoured than I had ever seen him before. I told Pablo later that his father had flirted with me, and it was almost true. He treated me like an equal, an old friend, a business associate of long standing, and he accepted the invitation to go upstairs and look around. We had carefully made a second bedroom look as though Pablo slept in it every night. We walked around together. He said that he loved the house, it was a real find, and he thought that it was better for Pablo to live here rather than at home. He had lived at home until he was married, he said, and he always wished that he had spent a few years living like this, hanging around with friends, being independent and accountable to no one.

Pablo told me that two friends of his from California wanted to visit him. He had put them off before because he did not think they would get on with his parents, but now he wanted to write to them to say that they could come and stay here. I said that it was fine; I was curious about them. He said that they had been his best friends and he wanted to see them, but it was hard to imagine them anywhere in the world except California. I asked him what they did for a living, and he said that he had hoped I was not going to ask that. He told me to guess. They're in the movies, I said. No, he shook his head. They're swimming instructors. No, he shook his head again. They're in the oil business. No, he laughed, they're definitely not. They work for their fathers, I suggested. No, he said, only suckers do that. I gave up. I told him he had to tell me. They run a flower shop, he said. What's the problem with that, I asked. He smiled: it's just a bit of a cliché, two gay men running a flower shop, but that's what they do. I said I wished that gay men in Buenos Aires ran flower shops. Instead, they got married or worked for their fathers or were in the oil business. The Californians think that Argentinian men are the best-looking men in the world, he said. Pure meat. Tell them, I said, that we think the same about Californian men. Do they know about us living together, I asked. Of course they do, he said. That's good, I said, so we won't have to pretend that we sleep in separate rooms. He laughed. No, he said, we'll have witnesses.

Two weeks later, we stood in the airport waiting for them. I knew the road to the airport well now, I knew the times of the flights from all parts of North America, I knew how likely they were to be delayed. I knew how long it took between the plane landing and the passenger appearing at the arrival gates. But as I stood waiting with Pablo I felt I had not been here before, or a stiffer and more distant part of me had been here. Everything seemed different. I said this to Pablo, who smiled and replied that once I got out of my suit and tie and formal shoes, I changed completely and became a human being. I said that I hoped no one from the World Bank or the International Monetary Fund or the oil industry was on the plane with his friends from the flower shop.

They did not come through with the rest of the passengers. I was puzzled by this because if they had missed the flight they would have had plenty of time to phone us and let us know. I was sure that there was no point in going to the information desk to enquire. They would tell us nothing. Pablo was becoming worried.

'Maybe their bags have not come through,' I said.

'No, it could be something else.'

'What could it be?'

'Mart has AIDS. That's what it could be. I think he's really sick.'

I stood with him in front of the arrivals gate. Half an hour had gone by since the last passengers had come through the arrivals gate. I knew it was impossible that there would be other passengers inside. If their bags had not arrived then their names and addresses and details would have been taken, they would go through passport and customs control and have their luggage sent on later.

Neither of us spoke. We stood there and waited; I saw Pablo's two friends before he did. They both had trolleys and they moved very slowly.

'Are you all right?' I heard Pablo shouting.

'No, we're not all right,' one of them said. He had a strange, thin face and was leaning heavily on his trolley. The other man was taller, and older than I had expected, with cropped fair hair and a moustache. He was pale. They looked at us blankly. There were no greetings or embraces.

'This is Jack,' Pablo said, pointing to the older one, 'and this is Mart,' pointing to the one leaning on the trolley. I shook hands with them. Still they did not smile.

'I think we should go to the airline desk', Jack said, 'and maybe see if we could get the next flight out of here.'

'What's the problem?' I asked.

'I don't think they like sick men here,' Jack said. 'They went through all Mart's pills and his drugs. They realized what he has. I think they wanted to refuse us permission to come into Argentina. They treated us like we were scum. They tried to contact someone, and they left us sitting there. They wanted to confiscate the pills, have them checked out. One of them was very aggressive.'

'Why don't we get in the car and go home and talk about it there?' Pablo asked.

'There's another problem,' Jack said. 'Mart is running a temperature. It went down yesterday, but he's getting fevers, and he was sick on the plane. I think maybe we made the wrong decision about getting on the flight.'

Mart still leaned on the trolley. He looked at the floor.

'I think I'm going to need to see a doctor,' he said.

'Let's think about getting a flight later on when we're home,' Pablo said. 'And let's try to find a doctor from home. There's no point in staying here.'

Mart smiled and shook his head and looked at the floor.

'It's good to see you,' he said and grinned at Pablo. 'Give me a hug.' His skin was tight on his face.

'We're sorry for getting you into this,' Jack said.

'That's what we're here for,' Pablo replied.

As we drove towards the city Mart talked about his illness. Most of the words were new to me, but Pablo seemed to understand what Mart was talking about. He had been in hospital and home again and then in hospital.

'But I feel better just now in this car,' he said. 'I like your boyfriend.'

'I was waiting for it,' Pablo said. 'I was wondering when you would begin.'

'I mean he's cute. Do you think he's cute, Jack?'

'Yes, I do,' his voice was deadpan. He spoke as though he had considered the matter for some time. I could see Jack's face in the rear-view mirror, he was smiling.

'He doesn't look very Argentinian. We were hoping he would look Argentinian. But he's cute. Jack thinks he's cute. I think he's cute.'

'You're about to cross the line,' Pablo said.

'And he's quiet. I like that,' Mart went on.

They were surprised when they saw the house.

'Is this really where you live?' Mart asked. He put his hands to his face. 'Golly,' he said. Pablo and Jack took the luggage from the boot. I began to tell Mart the story of how I came to rent the house, but he was not listening.

'This could be wonderful,' he said. 'Jack, come and see the living room. This place really has potential.'

Jack came into the room and held Mart from behind and swung him around playfully. I realized that anyone could see them from outside and I thought of going upstairs and lowering the curtains. But I stood there watching. I had not spoken much since they arrived.

'You really could do a lot with this place,' Mart said. 'It is a most beautiful situation.'

'I like it as it is,' I said.

'You should see the place they have in San Francisco,' Pablo said. 'There's nothing left to chance.'

'Well, I think it's important where you live,' Mart said. 'Now, I am going to lie down here. I am the patient. I want Jack to unpack. I need water, pills, a pillow and maybe a thermometer. I like the view, but I could do with some colour on the walls, and I would change the light fittings. And I probably need a doctor too. I need Jack to call my hospital and ask them who looks after boys like me in this city.'

'I'll do everything you want,' Jack said. 'I am the guy who stuck with his boyfriend through thick and thin.'

'You want thick and thin? He's lying just here,' Mart moved into an obscene pose. I had to remind myself that I did not care who saw him through the window.

They spoke some of the time in a sort of movie-talk, which always made Pablo laugh, and then they moved back into normal speech without any warning. When Mart did not speak, when he lay back with his eyes closed, for example, he looked really sick. I wondered how long he had to live. Pablo must have known how sick he was; I was upset that he had not told me. They intended to stay for a fortnight. I had thought they would go on excursions, spend some time at the pool, but it looked now as though they would stay here.

'You must feel free to phone the hospital,' I said to Jack in the kitchen. He was taking some drugs from an icebox which they had carried with them and putting them in the fridge. He was wearing jeans and a black T-shirt and as he turned to speak he looked much less pale and frightened than he had when he arrived at the airport.

'How do you think Mart is now?' I asked.

'We were so worried about the fever and the vomiting that we put no thought into how we would handle the customs and the police. It was weird. I think we're still going to have to find a doctor.'

He went upstairs and phoned Mart's hospital in San Francisco. I was in the kitchen when he came back down.

'I think we're in luck, if you can use the word luck about what's going on. There's an American doctor doing research here, he used to be attached to the laboratory in the hospital Mart goes to. I have two numbers for him, a home number and a work number. The doctor I spoke to knows him and says that he'd be happy enough to see Mart and check him out. He's going to phone him first. His name is Cawley.'

Mart had fallen asleep on the sofa in the living room. Pablo had put a blanket over him. He put his fingers to his lips when we came in. Jack put his hand on Mart's forehead.

'I think he's a bit cooler,' he whispered. The three of us went out, closing the door soundlessly behind us.

When I phoned the work number Jack had been given I got an answer immediately.

'Can I help you?' the voice spoke in English. I said that I was looking for Doctor Cawley. As soon as I used Jack's name he said that he was expecting my call, he had just received a call from the doctor in San Francisco. He seemed easygoing, ready to be helpful.

'It's a matter of how we do this,' he said. 'I don't have a clinic here yet, so he would have to come to my office, and this would be slightly irregular, but I think we can manage it. And I think that I should see him as soon as I can, so if he could arrive here within the next two hours, then I'll still be here.' He gave me the address, it was a side entrance to the hospital which fronted onto the street.

'He sounds like a nice guy,' I said when I went back downstairs and found Pablo and Jack drinking beers out on the patio.

'Yeah, they all get like that,' Jack said, as though what I had said had irritated him. 'They know what's in store for you, so they keep smiling and making polite, friendly noises at you. They're going to watch you going blind, they're going to have to tell you the news that your brain seems to be diseased, or you've got skin cancer, or you'd better tell your parents real soon. So they smile at you. When I meet an AIDS doctor who's rude, I'll know this plague is over.'

It struck me from the bitterness in Jack's voice that he was sick too, but I saw no signs of illness.

'That is my sermon for today, dear children, now you can all go,' he said in a drawl. He sipped his beer from the bottle.

Pablo took Mart to the doctor. Jack and I promised to make dinner. We sat on the patio drinking beer.

'How long has Mart left to live?' I asked him.

'You can never say. It could be a few days, it could be a year, even two years, but that would be stretching it, I think. Even if a cure came, I don't think it would make any difference, his immune system has been destroyed.'

'That's terrible, it's unbelievable,' I said.

'It's happening to thousands and thousands of people. All we can hope for is that things are easy, that he doesn't go blind in his good eye and that he manages to keep his memory and his mind.'

'He must be devastated,' I said.

'He was at first, but now he's used to it, most of the time he can handle it fine. He's got a lot of strength inside him. I never knew that before all this happened.'

'How long have you been together?'

'Twelve years. We've lost our business, paying for doctors and drugs. We still run the shop, but we don't own it any more. We've lost everything, I suppose, but sometimes it feels okay. When he comes back, if there's no real problem, we'll have a nice evening.'

We opened fresh bottles of beer and sat there quietly as hints of night came down. I felt like a child listening to an adult talk. I was surprised at how calm and resigned Jack seemed, as though what was happening to Mart, and perhaps to him as well, were an essential part of life, something all adults understood. There were other things I wanted to ask him – when did he know that he was gay? when did he tell his parents? when did he meet Pablo? – but I felt that these questions were too basic and personal. I went into the kitchen to make dinner. He began to set the table on the patio. I watched him as he laid out everything perfectly. I made a salad and a salad dressing and put the steaks on the barbecue.

'Dementia is happening a bit less than it used to,' Jack said as we stretched out on the patio again, 'but that's always the worst fear if you've been with someone for a long time, you end up taking care of a man who doesn't know you, who can't remember what he said to you just now. Pablo went through it with Frank. Frank had this terrible anger, I don't know where it came from, he had been such a calm, placid guy. Now he was shouting all of the time, he was incontinent and almost blind and covered in Ks and yet he wouldn't die. He went on and on, and Pablo would let no one else look after him. Pablo was amazing.'

I listened and said nothing. There was no point in saying that I did not know who Frank was, that I did not know that Pablo had had a lover who had died of AIDS. In a few seconds on that patio as we waited for Mart and Pablo to return from the hospital, a whole new explanation for things came into my mind. It seemed odd, if Pablo did not want me to know about what happened before he left California, that he had not asked Jack and Mart to say nothing about Frank. Maybe he did want me to know, but he could not find a way of telling me himself. Maybe he had just decided not to think about it. This would be more like him, but since I was suddenly unsure that I knew him at all, I could not say. I decided not to let Jack know that all this was news to me.

'I think meeting you was really good for Pablo,' Jack said. 'I think he felt that he would never be able to have another relationship. We thought he was crazy to come back here, but maybe it was for the best. I'm glad we came down, if only it was to see that he's all right. I just hope that Mart doesn't have to be flown out of here in a coffin.'

I wondered what Frank looked like. I imagined someone blond and sun-tanned and skinny. I pictured his hairless torso, his curly hair, his white teeth. I tried to picture him sick, his body emaciated, his skin dry and drawn, but I could not. I could only see him as beautiful. I knew too that nothing in Pablo's background had prepared him for caring for a lover who was dying; his parents had trained him to be a pillar of society in certain suburbs of Buenos Aires, to marry, to look after a business, to have children, to let his wife take care of them, to maintain a steely distance from the world. I wondered if he was sick. I tried to think about medicines he had been taking but I could think of nothing. I believed that everything we had done together had been safe, but nonetheless I felt afraid.

I was at the door looking out for them when they came back. I had been down to the water's edge, I had stared out at the huge expanse of calm that was the bay, I had watched the light fading. I opened the passenger door of the car and helped Mart out.

'What did he say?' I asked.

'He drew blood, and thinks I might have an infected line, but he won't know for certain until tomorrow. He's a nice guy. He took a real shine to Pablo, but I think he's straight.'

Mart walked into the living room and lay down on the sofa.

'He says everyone has to be real good to me, do everything I say.'

When Jack came into the room he jumped on top of Mart and began to lick his face.

'Call him off,' Mart shrieked, 'this man is an animal.'

Jack then lay on his side, quietly holding him, making sure he did not fall off the edge of the sofa.

'This is not the sort of treatment Doctor Cawley had in mind. He said I needed peace and quiet, no hunks trying to jump on me. Those days are over, he said.' He put his hands to his face and closed his eyes.

'He was really cute, even Pablo thought that he was cute, but he still had that dry doctor look which sort of put me off. I really wanted to toss his hair, but I held back. Usually, I sit there wishing the doctor was sick and I was fine, but today it was fifty-fifty. I wanted both of us to be fine.'

'What did you think of him, Pablo?' Jack asked. His tone was serious, as though he were asking about Mart's illness.

'I wanted to toss his hair too,' Pablo said.

'Maybe we should invite him out for a hair-tossing session,' Jack said.

We had dinner, and then Mart said he wanted to go to bed.

He took some drugs from the fridge and went upstairs. Jack did the washing-up, while Pablo and I sat at the table drinking wine.

'Maybe we'll go into the city tomorrow if Mart is okay,' Jack said. 'Take a look around, check out the talent.'

'I'll drive you in,' I said. 'You're probably best to take a taxi back.'

'Mart doesn't have to go to the hospital. He just has to phone,' Pablo said.

When Jack went to bed Pablo poured another glass of wine for each of us.

'I didn't know that you had a lover in San Francisco who died of AIDS,' I said.

'Jack told you?'

'Yeah, Jack told me.'

'I meant to ask him not to, and then I realized I would have to explain to him why, and I wasn't sure why. Anyway, I didn't get much chance to see him alone. I thought he might talk about it while I was out.'

'You have to tell me things. You can't let me find out things casually like that.'

'I want to pretend that it never happened. I want to pretend that we separated amicably and he went to live in New York or Seattle. I know that's stupid.'

'Let's go to bed,' I said.

We put our glasses in the sink and left the empty bottle on the kitchen table. As we went quietly up the stairs we could hear Mart and Jack talking in their bedroom. We stripped and got into bed and turned off the light. We did not go to the toilet or brush our teeth.

'So tell me about it,' I reached out and held his hand.

'Tell you what?'

'Everything. How you met. Everything.'

'I met him on a gay beach on a summer Sunday. I was wading back in and he was swimming out and we both turned to look at each other, and I swam back out. It was like a moment from a gay porn movie. I was a much stronger swimmer than he was. We were both with friends, but neither of us had a lover. We messed around in the water, and then he wanted me to come and meet his friends but I didn't want to do that, and I didn't want to introduce him to my friends, so we met that evening in a bar in the Castro. I had only ever done casual stuff before. I had never washed and shaved and dressed up so carefully before meeting anyone before. He looked even better with clothes on. He was half-Mexican. And that was how it started, it was that night. He did real estate and he made a lot of money. I looked at him and I trusted him and liked him.' He paused. 'Do you want me to talk about him?'

'Yes, I do.'

'It's very hard to talk about him. I keep feeling that I'm going to cry. He took everything easy. He could work on a few hours' sleep. I think we planned to stay together for ever. I moved in with him, and it was he who organized my papers and my passport. Eventually, I went to work for him. He was great at it. He loved to make a deal. If he showed you around an apartment, you would look at him rather than the apartment, and believe everything he said and end up buying it. Everybody loved him, people always wanted him to come to dinner, to come away for the weekend. But most of the time in the middle of the week we would go straight home after work and see no one except each other. It's a strange thing, but a lot of men were like him just then, a lot of gay men, they worked hard, they had a lot of money, they enjoyed life, they had a lover and good friends. And then it all changed, it all changed.'

As he spoke I could hear the tears in his voice. I held him close to me as he began to cry.

'Billy, the guy at the reception desk, got sick. He was the first we knew, we had heard about other people, and we had read the newspapers. But he started turning up for work looking wretched, and taking time off. Frank thought he was on drugs and was going to fire him. And then he realized what it was. I remember him coming into my office saying 'Billy's got AIDS.' The poor guy was crying in Frank's office. We took him home. Frank kept him on the payroll and paid his medical bills, but he deteriorated really fast, he died of pneumonia. We couldn't believe it had happened. We went to the funeral and met his family. And then it happened all around us. You know the story, everybody knows the story. And because AIDS was all so public, so much a part of the news, we felt that it belonged out there somewhere. The more we read about it, and – I know this sounds strange – the more people we knew who were infected and dying, the less we believed it could have anything to do with us. We were under no illusions about it: if it got you, you were gone. But we thought that it had passed us by – that we had been together for two or three years, and this meant we had missed all those opportunities to become infected.

'I noticed Frank's weight going down, but he was trying to lose weight anyway. I noticed him not finishing his meals. And I knew at some stage, months before any diagnosis, that he had a problem. And I suppose he knew too. And we carried on. I hoped that he would put off going to a doctor for as long as possible. We never talked about it. He must have known that I knew. We would even speculate about friends who we thought might be sick. But Frank was sick. He knew that if there was an important piece of business someone else should go. He worked from his desk. He took over the writing side of things, the mailing lists and the legal stuff. I still thought that he might go to a doctor and be told that it was something else. I let myself imagine that it was something else.

'One day he shouted at one of the reps who had failed to make a deal. I thought he was wrong and I phoned his office from mine in the afternoon to say that he should apologize, that he had no right to be so short-tempered. He asked me if I was busy and I said that I had work to do but if he wanted to talk I was here. He came into my office and shut the door and told me that he had taken the test. He would get the results after work. I said that I would go there with him, and I was sure there was no problem. He looked awful, and I suppose I knew that he was going to die. We drove to this doctor who lived close to us. He said he would keep his office open and see us as his last patients. We sat in the waiting room for a while and then the doctor summoned us in. I knew by his attitude, but I still thought it might be an ulcer or even cancer. "I'm afraid I have bad news." I remember him saying that. And then "I'm afraid it's positive." Frank started to cry and rock back and forth. He said "Tell me it isn't" over and over. At the time people still believed that only a percentage of those who were positive would go on to get full-blown AIDS, but the doctor said that he probably had an AIDS-related illness in his stomach, and he would need to go into the hospital for tests. And I sat there watching this, wondering how we were going to go home with this information.

'Frank asked the doctor how long he had to live. The doctor said he could not say, but Frank insisted on some prognosis. The doctor said he had also drawn blood for a full blood count test, including a CD4 count – at the time we did not know what this was – and that was low, it suggested that Frank did not have much time. "How long?" he asked again. The doctor said it was always hard to judge, and it depended on the person, but he thought a year, maybe two. Frank said nothing. He asked no more questions, even though the doctor had a counsellor who was ready to come over. He said he wanted to go home. The doctor said he would make an appointment at the hospital for him, he hoped there would be a bed free in the next couple of days, and Frank nodded and shook the doctor's hand, and we drove home once more in silence. I told him that

I would stay with him, but he was locked up in his own mind all that night and for days and nights afterwards. He did not want me to come too close to him, he did not want me to contact his family who lived in New Mexico. He was on his own in a way which I did not believe it was possible for anyone to be. He would have given anything, I think, to have lived. He would have given the disease to me or to anyone, he would have paid any money, or moved anywhere, or promised anything for this not to happen.

'I drove him to the hospital and I helped him check in: somehow his name and his date of birth and his insurance number all seemed part of his death. I shared some of what he went through, but it was only a fraction of what he suffered. He could not believe that he was going to die. He kept saying that he had moments when he was sure that this was something he had imagined. He dreaded getting into bed in the AIDS ward, everybody looking at him, knowing that he was doomed. I saw him twice a day. I ran the business. And then he came home and he was well for a while. The next year was a nightmare that you could never wake up from. It was like he was being tortured and punished, blow after blow coming down with nothing at the end except extinction.'

'Richard, can you hold me?' Pablo leaned towards me and put his arms around me. I had never felt so close to him. 'I can't tell you any more just now,' he said. 'Will you hold me, please, and maybe we can sleep? I can't tell the rest. Just let's say he died and I came back here.'

'I'm glad I know all of this. I'm glad you told me.'

He began to cry uncontrollably. I knew that Jack and Mart could hear him in the next room. I held him. I patted his head as though he were a child. I felt as I lay beside him that I should have guessed all this, or he should have told me before.

★

I dropped Jack and Mart in the city centre in the morning and left Pablo outside his father's office.

'Why don't you invite Jack and Mart out to your parents' house?' I asked. 'It would give your parents something to think about, and the boys would enjoy the swimming pool. They would probably love your mother.'

Pablo shook his head and knitted his brow and looked at me. He turned and got out of the car.

There was a message to ring a contact in the Ministry for the Economy as soon as I came in. He told me when I phoned him that a few serious investors from the United States were on their way to Buenos Aires and would arrive around lunchtime, then they were going to catch a flight to Comodoro Rivadavia, the centre of the oil industry, and take a look around, have a few meetings and be generally reassured that they were not going to waste their money. The government had had plans to look after them, but the plans had fallen through. He asked me if I would take care of them, he was sorry for the short notice, and he was ringing on the off chance that I was free. I said I would, as long as it was made clear that I was operating from an outside agency and not on behalf of the government. I might want to work for these guys in the future. He said that was fine: the government would pay the bill, but I could remain independent. A few years ago, he said, such an idea would have been high treason, but now everything was changing. I said that I would take him to lunch when I came back and tell him everything that happened. He gave me the names and flight numbers and the details of arrangements which had already been made. I drove home, to collect some clean clothes and let Pablo know that I would be away for a few days, and then I phoned a taxi to take me to the airport. As I waited, I looked into Jack and Mart's bedroom to make sure they were not there. I saw the array of Mart's pills on the bedside table, plastic bottles of all different sizes and colours, maybe fifteen or twenty of them. I stood at the door and looked at them for a while, wondering what it would be like to be about to die, to know that you could go at any time and had no chance of surviving.

I met the investors in the airport and travelled south with them and stayed in the same hotel. I remained three days down there, translating and going to meetings.

On the second night I had a quiet dinner with the investors and I learned something I did not know before. One of the Americans spelled it out for me: the privatization was going to be smooth and successful, there would be not a whiff of scandal surrounding it, everybody would be happy at the end of the day, both the government and the foreign investors. These men seemed to view Argentina as a normal country, like France or Germany, they were not surprised or overwhelmed by what was happening. It was something I had always believed impossible, I had always thought that the idea of selling off the oil industry would be dropped, or would be a fiasco, that no one would take it seriously, that everybody was operating at cross-purposes. But now, just a year before the event, according to the three men I had dinner with, everything was in place, and nothing could go wrong. You can do business with Argentina, one of them told me.

I had drunk too much coffee after dinner and I stayed awake thinking about the idea. I had presumed that when a policy became public in Argentina you automatically knew that the opposite, or something close to the opposite, would happen. You learned to read every public statement placing a negative in the sentences which did not have one, and deleting the negative from the sentences which did. Everything was bluster and high-flown rhetoric, and nothing meant anything. The greatness of Argentina meant the nothingness of Argentina. For wealth, read poverty. For the future, read the past. For privatization, read corruption and economic short-sightedness.

It had never occurred to me that this could change, and I realized, in spite of all the meetings I had attended in the past year or two, all the faxes and newspaper articles and press releases, that something new was happening in Argentina and I had not noticed it. My mind was so fixed on the past, on the dictatorship and the war and the ridiculous figure of Menem, that I had missed something that I was myself part of. I realized that since I had met Pablo, I had not seen enough of Susan or Donald, and I had not been discussing what was going on in Argentina. I thought that I should see more of them when I went back to the city, and see my contacts in the various ministries to make sure that I was not deluding myself, to make sure that things had changed.

In the morning as I was paying for my phone calls at the reception desk I saw Federico Arenas. I felt afraid. He had often come into my mind, but I had not been in touch with him since the day I handed him the money. He walked over and put his arm around me and asked me to come and have coffee with him. I told him I had a flight to catch. Catch the next one, he said. It sounded like a threat.

Things were different now, he said, as we sat at a table in the room where the staff were cleaning up after breakfast. You have to work for a living, he said. Every move you make is watched, everything is countersigned. It's a new country. He asked me about work, and I told him what I had been doing. I think, he said, that the Europeans will invest more than the Americans in the privatization. I nodded. He moved his face close to mine across the table and whispered that I had missed out on a few sensational deals, a few real aces. I couldn't work with you, he said. You're the wrong type, ready to go to pieces. You have no nerve. But it's all over, there'll be no more deals like that again, big or small.

I wanted to ask him what the chances were now of our being discovered, but I thought the question would make him laugh. I sat with him for as long as I thought was necessary. He slapped me on the back as we said goodbye in the lobby.

*

WHEN I GOT HOME, Mart was in bed. His line was not infected, he said, nothing had come up in the blood tests, the vomiting had stopped, but he was still feverish and tired. Jack had met a couple at the marina who had invited him out on their boat. It was typical of him, Mart said, to disappear like that, just when things were rough. When he saw that I was taking this seriously, he sat up and said that he was joking. This was Jack's holiday too, he said, and he was glad that he had ingratiated himself with a couple at the marina. His pills still stood in rows on the bedside table. I asked him how he knew which ones to take.

'They're our children,' he said. 'We have no favourites. We brought them all into the world and we love them equally. They might look the same to you, but they are all fully formed individuals to us.'

He began to go through all the names of the pills and what they were for and when he began taking them and how much they cost. Then he gave each of them real names, most of them were the names of film stars.

'These,' he grabbed a case of capsules and shook them, 'are Woody Allen.'

He laughed so much that he lay back on the pillow exhausted. He coughed and spluttered and seemed to be about to get sick, but he closed his eyes and stayed still. I thought that he was dying and I wondered whether I should call downstairs and get Pablo. I held his hand. He clung to me, breathing heavily. And then he relaxed and opened his eyes and smiled.

'You should see me on a good day,' he said.

He began to get better. When he went to see the doctor again, I drove him there and sat in the car and waited for him at the side entrance to the hospital. After less than a half-hour the doctor came to the door with him. They were both smiling. The doctor was much younger than I had expected. He could only have been in his late twenties or early thirties; he seemed stunningly fresh-faced and good-looking. He did not look like someone who dealt every day with death or disease. His skin and hair were shiny with health. He smiled at me when I got out of the car, and he helped Mart into the passenger seat, smiling all the time. I shook his hand and thanked him.

'I like seeing patients,' he said. I supposed he meant that seeing patients was better than rats and mice and test tubes in laboratories, but as he said it, it sounded almost callous. I knew that he did not mean to sound like that; he wanted to sound warm and obliging. I thanked him again and got into the car. We waved to him as I drove off.

I took a day off work and drove Mart and Jack to an estancia with a swimming pool where Jack and I could swim and Mart could lie under an umbrella. I was surprised at how strong and bronzed Jack looked when he was in his bathing togs. I almost fancied him as he rubbed suntan oil on my back. I was careful when he went into the water not to get too close to him, but I felt that he knew the rules better than I did.

I wanted to talk more to Pablo about Frank, but he did not want to. I could imagine the rest, he said. Or he would tell me some other time, but there were things that even Mart and Jack did not know, that nobody knew, that he was not sure he would ever be able to tell.

'I don't believe in God or the devil or evil,' Pablo said, 'but in those days, it was hard not to feel that something unnatural had taken hold of his body.'

'There's something I've wanted to ask you,' I said. 'I think I have to ask you if you have been tested.'

He gripped me and started to whisper.

'I didn't take the test. Frank told me not to. I thought I would and then I didn't. Maybe I should.' He was silent for a moment.

'I inherited the agency, and sold it. The money is still in a bank account there. Frankie left his house and what money was in the bank to his family. I was thinking recently, when I heard you talking with my father, of investing my money in oil shares.' He kissed me. 'I love you,' he said. 'I came back here. I met you within a few weeks of coming back. I have never taken the test. I think I'm okay. Have you taken the test?'

'No,' I said.

'I think we've been careful, haven't we?'

'Yes.'

'I love you,' he said, 'and I need you more now that I've told you. But there are some things that happened at the end I haven't told you. Maybe I will tell you some time.'

★

ON JACK AND MART'S last night in Argentina, a Saturday night, we went to an old-fashioned steak restaurant in the city centre. Pablo told them the story of my old apartment, how I still paid the rent on it, but had abandoned it, and never went there.

'It's a case of denial,' Jack said. 'It's a textbook case, I'm not sure what book, but all I know is that any shrink would make you feel you've got to give it up, let someone else have it.'

'Could we talk about someone else, please?' I asked.

'You mean, could we play get the guest rather than hump the host?' Jack asked.

'Something like that.'

The main waiter at our table who looked Paraguayan flirted with us and smiled at us every time he passed.

'Ask him if he's married,' Jack said. 'Tell him I have the hots for him.'

When he took our dessert order, Pablo asked him if he was married. He told us that he had two children. A few moments later he returned with a photograph of a small-faced smiling wife and two young girls.

'It's such a waste, a guy like that being married,' Jack said. Each time the waiter walked by the table he smiled at us more and more.

'I think he's queer,' Mart said. 'I think that's why he's smiling.'

'Is there anywhere we could go?' Mart asked. 'A gay bar where we wouldn't get beaten up?'

'And guys like our waiter could be standing against the wall?' Jack added.

'There's one bar,' I said. 'I haven't been there for a long time, but everyone is frightened. They stare straight ahead as though someone is going to tell everyone their big secret.'

'There are two bathhouses,' Pablo added.

'Bathhouses? Are you serious?' Jack asked. 'Can we go?'

'You can go,' I said, 'but I don't want to go, and I don't want Pablo to go.'

'Come on, let's go. It's our last night. What about it, Mart?'

'I'll go,' Mart said. 'I'll wear my T-shirt so no one can see my line. Yeah, let's go. Will there be people there?'

'Yeah, this is probably a good time,' Pablo said.

'Pablo, you want to come. I know you want to come,' Mart said.

Pablo looked at me. I shook my head.

'I'll walk up to the door with you,' I said.

'Will you not come with us?' Pablo asked.

'Who said you're going?' I asked him.

'Come on, we're all going,' Mart said.

'Let's pay the bill and I'll walk you to the door. I'll get a taxi home and you can use the car,' I said to Pablo. We left the waiter a large tip.

It was a warm evening and everyone looked beautiful on the street. I realized that Jack and Mart had not seen enough of Buenos Aires in the hours around midnight when deeply suntanned people dress up and saunter in the street, when Argentinians look spectacular. I was about to say that the next time they came they could stay in my apartment and wander around here every night, but I realized that you could not talk to Mart about a next time. I wondered what Jack would be like on his own, without a companion, but he would probably not want to come back here because it would remind him of Mart.

'You're going to come with us, you are, come on, you are?' Mart linked arms with me as we walked along.

'And when I meet you in the steam room, or when I watch Pablo getting into a cubicle with some kid, what am I meant to do?'

'We'll all be good,' Mart said.

We walked casually in the direction of the sauna. At the door the other three stopped and looked at me.

'Okay, okay, I'm coming in too,' I said. Pablo squeezed the back of my neck with his hand.

At first we were loud, but soon the sullen rules of the place had their effect on us. It was strange, as we all began to strip, how quiet we became, how self-absorbed, as though we had nothing in common, except the beginnings of desire. Slowly we watched each other becoming anonymous, items on a fiercely competitive and merciless sexual market. Mart left his T-shirt on and tied a towel around his waist. He said that he would go and sit at the bar and he would see us all later. I said that I would sit with him.

'Look at those two bastards,' I said to him as we walked away.

'Look at us four bastards,' he replied.

We ordered beers and sat on stools at the bar. I did not feel bad about Pablo wandering around half-naked. As a few men came into the bar to have a coffee or look for cigarettes or, in the case of one very dark man, some condoms, I wondered if he would take any interest in them. Mart talked about Pablo and me coming to California, how we could stay with them and use their car to travel around and see things, go into the desert. For most people, I explained, Argentina was not Buenos Aires, it was everything except Buenos Aires and the next time – I had mentioned the next time, having promised myself that I would not do so – Jack and he would have to go to Patagonia and Mendoza and Tierra del Fuego. He nodded and sipped his beer.

After a while I decided to go and look at what was happening. The place seemed to be filling up. I walked into the main area, where the small pool was, but I saw neither Jack nor Pablo. I looked into the sauna, and they were not there either. I walked down a corridor towards one of the cubicles and I saw Jack standing against the wall. He did not see me. He looked dark and predatory; he had taken on a whole new personality. I moved slowly towards him in the half-dark and crouched down low until I was right beneath him. He still could not see me. Suddenly, I sprang up and said 'boo' to him and put a grotesque expression on my face. He was startled for a moment and then he laughed.

'You look like a different person in here,' I said.

'I know,' he said, 'so did you just there, but have you seen Pablo? He's walking around like he really means business.'

I stood close to Jack and we watched Pablo move up the corridor, walking slowly, his gaze tense and concentrated. I realized that if I had not known him I would have wanted him immediately. He stopped and spoke to us. He smiled and laughed. I wanted to suggest that we get to hell out of here, but I said nothing. I said that I was going to return to the bar. But when I went back there Mart had gone. I ordered a coffee.

Earlier, I had noticed a guy watching me. He had his hair

cut really short as if he was doing his military service; he was white-skinned and fleshy. He came to the bar and ordered a coffee. I knew – I remembered the rules – how important it was to say nothing, to remain cool. I had not much time. If any of the others came back, I would have to forget about him. As soon as he sat down, I brushed my leg against his and noticed that he did not recoil. Slowly, he moved his ankle so that it touched my leg. I looked at him again and felt definite stirrings of desire for him. I did not move or make any gesture. I drank my coffee and he drank his. And then I stood up, and looked at him as though I were waiting for him to stand up too and follow me. When I looked back he was already on his feet.

It was so long since I had been with anybody else that I enjoyed this stranger's body. I felt relieved to be with him, somehow glad that I did not have to worry about his moods or his parents. We did not talk much: once, he asked me if I was well, and I said I was fine. I liked his body, and I liked the idea even more that I needed nothing from him except this, and that Pablo would be waiting for me when I had finished.

Pablo was in the bar with Jack and Mart and a thin boy called Jesús. I could not work out whether Jesús had just been with Mart or Jack. Mart was trying to talk Spanish to Jesús and we were all laughing. Jesús was sporting a soft downy moustache.

'Do you want to go?' I asked Pablo.

'Yes,' he said. 'It's all over.'

'What about Jesús? Does he want to come?'

'All the way to California,' Mart said.

In the dressing room Mart wrote Jesús his phone number on a piece of paper, and Jesús gave Mart his address. He said that he did not have a phone. We showered and put on our clothes, except for Mart, who had to dress without having a shower because he could not get his line wet. We walked back out into the city. Cars were still parading up and down the boulevards, bars and cinemas were still open and the streets were full of people.

'Yeah, we've got to come back here,' Mart said. 'This is a really good place.'

*

THE MORE I WATCHED the government prepare for privatization the more impressed and interested I became. It was as though each move had been planned as part of some grand strategy and any possibility of error had been covered. Soon, the telephone system and the national airline would be for sale. At the beginning of 1988 I attended meetings at various ministries to discuss how the last months of the campaign would be handled. It was decided that I would attend a number of conferences where prospective investors and, more importantly, journalists covering the oil industry would be. There was a public relations firm in New York and in London employed to deal with day-to-day matters. There would also be civil servants from the oil sector available. My job was simply to translate for Argentinian officials and to talk to as many people as possible at conferences, to make sure that nothing negative about the privatization would circulate for very long and to report back to the New York firm and to the ministry.

There was a man from the New York public relations firm at the first of the strategy meetings which I attended. I took in his pale green linen suit, his white shirt and pale green tie, his tanned skin and white teeth, his blond hair and winning smile, and he looked back at me and nodded his head and curled his lip in friendly amusement. He talked in a lazy, easy sort of way as though he knew all the tricks, and believed that the world could be relied upon not to do anything strange. I hoped that he was going to come to one of the conferences with me. I liked him.

He talked about how to deal with journalists and opinion-formers: we should make clear to them that we needed nothing from them. He saw no reason to offer free trips or other inducements to journalists, but once anyone was prepared to take the trouble to write about us, we should pull out all the stops and be open and hospitable, simply state our case in the best possible environment. We should not be seen to be craven or Third World in the way we operated. We must behave like a large, rich country selling something that people wanted to buy. Anything that smacked of Third World inferiority must be kept out of the picture. Most of this had to be translated for the civil servants, one of whom was frantically keeping notes for a memo which would be read personally by Menem. I could see them becoming tense when 'Third World' was mentioned. I made a note to suggest to the American that we find a euphemism.

I sat beside the American at the lunch afterwards. He was called Tom Shaw. He asked about my background and where I had learned my English. He was different from other North Americans who had come here: his background was in public relations rather than oil. He said he had worked as a disc jockey for a number of years, the years when everyone else was at college. But for the past ten years or so, this is what he had been doing. I noticed that when a tall, young, good-looking women left the private dining room and several of the men at the table began to talk about her he did not join in, he changed the subject. I told Pablo about him when I went home. Pablo smiled and shook his head and sighed. He said that he wished guys like that came to his father's office, that might help him get through the day. He would not even mind if a good-looking women came by, even that would be something.

Pablo agreed that I could tell Susan about us, and let her tell Jorge. Susan, he said, could come around to dinner, but not Jorge, and not Donald either. He did not like the look of

Donald, nor the sound of him, he said. Poor Donald, I said. Nobody likes him.

When I went to see Susan, I learned that she knew nothing about the new plans to market the privatization. I told her about the meeting and the use of public relations firms. I realized that she had not been consulted in any way.

'They're getting very confident, these oil people,' she said. Her tone was bitter. I said nothing.

'Well, we set it up for them, did what we could, and we can hardly complain,' she said. 'And we've made a man out of you.'

'Well, that's stretching it a bit,' I said. 'In fact, I was going to tell you that I have been living with Jorge's brother for the past while, I mean sleeping with him.'

'We have one each then,' she said.

'True,' I said. 'That is, if you still have Jorge.'

'I do.'

'Did you suspect about me and Pablo?'

'No, I thought you just went for straight men. I thought you lay in bed at night thinking about him while he lay sleeping in the next room.'

'He isn't straight. He doesn't sleep in the next room.'

'Well, that'll be news to Jorge, and to that old snake his mother.'

'I don't think you should tell her.'

'She's an old bat.'

Donald was sitting in the kitchen reading an American newspaper. We went out into the garden while Susan had a shower. I noticed that the swimming pool had been drained.

'We were going to have it fixed,' Donald said, 'but I don't think we'll be here that much longer.'

'What do you mean?'

'Our term's up, or something like that. I think it's time to move.'

'Susan didn't mention anything.'

'No, I was detailed to tell you.'

We walked in silence to the front of the house.

'Do you know where you'll go?'

'Back to Washington. At least for the moment.'

'And then?'

'I don't know.' He said nothing. We turned and walked back towards the garden.

'How long have you known that my wife has been seeing your friend Jorge?'

'Seeing?'

'You know what I mean. I mean fucking.'

'For a long time.'

'Well, he won't be doing it much longer. Maybe you could tell him that.'

'I'm not really in the business, Donald, of conveying messages of that sort.'

'Then maybe I'll tell him.'

We walked in silence for another while. And then we went into the kitchen, where Susan was setting the small side table. They were in a melancholy mood that evening until the wine took hold. Susan told Donald about me and Pablo.

'You mean he's fucking Jorge's brother? Well, in that case I get regular blow jobs from his father while his mother sticks her tongue up my ass. Are there any sisters?'

'Hey, Donald, give us a break,' I said.

'You mean, you're serious?'

'Yeah, I'm serious.'

'Well, that's good because I think Pablo's cute. He's cuter than his brother. His brother's an asshole.'

'Go easy on the language, Donald,' Susan said.

'Maybe you should go easy too,' he said.

'Maybe we should all go easy,' I said.

He began to laugh.

'What a stupid thing to say: "Maybe we should all go easy,"' he said. 'You're beginning to sound like an asshole too.'

'We all love you, Donald,' Susan said snidely.

'It was all done right in front of my nose,' he said. 'One weekend we decided to redecorate the bedroom, and Jorge came to help us. We had fun, all of us, except I didn't know that Jorge and Susan would be swooning in one another's juices before the paint was even dry. I'm busy rewriting the past two years with these two on top of each other every time I turn my back.'

'I said we all love you, Donald,' Susan repeated.

'Everybody here is up to something,' Donald said. 'You can trust nobody. I think we're going to go home and open a store. Something straightforward. A shoe store. A deli.'

'We all love you, Donald,' I said. Susan and I began to laugh.

'So you're just a fucking fairy. Well, we knew that all along. A fat-assed fairy.'

'That's what I am, Donald, a fat-assed fairy.'

'Stop calling me Donald. I don't like your tone when you call me Donald.'

'I don't mind you calling me a fat-assed fairy.'

'I think we should all have another drink,' Susan said.

They told me that night that they thought I should get out of Argentina, that I should talk to the British and American public relations companies about finding work for me, that it was and would always be a dreary backwater here. I said that I was happy now and would make no plans. Susan shook her head.

'You've always been like that, a mixture of such good sense and an amazing lack of something. I don't know what it is.'

Donald was enjoying his new role of cuckolded husband about to transport his wife from the scene of the crime. He could not stop talking about it.

'So you can tell Jorge then to take his Argentinian pecker and stick it somewhere else,' he said.

'I'll tell him nothing,' I said. 'I hardly ever see him. Does he know you know?'

'No,' Susan said. 'Donald can only talk about him behind his back. He's not a courageous man, Donald, that's one of the things I like about him.'

'You're the one with the courage,' I said.

'I don't claim credit for much,' Susan said, 'and there won't be any statues put up to me or to anybody else. And there are people around here who think Ronald Reagan is some sort of joke and he is – he certainly is – some sort of joke. But we set out to create democratic structures here, and we had his full support for that, and we did it, and we're going. It's made up for other things in the past that I told you about once, things that happened when we were younger that we are not proud of. But you have money now, and you're not yet forty, and you're gay, and you know you're gay, and you should get out now, there's nothing for you here, and everything for you elsewhere. That mixture in you, whatever it is, makes you very attractive. Don't grow old down here. You'd be insane to do that.'

'Is Pablo circumcised?' Donald asked.

'He has beautiful nipples,' I said. 'They go hard when I lick them.'

'I was going to say something,' Susan said, 'but I think I'll make no comment.'

*

THE TAXI DRIVER who drove me home wondered who I was that I would visit a house so strangely guarded as Susan and Donald's and live in a place so isolated with no other houses around. I hardly spoke at all. I was too drunk. I got into

bed beside Pablo without waking him and went into a deep
sleep.

★

SOON AFTERWARDS, I went to New York for the first time.
I believed as I travelled due north that I was moving from a
shadow world into a world of substance. I expected everything
to be ordered and opulent, shiny and glamorous. And instead it
was chaotic and run-down and also amazing in its wealth and
sense of energy and expectancy.

I think Americans who knew the oil business were surprised
at how little serious opposition there had been to the plans for
privatization. I began to think about it one night after another
of those all-male dinners, where people are friendly and jaunty
and half-familiar with each other. Argentina after the humiliation of the war and the disappearances would have done
anything to please the outside world, and privatization was the
price the outside world required. Everything the country had
that was valuable would be sold, and this would tie Argentina
to outside interests so that it would never be able to behave
badly again. I thought about this as the rest of them were
talking and laughing. They asked me what I was thinking about,
why I was so serious.

'Home,' I said. Once more, I noticed that Tom Shaw did
not laugh at the same jokes, even though he remained friendly
and charming. He was younger and better-looking than the rest
of them. He was employed to be young and good-looking.
Over that weekend in New York I began to believe that he
was gay and that he was watching me. I was not flattered by
this. I was frightened. He was too attractive, too big a prize, for
any attention from him to be taken lightly. I made sure never
to sit beside him, but at a table, or in the conference room, he
always watched me.

At some point during one of these conferences I became convinced that the privatization of the oil industry would be bad for Argentina. It struck me that everyone involved understood this too, but behaved as though the details of the privatization were too fascinating to make the overall idea worth considering too much. If the government held power over the industry, then developing it, trying to find new sources of oil and controlling prices would all become priorities. But my job was not to work out whether it was a good idea or a bad idea, but to make sure that no rumours about Argentina or bad vibes about the industry took hold among people who worked in oil.

Over the previous few years I had met and looked after maybe a hundred people, and now most of them began to reappear in hotel lobbies, in conference rooms, at dinner tables. I enjoyed the camaraderie which had built up between us. A few of them seemed funnier, looser, more friendly than they had been in Buenos Aires. They viewed the Argentinian privatization with great interest; most of them had some oil shares and were curious about who was going to buy the new shares and at what price. I found a few times that when groups gathered late at night, the conversation would come round to what would happen. Men would nurse their whiskies and ask me how I thought things were going, and I knew I had to be careful, that everything I said would be remembered, that somebody else in the company would probably be reporting back to the ministry. My job was to say how important this privatization was for Argentina, it was one step in an overall strategy to move the economy from a dormant South American economy, with constant inflation, heavy borrowing, importing of raw materials, regular political crises, and serious crime, such as Venezuela or Colombia, to a country which could do business with the United States. We had the discipline and the European background to put through these reforms, I said.

There would be no more inflation or currency speculation, the peso would be pegged to the dollar, and this would mean hardship, but we, as a society, could handle that hardship. We expected the privatization to go smoothly, and the revenue would be used for investment and to pay off certain debts. I told them we expected the leading oil companies in the United States and Europe to purchase the shares.

I was travelling once or twice a month now. I remember that I had been back from a conference in Europe just a few days when Susan and Donald had their farewell party. I remember that I was exhausted and that I had a chest infection which would not go away and I worked from home writing reports between long bouts of sleep. I told Pablo that soon this would all settle down and we would be back to normal. He had the car most of the time and he came home straight after work and made dinner and did the shopping and the cleaning.

Susan and Donald sent out handwritten invitations to me, Pablo, Jorge, Señor and Señora Canetto, and, we hoped, to numerous other people. I didn't want Pablo to go and Jorge didn't want his parents to go. The evening promised to be a parade of pretence. Donald would simper over the parents, discuss their two sons' virtues with them and go away laughing. At least this is the idea I presented to Pablo. Pablo said that if his parents were going, then he wanted to go. How could he explain to them why he wasn't going? He could just not turn up, I said, it could become a mystery. Maybe, he said, maybe he would do that, but in the meantime he would accept the invitation.

Once more, I was back in the room where I had met Susan and Donald for the first time, but now I knew at least half the people in the room, and could easily avoid Donald and try not to hang around too long beside Pablo, Jorge and their parents, who stood and stared at everybody as though they had spent their lives in the wilderness and had never seen people before.

I was shocked when I saw Federico Arenas there. I asked Donald if they knew him well. I searched his face as he replied to see if he and Susan knew about the deal, but he gave nothing away. He said they had found him helpful now and again during their stay. Federico came over and put his arm around me once more. He admired my suit and said that he had heard good things about me. I asked him if there was a chance that the period before privatization would ever be investigated. I knew it was a stupid question. He shook his head. It's all been forgotten, he said. Too many people did too well out of it. You're a worrier, aren't you, he said. Forget about it, everybody else has, it was nothing, he said and turned and walked away.

I was wrong about Donald. He avoided Pablo's parents and Pablo too. He moved quietly and timidly through the room talking to people. When Susan found me she told me not to leave her side until further instructions. I asked her what the agenda was; she said that there was no agenda. I desperately wanted to go home. I told her that I needed to rescue Pablo from his family and when I found him I brought him out into the garden, showed him the empty swimming pool. He was anxious not to stay away from his parents for too long.

★

I CANNOT REMEMBER when it became clear that Mart was going to die. It was either that night or the next day. I remember that the next day was a Saturday and Susan came around, and by that time we had heard the news from Jack and from another friend of Mart and Jack's who had phoned us as well. Pablo decided to go to San Francisco.

I had a conference in Miami early in the following week so I asked Susan to call by before I left. She said that they regretted giving the party the previous evening. They knew as soon as they sent the invitations out that it would be a bore. They should have seen the people they wanted to see in smaller groups, or maybe just left the country without seeing anybody. I walked out to the marina with her while Pablo made another call to San Francisco. She was wearing a light blue silk bow across the top of her forehead. She gazed at the water as though it were some old enemy of hers.

'We've really enjoyed knowing you here,' she said. 'I came out to tell you that.'

'And I've enjoyed knowing you too,' I said.

'I have a number of addresses and phone numbers where you would be able to find us if you needed us in a hurry. My mother's number is probably the quickest way to get in touch with us over the next few months.'

'Your mother?' I said. 'I didn't know that you had a mother. I thought that you came into the world some other way.'

'I'm going to miss you,' she said.

By the time we came back to the house, Pablo had booked a plane ticket to San Francisco. He was going to leave that night. Susan had a cup of coffee and then left, beeping the horn incessantly as she made her way into the distance. Pablo cleared away the lunch things. I held him as he stood at the sink in the kitchen. He turned and kissed me; soon we went upstairs and lowered the long white curtains. We made love in the bed and then slept for the rest of the afternoon.

He phoned the next day from San Francisco. He had seen Mart, who was receiving no more treatment. The doctors said that he would last no more than a few days. He was on morphine so there was no pain. Jack had finally managed to contact Mart's mother, whom Mart had not seen for twenty years, and she and Jack were keeping vigil at the hospital, never leaving the bedside. Mart held her hand. He could not stop looking at her, he asked her to take him home, and this was difficult and strange for Jack.

Pablo was staying at a friend's house. He wasn't sure that he was needed, but he was glad he had come. Mart and Jack were asking for me. It was all very sad, he said, he kept finding out about other people who were dead, or who were sick, and no one was talking about a cure. He was tired, he said, and he was going to go to bed now. I gave him the number of my hotel in Miami and I took his number and we said that we would speak the next day.

On the Sunday night I flew to Miami and checked into the hotel early in the morning. My room was not ready, and I was grumpy at the desk and said I needed my room as soon as possible. The receptionist looked as though she had no sympathy for me, and left me sitting in the lobby. When I finally made it to my room the phone was ringing. It was Pablo, who asked how long I was going to be in Miami. Until the end of the week, I said. He said nothing until I asked how Mart was. He's sleeping a lot, he said, and then he's making jokes, and he's introducing everyone to his mother. His mother and Jack sleep in the room.

I told him how I had just arrived, and had had no sleep. He left silence. I thought that he must be tired too. He said that he would ring me later. I said that I was going to sleep now, and I would be there all day and he could ring me any time.

I rang back in the afternoon, but there was only an answering machine. I ordered food and newspapers on room service. I had a shower and then I lay on the bed dozing, half-watching something on the television. Some time later, the phone rang again. I presumed that it was Pablo, but it was not. It was a different voice. It was Tom Shaw. He said that he had just checked in and had noticed that I was here too, and since most of the others would not arrive until later, or until the morning, he thought that we might have dinner together. I told him I would see him at eight o'clock in the hotel bar. He said he would book a restaurant. I phoned Pablo again before I dressed and went downstairs, but there was still only an answering machine.

I wondered if I could be wrong about Tom Shaw as he came and sat at the hotel bar, ordering a dry Martini and insisting that I have a second gin and tonic. Maybe he felt that it was part of his job to smile at me in that all-absorbing way. He looked at my clothes, touched one of the buttons of my shirt, spoke to me in a tone full of mocking intimacy. He had been sitting beside me for less than five minutes when I was sure that he thought I was going to go to bed with him. We finished our drinks and left the bar; it was only when we crossed the hotel lobby that I realized he was taller than me. As he opened the door of the taxi to let me in first, it struck me that he was treating me as though I were a woman.

Over dinner he was funny and attractive and easy, but still he gave nothing away. He lived alone on the Upper East Side in New York, he said. It was safe and dull, and that was how he liked it most of the time. He loved Buenos Aires, he said. It was his favourite place.

'I love the meat,' he said, and grinned at me. 'Most of the time I like it cooked, but there are times when I like it raw.' He laughed.

'I think I know what you mean,' I said.

'I think you do too,' he said.

I looked at him carefully as he spoke, and I realized that if I were a woman I would not trust him. I saw no reason to trust him now either. It was only when I noticed the blond hair on the skin around his wrist that I felt any desire for him. He wanted to know about my life in Buenos Aires; I told him about the house I rented, but I did not tell him about abandoning the apartment. I told him that I was seeing someone who was important to me, but I did not give any details. I watched him ask for the bill like a skilled professional. He paid by credit card, and then we left together. Once more, he escorted me to the door and opened the taxi for me.

'Would you like a nightcap in my room?' he asked as we

drove towards the hotel. 'I have a suite so it's pretty comfortable up there.'

'Just one,' I said, 'then I have to go to sleep.'

He put his hand on my crotch and held it there.

'I have been waiting to do this for several months.'

'I know.'

'You always slip away.'

'I'm going to do that tonight too.'

I rang Pablo when I got to my room, but the answering machine was still on. I left a message for him to ring me and then I went to sleep. I thought that he would phone during the night when it would be early evening on the west coast, but he did not. I had no number for Jack and Mart, but even if I had had their number I felt it would not be right to phone them. Maybe Mart was dead, and Pablo and all the others were taken up with arrangements.

He did not phone me the next day. I went to the reception desk several times to ask. Every time I moved from the conference room to the dining room or to the bar, I let them know at reception so that they could divert the call to where I was. By the time the following day was over, I knew there was something seriously wrong. I phoned home and there was no answer; I phoned my secretary and there were no messages. Maybe it was simply that he could not bear to talk to me in the days after Mart's death. I wondered if I shouldn't go to San Francisco. On Thursday I decided to phone Pablo's parents' house. I could say that I was a friend from North America. I tried out different voices before I dialled. The maid answered the phone. She said that Pablo was sleeping, and he could not be disturbed. He had flown in from North America the previous night. I presumed that he did not want to go back to the house alone, and I was sorry that I had not skipped the conference and gone to San Francisco with him. I still thought it was strange that he did not phone. I left no message for him.

That night Tom Shaw phoned my room when I was sitting up in bed watching television. He wanted me to come to his room for a drink.

'I'm already undressed,' I said.

'That sounds cool,' he said.

'Seriously,' I said.

'There's a dressing gown that goes with the room. Put it on and come down.'

I flicked through the channels and thought about it for a minute.

'Okay.'

I had a shower and dressed myself fully and walked down the corridor towards his room with the key in my pocket. He was in pyjamas. He was wearing expensive-looking oriental slippers.

'You put your clothes on?'

'If I had nice, stripy pyjamas like you, I would have worn them.'

'What are your pyjamas like?'

'I don't wear pyjamas.'

He made me a gin and tonic from his minibar and we sat down in the living room.

'When will you be in New York next?' he asked.

'I don't know.'

'I'd like to show you around. It's all a bit calmer now than it used to be, but I think you might find it exciting. That's if you don't know it already.'

'No, I don't know it.'

He walked into the bedroom and played with the remote control and stood for a minute looking at the television.

'There's a good film coming on,' he said. 'Do you want to come in and watch it?'

We sat up on the bed together watching the beginning of the film, which was a dark crime movie I had never heard of. I put my drink on the bedside table, or I held it in my hand. When I took off my jacket and my shoes Tom leaned over to kiss me. I could feel the heat of his body. When he opened my shirt and began to play with my nipples I could feel his erect penis against my thigh.

I woke in the night. The central heating system was on too high; I felt a dryness in the air which made it hard to breathe. I went to the bathroom, where I felt short of breath. When I came back I looked at Tom lying naked on the bed. He looked beautiful and perfect: I watched him while I was dressing. I slipped out of the room. In the morning as I was packing to go to the airport, he rang and made me write down his address in New York and his phone number. He wanted me to ring him over the weekend. I told him I was not sure that I could.

*

AS SOON AS I CAME IN from the airport I went upstairs. I knew immediately that Pablo had left. His clothes were gone; nothing of his was hanging in the wardrobe. He had taken his toothbrush and a special shampoo that he liked. And downstairs there was a note on the kitchen table in his scrawl. It read: 'Things haven't been working out between us recently. I wanted to leave before it became any worse. Maybe I should have stayed and talked about it, but I felt this was the best way to do it. I want to end our relationship. I also want to thank you for everything. Love, Pablo.'

I walked down to the water and thought about what I should do. I had always believed that things between us would go on for good. Maybe I should have put more effort into it. Maybe I should have travelled less in recent times. I went back up to the house and phoned his parents' place. He answered the phone, and then transferred the call to another room so that he could talk quietly.

'I want to meet you,' I said.

'No, I can't,' he said. 'I made a decision. I'm absolutely sure about it.'

'Thanks,' I said. 'I'm glad that you're so sure. It makes me feel good.'

'That's what I mean, there's no point in us meeting. It's easier just to end it like this.'

'Easier for you,' I said. He said nothing.

'I phoned a few days ago but you were asleep,' I said.

'I've been back two days. I was with Mart just before he died. It was very hard for everyone. Maybe because he was so brave it was hard. It seems unbelievable that he is lying under the ground. I keep feeling that someone could just go to the graveyard and dig him up and talk to him and make him come alive.'

'Pablo, I need to talk to you.'

'No, I can't talk to anybody. I think I'm going to go back to San Francisco, maybe in the next few days. At his funeral he asked that they play "Mad About the Boy" as his coffin was being wheeled down the church. It wasn't funny, like he meant it to be. It was unbearable. I couldn't wait for it to be over. No one is prepared for death. I thought we all were, but we weren't.'

'Can we meet in the city?'

'I'll phone you in a week or two.'

'Are you sure that you're not just upset?'

'Hey, I'm sure, I told you I was sure.'

'I really miss you. I really want to see you.'

'You're going to have to find somebody else.' He put down the receiver.

I was crying as I went to the bathroom. I could not imagine what I was going to do for the rest of the day and the next day. He had left it so that I could not telephone him again. I tried to think what I did before I met him, how I filled my days. I began to brush my teeth, as though that might help in some way. I felt that if I met him I could convince him to come back. I was still crying when I went downstairs.

I lay on the sofa and tried to go to sleep. It was the early evening. As I lay there an idea came to me. I went to my jacket pocket and took out Tom Shaw's address and phone number. I phoned him. He recognized my voice as soon as he picked up the receiver. He laughed.

'I don't know why,' he said, 'but I thought that you might phone.'

'Are you busy this weekend?'

'I would be if you came up here. Otherwise, I'm not.'

'I should be able to make it by the morning. What will I do – just get a taxi from the airport to your address?'

'Yeah, or phone if you're going to be late. Or phone in any case, so I'll be ready for you.'

As soon as I stood up from the sofa I began to have difficulty breathing. I felt a sharp pain in my back but it did not last long. I phoned the airport and got a seat on a night flight to Miami. I did not know when I was going to return. The ticket was expensive, but I reserved it nonetheless. I filled a small bag with clothes and a few books and toilet stuff. I made sure that I had my passport and money and my keys and my address book. I wrote Tom's number and address in the book. And then I drove to the airport. I did not think about Pablo.

I slept as soon as I got on the plane, and I was still groggy and sleepy when we touched down in Miami. I had to walk for what seemed like miles before I found the desk for the connecting flight to New York. I wondered why I had not just got drunk at home and fallen into a sleep. I even thought of turning back and ringing Tom Shaw to say that I would not be able to make it after all. But I got on the plane. I had a window seat and I looked out at the clear blue of the sea and the bright yellow sand of the beaches and then the calm, creamy endless cloud as we made our way north and I was glad that I was alive, and I lay back and thought about Tom Shaw's body, his gleaming smile, his energy, and I thought that everything was all right as I began to doze.

I could not find a working call box which took credit cards in Kennedy Airport; I had no coins. It was eleven thirty in the morning. I took a cab into the city. When I saw myself in the mirror I knew that I should have shaved. I needed a haircut. But I could do all that later. I hoped that Tom had not gone out. The apartment was on east sixty-ninth, and the cab driver wanted to know which streets it was between, but I did not know and this meant that he had to drive around several times to find it. I paid him and stood at the reception desk and asked for Tom Shaw. The porter phoned his apartment, and told me to go to the ninth floor. In the lift I was excited at the idea of seeing him again. He was wearing jeans and a denim shirt and no shoes and socks when he came to the door. He lived in a two-room apartment with a small kitchen and bathroom. The bed was enormous, and one wall of the bedroom was all mirrors.

'Look what the cat brought in,' he said. 'You look like you've been up all night.'

'I've been on a plane all night.'

'Why don't you have a bath and a shave and I'll go out and get stuff for breakfast and then I'll make coffee.'

I could tell that he did not want me to talk about why I had come. Before he went out he opened the bathroom door and left a bathrobe on a hook.

'You can wear that when you dry yourself.'

We had breakfast and then he led me to the bedroom. He had left some cream and condoms conspicuously on the bedside table. He stripped and then made me face the mirror while he removed the bathrobe. I was so tired that I felt the urge to make love, to satisfy myself, much stronger than ever before. There was nothing I would not have done. He left me lying on the bed and came back into the room with a small mirror and what I took to be two lines of cocaine.

'I have never done this before,' I said.

'All the more reason why you'll enjoy it.'

He used a rolled-up ten-dollar bill to snort the cocaine, and then he handed it to me. I snorted it, and I immediately felt a bitter taste on the roof of my mouth and a strange numbness. He pulled the bedclothes back and we got between the clean white sheets.

'We're going to have to make the journey worth your while,' he said.

In the late afternoon, he went out and left me sleeping. When I woke I could not remember where I was. I reached out and could not find the lamp. I got out of bed and found the door and opened it and looked out into the hallway, but still I could not think where I was. There was no one in the living room or the kitchen. I went into the bathroom and began to cough. Each time I coughed I could feel the cocaine at the roof of my mouth. I felt that I had no breath at all. I kept heaving and coughing as I stood there. The clock said seven thirty. I went back into the bedroom and turned on the lamp beside the bed and fell into a light sleep until Tom returned.

He was smiling and cheerful, as though my arrival had provided him with immense amusement. I almost wanted to tell him what had happened, but he seemed to have no curiosity. When I got up and had a shower, he brought me in two huge soft towels which he had heated on the radiator. He said that we were going out to dinner. The good times were just beginning, he said.

We got a cab to take us down the potholed and bumpy streets of Manhattan to Greenwich Village.

'In Buenos Aires,' I said, 'when the streets are in bad condition people really are ashamed.'

'No one around here is ashamed of anything,' Tom said.

For a moment I thought that he was Pablo. I held his hand.

'Don't go all quiet on me,' he said.

'I'm not sure what I'm doing here,' I said.

'Concentrate on the next half-hour, and I've brought some magic powder which will help you along.'

He told the cab driver to stop on a dark street which was crowded with people.

'Let's get out and walk around,' he said.

I was amazed that the shops selling clothes and books and tapes and more clothes were still open. People walked the streets with carrier bags. Each person I saw as we went along would have stood out in the streets of Buenos Aires. We went to a restaurant on a corner: the ceiling was high and there were plants everywhere, and the woman who led us to our table looked even more snobbish than any of the people eating at the tables or sitting at the bar, and behaved more imperiously.

'You look like a country boy who's just come over the bridge or through the tunnel,' Tom said.

'Yes, that's what I am.'

'The woman who brought us to our table is probably bridge and tunnel too, except she has learned not to look like that.'

'And what about you?'

'New Jersey born and bred.'

'Is that so terrible?'

'It means that I couldn't wait to get in here and have a good time.'

'I've never eaten lobster before, maybe it's because I live too near the sea.'

'Well, now's your chance.'

I ordered lobster with ginger and Tom ordered some sort of chicken. The waitress did not seem amused when he said we would have Bloody Marys for starters. Tom still did not know why I was here and when I was going back. I felt that he wanted to make clear that he had no interest in getting involved with me. He spoke about the prices of apartments in New York, how this area used to be cheap, but now everybody wanted to live here. He would not want to live here himself, he said, there was too much going on. He liked to take visitors from Argentina down here.

I was still tired and only barely able to concentrate. He noticed this and slipped me a package under the table. He told me to go into the bathroom and have a snort and then I'd feel better. I put the package in my pocket and went to the bathroom and locked myself into a cubicle. It was all here: the powder, the mirror, a tiny plastic spoon to make the line. I rolled up a ten-dollar bill and snorted. Once more, I felt the bitter taste in my mouth and the numbness. I shivered as though the temperature had suddenly gone down. I washed my face in cold water, and stood looking in the mirror.

After dinner we wandered in the streets for a while and had a drink in an old-fashioned hotel where the lights in the bar were so low I could barely see Tom across the table from me. The cocaine was working: I felt alert to everything that moved, I loved the alcohol in my vodka and tonic, I was ready to talk about minor details of the decor, or the barman's uniform and gait, or how good I felt. And this seemed to make Tom happy. He laughed and smiled and showed his shiny white teeth. I was glad I was with him, glad I had come all the way up to New York to experience this.

Later, we got a taxi to a gay bar for older, professional men, as Tom put it. Are you a professional man, he asked me. I said that I was. He laughed. Most of the men there wore suits and ties. The place was full of easy chairs and sofas, and the atmosphere was cheerful. We had several drinks. Tom knew a few people, whom he introduced to me, and we all talked for a while, about Argentina and New York, making vague jokes about sex. It seemed as though these men were tired of hunting for sex on a Saturday night and decided instead to look for company, mild conversation and some laughter. But maybe at a certain time of the night they stiffened and stopped standing around with drinks in their hands talking to people they knew, and they went in search of sex. It was all so casual and civilized, like a gentleman's club. I thought that if I lived in New York I would come here all the time, it would be easier to meet somebody here, it would be easier to grow old here feeling that you were not alone.

'You've gone all dreamy on me again,' Tom said.

'Another drink, maybe,' I said.

He called the waiter and we had two more vodka and tonics.

'I think we should go home soon, now that I've shown you a bit of New York. I think we're going to have a long night.' He put his hand on my crotch. 'In fact, I'm sure of it.'

We walked from the bar to his apartment. It was starting to rain. I still felt elated, full of energy. I could feel the alcohol throbbing in my blood. As soon as he went in the door of the apartment Tom made two more lines of coke and we snorted one each.

'I'll toss a coin,' he said. 'One of us strips, the other keeps his clothes on.'

He won the toss to keep his clothes on. I stripped in the bedroom, dropping my clothes on the floor, and then I walked out into the living room. He put his finger into the bag of cocaine and daubed some on the top of my dick and then on my asshole. We lay on the thick carpet together. He began to bite my nipples and then squeeze them with his thumb and forefinger until it hurt and I tried to stop him, but he carried on as though it were vital to continue. Slowly, a feeling built up inside me that I could endure any pain. He put his finger once more into the bag of cocaine and daubed me with the small white grains. He lay beside me and kissed me, refusing to allow me put my hands inside his clothes. I felt invulnerable, ready for anything.

I woke at about three o'clock and the coughing would not stop. Each time I coughed I felt a sharp pain in my back. I felt hot and sweaty. I lay there trying to stop but I had no control over my breathing. Tom woke up.

'Hey, that cough's becoming a real problem.'

'Maybe it's the cocaine.'

'It sounds serious to me.'

I lay there with my eyes closed trying to breathe calmly. He turned and tried to go back to sleep. Slowly, the coughing started again. I felt a burning in my lungs. I was aware that I was disturbing him. He turned on the lamp beside the bed.

'You sound sick,' he said. 'Have you been to a doctor with this?'

'No,' I said. 'I don't know what it is. I think it might be the cocaine.'

'Do you think you're going to cough much more?' he asked.

'I don't know.'

'Because I think I'm going to go out and sleep on a mattress in the living room.'

He stood up and took two pillows with him and rummaged in the built-in cupboard for a mattress, which he dragged across the room. He came back for some sheets and a duvet. He closed the door behind him without saying anything. I began to cough again. I felt as though I were on fire, and I was sorry that I was in a stranger's bedroom and not in my own house. I thought of getting up – it was three thirty – and going out to the airport to catch the next flight home, but I decided to wait and get some rest. I was sweating. I felt helpless.

I must have dozed for a while. I woke with Tom's lamp still on at twenty to five and I decided to go. My bag was in the corner of the bedroom. I checked what I needed – passport, ticket, money, keys – and I put on my clothes. I went into the bathroom and collected my things. I stood in the living room like a long shadow and asked Tom if he was awake. He mumbled something. I told him that I was going to go. He sat up and asked me if I needed anything.

'I'm going to go,' I said.

'Okay.'

'I don't need you to get up.'

'Okay.'

'I'll see you at the next conference.'

'Are you going to Argentina?'

'Yeah, that's where I'm going. I'd better hurry or I'll miss my plane.'

I opened the door and slipped out into the corridor, and I walked quickly to the lift. In the street I hailed a cab and told the driver I wanted to go to Kennedy. I did not know what airline I was going to use to get back, but I told him to drop me at the departure gates of the Argentinian airline. Since it was Sunday, I discovered, there would be no flight to Buenos Aires until the late afternoon, but if I went to LaGuardia, I could catch a flight to Miami and get a connection there. It would cost more money, but I felt I needed to go home. My skin was on fire and I had a terrible thirst. I could barely carry my bag. I paid for my ticket by credit card.

As soon as I got the ticket I felt that I was choking. I walked away and lay down on a bench. I tried desperately to catch my breath, to breathe calmly. People looked at me as I lay there spluttering and coughing. Eventually I managed to stand up and go outside and get a taxi to LaGuardia.

The plane to Miami was almost full. I had a window seat, and I sat back with my eyes closed and my face burning with heat. As soon as the plane took off I started to cough. The woman beside me seemed affronted by this, as though I had been put beside her as a way of annoying her. Each time I coughed she tried to move away from me. I had my head between my knees. It was as though I were trying to cough the cocaine out of my system. I braced myself each time, I knew how sharp the pain was going to be, as though my lungs were going to explode. An air hostess came and stood watching me, and then another. I pretended that they were not there.

'Are you asthmatic?' one of them asked.

I nodded.

'It will be okay,' I said.

'Could I be moved?' the woman beside me asked. The air hostess walked up the aisle and found her a new seat. She moved, muttering and making a great fuss. I lay back and tried to sleep. Every bone in my body was sore, and I felt that I was not going to be able to continue breathing. I wondered if I should stop in Miami and go to a doctor there; maybe they would have more experience of people who were allergic to cocaine. In Buenos Aires I had not been to the doctor for years, not since before my mother died. I knew that doctors had to maintain some sort of confidentiality. I had, in any case, taken the drugs in New York rather than Buenos Aires. Soon, I fell asleep, and when I woke I was coughing once more; at the end of each cough I hit a loud uncontrollable high note which made everyone look around. I desperately wanted to be home.

'Do you want medical attention as soon as we arrive?' one of the air hostesses asked me.

I shook my head. I said I would be okay. I made sure not to say that I was catching a connecting flight to Buenos Aires. I closed my eyes again and she went away. When the plane landed and we collected our hand luggage and made our way into the terminal, I tried not to breathe at all. I was afraid that if I did not concentrate, I would double up coughing in the aisle of the aircraft.

As I pushed my trolley along passageways to get to the Buenos Aires plane, I found that I could not continue. I leaned on the trolley coughing, the sound was rasping in the echoing corridors, and I ended up kneeling on the floor not able to take a breath. I did not know what I would do when I got home. It would be late on a Sunday night, I did not suppose that many doctors would be on duty. I wondered if I should not go straight to a hospital, but I did not know what I would tell them.

Slowly, I picked myself up and moved towards the departures gate. I thought about a strong sleeping pill, something that would put me into a deep sleep for the journey home. I wished I had some pills. I thought that this reaction to the cocaine might last some hours and then fade. Once more, I was given a window seat, and as soon as the plane was in the air I began to cough again. As we flew south most people around me fell asleep, but they woke up to the sound of my cough, which seemed louder now on this plane, as though all of my insides were going to come up. The air hostess asked me if I wanted her to see if there was a doctor on board and I said that I did not, but later, when it became worse, and everyone around me was awake and listening, I nodded to her. She moved around the plane asking people, but there was no doctor on board. She brought me an extra blanket and a pillow and moved the people around me so that I could stretch out across three seats. As soon as I lay down I knew that I was really sick, and getting sicker, and that maybe it was something else, which the cocaine had merely brought on. I fell asleep, and woke again covered in sweat.

I managed to drive home from the airport. I thought that I was going to die at the wheel, that I would collapse. I knew that I was running a very high temperature. Several times I had to pull in on the highway and cough until I was shivering with exhaustion. It had never occurred to me before that I should be grateful for being well, but now I saw the time when I was not like this as something I wanted to experience again. When I got home, I rang the Juan Fernandez Hospital in the city centre. I had passed it many times and paid it no attention. There was no answer. I checked the phone book again and found an emergency number. I described my symptoms to the woman who answered. I did not mention cocaine. I told her that I had comprehensive health insurance. She told me to come in now to the casualty gate, immediately, and someone would look at me. I phoned a taxi and put the things I thought that I would need into a bag. By this time I believed that they were going to detain me in the hospital overnight.

As soon as I walked in the door marked 'Casualty', I was stopped by a porter. He made me stand while he phoned to see if there was anybody there and I began to cough again. The pain brought tears to my eyes. He turned and looked at me sharply, then dialled another number. He brought me a chair to sit on; he patted my back to reassure me. My skin was still burning and I was short of breath. The journey from New York seemed like some interminable dream. I wanted to lie down on the floor and die.

A nurse came and led me down a corridor and then through double doors down another corridor. When she put me into a curtained-off cubicle with a narrow bed she told me to sit down and pulled back the curtains. She began to ask me questions and wrote the answers down on a chart. I told her about the coughing and about being in New York, but once more I did not mention the cocaine. She took my temperature with a thermometer under my arm and told me it was one hundred and four. She said she would go to get a doctor.

I thought about the difference between now and when I was well. Effortless evenings, having dinner, drinking wine, lying on the sofa, talking to Pablo, going to bed with him and making love, and then sleeping. I realized that my temperature had been high for at least a day, maybe more, and I thought that this was dangerous, or at least not a good sign. After a while, a young doctor came and asked me to remove my jacket and shirt. He asked me to breathe deeply and placed the cold steel of the stethoscope on my back and chest. He put me lying on the bed and came back a few minutes later with an older doctor and a nurse.

The doctor looked at me suspiciously, and then listened to my chest and back through the stethoscope, and said that I had a severe pneumonia. He would need me to fill in forms, and then he would find me a bed and begin treatment. It looks bad, he said. You've let it go too long. He looked down at the chart and wrote something. How bad, I asked. He said that they would have to do tests to find out. I filled in the form, my name, my address, and then my next of kin. I realized that I did not have a next of kin. I did not want them to contact any of my uncles. I wrote down my mother's name, and the address of my apartment. I gave them all the other details they wanted. I thought of them phoning the empty apartment with news about me, and nobody answering the phone.

A porter led me in a wheelchair to a ward. I put my bag on my lap. It was like something from a movie, the long corridors, the strip lighting, the half-glimpses into rooms where people lay in bed, the silence of the night. He wheeled me into a ward with five other beds, all with figures in them lying asleep. A nurse came and pulled the curtains around my bed and told me in whispers to undress here and get into bed. The doctor, she said, would be around shortly. As soon as I began to undress I started coughing again. I lay on the bed with my shoes off until it stopped. I was sure now that I was going to die. Slowly, I took off my clothes and put on the pyjamas I had brought with me. I was too hot for blankets. I waited for the doctor to come. I began to feel thirsty, but when I tried to drink from the jug of water beside the bed, it was impossible to swallow. More time went by and I lay there waiting.

I was half-asleep when a doctor and a nurse came with a trolley of instruments. They turned the light on over my bed.

When I saw one of the nurses prepare a needle I felt afraid. I suddenly did not want this. A doctor told me to take down my pyjama-bottoms and turn around. He had the needle in his hand. The nurse daubed cotton wool on the skin of my hip, and the doctor put the needle in. At first I felt nothing, but when the pain came it was sharp and made me tense. The nurse put her hand on my shoulder and told me to relax. The needle went in further now, I could feel it tearing something inside, and then the doctor withdrew it, and the nurse put more cotton wool on the skin. I pulled up my pyjama-bottoms and lay back. Another needle connected to a drip which the nurse set up beside me was put into my arm. The doctor listened to my chest on the stethoscope once more. Neither of them spoke to each other or to me. When they had finished, they walked away as though I did not exist. The nurse who worked on the ward came and pulled back the curtains.

I lay there all night without sleeping, watching everything that moved in the ward and the corridor outside like a baby who has just come into the world and opened its eyes. I watched as the man in the middle bed across the way soiled himself in the night and a couple of nurses came and led him out to the bathroom while they changed the sheets on his bed. I watched the boy in the bed beside me quietly go out to the toilet and come back in again. I watched the man in the bed opposite me wake and sit up and call the nurse and then lie down and go back to sleep. And I watched the dawn, and then the lights coming on in the corridor and the ward, and then breakfast starting. I had not moved all night. A nurse came and took my temperature and my blood pressure. She told me not to take any breakfast as I would be going soon for a bronchoscopy. I asked her what that was; she said it was a test on my lungs. I asked her what my temperature was; she said it was high. She looked at my chart and she could not believe that I had not slept.

About an hour later, I was wheeled down to a sort of operating theatre and left waiting in an ante-room. I wondered if they were going to use needles again. I had a vision of them sticking a needle in my back, all the way into my lungs, and sucking out some liquid which they could test. It only occurred to me when they wheeled me into the theatre that they were going to stick a machine down my throat. I asked the doctor if he could make me unconscious for this. He was a tall man in his fifties. He reacted as though he had not been listening, and then he looked at me and nodded ruefully: if I wanted to be asleep then he was sure he could do something to help. I watched the nurse prepare another needle. But when the doctor came over with the needle he could not find a vein in my left arm. He told me to open and close my hand. Eventually, he stuck the needle in. I gasped and he told me to keep still.

I woke in a small room with a window looking over a lawn. There was a machine beside me with tubes coming from it. One went into my arm, another into my neck. I felt pain in my chest and my back. The room was painted white; there was a window looking onto a corridor. I did not know what time it was, or what day, but I realized that I should send a message to my secretary. Every breath was difficult. I saw two figures at the window looking in at me. I turned and stared at them, but I was too exhausted, and I closed my eyes again and let my head rest on the pillow. It was a moment or two later that I turned and looked again, and by that time I knew that I had seen one of the doctors before; he was the American doctor who had seen Mart. Now he had a chart in his hand and he was looking down at the chart and nodding and then looking in through the window at me.

I suddenly realized that I had AIDS, that's what it was, that's why the American doctor was looking at me. I closed my eyes again. A nurse came to take my temperature. I asked to see the doctor in charge and she told me that the team would be around later. I asked her what time it was. She said it was four o'clock. I gave her my office number and asked her to contact Luisa and get her to call personally at the hospital. I lay back thinking that this would be the end, then, that my body would be covered in a sheet and pushed on a trolley to the morgue, that before then I would spend weeks, maybe months, languishing here or at home, becoming thinner and weaker, waiting for the long ordeal that would result in being alive one minute, alert, with a full memory, and the next minute dead, everything gone. I would fade away. I wondered if there was anything I could do at this stage, if I could begin hoarding sleeping pills, if I could get it all over with easily, now.

No doctor came until late that night. I was half-dozing and when I looked up I saw the American doctor standing over the bed. He was not in a white coat. He was wearing a green pullover and an open-necked shirt. When he spoke in faltering Spanish, I realized that he must have learned it in Colombia or Mexico. He introduced himself as Doctor Cawley; he said that he was in charge of infectious diseases, and he wanted my permission to test me for a few things, including TB and HIV. These were more or less routine tests, he said. I had a serious form of pneumonia, and he needed as much information as he could get.

'Do you think I am HIV positive?' I asked him in English.

'Anything is possible,' he said. 'Anyone in this hospital could be positive.'

'I mean do you think that this pneumonia is part of AIDS?'

'I need to do a test,' he said. 'Otherwise we're just speculating.'

'How long does a test take to do?'

'If I send someone in to draw blood in the morning, I could probably have the results by Friday. The TB test is quicker.'

'Will I still be here on Friday?'

'Yes, it will take quite a while to deal with your pneumonia. It is quite serious.'

'How serious?'

'Only the next few days will tell that. Can I ask you about your sexual history? Are you married?'

'No, I'm gay.'

'Have you been at risk?'

'I don't think so.'

'What do you mean?'

'I mean I have not had unprotected sex since about 1984.'

'And before then?'

I shrugged. He looked down at the chart.

'Can I send in my registrar in the morning?' he asked.

I nodded.

'Is there anything else you want to ask me?'

'Yes, I took a lot of cocaine over the weekend. Do you think that has affected me?'

'No, probably not. I think that the pneumonia has been there for quite some time.'

As he turned to go out he smiled, and I remembered him vividly from that moment when he had accompanied Mart to the side door of the hospital. But then it struck me that it was a different hospital.

'Are you attached to this hospital only?'

'No, I'm involved with infectious diseases overall. I move around.' He smiled again, and then his face became serious and he left the room.

As the young doctor took the blood in the morning, I tried to pray, but I discovered instead that I was talking to my mother and my father and I was asking their help, asking them to make sure that I was okay. For some of the time I was sure that I was infected, and I knew that the results would come back positive, but I found myself going over every phrase the doctor had used, how anyone in the hospital could be HIV positive, how the test was routine. I noticed that since I had been moved into this room, nurses and doctors put on gloves when they came close to me. I wondered if pneumonia was infectious.

When my secretary came, she looked surprised and asked me what was wrong. I told her that I had appendicitis. I said to tell anyone who rang that I was in Comodoro Rivadavia, and I would be back next week. I asked her to call in every day, in case there were messages or important letters. I gave her a list of newspapers, magazines and books I wanted. She wrote everything down. I told her not to come in on Friday.

Every two hours, even in the night, my temperature was taken and my chart was written up and the tubes were checked. Doctors came and went; further blood samples were taken. Sometimes, doctors and nurses spoke about me as though I were not there. I slept and woke and dozed and slept again. I listened to the radio. I felt weak and breathless. I hated the bedpan, trying to shit while lying on my back and calling for the nurse when I had finished. I hated injections, the thin needle coming towards me. But mostly, I thought about my blood being tested. I did not know what the testing system looked like, or why it took so long, or what process they used. I thought about my blood lying there in some laboratory in the night, slowly sending out its messages and signals. I concentrated on it, I willed it to be okay. I thought that if it was positive I would try to kill myself, and then I thought that I should ring Pablo and ask him to help me, but I did not think I could do that, and I did not think that I would kill myself. I was reassured by the fact that I had not become thin. There was nothing wrong with my stomach. I was not sweating too much. The fever came from the pneumonia. And anyone could get pneumonia, just as anyone in this hospital could be HIV positive.

I waited all day Thursday, watching the window for Doctor Cawley in case the results came early. I went through the post which Luisa brought me, and tried to read the newspapers, but I was too tired. Two nurses came with soap and hot water to wash me. They dealt with my body as though it were a piece of furniture, as though touching it was of no interest to them. I lay there trying not to be embarrassed.

I woke on Friday thinking that this would be the most important day of my life. If the result was negative, I promised myself that things would change. I would live a better life; I would work out what I must do. Around lunchtime I dozed for a while and when I woke I could not remember what was wrong, and then I realized that I was waiting for the result, someone was going to come and tell me whether I would live or die. I became desperately afraid and anxious, and watched the corridor all the time for signs of the American doctor.

I knew that the HIV virus was mainly passed on by anal intercourse, by letting someone come inside you. I thought back over the times I had done this, but it had been years ago. A nurse arrived to take my temperature; a doctor came to listen to my chest. Another nurse took my chart away. I lay there wanting this to be over. I thought about swimming in warm water, of lying back and floating in the sea. I thought about sex with Pablo when I met him first.

And then, it must have been about five o'clock, the American doctor appeared. I smiled at him and tried to sit up. He did not smile. I thought that he was here to tell me it was negative, but I must be careful in future. I was absolutely sure that it was okay. He closed the door behind him and walked across the room until he was standing with his back to the window.

'It's positive,' he said. 'I've checked it twice and it's positive. I'm very sorry to have to tell you this.'

'This is a nightmare,' I said. I wanted to push back the time, make it one minute earlier, make him cross the room again and tell me that it was okay. He looked calm as he stood there.

'I'm very sorry to have to tell you this,' he said again. 'We were pretty sure when we saw the strain of pneumonia, but obviously we had to do the test.'

'How long have I had it?'

'The virus? It's hard to say, ten years, eight years, six years.'

'Could I have got it in the last two years?'

'I would say not. It's very unlikely.'

'What's the prognosis?'

'We'll work at treating the PCP, which is the type of pneumonia associated with HIV, but it will take time, and, to be frank, there may be other complications.'

'Like?'

'Your immune system is very weak, and has been considerably weakened by the PCP, and there's very little we can do about that.'

'Do you mean that I don't have much time?'

'I don't know what's around the corner. You can never tell, but at the moment, well, at the moment, we'll just have to do our best.'

'How long do I have?'

'It always depends on the person. If you were in your twenties, you would be stronger, but we should concentrate on dealing with what you have now. I'll come back in the morning and maybe we can talk more then. Again, I'm really sorry for being the one who had to tell you this.'

'Is there no chance it could be something else?'

'I'll have a second blood test done, but I would say not.'

'Am I going to die then?'

He looked at me and said nothing. He turned and looked out of the window.

'Things do not look good. I must say that to you. I have a

counsellor outside, and she would like to come in and talk to you now.'

'What will she do?'

'Her job is to deal with all your worries and fears.'

He went to the door and opened it, and looked as though he were about to say something. He nodded and went out. I lay there trying to imagine that this had not happened. I kept saying 'I cannot handle this' over and over to myself.

The counsellor came in and pulled up a chair beside the bed. She asked me if I wanted someone to ring my mother. I told her that my mother was dead. She looked at the chart and said, no, her name and number are here. No, she's dead, I said, she died years ago, and I do not have anybody else who is close to me and you can ring her if you like but you will get no reply. The woman held my hand. You must be devastated, she said, you must be devastated. Have you cried yet, she asked. Maybe you should cry. I shook my head and said that I did not want to cry. Did I have any friend whom I would like to see, she asked. No, I did not, I told her. I would be okay, I said, I did not want to see anybody. I might feel differently in the morning, she said. I wanted her to leave me. Had I made a will, she asked. It might put my mind at rest if I made a will. I told her I would think about it and talk to her in the morning. She said that she did not usually come in on Saturdays but she would come to the hospital in the morning in case I needed to talk some more.

I lay there believing that someone would come to talk to me, that someone would give me an injection and make me sleep, that I would have an hour or two away from this, in oblivion somewhere. When it got late I called a nurse and said that I needed a sleeping pill. She said that she would ask the doctor on duty. When she did not return I called her again. She said she had asked the doctor and would ask him again.

Later, she came back with a pill in a tiny plastic cup. I took the pill and lay back and tried to sleep. I dreamed that I was dead. I was lying in the hold of a boat at the marina beside my house. I was naked, my body was all white and washed, ready to be taken out to sea, my dick was all slack and my eyes were closed and my mouth was closed, and I could hear the motor starting and the rush of water against the body of the boat. Two men were talking. I lay there, dead, inert. But my mind was still there, and I could feel everything and know everything and remember everything. But I could not move or speak and soon I would be lowered overboard and there would be nothing I could do. When I woke I realized that the dream was real, that being awake was no relief. I watched the lights come on in the corridor outside and the morning begin in the hospital. I thought of the American doctor lying asleep in a bed somewhere in the city, at ease and warm. I lay there repeating to myself the phrase 'I cannot handle this' as though it would save my life.

★

I GAVE THE OLD APARTMENT as my address, and I constantly thought of going back there. I dreamed of sitting in the tiled hallway looking out of the window, I dreamed of moving quietly and slowly from room to room like someone frail and retired, with not long left to live. I told them that I wanted to go home, that my mother would look after me. I hoped that Gloria, the counsellor, who came to see me sometimes, would not mention to the medical people that my mother did not exist, she was buried under the ground. Gloria thought that I was strong; other people, she said, had cried for days and could not be consoled. I had not cried at all. I simply asked the doctors when I could go home. I no longer had a temperature, and I was able to eat and drink and sit up in the bed. This was good, the doctor said, as some people became worse in the early stages of treatment. When my secretary came every day I went through the post and the list of messages. I had to turn down work, but nobody, as yet, knew that I was sick. She asked me if I had had my stitches taken out, and I remembered that I had told her that I had appendicitis. I said the stitches would be taken out any day now.

I asked her to buy me some Agatha Christie novels in English. I had not read them for years, but I remembered staying awake into the small hours to find out who had really committed the murder, and I thought they would be useful when I woke in the night and began to think about how I was going to die. But the books never worked, even though Luisa brought me five or six paperbacks. When I woke, the thinking took over, and no plot, no matter how exciting, could disturb my thoughts about how my blood was poison and my sperm was poison, how my body was a danger to anyone who came too close to me. I have AIDS, I said to myself over and over, I have AIDS and I am going to die.

Sometimes, it seemed easy: I thought about death as a falling asleep, a long rest. But then in one sudden, unexpected moment, it would come: I would realize what was going to happen, I would gain the sharp knowledge like a needle in my back that there would be more times in hospital, with pain and weakness and nurses putting on gloves before they would approach me. Soon there would be nothing. My body would be put under the ground and left there. Sometimes, I lay in that bed terrified. I could not believe that this was happening to me. It was like worrying about money or work, and then trying to put the problem out of your mind, and realizing that it was not a problem that would ever go away, or be solved.

I asked Gloria how much longer they would keep me in hospital. They were always hesitant about letting people out, she said. There was always one more test they wanted to do; it was always easier to postpone decisions. But once they needed a bed, they would look down a chart and make an instant decision to let you go. It usually happened when you least expected it, she said. And what she said turned out to be true. On a Tuesday morning when I had been in the hospital for just over two weeks, the staff nurse came and said that I could go home on condition that I had someone to look after me there. I had the keys of the apartment in my pocket. I said that I had someone to look after me. I think she thought that I meant I had a boyfriend and she looked at the ground and said nothing.

Gloria came and gave me her number in case I needed her help. I had to wait until I made an appointment with Doctor Cawley for the following week and then I had to sit in the room and wait for all my drugs. Up to now, I had swallowed whatever I was given, but before I left the hospital I had to go through each drug with the pharmacist so that I knew what it was. I wished that Mart and Jack were here to see me now; I wished that someone I knew would be at home when I went there.

I got a taxi from the hospital to the apartment. I looked at the people in the street and the back of the driver's head and thought about them: they were not full of disease, they were not going to die soon, they were wandering around believing that they were going to survive. I selected people at random from the taxi window and wished that they were sick, that they had AIDS, and not me. Gloria had asked me if I felt angry, and I said that I did not. But now I felt singled out for all this pain, I felt that I had nothing in common with all of these people in the street.

When I arrived at the apartment building, I stood at the bottom of the stairs for a while leaning against the wall. I walked up the stairs. I opened the door and went back into the apartment. It seemed darker than ever before, and smaller. I opened some of the windows and I sat down in the hall as I had planned to do and closed my eyes. I wished I were a baby again, or a small boy, I wished I could go down now to my parents' bedroom and get into bed between them, tell them I was sick and I was having bad dreams and lie there in the warmth between them and the smells of perfume and lavender and talcum powder, snuggle up there and sleep, and wake knowing that it would be all right. You gave me ten talents, the voice from Sunday school came back to me, and look what I have returned with, a poisoned bloodstream, a terrible disease. I sat in the chair in the old apartment with my eyes closed and then I went into my old bedroom and lay on the bed and tried to sleep.

★

TWO DAYS LATER I went out to the house by the marina and I collected my clothes and other belongings and threw them into the back seat of the car. As I went through a drawer in the bedroom I found the numbers which Susan had given me in case I needed to contact her. I rang her mother's number; her mother picked up the phone and said that Susan had just gone out but would be back in twenty minutes. I told her who I was and said that I would telephone in twenty minutes. I felt easier and lighter, the mere knowledge that I would be able to tell somebody whom I knew the story of my illness had relieved me of some of its weight. I walked down to the water, looking forward to telling Susan my news, the way other people might look forward to telling a friend that they were going to get married, or were going to have a baby. It was a cold windy day, the ropes were beating against the mastheads of the boats, white clouds were blowing across the sky and the water was tawny, almost red. I sat down on the stone steps, and for the first time I felt almost happy, glad to be alive now, no matter what was going to happen in the future. I thought that maybe I should come back to live out here, and maybe I should go back to work as well, try to live normally, as though there were nothing wrong, rather than waiting for the worst, as I was doing now. I also knew that I would have to get in touch with Pablo.

I walked back up to the house and telephoned Susan once more. I knew that I was going to tell her everything that had happened, but I did not work out how I was going to begin. This time she answered the phone herself. Her voice was warm and her tone familiar and friendly. I wished that she was in the city, and I could see her now or soon.

'Susan, I wanted to tell you that I have AIDS. I was diagnosed.'

Suddenly, I began to cry. It was as though saying it made all the difference, brought home that it was true, made clear what it meant. She kept saying that she was sorry, she was sorry.

'I always thought that you had been careful,' she said. 'I don't know why.'

'I have no idea who infected me, or when,' I said. 'But they don't think it was recently.'

'There has been stuff here in the papers about new drugs,' she said.

'I'd be grateful if you could see if there's anything new.'

'I know a few doctors, I'm sure I'd be able to get you whatever drugs are available.'

I told her the story of my stay in the hospital. She said she would find out about doctors and call me back.

I told her that I would be at the apartment. That night, she rang from an office in Washington to say that she had material which she wanted to fax me and she also had the name of an American doctor who was in Buenos Aires, Doctor Cawley. I told her that I had already been in touch with him. He was, in fact, the doctor who broke the news to me.

'Everyone I spoke to thinks very highly of him,' she said.

'He says there's no cure.' I could feel my eyes filling up with tears.

'I'm going to fax you all the information I have,' she said. 'You should perhaps go and collect it yourself, you probably don't want your secretary to see this stuff.'

'I've broken up with Pablo,' I said.

'You've done what?'

I told her what had happened.

'You mean you're on your own down there?'

'Yeah, I'm on my own. No one else knows. I don't know what I'm going to do.'

'I can't ask you to come and stay here, because it's my mother's house, and Donald is behaving like a wild animal, but I'll come down if you need me.'

'I'm all right.'

'You should get in touch with Pablo.'

'I tried before, but I'll try again.'

When we finished speaking I walked over to the office and stood by the fax machine. Soon the paper began to roll out, page after slow page, explaining the disease and all its strange manifestations, eye disease and how it could be treated, brain disease, stomach disease, skin disease, and all the strange new words which I had never heard before and barely knew how to pronounce – toxoplasmosis, cytomegalovirus. Each page gave details about what they called opportunistic infections, AIDS-defining illnesses. I glanced at the beginning of each section, looking at the words and the descriptions of symptoms and treatments, wondering which of them I would get, which would come first, which words I would hear in the hospital, would it be my brain, or my stomach, or my eyes, or my skin?

Reading the pages which came out of the machine was like catching a glimpse of hell in some story-book version of life and death, all the possible punishments, all the different tortures which could be inflicted, except this was all true. Some of this was going to happen soon, these words were for actual things which I was going to suffer, which were going to happen in my own body, as my immune system was washed away by disease. I sat there reading versions of how I was going to die.

When the last pages had come through, the line went dead and then the phone rang. It was Susan again.

'I thought that this information might be useful. I'm still really shocked by what you told me. I think you should be reassured that this doctor of yours is very good. He's done some important research.'

'But things don't look good, do they? There's no one talking about a cure.'

'No,' she said. 'I don't think so.'

It sounded like a death sentence, like the final confirmation of something which I had not been able to admit fully to myself. I began to cry again and she stayed on the phone and listened as I sobbed.

'I'm sorry,' I said. 'I don't know why I'm crying now. I should have cried ages ago.'

'It's okay, I'm here, you can call me any time.'

★

I WORE A SUIT and a collar and tie to my first appointment with Doctor Cawley, as if I were going for an interview. When his secretary smiled at me, I remembered what Jack had said about doctors smiling all the time at people who had AIDS. I smiled too, I was only too willing to collaborate. Doctor Cawley's tie did not match his shirt, but everything about him was neat and shiny. I liked his eyes. He spoke in English, asking me if I understood the illness. I said that I did. He took a piece of paper from a rack of forms on his desk and began to draw a diagram on the back. He drew a large L and then put the biro at the top of the vertical line.

'This', he said, 'is the state of your health now.'

He then slowly drew a declining graph until it hit the edge of the bottom line.

'This,' he said, 'is the way things are going to go. Do you understand?'

I was going to say that I was not a fool, that I did not need a graph to understand what AIDS did to the body. He was like a small boy who had mastered a new game. He now wanted to list for me the drugs I was on, or might need in the near future. He took another piece of paper from the rack and turned it around so that he could write on the back of it. But there was already a graph drawn showing the decline of the immune system on this piece of paper. He cast it aside and picked out the next piece of paper. It, too, had the drawing of a graph. Clearly, this was what he did for all his patients. It looked so innocent, so easy to draw. I wondered who the other poor victims were who had had their imminent deaths so casually illustrated.

'How are you?' he then asked me. 'I mean how is your state of mind.'

'Fine, thank you,' I looked at him coldly.

He told me that he would need to see me in another four weeks, and he gave me a prescription to give to the pharmacist at the hospital, and a list of things which he wanted checked in a blood test. Then he stood up and smiled and shook my hand. I wondered if he was shaking my hand to show that, even though I had an infectious disease, he was not afraid to touch me. I thought as I stood there that drawing graphs for people showing them how they would die was a strange way to make a living. I did not smile at him.

I began to work again. I lived in the apartment and constantly intended to telephone John Evanson and give him back the keys of his light-filled house by the marina and tell him that I could no longer live there, but I postponed it. I travelled to New York for a lunch with potential investors and a few days briefing various journalists. I saw Tom Shaw a few times. I even had a drink on my own with him once, but we talked about business and strategy. I did not know if he could tell that I was sick. He was too guarded in his manner and his responses for anyone to know anything about him. I did not think about sex.

Slowly, I became used to the idea that I was going to die. I became afraid only if I thought that something specific was wrong, especially if I woke in the night. In New York the heating was too high in the hotel and I woke in a sweat a few nights in a row. I wondered if this was the beginning of night sweats, and I lay there worrying if I should see a doctor now, if I should telephone Buenos Aires and tell Doctor Cawley about my symptoms. I had lost weight in hospital; often, I looked in the mirror to see if I looked like a man with AIDS. If I came across the reflection of myself I found that I looked frightened, insecure.

*

MY SECOND APPOINTMENT with Doctor Cawley was at eight o'clock in the morning on a Friday. I got up early and had a shower and, once more, I dressed carefully in the most expensive clothes I owned. I put gel on my hair. He wanted to go through the results of my blood test and talk about starting on AZT. My T-cells, he said, were less than one hundred. At best, patients lost between fifty and one hundred per year, he said, but the AZT would bring the count up for a while, and improve things generally, though he did not know for how long this would last. I understood what he was saying. I did not ask him any questions. He told me if I noticed anything in my eyes, I should contact him immediately, and he asked me to take off my shirt and tie so that he could examine me.

Afterwards, I paid his secretary and made an appointment for two months later. And then when I opened the door to leave I saw Pablo sitting in the small waiting area reading a magazine. He looked up and our eyes met. The secretary told him that he could go in. It was like meeting someone who has been dead for years, who comes into a dream. He looked frightened. I knew that he must be sick. He stood up.

'I'll wait for you here,' I said.

He touched my hand for a moment, it was a gesture of reassurance, of recognition, before he went into the office. I sat and waited for him. I wondered what was wrong, whether he had just the virus, or any symptoms, whether his family knew or not, whether he would want to see me or not. I flicked through the pages of a woman's magazine, and then left it down. Maybe he was here to get the results of a test, and maybe he was all right. If he came out now, I thought, and told me that he did not want to see me and did not want to talk, I would understand, I would go home on my own. I would have other things to think about. But if, on the other hand, he came out of the office and said that he wanted us to go for a walk, or a cup of coffee, have a drink together, go back to the apartment together, then, I knew, it would make all the difference to me, it would lift me in a way that I was too scared to contemplate.

I waited. I looked at my watch and realized that I had been waiting for half an hour. What could they be talking about? What could they be doing? I had been in there only ten minutes. I walked down the corridor to see if there was another way out of the office, another door, but there was not. I went back and sat down and flicked through the magazine again. I wondered if the doctor was examining him as he had examined me. I thought about Pablo without his shirt on, vulnerable as the doctor listened to his heartbeat. I hoped that he was not sick. I had no family; I could die in whatever way I pleased. I smiled to myself at the thought of that. But he had his mother and father to think about, he had to worry about when he would tell them, when they would find out. Maybe that was what he was talking to the doctor about. He had been in there for forty-five minutes. I was hungry.

When he appeared his eyes looked glazed and his manner

seemed distant. Doctor Cawley came to the door and smiled at him and shook his hand and then looked at me as though it were perfectly natural for me to be still sitting there, and then he smiled at me too. I could think of nothing to smile about. Pablo and I walked silently out of the clinic and into the street.

'Have you got it as well?' Pablo asked me.

'Yes, I do,' I said.

'Have you been seeing him for long?'

'About six weeks.'

'Is that when you found out?'

'Yes.'

'It never occurred to me that you might have it as well. I was really frightened when I saw you there.'

'I couldn't believe it,' I said. 'If you'd been late we'd never have seen each other. You should have contacted me.'

'I have a terrible problem,' he said. 'I have CMV.'

'What's CMV?'

'It's an eye disease.'

'It's the one that makes you go blind if it's not caught in time, is it?'

'Yes, that's it. I have it. It was diagnosed yesterday by an eye specialist. I have to make a decision about it. I have to decide whether to have treatment here, which will involve me going into hospital for two weeks, or whether I go to San Francisco and try to get into a hospital there, which might be difficult since I have no health insurance.'

'What's the problem about here?'

'My family. I don't want them to find out. They'll have to hear the news sometime, but I don't want it to be now. But the main problem is time. The treatment has to begin in the next day or two.'

'You could tell your parents that you are going to San Francisco.'

'Yes, I think that is what I am going to have to do.' He stopped then and turned and looked at me.

'I have just been talking about me,' he said. 'Maybe there's something worse wrong with you.'

'I need to know how long you've known,' I said. 'We can talk about me later.'

'I did the test when I went to San Francisco when Mart was dying. I got the result the day he died. But I guessed that there was something wrong for a while.'

'Who did you tell?'

'I told a few people the day of the funeral. And then I just came back here and pretended that nothing had happened.'

'That's typical of you,' I said. We both laughed.

'I want you to come home with me,' I said. 'We can talk there.'

We got a taxi to the apartment and walked up the stairs as though we had never done anything else in our lives.

'I have to phone the doctor and let him know,' he said.

'Phone him and tell him that you'll do the treatment here.'

He went to the phone and I lay on the bed waiting for him. I could hear him clearly in the hall making arrangements for the next day. Then he came and took off his shoes and lay beside me on the bed.

'Maybe I should have told you what the problem was when you rang me that day. I just couldn't face it,' he said.

'We've got to stick by each other now,' I said.

We lay cupped against each other as I told him what had happened to me. He held my hand. And then neither of us spoke. There was not a sound in the room.

'I'm going to have to get a line in my chest like Mart had,' he said, 'and I'm going to have to store drugs in the fridge and inject them every day.'

'It's funny. When Mart was here we thought he was different from us, but he wasn't.'

'Do you mind if we don't make love?' he asked.

'No, I don't mind. I just need you to hold me.'

He went home that night and told his parents that he had been left money by a friend in San Francisco and had to go there personally to sign the papers. His father wanted to drive him to the airport, but Pablo told him that he had to go into the city centre to collect a parcel to take with him to San Francisco for another friend. His mother quizzed him at length about the parcel, where he was collecting it, and to whom he was taking it, and how he was to make sure it did not contain drugs. He was sorry he had not made up a better excuse. He arrived at my apartment the following morning with a small suitcase which his mother had packed for him.

'I hate going into this hospital,' he said. 'I'd do anything to put it off.'

'Let's lie down for a while.'

When one o'clock came I said that it was time that we set off for the hospital.

'My eye is doing really funny things,' he said. 'There's a dark shadow in one entire corner.'

'Do they operate on the eye?'

'No, they just fill you full of drugs all day and night.'

I waited in the hospital corridor while he changed into his pyjamas. He was in a room three doors down from where I had been. I stood with him then while he filled in the admission form. He gave my name as his next of kin, and gave my address and phone number to be used in case of emergency. He got into bed; the nurse told him that the doctor would be along soon and put a line into his wrist, and then the treatment could begin. She left us alone in the room.

'If this was San Francisco,' he went on, 'everyone on the ward would be getting the same treatment, and some of the doctors and nurses would be gay. It might be easier.'

He had beautiful thick, black hair on his arm. I began to

stroke it and play with it, and he looked down, half-amused, as though his arm did not quite belong to him. He lay back and made purring noises. When the doctor came with two nurses to put in the temporary line and start the treatment, I went out and stood in the corridor. I was more in love with Pablo than I had been in all the time we were together. I began to think about how much money I had, and how much he had, and how long we were likely to live, and how much it would cost us for medical treatment in San Francisco, and whether we should go there when Pablo had finished his treatment. I had to stop calculating, I had to promise myself that I would not mention anything to him. All I wanted now was to be with him, to spend the day here with him, to make things easier for him.

I pulled out of a trip to Comodoro Rivadavia, and cancelled another trip to New York. I told the ministry that I was overworked, and they seemed to accept this. On the first morning he was in hospital I woke when it was still dark, and I felt that my mother was in the room, alive and watching every moment, knowing everything, every detail, every thought in my head. She could see the battle going on in my body between the virus and the immune system; she watched as the virus wrote itself into each cell. She was full of pity and worry. I thought as I lay in a half-sleep that I could hear her sighing. I thought that if I reached out I would be able to touch her, but slowly I realized that there was no one in the room.

I bought the newspapers every morning and walked from the apartment to the hospital, which took me about half an hour. I brought flowers, or orange juice, or chocolate, or fruit, and I tried when I arrived to talk about the outside world, things I had seen or heard since yesterday, and not to ask him what was going on in the hospital. I knew that he was having trouble sleeping, he was on a mixture of two drugs – Foscarnet and Gancyclovir – and they seemed to make him sick. I began to name the two junior doctors, both slightly overweight and gruffly pompous in their mid-twenties, Foscarnet and Gancyclovir. One of the nurses, Patricia, thought that this was funny, but made clear to us that it was, perhaps, a joke we should keep to ourselves. Pablo often slept when I was there, I tried to make sure that everything was quiet, that no one disturbed him. I loved sitting there beside him, guarding him, looking out for him, pulling the blankets up around his neck, or opening the window a small bit if the room became too warm.

He would wake and see me watching him and smile and try to sleep again. And then he would sit up and read the newspapers. A few times he almost broke down, and said that he could not believe that this was happening. I asked him if he knew how he had become infected, and he said he thought that he did: someone in San Francisco he had met casually a while before the real scare began, who died later. He had let the man fuck him, and the man had come inside him. They had done it a few times, and then not seen each other for years. He knew the man was dead; it had always worried him.

A few times in that first week Doctor Cawley did a round of the wards, accompanied by Foscarnet and Gancyclovir, who stood to attention in his presence, and two nurses, one of whom we called The Duck. I waited outside. After the second visit I asked Pablo if he had ever thought of fucking Doctor Cawley.

'Yes, I have, it's strange you should ask.'

'What position would you put him in?'

'On all fours, I thought,' he said.

'With his head in the pillow?'

'No, I'd like his head up in the air.'

'Funny,' I said, 'I'd like his head in the pillow.'

'Just shows,' Pablo said, 'no two people are the same.'

'What about Foscarnet and Gancyclovir?'

'I'd give them a miss.'

'And The Duck?'

'You are really shocking,' he said.

Although visiting ended officially at nine o'clock, they let me stay until later. Sometimes I read a book while Pablo lay there staring at the ceiling. Each cycle of the treatment was scheduled to take two hours, but usually it took much longer. With the help of Patricia, I learned how to manipulate the drip and make it work faster. She warned me not to let anyone catch me touching it.

'What would Foscarnet and Gancyclovir do if they caught me?' I asked.

'Or The Duck? What would she do?' Pablo asked.

Patricia told us to keep our voices down. For the first week she was on night duty and a few times she came and sat with us when she was not busy. She was careful not to ask us any questions. When Gloria, the counsellor, came to see if there was anything she could do for Pablo, she was surprised to see me. One morning, we told her the story of our relationship. I do not think that she had ever met two men who were in love with each other before. She was full of curiosity and amazement. When she asked too many questions about Pablo's family, we had to tell her that we did not want to talk about it. We accused her of being in love with Doctor Cawley, and asked her to tell us what her fantasies about him were, but she giggled and refused and said that she did not fancy him at all. He wasn't her type, she said.

'What about Foscarnet and Gancyclovir?' Pablo asked her.

I woke each morning feeling contented. I thought about what I would take with me to the hospital, what I would talk about when I arrived. After his first week on treatment, Pablo had to have minor surgery in his chest to have a line put in. He had asked Doctor Cawley how long the line would remain in place, the doctor had told him it would be there for good. That, I think, had brought home to him like nothing else how bad things were. He would never be able to swim again, or walk around in shorts with no shirt. He was worried, too, about being cut open. I had to be careful not to make jokes all the time, to let him talk about how afraid he was, and how shocked he was, to let him dwell on his illness if he wanted. I realized that all this made me feel well by comparison. I could go out and have a cup of coffee, or I could go home at night. Pablo was the patient.

Once when I was sitting there and he was coming back from the toilet, I noticed that his pyjamas were at half mast, and I could see his bottom. I realized how much I loved his body, how much I savoured being close to him, and how easy and comfortable it was for us to be together without the possibility of sex. We found pleasure in the aura of each other, in the fact that we knew each other's bodies, had possessed each other. We did not need to do that now. We had other needs.

The operation was short and simple, and did not cause Pablo much pain. He liked the surgeon, he said. Still, he was tired afterwards and needed mild painkillers. The temporary line was removed from his wrist; from now on the drugs, the Foscarnet and Gancyclovir, would enter his system through the line in his chest. He spent a few days learning how to manipulate the line and keep it clean. It was important that it did not become infected. As I watched him sleep the day of the operation, I began to wonder what he would look like when he was dead. Maybe he would have suffered more, and his face would be thinner, but maybe too he would look as peaceful and serene as he did now. Maybe his death would be easy. He woke and looked at me and smiled.

It was still unclear whether the treatment was working or not. Pablo still complained of a shadow in the corner of his eye. Doctor Cawley said that the specialist would have to look at the eye, and further treatment could take four or five days more, or maybe longer. We made plans to keep the drugs in my fridge and Pablo could come around every day and take them. I wanted him to come and live with me again, but I did not mention this. Sometimes, he seemed distant from me, as though he had decided that we would never be lovers again. I did not want him to spell this out, so I did not talk to him about our relationship, or our future together.

He was worried about his parents. He knew that he would have to make sure that they did not notice the line in his chest. As the time approached for him to leave the hospital and enter the real world again, he became silent. I said nothing to him about the plans I had harboured to go to San Francisco and stay there. I did not think that we had enough money.

One morning I was going down the stairs of my apartment building when I noticed painters at work through the open door of Señora Belucci's apartment on the first floor. I had walked about a block from the building when it struck me that I should go back and ask them to come and paint my apartment. The chief painter was standing at the door in overalls, he was a stocky man in his fifties, soft-spoken with calm blue eyes. I liked him immediately and asked him if he would come up with me now to look at the apartment and give me an estimate for how much it would cost to have it all painted. He said that he would leave the estimate under my door. I read it when I came back that night. He wrote that he would be able to start immediately, and the work would take about a week. He also said that the estimate included wages, the cost of materials, and a small profit, and he could not do it for less. I thought it was high, but I trusted him, or at least I felt that he was not the sort of man who would want to cheat, and the following morning I asked him to do the job.

He wanted me to decide on the colours there and then, but I told him I would let him know the following morning. He gave me a book of colours and I brought it to the hospital. Pablo was low that day, depressed about the line in his chest and the feeling that this was only the beginning of his problems. He had asked Doctor Cawley about Ks, and could not stop thinking about huge bruises appearing on his face and all over his body. I showed him the book of colours and slowly he became interested and animated. White was a cop-out, he said, he wanted rooms painted in red and blue. He began to write out a list of the rooms and a list of colours from the book. I felt that he was thinking about the apartment as though he himself had some stake in it. I sat and watched him and argued that the colours were too bright. I wanted everything to be white; he agreed that the hall could be white, but the bedroom had to be pale blue, and my mother's bedroom red, and the sitting room a steely grey. And you should throw out all the furniture, he said, everything.

'If I threw out all the furniture, would you come and live there?' I asked.

'I prefer the other house,' he said.

'It's too expensive,' I said. 'But we could go there for a while.'

He said nothing. I was sorry that I had raised the subject so directly. I gave the painter a key and told him that he could go ahead and I handed him the piece of paper on which Pablo had written the colours. I walked through the apartment with him and asked him to throw out various pieces of furniture, including my mother's wardrobe and chest of drawers and the kitchen table and the dining room chairs. I thought of throwing out all of the furniture in my own bedroom, and I almost told the painter to get rid of everything, but I did not. I told Pablo nothing about this. Instead, I pictured us walking into the apartment and I saw him looking around in wonder and delight at the new paint and the missing furniture.

Doctor Cawley told Pablo that he could not be discharged from the hospital until the eye specialist had seen him. He could dress himself and pack his things if he wanted, but the room would be kept for him until the specialist had said that the CMV was no longer active. I turned up early that morning and I went with him in a taxi to the eye clinic. He was dazzled by the light of the warm spring day, and he was sure that the CMV was back again, he said he saw all these black shapes and floaters in front of his left eye. He could not face going back into hospital, he said. He had been all right until the idea that he could leave was established and then he was desperate to go. We sat in the waiting room. Everyone else had glasses, or something visibly wrong with their eyes. They must have wondered why we were in the queue.

The specialist was a mild, thin man. He called Pablo in and put drops in his eyes, and sent him back out. When he was called in again he stayed in the specialist's room for about half an hour. I began to worry about work, and realized that I hadn't even bothered to reply to various messages. I would go to the office in the morning and sort everything out, I decided. Pablo had not discussed with me where he would go if he was discharged from the hospital. I believed that he wanted to come home with me, but I knew that he did not want to talk about it.

When he came out he said nothing, but I knew that there was no bad news.

'He says that the spots and the floaters are a result of the infection, they are pieces of detached membrane,' he said when he got outside the door of the clinic. 'He says that the disease is gone.'

'You're a free man.'

'I'd love to go to a restaurant and have a big lunch.'

We went back to the hospital and collected his things. Patricia came and cut off the name-tag from his wrist and told us that the pharmacy had his drugs ready for him. I carried his case down the corridor. We got a taxi to my apartment and walked past the painters, who seemed to have barely started, even though they had been working for days.

'You should knock down some of these walls,' Pablo said. 'Make the rooms bigger, transform the place.'

'I thought that you preferred the other house.'

'I do. Can we go there now?'

'I haven't paid the rent this month, but I can write him a cheque now,' I said.

I had left the car down a side street. We put our bags in the boot and the box of drugs on the back seat. I drove to John Evanson's apartment building and left the cheque in an envelope with the porter there and then drove out to the marina. The sky was clear of clouds and the day was becoming warm.

'Why don't we have lunch at home,' I said. 'We can stop at the supermarket.'

'I'm feeling tired,' he said. 'I'm not sure I'll be able for lunch.'

'Let's try,' I said. I left him in the car while I bought supplies in the supermarket.

'I'm going to have to start thinking about work again,' I said as I drove towards the house.

'I know,' he said, 'and I'm going to have to make some decisions too. But I'll think about it in a minute. I'll work out what I'm going to do.'

'I still love you,' I said.

He did not reply. The house looked beautiful in the light of the afternoon sun. We unpacked and went back in. I opened a bottle of wine and poured him a glass, but he could not bear the taste of it. I poured him a glass of water and we toasted each other. He asked me to stay while he made a phone call. I watched him dial; he was ringing San Francisco. He spoke to Jack, but he did not tell him that he had been sick, or that I had been sick. He told him that we were expecting him to visit us. He asked Jack how he was and I watched his face darken.

He handed me the receiver and I spoke to Jack, who said he was finding it hard to manage without Mart. He had believed that he was prepared for him dying, but it was all much worse than he had thought it would be. I told him that he was welcome to come down here and handed the receiver back to Pablo.

Pablo spoke quietly, as though what he was saying was a big secret. He explained how his mother believed that he was in San Francisco staying with Jack. It was unlikely she would make contact, he said, but if she did, he wanted Jack to say he had just gone out for a walk, and then ring Pablo at this number to alert him to the fact that his mother was on the warpath. Pablo made wah-wah sounds like an Indian in a cowboy movie. When he had stopped laughing he said that maybe he should not burden Jack with inventing an alibi to keep his mother at bay, but Jack seemed to say that it was all right. Pablo said that he would phone him again soon.

He put down the phone and dialled his mother's number. He told her that he was well, and he was thinking of staying on for another while, and he gave her Jack's number. He listened patiently as his mother spoke. He made a sign to me as though he were conducting an orchestra. He listened some more, and then he told her that he would have to go. He put down the phone and lay back on the sofa.

'I shouldn't be doing this,' he said. 'At some stage I will have to talk to my family about being sick, and it will be difficult. Will you promise to help me through all of that?'

'Yes, I will,' I said. 'I will promise that.'

I made lunch and watched him as he tried to eat.

'I hated the hospital,' he said. 'It's only now I realize how much I hated it. If I ever see another tray of food I will get sick. I hate all those doctors and all those corridors. I'd love to feel that I would never have to see them again, but there's no chance.'

We walked down to the water and watched as two teenagers undid the ropes of a small sailing boat and tried to raise the sail.

'It's hard to imagine what it's like to be them now,' Pablo said. 'Being healthy and young like that, having it all ahead of you.'

'I like the dark one,' I said.

'Yes, so do I.'

We sat down on the quayside and watched them working at the sail. There was hardly any wind, but the sky was filling up with clouds. We looked out at the water and said nothing. I noticed that Pablo was shivering with the cold. We stood up and walked back towards the house.

'You're going to stay for a while then?' I said.

'Yes, I am.' He leaned over and put his arm around me. 'I'm going to stay for a while. Is that okay?'

'Yeah, that's fine.'

We went into the house and closed the door behind us. He asked me to turn the heating on and said that he would go to bed for a while. Maybe, if he was well enough, I said, we could go back into the city in the evening and go to a movie. Maybe, he said, maybe we'll do that. He asked me to wake him in an hour or two if he was still asleep.